Lynda

PRAISE FOR NICOLE BYRD'S NOVELS

Dear Impostor

"Madcap fun with a touch ... Regency-era romp ... s...

—*New York Times* bestselling author Cathy Maxwell

"A charming tale of an irresistible rogue who meets his match. Great characters, a plot that keeps the pages turning, and a smile-inducing ending make this a must-read. Delightful, charming, and refreshingly different . . . don't miss *Dear Impostor.*" —Patricia Potter

"*Dear Impostor* is the real thing—a story filled with passion, adventure and the heart-stirring emotion that is the essence of romance."

—Susan Wiggs, author of *The Firebrand*

Robert's Lady

"*Robert's Lady* is a most excellent debut."

—*The Romance Journal*

"A moving tale of love lost and love found."

—*Romantic Times*

"Nicole Byrd has created a masterpiece . . . with the perfect blend of mystery, suspense and romance. This is one romance story you hate to see end."

—*The Romance Communications Reviews*

"Highly recommended . . . more than a fabulous Regency romance. Rising star Nicole Byrd shows much talent and scope." —*Under the Covers*

"Vivid . . . fully developed characters and a story set at a fast clip." —*The Romance Reader*

"A very strong debut . . . I'll be looking for Ms. Byrd's future releases." —*All About Romance*

Titles by Nicole Byrd

ROBERT'S LADY
DEAR IMPOSTOR
LADY IN WAITING

Lady in Waiting

Nicole Byrd

JOVE BOOKS, NEW YORK

If you purchased this book without a cover, you should be aware that this book is stolen property. It was reported as "unsold and destroyed" to the publisher, and neither the author nor the publisher has received any payment for this "stripped book."

This is a work of fiction. Names, characters, places, and incidents either are the product of the author's imagination or are used fictitiously, and any resemblance to actual persons, living or dead, business establishments, events, or locales is entirely coincidental.

LADY IN WAITING

A Jove Book / published by arrangement with
the author

PRINTING HISTORY
Jove edition / May 2002

Copyright © 2002 by Cheryl Zach and Michelle Place.
Cover design by Leslie Peck.
Book design by Kristin del Rosario.

All rights reserved.
This book, or parts thereof, may not be reproduced in
any form without permission.
For information address: The Berkley Publishing Group,
a division of Penguin Putnam Inc.,
375 Hudson Street, New York, New York 10014.

Visit our website at
www.penguinputnam.com

ISBN: 0-515-13292-6

A JOVE BOOK®
Jove Books are published by The Berkley Publishing Group,
a division of Penguin Putnam Inc.,
375 Hudson Street, New York, New York 10014.
JOVE and the "J" design
are trademarks belonging to Penguin Putnam Inc.

PRINTED IN THE UNITED STATES OF AMERICA

10 9 8 7 6 5 4 3 2 1

Prologue

*O*h, dear God, she was going home. Already she could feel the cage doors closing about her.

Circe Hill paced the Calais dock, pausing only to gaze across the heaving water of the Channel, toward England and a future she was certain she did not want. Overhead a gull called, raucous and impudent, and the stench of dead fish tainted the otherwise fresh sea breeze. Shaking her straight dark hair free of the last of its pins—her hat had been discarded long ago—she took a deep breath. Better enjoy the last moments of her freedom. . . .

Her fingers itched for a brush. Or at least a pencil, to sketch the sailors as they toted barrels and boxes below decks and readied the neat little vessel to lift anchor. But she couldn't concentrate, not today, not when her sister's pleas were at last bringing her home.

Psyche meant well, of course. Most younger sisters would have been delighted—what proper young lady wouldn't love a London Season? But despite her faultless pedigree, Circe had never *been* a proper young lady.

She gazed down at the sun-touched skin of her forearms. For two blissful years Circe had been free to follow her childhood dreams. She had wandered amid Italian vineyards, on Spanish beaches, and in French villages and had sketched and painted and listened attentively to the best art instructors her wealth could hire—or the best ones who were willing to teach a female, at least. After years of yearning, of struggling to learn on her own in her schoolroom, it had been heaven. And she had felt so untrammeled, with no one except the long-suffering Miss Tellman to chaperone, and Telly had long ago given up lecturing Circe about propriety.

Now the dream had ended, and reality reared its ugly head. Circe muttered a few words in street French that would have made the sailors drop their bundles if they had heard. Then a movement on the docks distracted her, and she lifted her head.

"Attention!" Two men draped in dark cloaks and wearring heavy frowns accosted the very proper bourgeois French family whom Circe had noticed earlier. Papa looked like a prosperous merchant, and Mama was also sedately garbed. She called often after her clutch of dark-eyed children, but she and the nanny together could hardly keep them away from the briny waters that sloshed the pier.

Strangely, it was the young nanny the two men eyed, and although Circe was too far away to hear their questions, she saw Papa swell in indignation and Mama frown protectively. Why were the officials—if such they were—interested in a servant?

Nearer to Circe, a petite young woman in a shabby traveling cloak, a bundle under her arm, spoke timidly. "Signorina?" The girl stood mere inches from the edge of the dock, and her head was down beneath her hood, as if she tried to hide her face.

"Prenez garde," Circe said, a bit absently. "The wood is wet and quite slippery." Then she realized that the girl's salute had been in Italian, not French. Who was she?

"It matters little," the girl muttered in accented but understandable English. "I might as well throw myself into the deepest depths!" She glanced up for the first time; she was young, perhaps younger than Circe herself, and Circe was shocked by the desperation she saw in her eyes. More than that—

"I've seen you before," Circe said slowly. "In front of the bakery in Genoa, and later—later—" Circe almost gasped. "You were the solitary young nun on the coach ride from Nice! You kept your face down then, too, but I saw you look up once or twice. Why—"

The girl's brown eyes widened, and she made the sign of the cross. "Do you have the Inner Eye?" she whispered, one dread for a moment apparently superseded by another, more primitive fear.

Circe was startled into a laugh. "Of course not. But I am an artist, and I look at people's faces, bodies, the shapes of their eyes—everything. Why were you dressed as a nun, since you are obviously not of a religious order, and why—"

The girl trembled, and Circe saw the two men in black coming closer. "Are you a thief?" she asked very low. The girl did not have the look of a criminal, but she would not be the first to use her fresh-faced youthful mien to deceive.

"Oh no, I swear it by the Blessed Mother," the girl whispered. "Signor DuPree told me to follow you—he said you might help. Those men are Austrian secret police, and they want me because of my father."

Her thoughts racing, Circe gazed at the girl. Her own painting instructor had sent this waif—why on earth? But the men walked up and paused in front of them, and one glance at their closed faces and cold eyes made Circe suppress a shiver of her own. She had been on the Continent long enough to have heard of the wide reach of the Austrian Empire's notorious secret police; their methods were equally infamous—she glanced down at the girl, whose face was now pale with fear.

"Comment vous s'appelez vous?" the first man demanded.

"I am English," Circe said, though she understood his French perfectly. She met him stare for stare. "My name is Miss Circe Hill, and why should you require it?"

The agent shrugged and turned to glare at the girl in the threadbare cloak, who looked as if she might faint dead away, her terror was so palpable. The man's expression sharpened. "And you? Are you English, too?"

Silence, and the girl drew a deep breath.

"This is my maidservant," Circe said, surprising herself as much as anyone. The girl's eyes widened, but she threw Circe a grateful glance, then stared at her feet again, avoiding the man's suspicious gaze.

"I do not understand why you are asking such questions. We are about to embark on this vessel to return home," Circe added. "And I believe it is time to go aboard. The captain will not wish to miss the tide."

Indeed, the French family had already disappeared into the main cabin. Circe saw Miss Tellman, her companion and former governess, gesturing to her from the deck of the ship. Telly had gone on board earlier with the luggage to check on their cabins, while Circe lingered on the dock, wrestling with her private misgivings and her reluctance to make the final commitment to this journey home.

"Are you an official of the French government? Because if not, I fail to see what right you have to delay me." She kept her voice icy and, to her relief, the agent hesitated.

"Come along, *Mary*." Without looking at her "servant," Circe turned away. From the corner of her eye, she could tell that the girl had wit enough to follow silently, her face still tilted down.

On board, they were swept up into the tumult of the ship leaving its anchorage, sailors shouting orders and bustling about. "Oh, there you are, Miss Circe," Telly said, wringing her hands in relief. "I was afraid you would be left behind. Come inside, I have some tea waiting in your cabin."

Circe followed, and as she wondered how to explain this new acquisition, she glanced back and found that the girl had disappeared. Perhaps it was just as well; anyone who had traveled alone through two countries could no doubt take care of herself. But then, recalling the girl's anguished eyes and her earlier statement about throwing herself into the sea, Circe made a quick decision. "I must go back to the deck."

"I shall go with you, Miss Circe," Telly assured her. Pulling her shawl closer around her sloped shoulders, she gathered up her ever-present knitting and prepared to follow.

"No indeed, the wind is cold. Drink your tea, I shall be back shortly," Circe assured her old friend, wanting to speak privately—and candidly—with the stranger. She hurried outside.

As the sharp sea breeze touched her face, Circe located the girl at once. The thin figure in the worn cloak stood clinging to the boat's rough railing as she gazed back at the retreating shoreline.

Good, the mystery girl had done nothing foolish. But the question remained, why was she a fugitive? What would have made her flee so far from the kingdom of Piedmont, at the top of the Italian peninsula? What had she, or her father, done? Circe would have to ask, though she hated invading another person's privacy. She felt her own lack of autonomy keenly just now; how dare she impose herself on a stranger?

For a moment, she hesitated. Circe braced her legs as the boat dipped and the wind whipped her long skirts back against her body and blew thick locks of hair into her face. Her thoughts returned to her own dilemma. How was she to suffer through a London Season? She didn't want to waste her time making polite conversation, appearing at boring balls and dinners. She had her art to focus on, and that was all she wanted, all she needed.

She should have been contemplating a new painting just now. The churning gray water and moody sky should have enchanted Circe. With the intoxicating feel of the moist air against her face, she should have been planning just what method she would use to capture that brilliant shaft of sunlight that peeked out every now and then from a break in the clouds.

But now she wavered, because with every league closer to England's shore, the more restricted she felt. There would be no more painting all day in a field or meadow, no more ignoring society's rules. She would have to be prim and proper and put aside her painter's smocks for silks and satins, or well-bred men and women alike would despise her. At the thought, a knot of resentment hardened inside her belly. If only Psyche had not insisted—

Circe sighed, knowing she was being terribly ungrateful; her older sister only wished for her happiness. Just because Psyche moved easily through the confines of English society, how could she comprehend her sibling's difficulty?

Remembering Psyche's letters—"just one Season," she had urged, sensibly, sisterly—Circe wrestled once more with her own feelings and the duty she owed to the sibling who had raised her. Circe should be delighted at the social season ahead of her. If she were a proper young lady, she would be. And if she could sprout wings, she would fly.

Cautiously, she looked toward the other girl, standing with her face still averted, who shivered as if damp from the spray that flew over the ship's rail and touched even Circe's cheeks and increasingly tangled hair. The ship leveled out once again and cleaved its way through the water toward the distant haze that was England.

Circe made her way across the slick deck, stopping a pace or two away. What was the stranger's problem? Why had her instructor sent her this slip of a girl? Circe rubbed absently at a smudge of vermillion paint on her thumb; she could see it even beneath her thin glove. "I sincerely hope you are not still considering throwing yourself to the 'deepest depths'?"

Her question was met by silence.

"Is your plight so serious? Would you not tell me more? I promise to respect your confidence."

The only response was a small sniff.

Circe hesitated. How could she help the girl if the stranger was not willing to be candid? Circe gazed out at the billowing waves, and her thoughts slid back to her personal woes.

"How am I to change for everyone else, when I don't want to change?" she muttered as a wave hit the ship's side with a hollow thud. "Minding my steps in a formal dance, minding my words, my very gestures—intolerable! No one will understand me; the Ton will despise me, and I will detest them, even while I am beside myself with the longing to be elsewhere. If Psyche hopes to find me a husband, she will be sadly disappointed." Forgetting she was not alone, Circe brushed a lock of damp hair from her cheek and whispered the fear that sometimes rose unbidden from her most private thoughts.

"No proper English gentleman could love me, nor could I love any such colorless milksop. As different as I am, is it possible for any man to love me in the way I wish to be loved?"

And how could she settle for less? No, she knew the answer, had already decided that she would live for her art alone, and lucky she was to have such a passion, since more earthly ardors seemed out of her reach. Remembering the problem of the silent girl beside her, Circe turned to go. She'd retrieve a cup of the tea Telly had procured and bring it out to the girl. Perhaps then she could coax her inside.

Circe had only taken a few steps when she heard a muffled sound. The girl was weeping. Oh, dear. Circe hesitated, then turned back. She could see the stranger's face now, flushed from the sobs the girl had been struggling to keep silent.

Circe felt as selfish as a two-year-old with a sugar bun; how could she have been thinking of herself? "You're safe now, you know," Circe said, her tone gentle. "No one will arrest you in England. Why were they searching for you, so far from Genoa?"

The girl raised her chin and met Circe's gaze defiantly.

"I am no criminal, me! My father was involved in the recent disorder in Piedmont. All he and his friends wished was to bring back the constitution of 1812, which promised more independence from our oppressors. But the Austrians have brought in their army, and always, their spies and secret police, and now my parents are in great peril, and I—I—" She sobbed again.

She was on a boat to a foreign land with, very likely, little money and no friends or family waiting on the other side of the Channel. Circe was appalled at her own thoughtlessness. How could she have been consumed with her own problems when here was an innocent—for she was sure now that the girl spoke the truth, and Circe was not an easy person to lie to—young woman in such dire straits? And besides, this girl defied convention in the most dangerous and most meaningful way; how could Circe fail to respond to that?

"You are not alone, I will not abandon you," she promised, reaching to take the girl's hand. "What is your real name?"

The young woman hesitated, then she blinked hard, and the flow of tears slowed. "Lucia—Luciana, if you please. Do you speak truth? Would you allow me to stay with you, to work for you, for a little while at least? I could save my wages and send them to my parents to help them escape, too. I am very handy with the needle, and I will learn all else I need." Hope dawned for the first time in the girl's brown eyes, and she clung to Circe's hand as if it were a lifeline.

"Of course." Circe gave Luciana's hand a warm squeeze before releasing it. "Now come inside and get warm, and let us get you tea and something to eat."

Luciana shivered again, but she followed Circe toward the cabins. Circe took a deep breath. Luciana's plight made her own worries look very small. Circe would help the frightened girl, and for herself, she would not repine; she would do what her sister requested. It was only a few months, after all, then she would be back at her painting, and her heart—her heart would give up this foolish yearning for something it could never have. How hard could it be to endure one Season?

One

No one had ever said Circe was beautiful.

But he didn't need a beautiful girl, only one who was well bred and respectable. No one could deny Circe Hill's lineage, which was above reproach, and as for respectable—well, she must have matured a great deal while she was away, and with her sister to guide her . . .

David Lydford, earl of Westbury, his morning coat hugging his broad shoulders, took the front steps of the elegant Mayfair town house with a bound, almost displacing the hat that had been placed very correctly on his head. Recalling his sense of dignity, he pushed the offending article back into place and knocked on the door.

But he heard no sound of a response, and he rapped again before the door swung ponderously open. An elderly butler gazed at him, his whole expression a reproof.

" 'Lo, Jowers," David said. "That is, good morning." His tone was most decorous; the butler did not seem impressed.

"My lord," Jowers intoned, "I regret to inform you that Lord Gabriel is out, and Lady Gabriel Sinclair is not at home to visitors." He began to shut the door again, but David put out one hand to hold it open.

"No, no, I know that, just spoke to Gabriel at his club.

I want to see Miss Circe. And I know she's back," David put in before the servant could deny the younger lady, too. "Gabriel told me, and I need to see her now, at once."

"But my lady is—" the butler tried to say.

Sometimes, being proper slowed one down too much. "Not to worry, I'll show myself up." Ignoring Jowers's sputtering protests, David slid past him and headed straight for the stairs. "Knowing Circe, I can guess where she'll be."

He took the stairs two at a time, passing the first floor with its formal drawing room, then the next level, with the family bedrooms, and continued on up a narrower flight to the old schoolroom, with its large windows that captured the morning light.

Important if you were a dedicated artist, as Circe most decidedly was. David tapped on the door, then pushed it open without waiting for a response. He saw just what he had expected to see, and for a moment the sight took him back six years to the first time he had met Circe, all gangly limbs and straight brown hair and those unexpected clear green eyes. He had once accused her of being a fairy child, with her strange air of knowing more than she should.

But her passion was painting, and at this hour of the morning she was almost hidden behind her easel and canvas, dabs of paint staining the coarse smock that protected her morning dress. As usual, Miss Tellman, who had once been Circe and Psyche's governess and now served Circe in the role of companion, dozed in a comfortable chair in a corner of the room, her knitting snarled in her lap.

"Hello," David said quietly, hoping that Circe was not so absorbed in her current work in progress that she would refuse to stop and talk. At the moment all he could see of her was a few stray locks of dark hair and an extra brush tucked behind one ear. Her face was obscured by the canvas that stood between them, and she did not bother to look up.

"I don't want any tea just now, thank you," she said

absently. Her voice still had the clear bell-like tone that had always pleased him.

"Pity, that. I had my heart set on one of your tea parties." David grinned, then remembered to smooth his expression into well-bred banality, with just a hint of the welcome due to an old family friend. But when Circe glanced around the easel, he forgot all about maintaining a seemly composure.

The big eyes, pointed chin, wide expressive mouth— all were still there. But what had been gawky and plain in a girl of twelve seemed suddenly to have come together just—well, beautifully. She was still unconventional, far from the ideal of classical beauty her older sister had always been. But yet, despite the disparate parts, the whole was a vision—she looked like a fairy princess with those startling green eyes and thick brown hair and a smile that flashed suddenly and took his breath away.

He gaped, then tried to pull himself together. This was Circe, only Circe, the fey little girl who had always said the unexpected. Yet, to see the woman she had grown into . . . *Good God,* he thought, and with great difficulty pulled his thoughts back to his original errand.

Meanwhile, she stared back at him, seeming almost as startled as he.

What had happened to David? Circe allowed her gaze to wander from the hat set so correctly on top of his glossy dark hair with its chestnut glints—when had he abandoned the rakish angle she remembered so well?—to his well-cut morning coat, down the subdued olive waistcoat and fashionably tight buff pantaloons to his carefully shined shoes. The old David had always been fashionably dressed, frequenting the best tailors, but he'd also had an almost careless elegance about him, as if he didn't care what anyone else thought and wore his well-cut coats only because they pleased him. The man standing before her, without a speck of lint on his dark superfine, looked as straitlaced and respectable as her most boring uncle. This man was a stranger.

"What are you doing here?" she demanded.

He looked wounded. "Surely I deserve a better welcome than that," he suggested, lifting one brow with a hint of the old David peeking through the proper façade.

Relieved, she smiled. "Of course you do. And I can stop now—the best light is almost gone." She put down her brush—funny, she had been using a mixture of blue-gray that was just the color of his eyes—and picked up a cloth to cover her canvas.

He glanced at the glorious disarray of her glossy brown hair, which looked almost as tumbled as if she had just emerged from her bed. It suggested thoughts of— No, no, this was Circe, he mustn't think about beds and disheveled hair and nightgowns slipping off one shoulder. With an effort, he tried to turn his thoughts into more respectable channels. To distract himself, David took a quick peek at the oil-covered canvas that stood on the easel.

He blinked. It was a simple setting, a towering English oak with a smattering of daffodils and hyacinths blooming in the grass beneath, and blue sky glimpsed between the green-leafed branches. On the grass, a woman in a white gown sat holding a baby in her lap. You could not see the woman's face as she bent over the laughing child, but the whole picture radiated love and contentment and ease, making him ache a little inside with the old secret longing. Circe was truly a genius with the brush, despite all the dictates of society that hindered a female artist from public acknowledgment. This deceptively modest scene was a masterpiece. He knew little enough about art, but any simpleton could see it. This should have been exhibited in the Royal Academy, and if she had not been a woman—

Then he glanced at her face. She had pulled off the smock and tried to smooth back her hair; its thick lustrous sweep softened the pointed chin and heart-shaped face. Her skin was smooth, if a little too brown from the sun for a fashionable miss, and her eyes—her eyes were clear and lucent as a still green pond into which sunlight poured. He had a dim thought that this was a masterpiece, too. How had he never before seen that she . . .

Then again he gave himself a mental shake. This was nonsense. She was nothing like the usual style of beauty that drew the Ton's admiration, nor did she resemble David's typical *amoureux*. It was only Circe, after all, taller now and more delightfully developed in figure, but much the same as the child who had once sat on the stair landing and quizzed him about his lack of costume for a masquerade ball. And he needed her help.

She waved toward the battered table and chairs that had graced the schoolroom for years.

"Ah, a tea party, after all?" he quipped, trying to recover his footing. He felt strangely shaken, and this was not at all part of his plan.

Why did he continue to refer to her childhood—would no one realize that she was grown up at last? Stifling a sigh, Circe glanced down at her less than voluptuous curves. She supposed it would be too much to expect him to notice the bosom she had finally grown, such as it was, she thought wryly. But she refused to be twitted as if she were still a child.

"I never gave you a tea party," she pointed out, hearing the exasperation in her tone.

His society face back in place, David nodded. "No, you were never the type for dolls and tea parties, were you, sprite?"

He should just tweak my blasted nose and be done with it. She stifled her ill humor and tried to keep her tone even, this time. "Not that I ever considered it a defect, but no, I had other interests."

Exuding solicitude, David crossed to her and bowed. He lifted her hand to his mouth, planting a kiss just to the right of a white smear on her thumb. "My dear, you could claim a defect as soon as I could claim sainthood."

His bent posture brought their faces level and Circe studied his handsome countenance. He was older, of course, the planes and angles of his face more defined.

His dark chestnut hair was as thick and wavy, his long, lean frame as dashing, despite the too meticulous outfit, and his nearness brought her a flicker of a different kind of awareness than she'd ever felt, years ago. It might be pleasant to stand close to David and allow this feeling to grow—but she was in England again, where nothing was allowed to come naturally. And anyhow, she didn't want it this way, not when David was being so—so not himself.

Drawing her hand back, Circe shook her head. "Don't do that, David."

He straightened, blinking in surprise. "I didn't—" He looked away a moment, collected himself and smiled again. "I beg your pardon, Circe. I am simply trying to treat you as the grown-up lady you have become."

Circe arched a brow in complete understanding. "If you were truly aware of me as a grown-up *woman*, I think your tone would be very different."

Surprised, David turned his laugh into an unconvincing cough "You don't really mean what that suggests—"

"You think not?"

"Methinks you've spent too much time on the Continent, Miss Circe."

"And I think you've spent too much time sipping lemonade at Almack's. What on earth has happened to you?"

David's eyes narrowed. "I have matured from the foolish antics of my youth," he informed her in the lofty tone that again made her want to take his correctly tied stock and twist his neck with it, till he crowed like a rooster. "I will soon be settling down, I do not hesitate to inform you, with a proper, most respectable young lady. I shall marry, become a pattern of rectitude, and avoid all the ridiculous exploits I used to engage in. After all, I'm an only child, and I must produce an heir someday, you know. Family name, and all that."

"I wish you very happy," she said, her tone carefully polite. If an unexpected and painful ache stirred deep inside her, it was only the last dying echo of a child's fancy . . .

nothing, really. "Who is the young lady who has won your regard?"

"Ah, well, I haven't actually found her yet."

She stared at him in genuine surprise. Circe motioned again to the wooden chairs that surrounded the scarred table. He held a chair for her, then seated himself.

"Why not?" she demanded.

"I don't really know," he admitted, forgetting himself and pushing his carefully brushed chestnut waves out of place; she thought they looked much better that way. She would have liked to reach out and brush the lock of hair away from his temple, feel the texture of it beneath her fingertips. She folded her hands upon her lap.

"It's not that I haven't looked a bit, now and then, but I haven't found just the one yet."

"No?" This was the most unreal conversation she could remember. "And these ladies are no doubt all languishing as they wait for you to make your choice?"

Her irony was wasted; he didn't seem to notice.

"They always seem to have one defect or another," David explained as he tugged his shirt cuffs into their correct position.

Circe's eyes widened in mock sympathy. "How very sad. Deformed, are they, poor creatures?"

David looked up, startled into an expression of genuine confusion. "Good God, no, Circe! Don't be absurd."

She swallowed her smile. "My apologies. I misunderstood."

"I'm referring to traces of real faults, faults that a countess should never possess."

Circe sobered. Perhaps he was serious about this bride search. "Such as . . ."

"Such as . . ." David responded, taking a moment to search for the words, "perfidy, infidelity, stupidity . . ."

Circe had just begun to feel a bit ashamed of herself for assuming the worst when David finished—

"And she must never think that Parliament is a new type of French lace," he said with utter disgust. "Or that

France has a Tsar, and Russia borders upon Italy."

Circe put one hand quickly to her mouth to hide her laughter, but soon gave up the effort. David grinned sheepishly but gave a decisive nod nonetheless.

"You may laugh, but these are the young ladies society—and my mother—deems appropriate for marriage. At any rate, I'm not ready to make such an important choice; such a decision can't be hurried, you know. But I do need a proper young lady, right away, at least for a little while." David had the uneasy feeling that Circe was not fully attending, and this was a most important dialogue. He really needed her assistance. Who else could he turn to?

"Only a little while? Are you sure?" Her voice wavered, and her green eyes seemed to glimmer. David wasn't sure if she was shocked or—damn it—still amused. He wasn't explaining this very well, but it was partly Circe's fault. She never responded as one expected her to.

"It's my mother," he said, falling back on his most oft used excuse. "She's on me to marry, and right away."

Circe lifted her delicately arched brows, and now her green eyes were knowing. "David, Psyche tells me she's been doing that for years. Why is it so pressing just now?"

"She's never been this bad before," he protested, annoyed that Circe would not accept the urgency of his plight. "She says she has contracted a lingering pleurisy and is likely to go into a decline." He rushed on before Circe could point out that his mother was always convinced she had one illness or another. "She says she will never live to see her grandchildren if I am not engaged at once and married before the fall. She's giving me no peace at all!"

"So how am I to help? You already know all the eligible girls in London, although they somehow do not measure up to your exacting standards. I've been away for years. Besides, you are surely not going to contract a rushed engagement just to placate your mother." This time her tone seemed guarded. She looked down at the smudge of paint still on her thumb, rubbing it absently. She smelled of linseed oil and turpentine, but somehow that did not displease him.

"Of course not. It's just—I've got too much on my plate just now to have to deal with my mother's tantrums."

The pretext about his mother was true enough, but it was hardly the real reason for his request. However, having been sworn to secrecy, David couldn't very well disclose to her the task his uncle had requested of him a few days before, or the seriousness of the job required. Not many people would have considered him suitable for such a commission, but Uncle William, who worked beneath the Foreign Secretary, had always declared that David had more bottom than anyone else gave him credit for.

"Not just a society gadabout, your David," he'd overheard his uncle tell his (David's) mother last Christmas. "And he seems to be settling down nicely this last year or two. Always thought he would grow up, sooner or later."

And although his mother had sniffed and shaken her head, David had felt an unprecedented moment of pride. Having turned over his shiny, new, and most proper leaf, he was prepared to step in and do his duty as an Englishman.

So he could not refuse this very confidential duty when his uncle had asked. But no one, absolutely no one, was to know. National security could be threatened, not to say a dreadful scandal stirred up if anyone guessed that David was shadowing a prominent European diplomat. So all he could do to gather Circe's unwitting assistance was smile and apply his usual masculine charms, which she so strangely seemed to abhor.

"David, even if you have not settled your affections, you always have a woman on your arm, or so Gabriel has told Psyche," Circe retorted.

"Ah, but they're usually not the kind of female that one could take into Society," David said in a rush of candor.

"Oh, I see. You favor *a chère ami*, or—what are such women called in England?—light o' loves?" Circe wrinkled her nose at him, looking mildly interested but not scandalized, which she jolly well ought to have been. He had really hoped that by now she might have learned to guard her tongue. For a moment, he wondered if this charade had a chance in hell of working. But he had no alternate plan, so he plunged ahead.

"Circe! You really must *pretend* to be shocked," David admonished her. "But yes, I need a proper lady for a bit."

"A bit?"

"Just long enough to relieve my mother's mind." He tried to sound convincing. "I thought I could do a bit of play acting myself, and you could help me, allow me to hang over you, pretend to be an item. Since I haven't settled on any young lady to pay suit to, I don't want to break some poor chit's heart, y' know, who might misinterpret my attentions and think that I was serious."

"Since you are such an eligible catch."

He grimaced. "Well, yes. And don't look at me like that, I can't help being an earl. Blame my father, if you like. It's just an accident of birth, the only legacy of value left me by my unlamented parent."

He had assumed his society face again, all scrupulous politeness and ease, as shallow as the sugar coating on a plum. What had turned David into this pattern card of a man? And why did he think she would believe such a ridiculous tale?

She should have laughed in his face. Instead, for reasons she did not care to examine too closely, she shrugged. "I suppose I could do it. I am to be your decoy, to keep your mother off your back while you—do what? Examine the other 'proper' young ladies at your leisure?"

David frowned and didn't meet her clear-eyed gaze. "No, no, not at all," he assured her. "And it won't be all one-sided. I can help you, too, y' know, in your coming out. Gabriel said as much—" He stopped, remembering that this also was not to have been repeated.

Circe sat straight in her chair, alarm evident on her face. "What did Gabriel say? That you should take pity on me, on poor charmless Circe in her first Season?"

"Gabriel adores you, Circe. He'd never say anything so shabby." David folded his arms, exasperated. Why was Circe taking a pet? She never used to be this touchy. Pity that girls grew up, he thought. Unless, of course, they turned into well-endowed opera dancers with flaming red hair and voluptuous charms. . . . Why had Annabelle gone off with that rich Cit? Dashed unkind of her, to sever their relationship so abruptly, just because he'd mentioned he would soon be looking for a wife. . . . With an effort, he pulled his mind away from his recently departed mistress and back to the schoolroom. "He just said I could check up on you once in a while, lead you into an occasional dance. Thought you'd feel more comfortable with an old friend to speak to now and then. Is that so unreasonable?"

"I suppose not." Circe relaxed, the bright flush of anger that had stained her cheeks fading.

Actually, there had been more to the conversation than that. "Psyche's having the devil of a time getting Circe to even agree to coming out," Gabriel had told him earlier over a steaming cup of morning coffee as they both sat in the well-worn leather club chairs. "She's only interested in her painting, as you might remember. But Psyche thinks it important that she have at least one Season before she returns to her art. We'll do what we can to guide her, but if you will help Circe, who has never bothered to practice any social skills, we'd be much obliged."

Since Gabriel had been his hero from the time David was in short pants, an older neighbor lad who had first taught him to fish and shoot and hunt and had allowed him to tag along in the field, he could not bring himself to refuse, though the timing was awkward.

And then it had occurred to David that this could be to his advantage, too. He could use Circe as a cover while he kept an eye on this Austrian diplomat, who, his uncle had said, tended to frequent the most stodgy gatherings, exactly the place to also find young ladies newly on the town. And of course, it would placate his mother, but hellfire, he had been dealing with his mother for years, just as Circe had so shrewdly pointed out.

"You're not going to tell your mother that we are contemplating marriage?" Circe interrupted his thoughts.

"Lord, no." David grimaced. "You know my mother. She'd have the betrothal announcement in the papers before we even attended our second ball. But just a hint here and there that you might be considering my attentions could save me a lot of grief."

Silence again. Circe gazed out the window, and her thoughts seemed far away. Probably planning another picture, David thought, resigned. But before he had to remind her of the object of the conversation, she surprised him with her reply.

"I think you're keeping something from me," Circe said with such simple directness that he was again reminded of the odd child she had been.

He tried not to look guilty.

"Nonetheless, I will assist you," she continued. "But remember, it is only one old friend helping another, David."

"Of course," he agreed a bit too quickly, and he took his leave soon after, leaving Circe to sit alone at the nursery table, drumming her fingers on the scratched surface.

How could she refuse David some trifling assistance? But he had something else on his mind, she could tell that easily—or someone else. Despite his protestations, perhaps he had fallen for some young lady, perhaps even some woman who was not quite a lady, or someone quite unsuitable. He should have told her the truth. She would not have hesitated to help him, as a friend, even if the thought made her spirits sink.

She was still sitting idly when Psyche came into the room. Feeling strangely depressed despite the progress she had made on her current canvas, Circe looked up at her sister. Psyche wasn't far past her thirtieth year, but she looked hardly older than the day she and Gabriel had married. Her skin was soft and delicately hued, her eyes a shining blue, her fair hair lustrous. Circe had long since given over the useless regret that she would never be as lovely as her older sister; it was a pity that Circe had straight brown hair, strange green eyes, and a more slender figure, but there it was. Just as well she had no intentions to seek a husband.

But Psyche did not seem as well disposed toward Circe's life plans.

"There you are, my dear. Did we have a caller? I thought I heard footsteps on the stairs."

"Just David," Circe explained.

"Oh, I see." Psyche had several sheets of paper in her hand, and she held them out for Circe to inspect. "I have the guest list for your coming-out ball. See if there is anyone you wish to add whom I have left off. Also, I've heard from the modiste. Your ball gown is coming along nicely, and the court dress for your presentation will also be done well in time."

Circe nodded absently as she scanned the list; some of the names were vaguely familiar, and she had no more to add. She had few friends in London, having lived abroad for the last several years. And she was usually oblivious to what she wore, being most interested in the newest tint of paint or a well-stretched piece of canvas. It was her sister, after all, who had been determined that she return to England so that she could come out formally and be presented this Season.

Psyche gazed at her, her tone guarded. "You are not angry at me, Circe, for persuading you to come home for a few months?"

Circe shook her head. "Signor DuPree has had another attack of the gout," she explained, mentioning her adored but demanding instructor. "He had already left to visit a spa and sip the waters before I ever sailed for home. It will be as well to leave him over the spring to mend."

"I would never ask you to give up your brush and

paints, Circe, but aside from the fact that we have missed you greatly, there is more to life than even great art, you know. I should wish you to experience some of the happiness that I have known."

Circe shrugged. She had heard this before. All very well if one were as lovely as her sister and had a husband such as Gabriel, who was not at all the conventional English gentleman. But as for Circe—no, she was sure it would never happen.

"Someday you might regret that you gave up your youth entirely to your painting. I know you say you don't mean to marry, but a loving husband, children, they can be a great blessing, I promise you." There was a catch in Psyche's voice, and then she looked even paler for a moment.

"Sit down." Circe pushed her sister into the nearest chair. "What is it?"

"I—I just—I think I may be ill."

"Telly!" Circe called. "Fetch a basin. My sister is not well."

"Oh, dear, oh, dear." The older woman awoke with a start. She hopped up and pulled a nosegay of flowers from a wide-mouthed vase. "Here, my lady, take this."

Psyche had put her head down almost to her lap, and when she raised it, she seemed more composed, though still very pale. "I'm all right now, the feeling has passed. But I think I will return to my room and lie down for a space."

"Poor Psyche," Circe crooned as she took her sister's arm, "let me walk you to your bedchamber." For the first time, she was genuinely glad that she and Telly had sailed back to England at her sister's repeated pleas. Surely this was just a little cold or some other mild malaise. Circe could not think of anything happening to Psyche. Since their parents' death when Circe was just a girl, Psyche had been both mother and father to her, and the thought of any calamity befalling Psyche—it just couldn't happen.

The two went along the hall and down the stairwell

until they came to the spacious and comfortable chamber that her sister and her husband shared.

Psyche's dresser, Simpson, who had served her for years, was brushing one of her sister's riding habits. She looked up in alarm as they entered. "Are you ill, my lady?"

"A moment of nausea, that is all," Psyche told her maid.

"Would you like a tisane, my lady? Or a cup of tea? Perhaps a biscuit?"

"Tea is enough," Psyche said firmly.

The servant hurried off to fetch it, and Circe held her sister's arm until she reached a chaise and could lie back against its damask pillows. A glance at her sister's well-shaped hips and generous bosom inspired a sudden thought, and with it a rush of hope. "Psyche," Circe asked, keeping her tone low. "Are you increasing?"

Her sister's blue eyes widened. "Oh! I'm not sure. It's possible." Psyche gripped her sister's hand tightly, unable to hide her joy. "Do you think it might be so?"

Circe did not attempt to answer, but she smiled, feeling both relief and anxiety. In over five years of marriage, Psyche had quickened only once, and then lost the growing babe a few months into her confinement. Circe knew how much her sister, and Gabriel, too, had mourned their unborn child and how they hoped for another chance.

Psyche shut her eyes, then opened them again. "Oh, it would be so wonderful, so joyous—so dreadfully timed! How am I to chaperone you through your first Season if I am always dizzy and ill and ready to cast up my accounts at the slightest notice?"

Circe laughed at the masculine slang coming from her proper sister. Gabriel's influence, she thought with affection. "It will be occasion for great rejoicing, and you will on no account tire yourself over me," she said. "I can always put off my coming out—"

"No, no, you are well past eighteen. I want you to do

it this year," Psyche insisted, her elegant chin set with resolve.

"Then we will find a way, but just now I want you to be easy," Circe said. "Or think how Gabriel will scold when he returns."

The mention of her husband made Psyche's blue eyes soften, and she touched her flat belly with a hopeful hand. "Yes, I'll try. And don't concern yourself, Circe. We will manage. There's always Aunt Sophie."

"She has retired to the quiet and serenity of Bath. You know she would not wish to experience another fatiguing London Season," Circe reminded her. "She found it tiring enough when you were unwed and in need of constant chaperonage."

"True." Psyche sighed and appeared to think hard. "There's Cousin Matilda, of course. Oh, I know!" She began to rise with excited purpose, but Circe eased her back down. "I will write a note to Sally. Having put off her blacks some time ago, I am sure she would love something to take her mind off her loss. I must admit I've been concerned about her."

Circe nodded and went to fetch her sister's stationery from the delicate writing desk. She was gone only a moment, but returned to find Psyche sitting up. Without a word, Circe swept Psyche's feet back up on the chaise. Psyche smiled at her little sister's reproachful look.

"We will work it out," Circe repeated sternly. "But for now, I want you to lie down. All I have to do is mention to Gabriel that you're not resting—"

Psyche lay all the way down on the chaise. "See, I'm resting. Circe, you mustn't say a word. He'll be so worried if he thinks I'm doing too much. And I don't think I could bear any more attention than he gave me the last time I was with child. He was so anxious to help that I was tripping over him at every turn."

"Then do as we ask, and I won't say a word," Circe promised.

Psyche sighed. "I will try, but I am going to write to

Sally." Her high forehead creased with a frown. "There is so much to be done."

Circe pressed a kiss to Psyche's brow, causing the lines to relax. "And none of it is as important as growing my niece or nephew."

Quiet joy shone from Psyche's eyes. "You're right."

When Simpson returned with the cup of steaming tea, Circe left her sister settled on the chaise and slipped out the door.

Outside, she said a silent prayer that this time her sister could carry a baby to term. Next to that, what did Circe's first Season matter? She had no interest in balls and parties, anyhow. Psyche was happy, and Circe would be happy for her; that would have to be enough.

Circe was destined for neither love nor marriage. And if the thought made her feel suddenly empty inside, it was only a momentary aberration.

Two

"*You are the most enchanting flirt who ever raised my hopes to near bursting point*," Mr. Elliston declared, his chest swelling with his declaration until the corset hidden beneath his expensive coat of superfine creaked alarmingly. They were seated side by side in the Forsyth drawing room, striking in its bold shades of teal and peacock blue, with the latest in French cabinets lining one papered wall, and a pleasing vista of spring flowers visible through the tall windows.

Sally Forsyth rather hoped his laces would break and end the tedium of his visit. "No, no," she murmured, batting her long lashes. "You wrong me, sir."

"Never would I malign so lovely a lady fair," her visitor declared. He put one hand to his heart, and she hoped that he was not about to break into verse again. Mr. Elliston fancied himself a poet. "Never would I suggest any impropriety, it is only your beauty, your charm, that tempts my errant heart!"

She knew that he was hoping for exactly that, the kind of impropriety that only a merry widow—experienced in love and with no husband available to demand satisfaction for any lapses in virtue—could provide. He was not the first elderly gallant who'd appeared at her door since the death of her husband.

Sally stifled a sigh. She still missed her sweet, slightly stodgy Andrew, who had succumbed to influenza two winters ago. She had cried herself to sleep for many a night after his death, dutifully worn black for a year, and then, being Sally, put on her colors once more and plunged back into the parties and luncheons and drives she had had to forgo during her period of official mourning. Life was short, and the span of a woman's attractions even shorter. She might as well enjoy some tasteful flirtations while she could still attract any gentleman callers.

Not that Mr. Elliston was going to obtain what he really wanted, an invitation up to her boudoir. But, again being Sally, she would not send him away without the slightest bit of encouragement. She smiled as he continued to spout nonsense, but pleasant nonsense, about the beauty of her curly brown hair and warm brown eyes, though she hoped that he was not going to go down on his knees, as the man would surely never get up again. At least, not without his corset reaching the bursting point.

To her relief, just as Mr. Elliston began to read her his latest literary effort, an unoriginal ode to a shepherd boy and his shepherdess love, a footman entered the drawing room. A single sheet of folded paper lay on the silver salver he extended to his mistress.

"The boy said this was urgent, madam."

"Yes, thank you," Sally murmured. Flashing a quick smile of apology toward her visitor, she broke the seal and scanned the writing inside. "Oh, dear. One of my friends is not well, Mr. Elliston. I must go to her at once. Please forgive me."

"Of course," her gentleman caller said, though he looked sulky as he folded his latest creation. About to push it back into his inner pocket, he paused. "Shall I leave this for you to peruse at your leisure?"

"Oh, no," Sally blurted, before remembering his delicate male sensibility. "That is, I'm sure it will need your own reading to bring out its most special allure." Rising, she turned toward the door, and he was forced to get to his feet and follow her out of the drawing room.

The farewells at last over, Sally sighed as the front door closed behind him. Really, the man was hardly an amusement anymore. Perhaps she could nudge him toward some other worthy lady in need of company. Sally was beginning to think that a nice lap dog—her last one had died peacefully of old age a few months ago—would provide just as much enjoyment as prosing poets with too high an estimation of their own worth and too little sense of humor. If only Andrew—

But she pushed such thoughts away; she always got a little blue when she reflected on her widowhood. Andrew had been such a comfortable husband, allowing her a free hand, but fond of her in his own way. Better not to think on it. Right now, she had to change her dress.

"I'm going out," she told the footman. "Order my carriage, I shall be down directly." She headed for the stairs and her bedchamber, calling ahead to her dresser, "Hodges, I shall need a walking dress, please."

The maid who had served her for years hurried in. "The blue, madam, or the new scarlet with gold braid?"

"The blue will do. I do not wish for bright colors to make her nausea worse," Sally said, trying to be considerate of a lady with an uncertain phlegm.

"Someone is ill?"

"Lady Gabriel Sinclair, and she wants to see me at once," Sally confided.

"Oh, dear, I hope it is not something serious," her maid worried aloud. "And the Season just about to begin, too."

Sally shed her at-home dress and put on the blue with the matching pelisse and the deep brown trim that brought out the honey color of her eyes. But she glanced into the looking glass only for a moment, and she was soon climbing into her carriage for the short drive to the Sinclair town house.

When she alighted, she hurried up the steps and was

shown into Psyche's bedchamber, where she found her friend reclining on a chaise, looking a little pale but not as distressed as Sally's fertile imagination had portrayed her.

"Darling." Sally hurried to Psyche's side. "What is it? I came at once."

"I didn't mean to alarm you," Psyche protested, smiling. "I only said you should come when it was convenient. I hope I didn't take you away from any pleasant diversion."

"Only Mr. Elliston, who was about to start spouting his broken verse—very broken verse." Sally shook her head. "So, no, I wouldn't say that it was a pleasant diversion exactly." Then she saw that her friend was baiting her. Sally made a face.

"You tease, you know I am tiring of him. But what of you, are you ill indeed?"

"I don't know, just a bit of dizziness and a touch of stomach distress." But Psyche's tone was significant, and Sally's expression changed to one of amazed delight.

"Oh, do you think—"

"I hope," Psyche said simply.

Sally reached for her friend's hand, and for a moment, clung to it. She found that her own eyes had dampened with a mixture of feelings, but mostly the sincerest good wishes.

"I hope this news does not—does not—" Psyche hesitated and pressed Sally's hand before she released it. She knew, of course, that in all the years of Sally's marriage, there had never been any hint of a child.

But Sally had resigned herself to her barrenness. "No, indeed, I am only happy for you, my dear. I am delighted to be a doting aunt, by courtesy if not by blood." She pulled up a stool to sit beside Psyche. "How overdue are your courses?"

Psyche told her, and together they discussed the probability, then went on hopefully to the best foods to maintain the health of a mother-to-be. "I have heard of a good jelly of beef broth that is said to have strengthening qualities," Sally remarked. "I will send your cook the receipt."

Psyche nodded, then appeared to remember the true purpose of her note. "Sally, I have a problem. If I am unable to take part in the Season—"

"In which case, I know Gabriel will not repine," Sally argued. "He would hardly chide you for missing a few balls."

"No, of course not. It is Circe. After months of persuasion, she has at last agreed to her coming out. I dare not put it off; she might change her mind again and return to the Continent to paint. I want her to have her chance to meet some eligible young men, not just farmers and village blacksmiths, no matter how picturesque they might be. She must have a little diversion, in addition to her devotion to her art. She says she doesn't want to marry, but she is so young, how can she judge?" Psyche frowned, her sisterly concern obvious.

Sally nodded in understanding. "Of course, I should have thought. You know I should be happy to chaperone your sister at any time. In truth, I hate going to parties alone. It is not the same without my husband, and it would be great fun to have a companion once more. And even when Circe is the center of attention, and I have to be one of the matrons sitting at the side of the room, too old to dance and flirt—"

Psyche laughed aloud at the absurd thought. "Oh, Sally, you're hardly gray-haired and infirm just yet!"

Sally, who was not yet forty, grinned. "And if my hair does begin to fade, I assure you, no one will ever know it. My maid is most accomplished in the French dyes."

Laughing, they shared secrets of face creams and powders, and Sally forgot all about her low moment. She felt quite exhilarated. She would never have a daughter to launch into society; what fun to have this chance to assist Circe. Then she recalled her acquaintance with Psyche's little sister and the child's tendency toward the unexpected. Ah, yes.

She was only too happy to help Psyche, and it would be the perfect diversion. If, mind you, Circe would cooperate, just a little!

⚞⚟

Circe was not feeling cooperative. "This waistline pinches me dreadfully!" she complained. "And how can one move with these heavy skirts? I'll need the help of all of the King's navy just to maneuver my way to His Majesty."

Sally gave a naughty shiver. "Delightful idea. Perhaps I will join you. I'm sure I have my old court gown somewhere."

Lying on her chaise to watch the fitting, Psyche laughed. "Behave, Sally. Now, Circe, you know that court dress is de rigueur for your presentation. It is only for one occasion, you will not have to wear it again."

A lot of fuss and expense for one event, Circe thought, gazing down at the elaborate, old-fashioned dress that the seamstress was adjusting to her measurements. She pictured all the art supplies she could have bought with the money that was going into this dress, which made her feel much like an overdecorated tea cake.

"Thank heavens, I can't imagine how anyone maneuvers in such costumes." Circe tried to stifle her rebellious feelings. She'd had to stop her painting early, yet again, with precious minutes of clear morning light still remaining. She'd known how it would be, despite all Psyche's assurances that her work would not suffer.

"It is quite necessary, Circe," Sally told her. "Everyone of quality must be presented at court."

"I know," Circe agreed, "and I said that I would do it. It's just such a dreadful waste of time."

The other two women exchanged exasperated glances, then, their expressions almost identical, turned back to Circe perched atop her stool while the seamstress, her mouth full of pins, measured a hem.

"Circe, really, please try—" Psyche began.

"It will be more diverting than you imagine—" Sally started. Then both paused, and all three women laughed.

"I'm not trying to be a nuisance," Circe told them. 'It's just that I really belong in the garret with my paints, not in the drawing room trying to make polite conversation. You know I can never do that successfully! And even if I could, I don't wish to be a proper society miss. Don't you recall what Mother said about education being more important than manners? Remember Miss Mary Wollstonecraft's treatise, 'A Vindication of the Rights of Women'—"

Psyche winced. "Circe, that woman was not at all respectable—please don't mention her name in polite company! And even Mother, although she valued the education of women highly and was sometimes—um, unconventional—understood the blessings of good birth. I know she would have wished you to have a proper coming out, and making your bow at court is just a necessary chore. I will not say it's the most stimulating occasion, but you will get to see the king, and sometimes—"

She paused, and a spasm of disquiet showed in her face.

"Quick, the basin," Sally told Simpson.

The lady's maid held out a large china bowl and Psyche leaned over it, while the dressmaker held up her apron to shield the all-important court gown.

Circe winced at her sister's bout of nausea. What a selfish wretch she was, she thought with a wave of guilt, to complain about one afternoon of boredom when her sister felt so miserable and had much more important matters on her mind. Circe would not complain any longer, she vowed. She would suffer through all of this and not worry her sister.

In a moment, Simpson took away the basin. Sally hurried to offer Psyche a cloth dampened with lavender water with which to wipe her face.

When Psyche leaned back against the chaise, her face was as pale as the white cloth she held. "This is dreadful. Last time I did not have this much distress."

"Yes, and look at the outcome," Sally pointed out, her tone matter-of-fact. "This is likely a good sign, Psyche, you will have all your doldrums now. In a few months the misery will pass, and the rest of your confinement will be uneventful and the birth simple and uncomplicated."

"Oh, I pray it may be so," Psyche murmured.

At Gabriel's insistence, she had been visited by Sir William Reynolds, one of London's most renowned physicians, who had announced in solemn tones what all the women of the household had already discerned: Psyche was officially with child.

The seamstress, with one wary eye on Psyche to sidestep any more sudden retching, announced that the fitting was concluded. "I shall have this delivered the day before your court presentation, Miss Circe," she mumbled, one pin still in her mouth.

"Thank you," Circe said, delighted that she could at last shed the uncomfortable formal dress. With the aid of the dressmaker and Luciana, who had been hovering shyly in the background wearing that abstracted expression she often had, as if her thoughts were far away, Circe was extricated from the heavy skirt and bodice and slipped back into her day dress.

Circe much preferred the simple, high-waisted design and clear yellow of her muslin gown. Today Luciana had attempted to twist her mistress's hair into a sleek chignon. To hold it in place the maid had had to use more than a dozen hairpins, which tended to poke her scalp at unexpected times, but Circe thought it looked reasonably proper.

"Let us withdraw, too, and let Psyche rest a little," Sally suggested after the seamstress had departed, her arms full of fabric. Luciana curtsied and retired, as well.

Circe glanced at her sister, who tried to protest.

"No, no, I am quite all right, it's just—" Her words were interrupted by a large yawn. Along with the nausea, she was easily wearied, as if her body needed extra rest while it performed its important task.

Circe nodded. "Yes, indeed. Nap a little, Psyche. We did not mean to tire you. Sally, come along to the schoolroom."

Sally grimaced, but she changed her expression quickly to one of polite pleasure. "Yes, indeed."

She should have taken their friend to the drawing room and ordered tea, Circe realized belatedly. But her fingers hungered for the feel of a brush. Sally would understand.

Indeed, Sally followed her up to the schoolroom and eyed the painting on the easel with appreciation. "How lovely!"

"I meant it for Psyche," Circe told her as she took up the paintbrush. She touched the bristles lightly. The paint had not yet hardened; unlike watercolors, oil dried slowly.

"You have done so much already?" Sally said. "Since you and she knew about the coming babe, I mean?"

Circe blinked. It had not occurred to her before to think about the subject of the painting—she painted the images that came into her head, without any pondering as to their import. "No, I began it as soon as I arrived home. . . ." She paused as the other woman stared at her. "It was just—just—"

"Yes," Sally agreed, her tone a little dry. "Very appropriate, don't you think?"

Circe sighed. If she had begun the painting before Psyche's symptoms were obvious, perhaps some hint of her sister's condition had slipped into her mind, that was all.

"I painted the villagers in Italy," she tried to explain to Sally. "The young mothers, women round with child, babies playing. Perhaps it was simply some understanding of the subtle changes in my sister's physique. Her breasts have already begun to swell, you know."

Sally's eyes widened.

"In preparation for the baby," Circe tried to explain.

"I know that, of course," Sally said, her tone astringent. "But I am a married woman, Circe. At least, I was a married woman, now a widow. But you are a maiden, and to speak so openly of such matters—you will shock the Ton if you discourse on such subjects."

Circe frowned. She could add body shape to the list of topics she must remember not to address in public. "I will never be able to do it, Sally!" she protested, putting down the brush again. "I've had two perfect years of freedom. Years where I had to hide nothing, pretend nothing. Now I cannot say anything without fear of disgracing myself, and Psyche, too. I should not be attempting this." Feeling tears too close to the surface, she bit her lip. "As well to try to make a goose into a swan."

"Circe, my dear." Sally came closer and put one comforting arm about her shoulders. "You will do splendidly, and anyone who knows you will love you for just what you are."

"A goose?" Circe's lips lifted despite herself.

"No, dear girl, for the swan in waiting that you surely are," Sally retorted, giving her a hug. "And despite your undeniable talents—" Sally glanced at the painting on the easel—"you should enjoy some of life's more mundane pleasures, too. Tasting the delights of the Season should not be viewed as a chore. You are neither ugly nor impoverished, and there is no reason you should not have plenty of admirers. You will learn to flirt and to dance and to chat with well-mannered young men. You will have a wonderful time."

Circe gazed at her, knowing that her expression was unconvinced.

"Truly you will!" Sally patted her arm. "And I shall be there to help you."

"Maybe," Circe conceded. The trouble was, she didn't wish for a circle of admirers, only one—and he had changed until he seemed nothing like he once was. David had been impulsive when he was younger, sometimes even foolish, but he'd also possessed an instinctive enjoyment of life that had spoken to the young Circe. Now he seemed as artificial as everyone else in the Ton. And besides, he was searching, so he said, for some correct and bloodless society debutante.

But hadn't she known she would never find a man who could accept her as she was, who could be a true soul mate? She would not think of it. She would push that youthful fancy of David out of her mind and someday, she hoped, out of her heart.

She sighed, but for Sally's benefit, tried to sound hopeful.

"I will try."

Three

*O*n the afternoon after Circe's court presentation, David came by to congratulate her on her success. At least, he had heard no rumors of a disaster of royal proportions, so he assumed she must have muddled through. Not long ago George IV had finally assumed the throne after his mad father's death and, like David, was newly reformed. So Circe should have had no problem making her curtsy before the former prodigal prince.

When the door opened, Jowers admitted him this time without argument, though he pointed out, "Lord Gabriel is not at home, my lord, and Lady Gabriel is resting."

David handed over his hat and gloves. "And Miss Circe? Is she in the schoolroom at her easel?"

The butler accepted the gloves glumly, his usual peeved expression even more disapproving than normal. But his reply sounded almost smug. "I believe not, my lord. However, I will inquire if she is at home to visitors." He disappeared into the interior of the house.

The wait seemed interminable; what was the man about? Couldn't he keep track of one slip of a girl? Not if it were Circe, David reflected. How could anyone keep up with her?

Perhaps Jowers had been mistaken. David climbed the

staircase rapidly, going all the way up to the schoolroom, but sure enough, it was untenanted. Where the deuce was she?

He left the room and started down the stairs. On the next wide landing, he caught a glimpse of a maidservant, her arms full of billowing lace-trimmed satin. The cast-off and much maligned court dress, David suspected. He called to the young maid as she was about to enter a bedchamber.

"Could you tell me where Miss Circe is, if you please?"

"I believe she's in the back courtyard, sir." The girl sounded flustered, but David smiled reassuringly and descended the remaining stairs.

He wondered, however, if the servant had been misinformed. Just in case, he made his way out the side door and walked around the house and into the rear courtyard. What would Circe be doing back here? If she wished to ride, a horse would be saddled and brought around for her.

David looked about him. Two ancient oaks shaded the yard, and the area was paved with gray stone. A groom could be heard whistling inside the stable as he brushed one of Gabriel's mounts, and a serving maid carrying a basket of apples hurried across the uneven pavement. A plump cat purred in a sunny corner, and sparrows squawked at each other atop the stone wall that enclosed the courtyard. But he saw no sign of his missing coconspirator.

Just when he was about to give up and return to the main house, he spotted a most peculiar sight. It seemed the tree nearest him had grown a new limb—a long, stocking-encased limb—and dangling from the tip of its toes was a narrow, yellow slipper.

Why was he not even surprised?

David stepped closer and raised his gaze to see that Circe had climbed up the stout old tree past the lower branches. She sat comfortably in a V formed halfway up where the trunk of the tree forked, and she held a sketch pad and pencil.

Why else would Circe be in a tree, he asked himself, trying to feel as shocked as he knew he should be. Regrettably, he felt a greater inclination to laugh.

Her attention directed toward the stables, she did not seem to notice him. She would likely sit there all afternoon if he did not haul her down to solid ground both literally and figuratively. As she shifted position slightly, her thin skirts rose higher, exposing a very shapely calf. David cocked his head and considered this new view of Circe—yes, a *very* shapely calf.

And David knew a thing or two about legs, especially long, curvy legs that stretched from a woman's delicate ankles to her even more delightful . . . David gave a low, appreciative sigh. He knew of no faster route to heaven than wrapped firmly between a woman's legs.

Circe shifted slightly, bringing David thudding painfully back to reality. He shook his head. What the *hell* was he thinking? And about Circe, who was practically a child! Well, not a child any longer, no, but in comparison to his world-weary person! And someone was bound to notice her soon. This thought did offend him, though he dared not examine why too closely.

"Circe!" he said sternly.

She looked down at him, blinking as if her thoughts had been far away. "Oh, David, hello."

She sounded so calm that his annoyance grew. "What do you mean, hello? I came to ask about your presentation at court. How was it?"

"Tedious." She chewed on the end of the pencil.

He tried to hold his temper in check. "Circe, what the hell—what are you doing up in a tree?"

"I wanted to check the perspective of my work in progress. I was not sure I had the angle just right, looking down upon the mother and child." She sounded so matter-of-fact that it was hard to hold on to his indignation, but he tried.

"The servants are going to see you, Circe!"

"And? They have seen me before, you know."

"Not up a tree! Or at least," he added, "I sincerely hope not. Come down at once."

"As soon as I finish my sketch." To his growing ire, she glanced back at the pad she held, as if to ignore any further protests.

He knew better than to try to scold Circe. She simply didn't think like any normal female. As he watched her pencil move across the paper, an old memory flashed into his mind. Careful not to speak too loudly and startle her— or embarrass her—he pitched his voice low and said, "I thought you were afraid of heights."

He had heard how her parents had died—an accident with a hot-air balloon. Her father must have been mad, too, as well as a brilliant inventor. Psyche had once told him that after the tragedy, Circe would not even fly a kite.

She stiffened and glanced below, and he thought that she paled.

"Ah, perhaps I am finished with my sketch after all," she said. "I didn't realize that—that I was up . . . that I . . . oh, God." Her voice had turned faint, and she was most definitely ashen.

"Do not swoon," he warned, alarmed. Even though one of her hands had grasped a nearby branch so tightly that her fingers were white, Circe looked disgusted at such a suggestion.

When Circe was absorbed in her work, she forgot everything else, David thought. He approached the tree and eyed a well-placed branch. "Just stay put."

Circe rolled her eyes. "Oh, don't worry," she said.

David peeled off his tight-fitting jacket, afraid he would split a seam, then stepped up into the tree, grasping the nearest limb, then the next. The grayish bark felt papery beneath his hands. He climbed another foot, then another, and at length was able to reach up to Circe.

"Take my hand."

She didn't move, biting her lip and gazing toward the earth below—too far below.

"Don't look down," David encouraged. "Focus on me."

She grabbed his hand and grasped it hard. "I'm not sure—I can't—"

"One step at a time," he told her. "I'm here for you."

Her face still white, Circe visibly gathered her courage. Turning to cling to the limb beside her, she lost her grip on the pad and pencil. They dropped through the branches, snagging a green leaf or two as they fell, then hit the ground with a dull thud.

Circe gulped.

"It's all right," he said calmly. "You're not going to fall. Move your foot to the next branch below you."

She drew a deep breath, then released her grip far enough to do as he bade her.

"Good girl," David said. He steadied her as she lowered herself and pretended not to see that she trembled.

She tried to go lower again, but her foot slipped, and she almost lost her grip. Crying out, she reached for the tree, but it was David she grasped.

For a moment, they clung together. God, she felt good pressed against him. Through the thin materials of their clothes he could feel her every heartbeat and her every breath. Her small, well-shaped breasts were high and firm, and her waist slim. He felt desire stir inside him and feared that she would sense his arousal. But if he loosened his grip, she would likely fall, and they were still at least six feet above the paved courtyard.

Circe's eyes had widened a little, and she met his gaze from only a few inches away. She smelled of apple blossoms, and he could see each and every faint freckle scattered across her nose, freckles that were not normally discernable. But then, he had never been this close to her before. As he gazed into eyes of such a clear green that he could have dived into them, he wondered why he never had. But before his mind could frame an answer, he was distracted by the press of her legs—long slim legs that he wished he could pull up and wrap about his waist while he pushed aside her skirts . . .

She stared back at him, unblinking; her confusion and her fear both seemed to have fled. He wished he could soften her inquiring gaze into languorous desire. His body heated another dangerous degree. Bloody hell, but he wanted her, wanted her to want him. He pulled her even closer against him. She seemed to fit so well against the hard angles of his own long, muscled frame.

What was she thinking? She didn't seem at all distressed by their unconventional proximity. In fact, Circe's generous mouth curved upward so sweetly that he couldn't help himself. He bent his head to touch her lips—

"Oh, mercy upon us!" a female voice shrieked.

They both jumped, and David almost lost his grip on the tree limb, which would have plunged them to the ground beneath. He tightened his hold just in time and held Circe flush against him. He twisted his head to see who had cried out.

A kitchen maid tilted her head to stare at them in shock, and now more servants were popping up, from the stable and out of the kitchen door. David wished them all to Hades.

"We are all right," he said, his tone stiff at being caught in such a scandalous position. "I was helping Miss Circe down from the tree."

It was a ridiculous statement, and a ridiculous predicament to be caught in.

And now Circe was laughing beneath her breath, damn it. He circled her torso with one arm and with the utmost reluctance allowed her to slip away from him, lowering her until she could find a foothold.

"I have it now," she said, then she released his hand and clutched the branch beside her, found another foothold, then jumped, landing with a soft flutter of muslin skirts.

Rapidly, David made his own way down. Dusting his

trousers, he scowled toward the groom, brush in hand, and the footman, his wig slightly askew, who goggled at the unusual spectacle. "You may return to your work," he snapped.

The groom disappeared into the stable at once, and the footman turned on his heel and headed for the house. The maids were still staring. David turned his gaze upon them, and the eldest flushed and nudged the other. They hurried inside, too, and David could at last turn his gaze upon Circe.

She looked remarkably composed, now that she was again on solid ground. She bent to retrieve her sketch pad and pencil and seemed intent on the pencil's broken point.

"Circe," he began. "You must behave like—"

"Like what?" Circe looked up at him. "I'm an artist, and I was behaving like one. And if you were going to say lady—and I can tell by the disagreeable set of your features that you were—remember that given the choice between lady and artist, I choose artist." She smiled ruefully. "It's best to not pretend something I could never be."

He spoke before he could stop himself. "Don't say that."

She tilted her head to the side and glanced at him in the direct way that was so uniquely Circe. To his fury, she laughed.

"It's the truth," she said, and then leaned closer to him and placed her warm lips against his ear. "And a few moments ago you didn't seem to mind how ladylike I acted—or didn't."

David drew in a deep breath from the shock of her candid observation. At least he told himself it was shock and not the most powerful attraction he had ever felt in his heretofore dissolute life. As he argued with himself, Circe turned on the narrow heel of her yellow slipper and headed toward the house, leaving David to seethe alone.

To make it even worse, the ache in his groin from unslaked desire lasted longer than his wounded pride.

❧

When the day of her coming-out ball arrived, Circe woke just before dawn. She rose and pulled on a warm dressing gown, eager for the comfort of her paints and brushes. Then, throwing a shawl around her shoulders, as the air was cool, she climbed the silent stairs to the schoolroom just in time for the clear pale light that flooded through the east-facing windows.

Soon she was absorbed in her work, adding the finishing touches to the painting on the easel as she added skillful dabs of green and blue, tints of cerulean and azure. Her ill-advised foray up the tree had allowed her to refine the unusual perspective she had adopted for this scene; she thought she had succeeded in catching the mother and child at an unexpected and revealing angle.

And if she still shuddered at the memory of finding herself so far above the ground, falling literally into David's arms had been worth her initial fright. Why did he refuse to admit his attraction to her? He had been attracted, she was sure of it. And she had felt a return of that new awareness that was so delightfully tantalizing. Too bad the servants had witnessed their leafy embrace and spoiled it all. Sighing, Circe added a dab of green to her palette. But at least she felt confident that beneath the new aura of propriety, the real David still existed. If she could only find a way to draw him out. . . .

Much later, Luciana came looking for her mistress. Bearing a tray with a pot of tea and toast, the little maid fairly quivered with excitement and anticipation. "Oh, there you are, signorina. I looked in your room, but it was empty, and then I thought you must be here."

Circe glanced out the window at the now golden sunlight. No wonder her stomach felt so hollow. But when she laid down her brush, awareness came rushing back. Oh, no. It was tonight, her coming-out ball was tonight. Her new gown hung in the dressing room, and the house, so quiet when she had climbed the nursery stairs, now hummed with activity. She could hear footmen coming and going on the lower flights of stairs as the drawing room was prepared for the dance, furniture rearranged, and fresh flowers brought in.

Luciana bubbled on. "Oh, the flowers are so lovely. And there are musicians coming later, Jowers says, and the goings-on in the kitchen! Mrs. McNilly is checking the ices, and I have taught Cook a new Italian dish for the second course, and she says I am a marvel! I'm having so much fun, and, oh, so will you, Signorina Circe."

Circe forced a smile and sipped her tea. If the ball were for anyone else, she would have had a much better chance of enjoying the festivity, she thought, trying not to spoil the young woman's pleasure. But to have everyone looking at her, listening as she played the part of a demure miss . . . The court presentation had been bad enough, all the girls lined up like a flock of nervous hens waiting to be plucked. But tonight it would be Circe alone.

Psyche thought she was giving her sister such a treat. Circe sighed and picked up a piece of crusty toast. After she ate, she returned to her room to dress for the day and then went to look in on her sister.

"How are you?" she asked, finding Psyche on her chaise in her bedchamber.

"If I lie here quietly all day, I am certain I will be able to make it through the ball," Psyche assured her. "Do not worry."

"I am concerned only about your health. I don't mind a jot about the party," Circe tried to tell her sister, but Psyche made a face.

"Of course you care," she argued. "And I will not spoil your grand occasion, Circe, so do not waste a moment's anxiety on me."

No one was going to believe Circe's feelings, not even Psyche. Circe gave up, concerned about the paleness of her sister's complexion. "Have you been able to eat?"

"Hush, I don't care to think about food just now," Psyche said hastily, putting a handkerchief to her mouth.

Circe nodded and patted her sister's hand, thinking that this did not bode well for the rest of the day. But she kept her thoughts to herself, not wanting to agitate her sister further, and when she left Psyche's chamber, she wandered downstairs to see how the preparations were going.

The folding doors between the drawing room and the smaller salon next to it had been thrown open to make a larger room; the furniture had been moved back and rearranged to leave room for musicians to play and guests to dance. The library downstairs would have extra tables set up for card games, and the dining room would be loaded with food for a late-night supper.

Right now, footmen were carrying in armloads of fresh flowers, which harried housemaids were arranging in vases and urns. Normally, Psyche would have been here overseeing such a task, but she was confined to her room by her indisposition.

Circe did not usually assist in the household affairs—Psyche and their London housekeeper were more than efficient—but Luciana had mentioned that Mrs. McNilly was occupied in the kitchen. The maids were trying their best, but they were more workmanlike than inspired in their placement of the cut flowers.

Her artist's eye could not help but be moved. Circe found herself saying, "No, no, not like that. Here, you must bank all the yellow flowers together, and then the white blossoms here and here, to stand out against the color, you see. And the big ferns in the back, to frame it all."

"What, miss?" The first maid looked confused. "We're just a-putting them in the pots, as Mrs. McNilly tol' us."

"Yes, yes, but you see, it looks better like this." Circe pushed up her sleeves and sat down with the flowers, showing them how to sort the blossoms for best effect, and when all the pots and vases were filled, she helped the servants cart them around and place them carefully about the room, stepping back often to observe the effect, then moving one vase here, one potted fern there.

It was quite an interesting study of color and form, she thought absently. Forgetting about the rest of the turmoil around her as footmen set out extra chairs and rolled up the carpets so that dancing could go on unimpeded, she set up the greenery and the colorful blooms in the most agreeable fashion. Then she sent one of the maids to fetch some wide satin ribbon she had glimpsed in her sister's dressing room and the other to summon a footman—she had an idea. . . .

Hours later she was quite pleased with the result, but as she rearranged one sprig of blossom, she suddenly found a new figure at her elbow, an elderly lady with snow-white hair and faded blue eyes, who leaned slightly on a walking stick and peered down at Circe through the lorgnette she held in her other hand.

"Child, whatever are you doing? Leave the flowers to the servants, you should be dressing for the ball."

"Aunt Sophie!" Circe jumped to her feet, scattering the blossoms in her lap, and hugged her great-aunt. "You have arrived. Are you very fatigued by your journey?"

"Yes, indeed. My witless coachman took the wrong turn and delayed us by two hours." Sophie shook her head. "But you are not attending. You must don your ball gown at once, and do something about your hair, child."

She looked Circe up and down with a gaze as keen as ever, adding, "I must say, the last two years have improved your appearance considerably. Though you must stay out of the sun, Circe! You are brown as a peasant."

Circe smiled at this qualified praise. It was so typical of Aunt Sophie to temper a compliment with a criticism. Mustn't risk anyone ever saying she had mellowed, Circe thought fondly. She noticed Luciana hovering in the hallway.

"Signorina, Lord Gabriel is about to sit down to dinner! We'll have guests arriving soon for the ball." Luciana's tone was frantic.

"What, already?" Circe looked out the tall windows,

her eyes widening with shock. Heavens, the lavender sky had faded into gray as the sunset waned. The day had slipped away as she set up her living palate of color.

"I shall come at once," she promised. "Lay out my gown."

"I did already," the girl protested. "But I can't put it on you without you there, now can I?" She blushed at her vehemence. "Oh, pardon me, signorina."

"Not at all." Circe grinned and saw her new maid's confusion fade. "A sensible observation. I am coming directly, I promise you."

Aunt Sophie directed the butler to have her things brought up, then allowed her own maid to help her up the stairs so that she could change for the ball. Circe followed, after stopping to peek into the dining room, where Gabriel stood alone, glancing at his pocket watch. Psyche was surely having a tray in her room, if she were able to eat at all, and Aunt Sophie, because of her late arrival, would likely do the same.

"There you are, Circe," he said. "Having nervous qualms?"

Circe thought it best not to tell him she had simply forgotten the time. "I have no stomach for food. Please don't wait for me," she told him. "I will be down in time for the ball."

"Of course." He moved closer to pat her hand, and Circe admired his easy grace. With his slim, yet muscular build and habitual air of assurance, Gabriel always managed to look as though he were doing exactly the right thing at the right time. Without intending to, Circe let out a deep sigh. The fine lines around Gabriel's dark blue eyes tightened with his laugh. "You will do splendidly, Circe, no need to be unsettled, you know."

If only she could believe that. "I'm just not much at making polite conversation," she tried to explain. "I hope I don't disgrace you."

Gabriel grinned and squeezed her hand. "Your candid comments are always a delight. Do not try to be less than you are, Circe. I have always loved your original observations."

Yes, but society's matrons might not find her unexpected thoughts so engaging, Circe thought, still uneasy about her presentation to the Ton.

Gabriel gave her a brotherly wink. "I predict you will have a wonderful time."

She hoped his skill at precognition was as strong as his luck at cards. Gabriel had once been a notorious gamester, but since his marriage he played less often, finding the care of his estate and other properties, he said, too time-consuming. Psyche said privately that he had simply grown into more mature responsibilities, but Circe would not repeat that bit of wifely wisdom.

She swallowed another sigh. "I hope you are right," she said, and left him to dine in solitary elegance while she flew up the stairs. In her chamber, Luciana was waiting, her cheeks flushed with nervousness.

"You must hurry, signorina," she said, as if Circe did not already know how late she was.

Circe slipped quickly out of her morning gown and bathed with her favorite apple-scented soap, rubbing herself dry with a linen towel, then pulling on her dressing gown while Luciana attended to her hair. Tonight it was pulled up into a pile of artfully arranged curls on top of her head, with a few white flowers tucked into the coiffure, and she winced at the pins that Luciana inserted to hold it all in place.

Then with Luciana's assistance, she very carefully donned the ball gown that she and Psyche and Sally had chosen, after endless consultations with the modiste and even more endless fittings.

But she had to admit that the result seemed to be worth the effort involved.

"Oh, signorina, you look *bella*—quite beautiful!" Luciana breathed, almost in a whisper. She sounded surprised, but Circe could hardly blame the girl; she felt a bit stunned herself.

She stared into the looking glass. Who was this slim girl with the upswept hair and the clear green eyes who gazed so calmly into the glass? The face was familiar, but different, too. Perhaps some of it was the absence of the usual paint stains and loose blousy smock, plus the neatness of the hair, but it also might have been the gown of purest white, trimmed in white seed pearls and tied with a smooth white satin sash, which made this stranger look so cool and poised and, yes, pretty. She actually looked pretty.

Circe was still trying to adjust to this new vision of herself when there was a knock. Luciana pulled herself away from the gratifying sight and hurried to open the door.

Psyche stood there, a little pale but lovely in a light blue gown with silver trim, a tasteful diamond necklace flashing at her throat and a matching tiara on her golden hair. The sight of her sister was enough to bring Circe back to earth, but still—she stole one covert glance back at the glass—even beside Psyche, tonight Circe thought she just might hold her own. Or very near.

Psyche's blue eyes misted a bit as she looked at Circe. "Oh, you look so beautiful." She moved to Circe and pulled her younger sibling into a tight embrace. After a moment, she stepped back, the tears in her eyes replaced with a gleam of laughter. "And even though you're as brown as a heathen—"

Circe laughed at this proof that Aunt Sophie had grumbled to Psyche, too. "Oh, good. I've been promoted from peasant."

"Even though you are darker than is the fashion," Psyche continued with authority, "I think your skin contrasts beautifully with your gown."

They stood there smiling at each other until Psyche sighed. "I have so many hopes for you, Circe. I wish for you to enjoy yourself tonight. I wish that your dreams will come true, all of them, not just your artistic dreams."

Circe swallowed a bit guiltily. She didn't really have

other dreams, at least none such as Psyche meant. None that she would admit, at least.

"Who knows?" continued Psyche. "Maybe tonight you'll be introduced to a man as wonderful as Gabriel."

Circe raised her brows. "I seem to remember you had a very different opinion of Gabriel when you first met him."

Psyche laughed. "Oh, you're right, of course. That man drove me crazy at first. Marching into our town house with all the presumption in the world . . . as if he really were the marquis of Tarrington."

Circe was still a bit amazed that her oh-so-proper sister had ever come up with such a daring plan—creating a fake fiancé and hiring an actor to portray him for one night. But fate—or Lady Luck, as Gabriel claimed—had intervened, and Gabriel had stepped into the role and into Psyche's reluctant heart. Whoever was responsible, Circe was grateful. She couldn't imagine their lives without her dashing brother-in-law.

Psyche held out the velvet box she'd been holding. Circe's ready curiosity stirred. "This was Mother's, and it's time for you to have it, dearest," her sister said.

Circe felt a lump in her throat. She took the case from her sister and opened it carefully. Inside lay a double strand of well-matched pearls, and eardrops with a large luminous pearl hanging from each post like a ripe fruit. Leaves of carefully set small emeralds held each dangling pearl, with a well-cut diamond at the apex of the design.

"They're beautiful," Circe whispered. Her vision blurred for a moment as she remembered her mother wearing this set of jewelry, and a young Circe hurrying up for one more hug and kiss before her parents swept out to the waiting carriage. "Thank you, Psyche."

"I kept them for you," Psyche said. "I thought they would be perfect for your coming-out ball."

Blinking hard, Circe turned so that her sister could clasp the pearls around her throat. Then she adjusted the earrings and looked at herself once more in the glass.

"Just right." She smiled at her sister.

Psyche cocked her head. "There's the knocker at the front door," she said. "Come, we must be ready to receive the first guests. Sally is already here. I sent her down to the ballroom with Gabriel."

Circe felt guilty again at her tardiness. "Thank you, Luciana," she told her young maid. "You don't have to wait up for me. It will be late, I should think, before the last guests leave."

"Oh, no, signorina," Luciana protested. "I want to hear all about your evening."

Circe followed her sister down the wide stairs to the reception room, now decked for the ball. Her sister's gasp as they entered the room gave Circe a moment of gratification. Her efforts with the flowers and the greenery had had their desired effect. The delicate yellow, lavender blue, and white flowers, instead of being set haphazardly about on the tables as the maids had first done, were grouped into bowerlike settings with the larger greenery behind them, and above, white ribbons and green vines twined amid narrow trellises to form miniature canopies behind groupings of chairs and settees.

"Circe, it is lovely! It feels like we're standing in the middle of a garden," Psyche exclaimed. "How did the servants manage without anyone to—oh, you did this, did you not? I should have known."

Sally came up to kiss Circe's cheek. "Of course, it's obvious that a skilled hand—and eye—went into this arrangement. It's truly a vision, my dear, as are you." She looked Circe up and down, then smiled. "I can see that I shall have my job cut out for me as your sometime chaperone."

Circe blushed, laughing at such an absurdity. Then she saw that Sally had brought her a gift, too. She opened the small parcel and found an elegant reticule, covered with seed pearls and gold embroidery, a work of art in itself. Her eyes widened at the delicate skill of the needlework. "How enchanting," Circe said. "Thank you, Sally."

"Your expression is thanks enough." Sally plied her fan. "I knew you would appreciate the grace of the design, quite nice, I thought. Oh, here's Gabriel to tell us that guests are arriving."

"You look bewitching, Circe," her brother-in-law told her. "And just in time. There are people on the stairs, dear," he added to his wife.

"Thank you, my love. Let us make a receiving line, Circe," Psyche said, the hostess in her taking charge at once. She took her husband's arm and glided back to the door of the big room, while Circe cast one last quick glance at the pleasing arrangement of the flowers. The candles were all lit, and the crystal chandeliers had been polished and cleaned so their brighter light was almost dazzling, reflecting off the bare wood floors in shimmering waves of light. She would like to paint that effect, Circe thought absently. The musicians were set up in the alcove at the rear of the room, and she heard one man touch his violin, tuning his strings.

Perhaps Gabriel was right, and all would be well tonight. Perhaps this time, she could act like a princess instead of a goose girl and accept her transformation with grace, without worrying about what happened afterwards. Perhaps she could carry it off, after all.

Psyche was beckoning. Circe hurried to her sister's side in time to greet the first guest, to smile and curtsy and put out her hand.

An hour later, she thought her smile had etched itself into her face. She felt just like a piece of stone statuary, and she was afraid she must look like one, too. How many people were going to come through the doors? Had everyone they had invited shown up? Gracious, there would hardly be room to move in the spacious double room that had looked so big only a short time before. The dance would be called "a sad crush," just as every hostess longed to hear. The fact that this added little to the comfort of the guests was ignored.

It occurred to Circe that David had not yet arrived.

What about the big pretense he planned for them; how could it be credible if he were absent from her first ball? Still, she cared little about his mother's nagging. David's designs were his own concern, she must remember that. Her concern was only to behave herself as a proper young lady, just for one night. And also—she glanced anxiously at her sister. Had Psyche gone even paler? Standing for so long and greeting the seemingly endless line of arriving guests—her sister must be worn down, and surely this was not good for her? Even though the tiny bulge in her belly did not yet show beneath her well-cut formal gown, the pregnancy was taking its toll on her sister's strength. And having such an uncertain appetite . . .

Circe wanted to tell Psyche to go and sit down, but she knew her sister would not listen. Then she heard the sounds of the unseen musicians, now hidden by the press of the crowd, change from the soft background music they had been playing. Yes, she remembered seeing Gabriel give a message to one of the footmen. The musicians were about to begin the dance music, which meant that Gabriel would lead her, as guest of honor, into the first dance. And Psyche could sit down and have a glass of lemonade; wine upset her stomach lately and she had quietly switched to other libations.

Circe thought, with an inner sigh, of her father—if only he had still been alive to do this honor. Perhaps her parents could see her tonight, she reflected with the old longing. Were they smiling down at her from heaven? If so, they would wish her to be happy, so she would try not to dwell on regrets or might-have-beens. But she did miss them so.

She turned to glance toward her brother-in-law, waiting for his cue to move to the dance floor, just in time to see Psyche's expression change. "What is it?" Circe asked in alarm.

"Nothing, only—oh, dear." Psyche put one white gloved hand to her mouth.

There was no servant close enough to assist her sister,

Aunt Sophie was sitting in a chair at the edge of the room, and even Sally had drifted out of sight among the crowd. "Gabriel," Circe said, her tone quiet but urgent. "Get her out of here, quickly!"

Psyche would be dreadfully embarrassed if she were ill in full view of all their guests. To Circe's relief, she saw her sister lean on Gabriel's offered arm. With his strong support, they disappeared in a moment into the hallway and out of sight.

But no one had told the musicians to delay the dance tune, and the beginning notes wafted through the crowd. People were turning to stare, waiting for Circe to come forward. Some of her male cousins were here, somewhere, and a couple of elderly uncles, but none of them was within easy distance, and she could not grab a virtual stranger from the nearest cluster of guests. As if guessing her thoughts, she saw the nearest man turn to gaze at her. He was middle-aged and stout, and the top of his head shone in the reflection from the chandeliers. At the moment she did not remember his name. No, no, she could not do it. She bit her lip, trying not to show her uncertainty.

But she had no partner. She had to do something but what? Feeling her cheeks flush, Circe hesitated. It was too late to stop the tune, and people would talk if—

"Miss Hill," a familiar male voice said. "You are late for your debut dance. Will you be kind enough to take my arm?"

Four

Circe turned with relief. It was David, smooth as aged wine in his neat black evening coat and waistcoat, his hair artfully brushed, one diamond stud winking in his shirt front.

"Oh, thank heavens, David. I've never been so glad to see anyone in my life," she said, releasing the breath she'd been holding. "Psyche was—that is—"

"I know. I saw her in the hallway showering a poor urn of daffodils. They will never be the same again," he said, his expression wry.

Circe frowned. "She cannot help it! If you felt so ill—"

"Ah, but I shall never experience quite that type of complaint," he told her, his eyes gleaming with a hint of the humor he would not allow to surface. "And it is most unsuitable of me to even comment upon it. Come, we are missing the dance, and it is in your honor, remember."

"Of course." She put her hand on his arm, and he led her to the dance floor. David might have turned too prim and proper again, but he still danced divinely, and it was a relief to allow him to bow over her hand. Couples formed in a line below them. She could not waltz, of course, until the patronesses of Almack's granted her permission, and that would not be at her own coming out, but still, with David beside her in the set, she could forget some of her worry about following the pattern of the dance. She would not take the wrong step or lead off in the wrong direction with David's skillful touch guiding her arm.

Not that she was usually clumsy, in fact she had learned some delightful dances on the Continent, but she had little patience for formal affairs and had not practiced the forms over and over with a dancing master as most young ladies did before their first ball. Psyche had suggested it, but Circe had had more important ways to spend her time. She had spent an hour with Sally reviewing the dance steps, hoping that would be enough. Still, tonight she did not want to disgrace her sister, and she was happy to have David's subtle assistance. For several minutes, they led the others through the pattern of the dance, and Circe made no missteps.

The formal tune lacked the wild beat of some of the Spanish and Italian peasant music she had grown to love, and it had been much more exciting to be actually in David's arms, pressed tightly against him. The memory of their encounter in the tree flickered inside her, and she was suddenly impatient with the slow, measured steps and the space that always stretched between them.

What would the Ton say if she rushed into David's arms right now? What would David say? From the careful way he held her at arm's length, she suspected he would only scold. Sighing, she was forced to make do with David's hand on hers, and David's too formal smile as they moved gracefully through the figures. She pushed aside her cravings for less artifice and more honesty and tried to enjoy the dance.

"You make a much more elegant picture," David told her, "when you stay out of trees. And you clean up quite nicely, without the paint stains."

For a moment she glared at him, then she took herself in hand and presented him with her most gracious expression. "And I like the way you dance, my lord," she replied demurely. "When you deign to show up at a party at all, even if an hour late."

"Lord, Circe." He raised one brow. "It is ill bred to be on time. I appeared at just the right hour, and certainly in time to rescue you."

The dance took them apart, which was just as well as she almost blurted something most inappropriate. By the time she circled back to his waiting arm, she was able to say coolly, "My thanks for your timely assistance, then. I hope not to detain you for too long."

"Not at all," he said. "We have to keep up our pretense, do we not? Besides," he added before she could think of something even more cutting to say, "you do look a picture in that dress. Beautiful, and decorous, too. I hardly recognized you."

Swallowing her retort to that backhanded compliment, she made her curtsy as the music faded. "Thank you, my lord," she forced herself to say. "I hope your mother will be pleased."

David smiled a bit absently. He seemed to be scanning the room. "My mother is in Bath, thank God, but I'm sure she will hear the gossip from all of her friends," he agreed.

Then Gabriel was at her elbow, nodding a thank-you to David. She felt a flicker of irrational disappointment that David would now leave her, but hid her feelings at once and asked, "How is Psyche?"

"I have persuaded her to lie down, and Aunt Sophie is with her. If she feels better, she will rejoin the party later," Gabriel said. "I am so sorry I missed your first dance, Circe."

"Not to worry, David was an adequate replacement." Circe smiled sweetly at her erstwhile partner.

"Adequate?" David raised his brows. "I never do anything that is merely adequate."

Gabriel grinned at them both. "I am glad he was able to step in. May I have the honor now?"

"Delighted." Circe took his arm and left David without

a backward glance. *There,* she thought. *Go escort a truly proper and boring young lady.*

But she said to Gabriel, "If you would rather stay with Psyche—"

"No, she insisted I hurry back to you. She wishes only that you enjoy the ball, Circe," Gabriel told her as they took their places for the next dance.

Circe knew she shouldn't, but she couldn't help stealing one quick glance to see whom David was partnering now. But he had instead retreated to the side of the room and was speaking with Sally, who said something that made him laugh. The decorous mask that he wore too often was replaced for an instance by a more natural expression, and Circe detected the sensual gleam in his blue-gray eyes.

If only she knew how to bring back the real David, lure him to drop his pretenses as Sally had done. With an effort, she pulled her thoughts back to the dance.

More young men waited to claim her when the tune ended. Circe had always been light on her feet, and now that her first rush of nervousness had passed, she had no trouble with the dance figures. It was the conversation that she dreaded.

After half a dozen dances, she stopped long enough to sip a glass of champagne to ease her dry throat. She had begun to think she might carry this off after all, when an astringent voice broke into the stammering compliments her most recent partner had been offering.

"So, Circe, have you learned to comport yourself like a seemly young lady at last?"

Circe stiffened instinctively, then forced a smile, though her lips felt stiff. "Hello, Aunt Mavis. How nice to see you. We had no time to talk when you came through the line. Where is Cousin Matilda? I did not see her come in."

"Probably because she's not here—increasing again and feeling a bit peckish this evening," Circe's vinegar-tongued aunt replied. But her usual dour expression softened for a moment. Circe knew that she was enormously fond of the two small girls that her married daughter had already produced.

"How splendid," Circe said with genuine pleasure. "Give her our very best regards. We shall have to call one day this week and see how she is feeling. I hope she is soon recovered."

"Told her to sip a cup of chicken broth and buck up," her aunt retorted. "I never had such problems before she was born. Girls these days are too prone to vapors. And where is Psyche gone off to, by the way? Haven't glimpsed her this half hour."

Circe thought quickly. She knew that Psyche didn't want her condition known just yet, and she surely had no wish for the kind of family gossip that Mavis could incite. Besides, their aunt was not exactly the most sympathetic person to confide in. "Oh, she went to see about the supper, I think," she said vaguely.

Several more matrons came up, friends of her aunt's, and the conversation became more general.

"Such charming flowers," Mrs. Caros remarked. "And so original."

"Thank you," Circe said, smiling with genuine warmth.

"And all who are here are the very best of the Ton," a second lady added, her purple plume drooping a bit into her face. "You have even enticed the earl of Westbury, I see. Your ball is a grand success, my dear."

Mavis fanned herself energetically with her fan. "Yes, such a crush, though it's too warm in here by half."

Circe nodded. "Would you like a glass of wine, Aunt?" she asked, hoping for a chance to slip away. But she was not to find her escape so easily.

"Tell us about your time on the Continent, my dear," Mrs. Caros asked. "France is such a delightful place to shop. Did you visit Italy as well?"

"Oh, yes, I wouldn't have missed it, so much art treasure." Circe knew that her expression softened as she remembered. "And the light—the light is so special there."

"Light?" The matron looked perplexed. "How could the sunlight differ?"

"On the hillsides it is golden, soft, and it changes the whole outlook when one is painting," Circe tried to explain. "The luster of a ripe pear, the gleaming play of water in a stream, the soft sheen of sun-browned skin . . ."

There was a sudden silence as Circe realized what she had said.

"Naked skin?" Mrs. Caros sounded scandalized. "What on earth would a young lady of good breeding know about bare skin!"

"But artists must paint people as they are, you know," Circe tried to explain. "Even centuries ago, Michelangelo understood that an artist must understand physiology in order to—"

"Circe!" Aunt Mavis eyed her with a stern gaze. "You have not painted unclothed men, surely!"

Around them, other heads were turning. Oh, Lord, here it was, the scandal she had known she would incite, just by opening her mouth.

"The naked person in question was two months old," a lazy voice drawled from behind them.

The whole group of ladies turned toward David, like bees drawn instinctively toward a particularly succulent flower.

"Oh, I see." Mrs. Caros dissolved into a twitter of nervous laughter. "For a moment I thought—"

"Really, Circe, you should not lead us on like that," Mavis interrupted. "You will have everyone talking."

"I'm sure no one would be so unkind as to willfully misunderstand, Aunt." Circe kept her tone sweet.

"She's such a wit, she cannot help herself," David said almost at the same time, then grinned at Circe's frown. "Come along, my dear, I have the honor of taking you in to supper. Psyche and Gabriel await us."

"Oh, good," Circe said, diverted by the news that Psyche was feeling recovered enough to come back to the party. "Excuse us, please," she told the ladies, then ac-

cepted David's arm. As they walked away, she looked up
to see him lifting a brow.

"Circe, you must remember to mind your tongue!"

"Yes, Grandfather."

"Humph."

Circe laughed, she really couldn't help it. "You see.
Only old men and my aunt Mavis actually say,
'Humph.' " Circe twisted her face comically as she pro-
nounced the silly word. It did not seem to amuse him.

David might pretend not to hear her, but she could see
his smoothly shaved cheek tense as though he were
clenching his jaw. After a moment, he cleared his throat
and asked, "By the way, how old was the model in question?"

"A good deal older than two months," she retorted with
less grace than she might have shown. Circe was tired of
being scolded; still, he had come to her aid. "Though it
was a clever rejoinder. What made you think of it?"

"I've seen your current work, that is all," he said. "The
mother and baby on the canvas upstairs. So it was not a
complete untruth. But you will have to learn to guard your
tongue, chit, if you wish to avoid being censored by all
the old cats in the Ton."

She pressed her lips together, wanting to lash out, but
knowing that he was right. "So I should learn to express,
um . . . not total untruths, as you put it?"

He looked almost condescending. "Yes, if you cannot
manage real decorum, a good imitation will have to do."

"And this is the way society operates? Don't you ever
wish to be straightforward, just tell the truth?" Circe found
it harder and harder to maintain a pose as a demure young
lady. "What is so wicked about the way people are
shaped?"

David's expression changed for an instant, then he
cloaked his thought, whatever it was, and said firmly,
"The topic does not do for ladies' conversation, trust me,
Circe."

"A stupid rule," Circe countered, but she kept her tone

low. Human bodies were beautiful things, she thought stubbornly. What would David's body look like, to sketch without the cloaking fabric? The idea brought her a surge of feeling, and she felt her cheeks burn. She had never felt a personal response to her models, whatever their age. They were merely interesting arrangements of angles and curves, a challenge to the artist's skil!. With David before her, she would never be only an artist. And what did that say about her feelings for him?

With a jolt, she saw that they had arrived at the dining room. Psyche and Gabriel were sitting at a small table with Aunt Sophie beside them. Her sister was pale but composed.

"How is the ball going?" Psyche asked.

Circe was saved from any prevarication by David's easy response. "Very well—Circe is the darling of the hour."

"No doubt," Aunt Sophie said drily, her pale blue eyes skeptical, but Psyche smiled, and Circe did not regret David's omission of her near gaffe.

They tasted the cold meats and delicious candied fruits, the ices and meringues that Cook had labored over. Psyche was able to eat a few bites, while Aunt Sophie chatted about Bath. The men discussed a recent horse sale at Tattersall's, but Circe said little, allowing her mind to wander. Perhaps she should take a vow of silence—there were simply too many things to remember not to speak of. How did the other young ladies manage it?

Other young ladies had had more conventional pasts, she thought. They had not spent the last couple of years living in French cottages, painting peasants at work in the fields, or dwelling happily in Italian *pensioni* where they could sketch vistas of vineyards stretching over the hillsides, complete with bare-armed young men harvesting grapes.

And there had been the trips into Spain, with its sunny vistas, and Switzerland, where she had been awed by the sight of the towering Alps, attempting to capture their majesty on canvas. She'd had little time to worry about proper conversation, sitting in the middle of a field surrounded by her paints and canvases, and life had been so much simpler.

And so much happier.

No sooner had the thought crossed her mind than she felt guilty. Glancing at Psyche and Gabriel and her greataunt, Circe was reminded of how very lucky she was. All the other girls she had known had looked forward to their coming out and their advent into adulthood, but not Circe. She would have been content to remain in the nursery with her paints and canvases. The images she created on the blank canvas were more real to her than any of these people, except for her family, of course . . . and David, but she couldn't have him.

As Circe licked the last of the raspberry ice from her spoon, the rest of the party rose, and they all strolled back to the ballroom. There, they found a convenient chair for Aunt Sophie, and Psyche and Circe sat next to her, with the gentlemen standing near them, still chatting.

Aunt Sophie raised her fan to cover her mouth and whispered fiercely to both her great-nieces. "Here comes that old fool Bircham. I wouldn't have him fifty years ago but he never gives up. Don't you two dare leave me alone with him."

Spotting the "old fool" who was headed their way, Circe hid a smile. Imagining the tiny, shrunken old man slowly approaching them as an overeager suitor was too much. Circe wasn't certain whether the man could even have walked unaided if it weren't for the young man who was lending him an arm. The two finally arrived at their table, and Mr. Bircham visibly caught his breath before he could speak. The man holding him so carefully looked down at him with obvious affection. Finally, Mr. Bircham spoke.

"My dear Sophie," he said with a smile. And what a smile—the man's creased face shone as if it were lit with a hundred candles. And his nondescript eyes twinkled with such vitality and humor that Circe wanted her sketch pad in the worst way. She smiled back.

But Aunt Sophie was her usual gruff self. "Arthur." She gazed at him through her lorgnette.

Circe could tell by Psyche's face that she was horrified at her aunt's abrupt manner, but Circe felt even more amused. She was so taken with the adorable old man that she stood and spoke before anyone else could do so. Ignoring her aunt's—and probably David's—disapproval, she extended both her hands to the old gentleman.

"How do you do? I am Sophie's great-niece, Circe Hill."

Looking pleased, Bircham grasped one of her hands in his own gnarled one and pressed a gallant kiss upon the back of it. "I should have known you anywhere, my dear," he said in a surprisingly youthful voice. "You are the very image of your aunt and just as charming, too."

Aunt Sophie snorted with derision. Gabriel and David suddenly found it necessary to look elsewhere while they fought to control their expressions, while Psyche merely looked resigned.

When it became obvious that Aunt Sophie wasn't going to provide a proper introduction, Psyche stepped in.

"How lovely to see you again, Mr. Bircham. I am so happy you could attend our Circe's debut." With admirable grace, she completed the introductions. Mr. Bircham was all that was gentlemanly and fine. After greeting the younger people, he turned again to Sophie.

"You remember my great-nephew, Sir John Templeton, Baronet, do you not?"

Circe was relieved to see that Aunt Sophie wasn't going to repeat her rudeness. Whether or not Aunt Sophie really remembered him, she nodded and unbent enough to smile and say hello. Sir John was a square-built young man with a face that should have been pleasing. He was of medium height, standing several inches shorter than David. But his formal attire was ill fitted, his fair hair clipped too short, and he did not meet their gaze. Circe would have been hard-pressed to reveal the color of his eyes should anyone have asked because Sir John was studying the gilt legs of Aunt Sophie's chair. They all greeted Sir John, who looked up and acknowledged them as briefly as decency would allow.

Gabriel nodded politely in the newcomer's direction, but his expression held no recognition.

"I'm afraid I—oh, wait, you are the scoundrel who nipped that gorgeous filly from beneath my fingertips."

Psyche tapped her husband's arm playfully with her fan. "I beg your pardon, Gabriel?"

Gabriel looked down into the quizzical expression on his wife's upturned face and smiled charmingly. "A horse auction, my love."

"Indeed." Psyche nodded. Circe watched the laughing glance her sister offered to her husband. *Ah, yes. It's that flirting business*, Circe realized. Sally had mentioned that she must learn to flirt; Circe was beginning to think some aspects of her education had indeed been neglected during all those years she had spent isolated with her paints.

"How you could dare show your face here after outbidding me, I'll never know." Gabriel grinned as he leaned toward Templeton and offered a hand.

Sir John, who after absorbing all the secrets of the furniture had been staring at the wall behind Circe's head, now looked directly at Gabriel and shook his hand. A shy smile spread across his face.

"I simply wanted her more, my lord," he said in a mellow, cultured voice.

"Sinclair, please," Gabriel said pleasantly. "We are all friends here."

Sir John seemed surprised at Gabriel's casual ease, but his shoulders relaxed a little.

Mr. Bircham gave his young relative a not so subtle prod. "In addition to outbidding you at horse flesh, he has another avid interest."

Sir John's face lit up at the reminder, and he turned to Psyche.

"Oh, yes, my lady. I am something of an amateur horticulturist. I wished to commend you on the sumptuous flower arrangements. May I be so bold as to request a meeting with your housekeeper. Her use of color and form are un—"

The smiles around the table must have made Sir John uneasy because he faltered. Psyche and Gabriel did not try to hide their pride, and even Sophie smiled.

"That will not be necessary, sir," Psyche said with her usual cool composure. "The person you seek is right here."

Sir John frowned at his error and then settled his gaze on Psyche. "Forgive me, Lady Gabriel. I did not know you shared my interest in plants."

Psyche laughed in delight. "Oh, my, no," she said. "If I had arranged the flowers, they would be thrown all together in one big pot. I haven't the skill nor the patience, I'm afraid. But"—she gazed at Circe—"my sister does."

Circe, who had been observing the newcomer with curiosity, now spoke. "Psyche enjoys boasting about me, but what I did was very simple."

Sir John blinked. "Simple! Nothing simple about it. Your creativity and aesthetic sense are enviable. My society and I—we have a small salon where we discuss horticulture—would be delighted to have you explain your ideas at one of our meetings."

Circe was flattered but a bit disconcerted. She was no expert on horticulture, and the thought of speaking to a group made her stomach roil. Still, as she looked at Sir John, who had dropped his gaze to study a silver candlestick, she realized she was not the only one ill at ease in polite company. Suddenly feeling a companionship with the gawky young baronet, Circe found herself saying, "I would be honored, sir. I shall speak with you further about your salon."

His face lighting up, Sir John's smile was so unexpectedly appealing that Circe grinned back. Sir John's enthusiasm made his usual diffidence less obvious. He was, after all, a pleasant-looking young man.

Psyche laid her napkin on the table and rose. "My lord," she spoke accusingly to her husband, "you have not danced with me the whole evening."

Raising his brows, Gabriel stood at once.

But Psyche was not done. "May I suggest we all take advantage of the music?"

And though Sir John blushed from brow to cravat at the obvious hint, he took a small step toward Circe as Gabriel and Psyche headed for the dance floor. But before he could stutter an invitation, a new voice spoke, a deep, cultured voice with a hint of a Continental accent.

"Good evening, ladies. Might I have the distinction of leading our guest of honor into the dance?"

Circe turned quickly, intrigued by the pleasing bass tone. The sight of the strong masculine face with its sharp planes and angles made her blink in surprise. The stranger had vivid dark eyes, wavy black hair, and a neat beard; for an instant, she pictured him as a virile, untamed Satan amid one of Michelangelo's incredible frescos, glaring from behind a bush while God reached out to Adam. The stranger had a devilish gleam to his dark eyes and a firmness about the lips that—that . . . Then the silly fantasy dissolved as he smiled, and the sternness about his face melted into a sophisticated charm that made the blood rush to Circe's cheeks. "If I may have the honor?" he repeated.

Mr. Bircham's kind eyes held concern, and Aunt Sophie frowned, but Circe paid no heed. She took his hand and allowed him to lead her toward the bigger room and the dance floor, without a glance toward David or the hapless Sir John. Circe had eyes only for her new escort. He was older than she, older even than Gabriel perhaps, but not at all fatherly. Beneath her hand, she could feel the hard muscles of his arm, and underneath the well-tailored evening clothes, she suspected that the rest of his body was just as firm and conditioned. Painting this man in the nude would be—she pulled her thoughts back, aware that she was blushing.

He looked down at her, obvious admiration mixed with a touch of amusement.

"I'm afraid, that is, I'm sure I did not see you in the receiving line, and I regret I do not know your name," Circe admitted. This face she could not have forgotten, even amid the rush of arriving guests.

He took her implied criticism with good grace. "Ah, forgive me, Miss Hill. Of course I should have waited for a proper introduction. I'm afraid your beauty has made me forget my manners."

Her beauty? Although one corner of her mind protested that this astute gentleman never forgot anything of significance, she couldn't help but feel flattered.

"I was somewhat late arriving," her escort confessed. "I was detained by last-minute business from the Continent. But I am well known to Lord Gabriel Sinclair, Miss Hill, so this is not at all improper. I am Count von Freistadt, at your service."

He lifted her hand to kiss it, and the light touch of his lips made Circe's whole arm tingle. This man made poor Sir John disappear into faint memory, and even David, she thought, looked a trifle brash compared to this man's sophisticated charm.

Circe gave herself a mental shake, and common sense reasserted itself. His ease with young ladies undoubtably came from long practice. In fact, now that she knew his name, she remembered snatches of gossip. The count had a habit of wooing young ladies just out, only to drop them in a Season or two for fresh prey, to the despair of matchmaking mamas. But Circe was not looking for a husband, so the likely intransigence of his suit did not alarm her. And in the meantime, as he led her into the set forming on the dance floor, she was aware of envious glances from the other ladies.

Circe had never been the cause of envy among her

peers—even David, for all his good looks and charm, came under the heading of "old family friend," not a genuine suitor, and she suspected that his attentions were thus discounted. But this worldly and elegant stranger was another matter entirely.

A violin trilled, and the count bowed low over her hand. Perhaps this coming-out business would not be as tedious as she had feared!

Five

As she and her husband took their places for the next dance, Psyche glanced back at the table. She swallowed a gasp.

Circe and the elegant Austrian count were walking away, arm in arm. "Oh, my," Psyche said. "That is not the escort I would have chosen for Circe. I would not even have invited the man, except that Princess Esterhazy would have been insulted if we'd snubbed him. He's her countryman and a great pet of hers."

Gabriel frowned, but his reply was soothing. "No need to worry, love." Gabriel squeezed his wife's slender fingers. "Circe is no fool, and we will keep a close eye on von Freistadt. He's polished enough. In fact, he's quite popular with many of the ladies."

"That is what worries me!" Psyche pointed out, her tone astringent. "He's hardly husband material."

"True." Gabriel grinned. "But do not distress yourself. After all, Circe is not unprotected."

Psyche smiled wryly. "Thank heavens. But poor Sir John, so neatly cut out. And he seems a nice young man, too." As the music grew louder, she curtsied and Gabriel bowed and the dance began. It did not help ease Psyche's irritation, however, to see that, back at the table, even David was scowling.

Left standing awkwardly by the empty chair, Sir John made a stiff bow to Aunt Sophie. "If you will excuse us," he muttered, but his great-uncle shook his head.

"No, John." He patted his nephew's arm. "You needn't spend all evening propping me up. I'll just sit right here next to the lovely Sophie." John nodded, his face slightly flushed, as he eased Mr. Bircham down into the next seat.

David wasn't certain that Sophie's sour expression could be described as lovely, but perhaps Mr. Bircham had a better imagination than he—or worse eyesight.

With a few mumbled words and another bow, Sir John walked away from the table. David hardly noticed, his attention again on the Austrian. *Damn the fellow.* Sir John was a perfectly inoffensive gentleman, a bit older than Circe at eight-and-twenty, a bit shy, but perfectly proper. The count, on the other hand . . .

Of course, it would make David's secret mission easier if von Freistadt chose to make Circe his flirt of the Season. David had in fact expected that the man would show up, having ascertained earlier from Gabriel that he was on the invitation list. Despite the Austrian's slightly smoky reputation, he was a fully accredited diplomat who claimed friendship with Princess Esterhazy, one of the Ton's social lionesses. So he could not be excluded from society's most exclusive gatherings, and his preference for young girls was well known. And since David wanted to keep him under his eye, it was convenient that he should be here. But not paying such close attention to Circe, damn it.

David glanced toward the dance and saw Circe smile at her partner. International intrigue was one thing, Circe's welfare another!

On the dance floor, Circe found that she had to mind her steps. Her earlier nervousness had returned with a rush, and her heart had an alarming tendency to beat too quickly. The count was an unexceptional dancer, for though his steps had an almost military precision he lacked David's easy grace. But the older man had such strength in his grip that she had the impression of great will carefully contained.

He glanced down at her as his heavy lips lifted into an assured smile. "Are you enjoying your coming-out ball, Miss Hill?"

"Oh, yes indeed," Circe assented, then realized with a start that her words were true. She had forgotten her worries about holding her tongue and not disgracing Psyche and Gabriel. Surely it could not be because of this man?

The dance parted them for an instant, and Circe took the opportunity to wonder at herself.

This was not like her. She had met handsome men before, men who were popular with women because of their good looks or smooth charm, so why—but then the count took her hand again and led her through a smooth series of steps, and she had to give all her attention to the pattern. Somehow, von Freistadt had a way of jumbling her thoughts in a most unusual manner. Not until he released her to circle another set of dancers could she glance at the side of his face and observe the harsh lines that etched the corners of his eyes.

This man had secrets hidden deep inside, secrets that no one would easily fathom. This was a dangerous man, Circe thought. So why, when the dance brought them back together, did she find it so easy to forget her moment of intuition when he held her hand, when he looked down at her with those gleaming lights behind his dark eyes?

Circe swallowed hard and tried to think of something polite to say. "It is—it is a most pleasing turnout," she offered, then could have groaned. How insipid could she be!

She thought the count was laughing behind his expression of polite attention. "Yes, you should feel most honored."

"Oh, I am," she agreed. "Honored that my debut has crushed my guests and left them overheated and voiceless from screeching at each other over the din of general conversation."

There, at least that was more like herself, Circe thought, at the same time that she knew Psyche would censor such a candid remark.

But the count threw back his head and laughed. "Oh, indeed," he said. "You have a wonderful way of getting to the heart of the matter, do you not, Miss Hill? Or may I call you Circe?"

"That would be most improper." She retreated at once, almost withdrawing her hand, but he tightened his grip and she found it impossible to pull back. Her heart jumped again.

"Very well, *Miss Hill*," he told her. "I will restrain myself. But I still think that you are not, at heart, a creature of polite inanities."

"You doubt my proper upbringing?" She gave him her best imitation of Aunt Sophie at her iciest.

The count frowned. "No, no, my most abject apologies. I would never suggest such a thing. Your family is of the most irreproachable. I would not have chosen to escort you otherwise." Then his brows rose. "You little devil, now you are the one who is making sport of me, is it not so?"

"Yes." Unrepentant, Circe flashed a quick smile. "But I thought you might just need a reminder, you know."

"That I must mend my manners?" The count laughed again. "You are a formidable opponent, Miss Hill."

"Are we opponents?" She blinked, considering his choice of words.

"Love and war, they are much the same, no?" As the music ended, he bowed once more over her hand. "And the dance floor is much to be preferred over the battlefield," he added, "for pleasurable maneuvering."

This man did not confine his "maneuvers" to the dance floor; he would be just at home in a lady's bedchamber, Circe suspected. The perception only added to her strange confusion. She wished he would not take the slightest excuse to kiss her fingers—no, actually, that wasn't true. To be honest, she enjoyed the rush of sensation evoked by the feel of his lips against her thin-gloved hand. If he were to kiss her like this against bare skin—

She had a sudden disconcerting notion that he could read her thoughts; his eyes gleamed and his smile was too knowing.

"If we are opponents, do not discount me too quickly," she told him, again speaking before she thought.

But he did not look shocked, and he did not pretend to misunderstand her. "I should never underestimate you, my dear," he answered, his voice very low.

He still held her hand, and she felt self-conscious, as if eyes in the crowd were watching them, and anger suddenly replaced her momentary chagrin. He was going much too fast, and she did not appreciate the feeling of being maneuvered, like a stupid ewe herded by a sheep dog.

When they reached Psyche's side, Circe withdrew her hand, somewhat abruptly. She gave him her best curtsy and turned to her sister, but she could feel his gaze upon her before he walked away, as surely as if he stroked the bare skin on the back of her neck. Circe shivered, and whether from pleasure or alarm, she could not have said.

❧

Sally had been standing with a group of nearby guests when Sir John had made his retreat, so obviously vanquished by the Austrian's offensive. Von Freistadt led Circe to the dance floor, and Sir John wandered away to study a potted plant. Sally felt a stab of pity; he was so palpably entranced with Circe, and yet, it was easy to deduce that the young man hadn't a clue as to how to fix his interest with her. And Circe, despite her lack of confidence in her social skill or her beauty, was too attractive and too wealthy to stand unpartnered at any ball, much less her own coming out.

The young man had little chance, Sally thought, fanning herself as she pretended to listen to Mr. Elliston natter on. The prosy old bore had managed to find her, of course, the first time she had walked among the guests, chatting and socializing and, in Sally's role as assistant hostess, attempting to take some of the strain off Psyche.

"And the next line shall be directed to your flawless complexion and luminous eyes," the would-be poet told her.

"How nice," Sally answered absently. "Oh, Sir John," she said as the young man left his observation of the palm and made to walk past them. "I was waiting for you."

"You were?" The baronet gaped at her.

"Of course, I did promise you this dance, did I not? I would not be so unkind as to forget my pledge." She smiled sweetly.

Sir John blinked, but he could only bow in agreement. He was a gentleman at heart, that was good, Sally thought. She could not have a lesser man courting their precious Circe; as for that Austrian, she had heard disturbing things. She would have to speak to Gabriel in confidence at the first opportunity.

Sally looked toward Mr. Elliston, who had paused, his narrow lips pursed into a frown. "You will forgive me, duty calls," she told him, her tone airy. "But do hold that thought about my luminous eyes—I liked it amazingly well."

It was obvious that the befuddled poet couldn't decide whether to be gratified or affronted. He sputtered as he struggled for words, and she walked away without waiting to see what his final response would be.

Sir John took the hand she offered—really, it was as easy as luring a baby with a sweet, she thought, the man was a total innocent—and led her into the set that was forming.

"I'm afraid I had forgotten, that is, I did not recall—" Sir John seemed to realize his double blunder because he reddened and almost stumbled as they began the first steps.

"You did not recall our engagement because I just made it up," Sally told him, smiling again to soften the admission.

"Oh, I see." Sir John stared at her. He obviously didn't.

"But I felt sure you would not mind rescuing me from a tedious gentleman who has been dogging my steps at every party." She gave her young partner a wistful glance, and his expression changed.

"Of course, only too happy!" Sir John looked at once more committed and more at ease.

"And it's always a pleasure to have such a capable dancer as partner," she added.

His steps seemed to become more crisp.

She had forgotten how malleable, and how sweet, younger men could be. Sally smiled up at her partner with genuine affection, and he reddened. Really, the man was too adorable. He could not be allowed to continue blundering along in such a ham-hocked fashion; he deserved better. Beneath that awkward exterior lay a sterling spirit, she was sure of it. Someone only had to offer him a little guidance. Perhaps she would speak to Gabriel—no, Gabriel had enough on his plate just now. And there was David, but David would not do, either, Sir John might take offense at being tutored by someone much the same age as he.

Perhaps . . . perhaps she should take him in hand herself. He offered his arm as they swung round, then clasped her hand as they moved into the next step. The feeling of his firm grip brought back a rush of memories of her own. One missed a man's touch, when one had been widowed. . . . Yes, she would do it. It would be a good deed, and she already could tell that she liked this pleasant, unassuming young man, so it would hardly be a chore.

Really, Sally thought, what with chaperoning Circe and giving lessons in deportment to Sir John, she was at risk of becoming downright angelic. And Sally had never before been called an angel. The idea made her laugh, and Sir John smiled down at her as if attracted by her mirth.

But then his expression changed, and his tone sounded anxious. "Did I make a misstep?" he asked.

"Of course not, I am enjoying our partnership. You have a firm grip, and you dance beautifully," Sally assured him. "And even if you did not, I would never be so unkind as to make sport of you!"

He smiled again, and they continued the dance in quiet harmony. While they moved smoothly through the pattern, Sally's mind was busy with plans for the baronet's future, plans that would have made him blush in earnest if he could have guessed them.

At least he seemed more cheerful already, and when the music faded and the other dancers paused, he bowed to her. "Do you have a commitment for the next dance?" he asked, his tone diffident.

She glanced around and ascertained that Circe conversed with an unexceptional young man who seemed to hang on her every word, and Psyche sat on a gilt chair at the edge of the dance floor, Gabriel standing at her shoulder, both chatting with guests. Sally was free to indulge her own inclination for a few minutes more.

"No, I do not. May I be so bold as to hope that this is an invitation?" She lowered her long, artfully tinted lashes just a little to glance up at him through their veiling.

He reddened again, but his smile was wide. "That was my intent, yes," he agreed, his tone serious.

The dear boy had much to learn about flirtation, Sally thought. And she was just the one to teach him. "Then pray, let us continue." She gave him her hand.

However, as the notes flowed from across the room and the tune became clear, she discovered that the next dance was a waltz. While this was undoubtably delightful for Psyche and Gabriel, who were now gliding about the floor, looking as entranced with each other as they had ever done in the first days of their own courtship, Sir John had, alas, much to learn about the art of waltzing.

The first time he stepped on her foot, Sally blinked but was able to hide her grimace. The next time he lunged too widely, he trod on the hem of her gown, and she heard the delicate fabric rip.

"Oh, dear," she said faintly. They paused in the middle of the dance floor. Sir John looked stricken.

"I am so sorry," he muttered, his light-hued complexion flooding with another of his ready blushes.

"It is nothing," Sally assured him, less concerned with her delightful ball gown than his embarrassment. Then she stepped back. Another couple had almost careened into them; Sir John was not the only dancer who needed more instruction in the challenges of the waltz. "Let us stroll off the floor, and I will summon a maidservant to help me pin up my hem."

"Of course." He gave her his arm and guided her to the side of the room, where Sally lifted her hand to summon a footman and deliver her request. "If you will excuse me for just a moment," she told Sir John.

The young man still looked flustered. "I am so sorry, it was all my clumsiness—" he began.

She lifted one finger and touched his lips gently. His hazel eyes widened, but at least the apology was stifled. "It was nothing, it can happen to anyone," she assured him. "I shall claim the rest of our dance later—I will not be denied the pleasure of finishing it with you."

He gazed at her with an expression she could not quite decipher, but a young female servant had hurried up, and Sally turned away.

The two women withdrew to a quiet anteroom to examine the damage to her dress. It was not as bad as Sally had feared. A few minutes to allow the maid's nimble fingers to fly with a needle and thread, and she could return to the ball.

Back in the ballroom, Circe watched her sister and her husband twirl and dip so gracefully to the music that she felt a tiny moment of envy. She could not waltz just yet, of course, but soon she would enjoy that most uninhibited of dances.

"Too licentious, by half," Aunt Mavis muttered.

Circe glanced at her relative. Was there any pleasure in life that Mavis could not find reason to condemn? "It's very graceful," Circe pointed out, her tone gentle. "And such a delight to watch, don't you think, when it is done well?"

She loved beauty in any form; she couldn't help herself. But her aunt sniffed. "It should be limited to married couples only," Mavis argued. "Look at how the men put their hands on their partner's waists! I ask you, what do you suppose they are thinking?"

It was just as well that her tirade was interrupted. Circe felt the presence at her side before she heard the deep voice.

"I have some champagne for you, Miss Hill, and a quiet table where we can watch the dancers, since it pleases you so."

It was von Freistadt. She had known it even before she glanced his way. He held two wine goblets; he offered one to her.

"How did you know I love to watch?" she demanded, intrigued despite herself. "And Mr. Martin has just gone to get me a glass of ratafia."

"Yes, I heard him announce his intention," the count told her. "But I fear he has gotten lost on his way to the refreshment table."

"You know he has done no such thing," she said, surprised into a laugh as she accepted the goblet.

"But the press around the table is deep, and he will be delayed, no doubt," he retorted, his dark eyes flashing.

"So how did you obtain this glass so quickly?" Circe enjoyed the play of words between them even as she sipped the bubbly wine.

"I lifted them from a clumsy young gentleman who had more than he could hold," the man admitted.

Circe lifted her brows at such audacious behavior. "How rude of you!"

"No, ruthless," von Freistadt corrected, sounding not the least repentant. "I was doing him a favor. He would soon have lost his grip on the goblets and splashed wine on his lady's gown, I am sure. Besides, now we may retire and watch the dancers at our ease."

Circe felt as if the wine had already rushed to her head, or was it simply the count's presence? He was most unsettling. "I asked for ratafia," she pointed out.

"Nonsense, ratafia is too tame a libation for a lady of such passion."

Gracious, what nonsense, Circe thought, but it was very pleasant nonsense. The count was steering her toward the side of the room, and she had not even excused herself to her aunt. Oh, dear, more grist for Mavis's grumbling. Then she found that he was steering them not toward an unoccupied pair of chairs but into one of the curtained alcoves.

"We cannot withdraw alone," Circe said, her tone sharp. She might have spent her recent years on the Continent relatively unchaperoned, except for the faithful Telly, but she knew that slipping away from the party with a man like the count would stir gossip as quickly as any of her worst gaffes.

"I thought you might care to waltz a little, instead of simply being forced to watch," he told her, his voice smooth. "You do not strike me as the kind of lady who wishes to be only an onlooker."

That was so true that she gazed at him in surprise, then tried to recover the direction of the most unusual conversation. "There is not enough room in this small space to waltz."

He gave her a wolfish smile. "For one couple only, it will suffice."

Circe had to concentrate not to look away, his eyes held

such a knowing gleam. "Anyhow, you know I cannot waltz until one of the patronesses of Almack's grants me permission."

"A silly rule." He lifted one dark slashing brow.

"True, but that's the way it is," she tried to explain. "My sister has warned me about it often enough."

"But the Princess Esterhazy is my dear friend—she will grant you permission at once if I ask it of her," the count told her, his grin rakish. "In fact, you may consider permission given." He put one hand on the slight curve of her hip, too low to waltz correctly, she knew. Circe felt as if her head were spinning. No more champagne for her tonight, she thought, a little alarmed.

"No, really," she protested, trying to step back. But he was pulling her into his arms, and his grip was as forceful as always. "I'm certain this isn't a good idea."

The count didn't answer, and surely this was too close an embrace for dancing? It made her heart beat faster, but yet, it was not the same response elicited by the closeness she had shared with David. Something felt wrong.

"I think—" a new voice interjected—"that you should release the lady."

Still standing within the count's arms, Circe blinked in surprise. It was David, and she had never before seen him look so grim. For once, she couldn't think what to say.

The count had no such inhibitions; his tone was gruff. "This is none of your concern, Westbury."

"I fear you are mistaken," David retorted, his voice equally steely. "I have known Miss Hill since she was a child. As a friend of the family, I have every right to tell you to release her at once!"

A friend of the family? Is that all he would claim? Strangely hurt, Circe bit her lip and didn't speak.

But the count lifted his bearded chin, and his gaze was haughty. "Rash young men who interfere where they are unwanted often come to bad ends. I would suggest that you withdraw quietly."

"Strange, I was about to give you the same advice," David flashed back.

Von Freistadt lifted one arm, his fist clenched, and Circe stepped out of his loosened embrace. "Thank you for the, ah, dance lesson," she said. "But perhaps we should indeed part. I'm sure you do not wish to incite any untoward comments from my sister's guests."

The Austrian's dark eyes glittered. Circe felt a flicker of alarm at the emotions she sensed barely suppressed beneath the rigid set of his features. But after a moment of tense silence, he bowed to her, pointedly ignoring David.

"Until the next dance we share, my dear." He turned and pushed through the thick draperies and was out of their sight.

Circe rather expected that David would follow the count, but he didn't. If he were going to give her a lecture about going off alone with a man . . . Circe met David's stare with a cool gaze of her own.

To her surprise, he stepped forward and gripped her arms.

"What?" she blurted, unnerved by his touch.

"If you are in such urgent need of dance instruction, the least I can do is oblige," he said.

She could not place his tone, and his expression was equally hard to read, even by someone who had observed him so many times. She found that he had placed one hand on her waist, in the intimate contact Aunt Mavis had so recently deplored, and he lifted her other hand in the approved fashion.

"Now, two steps back and one to the side, thus."

"David! I know how to waltz." Despite her protest, she found that all knowledge of the dance had suddenly fled from her memory. They were almost as close as they had been in the tree, and she felt her awareness of him rush back. It was different from the heated rush of excitement and almost fear that the count had excited within her, different from the calm formality she felt with any other dance partner in any other dance. With David she couldn't seem to think at all, much less move gracefully through the steps.

She was too slow to follow his lead, and he pulled her gently toward him. Yet still her feet seemed weighted, and she hesitated, then stepped forward just as he stepped up, and suddenly they were pressed close together again, the thin skirt of her gown touching his pantaloons, and her breasts brushing the hard muscle of his chest beneath the superfine of his evening coat. She felt as if the shadowed alcove had suddenly been flooded with fresh morning light; everything seemed brighter, the colors more vivid. And the touch of his body against hers—sensations arose inside her that she had not dreamed of. . . .

She could not meet his gaze or she would blush, yet she had to see what his expression would tell her. Why was he doing this? She lifted her eyes and met his stare. The lines of his face were tense, and his blue-gray eyes curiously blank, as if he hid his emotions more deeply even than usual.

He lowered his face toward her, then, just when she thought that he would touch his lips to hers, he paused. They seemed frozen in this strange embrace, and Circe trembled.

"Why?" she whispered. "Why are you doing this?"

Her soft query seemed to release him from his trance. "Why? When you forget all the proprieties in such a way? Should I not be asking you why you would seclude yourself with a man whose reputation—"

"And is this my punishment?" Circe continued, a surge of indignation replacing her confusion. "If so, you are worse than he!"

He gazed down at her clear green eyes, just now flashing with anger. How could she be irate? He was the one who had every right to his simmering rage. The anger that bubbled inside him, barely contained, had led him to grasp her hand and pull her close, so close that he seemed near to exploding, but this time not with anger—he was not sure himself just what he was feeling.

"Leaving the party with a man you have just met, exciting just the kind of—what do you mean, punishment?" David demanded, as her comment at last penetrated the strange fog that had taken over his brain. "You think that dancing with me is punishment?"

"This is not dancing," Circe told him, unwilling to tell him the truth, that he was trifling with feelings he didn't know she had. Slowly, she withdrew from his grasp.

He wanted to pull her back, but after his moralizing about decorum, it would have seemed inane, indeed.

"This is—I'm not sure what this is, but I am sure I should get back to the guests before the scandalmongers strike up their second chorus." Her head high, she disappeared through the curtains without a backward glance.

David watched her go, and only then could he take a long, deep breath. Some of the tension flowed out of him, and he felt his knees go curiously weak.

What the devil had he been thinking? Of course he had every right to demand that the Austrian unhand an innocent girl. For all her eccentricities, Circe was as guileless as a babe, more so, in some ways. He could hardly stand by and allow some unprincipled rake to abuse her trust! His temper rose again just thinking of it. Bloody hell! He wished he could withdraw from the assignment his uncle had given him, but he had pledged his word.

David wished that he could call out this damned impertinent, licentious count instead of following him and observing his movements. One day soon he would be free to do it, he told himself, trying to find consolation from his mounting sense of grievance, trying also to avoid thinking of Circe and his own suspect behavior.

What had possessed him to take hold of her that way? After the episode in the tree, he had promised himself that his behavior would be flawlessly correct the next time he encountered Circe. What was that strange burst of almost uncontrollable anger that had seized him when he'd witnessed von Freistadt holding her so intimately? Circe could not like the libertine, could she? Surely she had not enjoyed the man's embrace.

When David had pulled back the curtain, he had seen the look that von Freistadt bestowed upon his partner, part pure lust, part scorn, both barely concealed. Circe might not recognize the gaze, but David certainly did, the look of an experienced roué who feels both desire and contempt for his next victim. No one should treat Circe in such a way, ever. For that matter, no one should initiate her into the steps of the more worldly dance, the more tempting coupling of the waltz—no one except David himself.

And that thought brought him up short. What—no, he could not be thinking—damn it, this was all von Freistadt's fault. The man incited all of David's natural inclination to . . . to what? Circe was not at all the type of proper, prim young lady he had envisioned for his future wife.

No, he was only being protective, David assured himself. He had been entrusted with Circe's care, hadn't he? Hadn't Gabriel said as much, more or less? David was only acting in place of her brother-in-law; she had no brother, no father to offer familial protection.

If anyone needed looking after, it was Circe, who often acted without thought to society's conventions. A poor friend he would be to allow her to cause a scandal. The problem was, she just didn't think the way a young lady should think, no doubt the fault of all that time spent alone, painting.

No, that was too easy an excuse. He knew Circe better than that. She had always been and would always be singular, different. That was part of her charm, he thought, suddenly depressed, and he could not expect that other men would fail to recognize her appeal. Yet the fact remained, no one could be allowed to take advantage of her, not while David had anything to say about it!

For the rest of the evening he watched from a discreet distance, but the count was back to his oily charming ways and did not attempt to pull Circe aside, though he danced with her once more. Was Circe aware of this man's clouded reputation? Perhaps David should have another word in private with her—whether she wanted to listen or no!

The Austrian did not single out any other young lady, though many of them threw him wistful glances, for all the world like silly fawns watching a fox, David thought in disgust. It looked as if Circe were indeed the count's flirt of the Season. David wished with all his might that the count should turn out to be guilty of all his uncle suspected. David hoped that he could throw the man into Newgate prison himself. That very satisfying thought brought the first smile to David's face in over an hour.

He himself stood aloof most of the evening, deciding only as the guests began to depart and the crowd on the dance floor thinned that he should dance at least once more with Circe. Psyche seemed to have slipped out of the ballroom again, and, weary from her journey, Aunt Sophie had also said good night some time ago. Gabriel was still about, but he had to say farewell to their guests, and he would expect David to keep an eye on Circe. Besides, it might look odd if people thought he was snubbing her, and he had not the heart to embarrass the chit. At least he told himself that was the reason.

So it was out of courtesy, no more, that he solicited her hand for the last dance of the evening.

Circe agreed, her tone polite, but as they walked into the set, she asked, "Do you feel you need to finish the ball with me, since you began it?"

He glanced down at her, not sure if she were essaying a jest, but her answering gaze was serious. "Merely doing my duty," he said, then wished at once he'd used another word as he sensed her palpable withdrawal.

"You're always the soul of courtesy," she told him, her tone as frosty as the champagne he had enjoyed earlier.

They danced the rest of the dance in silence, and David felt his anger once more simmering inside. It was all the fault of this Austrian. Now David couldn't even talk to Circe without the stranger's presence coming between them, making David, who prided himself these days on his propriety and social correctness, falter and say the wrong thing and, apparently, cause offense.

He circled a large lady with a purple turban, then when the dance brought him back to his partner, he tried to make it right. "You know that I enjoy dancing with you, Circe," he told her.

She lifted her long lashes and met his gaze. "Do you?"

" 'Course I do, you're a most graceful girl, really."

But she looked away, and somehow he felt he had failed her again. Damn it, what possessed him tonight? He had a sudden desire to pull her even closer; he would be glad enough when she was allowed to waltz. Although that would mean other men could partner her, too, he thought, frowning.

And he knew the count would be the first in line.

When the dance ended, Circe gave him her best curtsy. "You are an excellent dancer, thank you for the honor. And our felicitations also for fitting us into your crowded social schedule, my lord," she said.

"Circe, don't be ridiculous," he snapped. "We've known each other for years. Why are you 'my lord'-ing me?"

"I simply don't wish to be derelict in my *duty*." She emphasized the last word.

"And since when have you had a thought to social obligations," he demanded. "Stop it, you're making a cake of yourself."

"If it were not for social obligations, I would have thrown your arrogant invitation back into your teeth. That way, at least one of us could be honest!" She sounded much more like herself.

"There's no need to scowl at me like that. I never fed you any false coin," he told her, stung. "I don't think I deserve to be treated like one of your mutton-headed cousins."

"My cousins are perfectly bright, most of them," she argued. "And since you view yourself as duty-bound to be polite to me, the least I can do is respond in kind."

"Oh, that's it, is it?" The seething anger that had soured his mood for the last two hours suddenly erupted. "Just because I'm acting like a well-mannered gentleman instead of a hoyden—"

"Oh, unfair!" Circe interrupted his righteous tirade. "I have been minding my manners all night—"

"When you were slipping away from the party to enjoy a tête-à-tête with a man whose reputation alone should make any maiden blush!" David retorted. "Is that what you call minding your manners?"

A woman standing a few feet from them glanced across, her expression curious, and belatedly David lowered his voice. "I'm only thinking of your well-being—no need to take it as an affront."

But Circe's green eyes glittered. "Oh, no, why should I be affronted, just because you accuse me of enjoying the most improper behavior? I am all gratitude at your solicitude, my lord."

"Oh, Circe, act your age, damn it." David swallowed hard against the acerbic remarks that lingered on the edge of his tongue.

"Shall I meet you in the park to roll our hoops together?" she asked, her voice too sweet.

"Circe, I never said—"

"Yes, you did. I am not a child any longer!" Circe lifted her chin, for a moment reminding him strongly of her sister. "I am not. But I am me, and I will never be totally proper, even though I may affect the pose of a decorous maiden—oh, don't look at me like that, you know what I mean!"

"I do, but the rest of the world could read your unconventional words and acts very differently," David tried to reason with her.

"You sound just like my sister," Circe said. And although he knew that she adored Psyche, the comment did not sound like a compliment.

"I am . . . I am older than you," he began.

"And your conduct has been so above reproach?" She took a deep breath and seemed to master some of her anger.

He had the grace to nod. "Touché, my dear. But let the voice of experience be your guide, then. You do know that a man can . . ."

"Oh, a man can do so much that a lady would never dare to emulate. Of course I know that," Circe agreed, "and most unfair it is."

Her suddenly thoughtful expression made him pause. "Circe, don't even think about making some kind of lunatic statement about women's role in the world, or some other such nonsense."

She blinked and he was chagrined to see tears in her eyes.

"It isn't nonsense to me. I'm not trying to make a statement. I just want to get back to my brushes and paints," she said, her voice suddenly low. "I understand the challenge of a cloudy day and a reedy pond. I don't always have the patience to remember the silly rules that bind us—or me, as you so kindly point out, much more than you."

"Circe, don't." He had an urgent desire to reach across and wipe away the tear that trembled on her lower lash. He felt . . . he felt . . . David felt frozen with sudden awareness. How could he feel this way about Circe, little Circe with her coltish exuberance and candid and always unexpected comments?

But she wasn't a child any longer.

His silence had stretched on too long. She gave him another curtsy, and this time her expression was as formal as her words. "Thank you for the dance, Lord Westbury, and for assisting me earlier when Gabriel was not at hand."

She walked away before he could find any words to answer. And polite farewells were not what he had in mind.

David had just been struck by a thunderbolt, a revelation that left him as weak-kneed as a three-day drunk. Circe was no longer a little girl, no longer just a pleasing urchin who was related by marriage to his old friend. Circe was a lovely and unusual young woman, with graceful carriage and a lift to her chin that made him want to reach out and caress the lustrous skin at the base of her neck. Circe was quite grown up, and the feelings inside him were not at all brotherly.

He could not have been more astonished if the stars had fallen out of the sky and planted themselves in the garden outside. As he took his leave of Gabriel, who stood at the door saying good night to the last guests, David felt numb inside.

It was more than a flicker of impersonal desire, experienced when he had briefly held her close. It was much more.

He had feelings for Circe.

Six

*D*avid was so lost in thought on the ride home that he was startled when he found himself looking at his own front door. He sat in the library staring into the dying fire for over an hour, then went up to bed to find that sleep eluded him.

Circe?

It was not possible. Circe was not the conventional maiden he had made up his mind to marry. He had a firm picture of his future wife—well, perhaps the face was fuzzy and indistinct—but he knew that his bride would be meek and sweet and biddable and always, always the picture of propriety. There would be no angry shouting and dishes flying in his house, none of the endless disputes that had plagued his own childhood, to make his son cower behind a stout chair to avoid the breaking china as the young David too often had done. And though he had avoided the cutting shards, the angry words had been just as sharp, leaving behind their own scars.

To avoid repeating his parents' bitter and unhappy marriage, David would be a better man than his father, and his wife—his wife would be proper, too, proper and predictable. It must be so; he could not bear to repeat the unhappy pattern of his parents.

Yet feelings stirred inside him, feelings he could hardly begin to decipher. All he knew was that anything to do with Circe touched some deep nerve, that any possible threat to her well-being pulled him into instant action, that any sign of her unhappiness made him want to sweep her up and gather her into his arms.

And it was not a brotherly solicitude he felt. He wanted to kiss her soft sweet lips in a way that she had, he was reasonably sure, never been kissed before. He wanted to awaken the response inside her that no man had yet elicited, the kind of enthusiasm and joy that up to now had been awarded only to her artwork.

The thought of the count being the first to teach Circe about passion fueled a rage inside him that made David grit his teeth. No, by God, he would not allow it.

Yet, he had promised himself to make a suitable marriage with an appropriate young woman. He could never ask Circe to change, to be less than she was, so he must put aside his own longings. Sighing, David rubbed one hand across his face. No, marriage between them would not do. It would only make her unhappy; he had no right to force her into the kind of conventional mold he struggled to maintain, himself. He must not be tempted by his surprising attraction to Circe. Yet, trying not to think of Circe, he tossed and turned for hours.

The next morning he rose early. He drank a cup of tea brought by a startled footman, who stammered excuses for the bare sideboard in the breakfast room. "We wasn't expecting you up just yet, Your Lordship, but I'll send down to the kitchen right away, like, for some proper breakfast."

"No, this is fine. I'm not hungry," David told him. He had always had an instinctive courtesy with his servants; no real gentleman would do less, though he had seen his own father shout at the staff often enough. But it was Gabriel who had attracted David's youthful admiration, Gabriel whom he had modeled himself on. Thinking of his longtime friend reminded David that he must tread carefully—he would not offend Gabriel in any way, and upsetting Circe, offending Circe, could jeopardize the most important friendship he had ever had.

Cursing these suddenly treacherous waters—he should have confined his attentions to prim and meek young ladies, as he'd planned, David thought glumly—he made his way to his uncle's house in order to catch him before he left for the Foreign Office.

His uncle's butler let him in, and he found his elder relative in the breakfast room.

"There you are, then," his uncle said genially, a napkin over his rounded belly. He waved to the food in the platters behind him. "Have a bite to eat."

The overflowing dishes of eggs and kippers and steak and ham could hardly be called a bite. Perhaps he was hungry after all. David nodded to a footman, who filled a plate and brought it to him. David took a seat at the polished cherry table and sipped the steaming coffee that had already been poured.

"What have you found out about our—ahem—foreign friend?" his uncle inquired, with a glance toward the servants, only the keen glint in his eye betraying how important the question really was.

"Very little," David said. "We both frequented a ball last night, and he was his usual unctuous self, charming the younger ladies." Somehow, he found he didn't want to name the lady who had interested von Freistadt the most.

"Ah," Uncle William said, taking another forkful of ham into his mouth and chewing vigorously.

"And I have watched his house for three days and seen him go off to his club, to the embassy, to a long list of luncheons and dinners and parties," David continued. "The only thing . . ."

"Yes?" His uncle put down his fork, and his expression sharpened.

"I have twice seen a man of nondescript appearance, dark haired with a scar on his face, come to the back door of his residence, be admitted without question by the servants, and then leave after an hour or more spent inside. He is not a tradesman, not a vendor, by any sign I can note."

"Did you follow him?" his uncle inquired, his tone eager.

"Yes." David frowned. "The first time I trailed him as far as the docks, and he took a boat out to a ship of foreign registry, which I had no way to enter. The second time he eluded me, I regret to say, in a crowded street."

"Ah, well." His uncle's tone was resigned, not censorious. "A tricky bunch, these people, if we are right about our friend."

"So you think we are right?" David gazed at his uncle, who took another bite of ham.

"I suspect so." The older man nodded. He swallowed, then added, "You are doing a good job, lad, keep it up. This matter is of the utmost importance—we are still hearing rumblings from the Continent—and every instinct I have tells me this diplomat must be involved."

"It would be helpful if we knew just what we were looking for," David pointed out. "Is it some important person they have smuggled into England? Some document that should not have left Austria or one of its possessions?"

"If I knew that . . ." His uncle sighed, then glanced at the handsome clock on the mantel and pushed back his chair. "Must run—have an appointment with the Foreign Secretary at ten. Keep on with your observations, and perhaps we shall have a moment of luck."

David nodded. "With luck, I'll get to shove our dear *friend*'s nose to the other side of his head," he muttered.

"Eh, what's that?" Uncle William shrugged himself into the fashionably tight-fitting greatcoat that one of the footmen held.

"Nothing," David said. He realized he had not touched the food on his plate, and he picked up his fork.

"Keep me informed," his uncle said. "I appreciate

having your help; I dared approach only someone I trust absolutely to keep this secret. Would be an awful scandal if the man in question found out that we are watching him. He'd kick up the devil of a fuss, if we could not prove we had reason for our mistrust."

David felt a moment of warmth that his uncle had entrusted him with such a delicate matter. He could not let him down, despite David's eagerness to be free to deal with the count on his own terms. He could not disappoint his uncle, but neither could he allow Circe to be taken in by this satyr. The man was probably old enough to be her father, David thought in disgust. And the habits that the count was said to have, the gossip that was whispered behind his back would make a more hardened libertine than David blush. . . .

The young men David had once caroused with would laugh in disbelief if they could see him now. First his new respectable habits and now secret missions. He hardly knew himself, these days. No wonder that Circe should find his real meaning hard to decipher.

⤛

Sir John Templeton was arranging his neckcloth when his footman brought up the note. His valet stood behind him, grimacing as he watched his master mangle the snowy cravat hopelessly out of shape. But Sir John hated to be fussed over, and he found the more detailed nuances of fashion boring. Who cared, after all, about the style of a man's neckwear? His plants certainly didn't care if he mastered the Oriental. Sir John had no wife to please, no lady friend to impress.

At this somewhat doleful thought, an image of Circe appeared unbidden in his mind's eye. Gad, but the girl was lovely, and had such a talent for flowers and plants, arranging them as if she could sense their mute supplications for distinction and grace. There must be such a delicate eye, such a feel for beauty inside her. Surely they must have some affinity of spirit, the type of connection he had never managed to make with a woman. He really would like to know her better.

But with men around like von Freistadt . . . Sir John felt again the wave of embarrassment that had flooded him when the Austrian had removed Circe from beneath Sir John's hand, with the artless ease of any pickpocket. It was no use. Sir John was no lady's man; he should resign himself to the fact.

He turned his mind to more pleasant thoughts; he had two new China roses to repot this morning. Plants he understood, plants responded to his touch, whereas women never did. With plants, he never became tongue-tied and as awkward as an unseasoned lad. Sir John sighed again.

At last he noted the footman hovering inside the door, holding a silver tray with a folded sheet upon it. He nodded to the man and accepted the missive.

The paper was of good quality, heavy, and he did not recognize the seal. He broke the wax and shook open the sheet. The handwriting sprawled across the page with an energy and enthusiasm that was both attractive and, he felt instinctively, very feminine.

Sir John, please forgive my unceremonious manner and meet me in Hyde Park at eleven o'clock. I will be walking near the hyacinth beds.

He knew the location, of course; he knew the arrangement of all the plants in all of London's parks. The hyacinths were in their prime, and the nearby tulips, the bulbs imported from Holland, were also making a splendid display. But why—? He glanced at the signature and knew that his eyes widened.

It was signed *Mrs. Andrew Forsyth.*

Why was she sending him a note? And wasn't this behavior terribly forward? He wasn't sure. Unmarried ladies did not correspond with gentlemen unless they were betrothed, he knew that. When it came to widows, his knowledge of the finer points of the social code failed him. There was one way to find out. He could hardly ignore her summons; she had been very charming last night. It had eased his chagrin over losing his dance with Circe to find Mrs. Forsyth so appreciative of his company. The woman obviously had taste, he thought, tucking the note into his inner pocket.

"Shall I bring a cup of tea to you in the conservatory in an hour, as usual, Sir John?" the footman asked, his tone holding a note of barely veiled curiosity.

"Umm, no," Sir John said. "I am going out. I will work in the conservatory later. Keep the soil of the China roses damp until I can attend to them."

The two servants exchanged startled glances, but he hardly noticed.

He decided to walk to the park so that he would not have a horse to lead behind him; it would make for an awkward conversation if the lady were on foot. And while it was likely that she wanted him only briefly, that there was a question of some kind she needed to ask, though he couldn't imagine what it might be, still, he wanted the chance to walk with her and perhaps point out the new fringed variety of tulips with which she might not be familiar.

So he descended the steps of his own residence—the large house had become something of a nuisance after his mother died; he would have let it out and gone into rooms if it were not for the fact that he needed the spacious conservatory for his plants—and strode toward the park. He found that it was really a lovely day, the pale spring sunshine peeping through breaks in the clouds, and the temperature cool but pleasant.

When he reached the hyacinth and tulip beds, there was no sign of Mrs. Forsyth. Baffled, Sir John paused to look around him. He saw a nursemaid tugging along one young lad overbundled in shawls against the slight wind that stirred the flowers, and two older ladies walking sedately on a nearby path, but—

"Sir John," someone called gaily.

He turned and found Mrs. Forsyth's petite figure hurrying up the pathway as she waved a purple muff in his general direction. She wore a soft gown of lavender silk, mostly covered by a pelisse of deep purple, and her cheeks were becomingly flushed by the cool breeze. Her lavender bonnet with its purple plumes was tied beneath her chin and kept her thick ringlets in place, though he noticed one errant curl that had slipped out to lie against her cheek. He had an irrational urge to push it back into place, but he knew better than to indulge such thoughts.

"I am so glad that you came." Her tone was fervent.

He bowed to hide his confusion. When he lifted his head, he was reasonably sure that another of those dratted flushes that always made him feel so absurd would have faded.

"I would not leave a lady waiting alone," he said simply.

Mrs. Forsyth smiled up at him, her brown eyes glowing with her usual infectious good spirits. "You are such a dear man."

He was startled again. No woman of such charm had ever addressed him so. What . . . ? She smiled even more widely, and he lost the dawning wisp of thought.

"How may I be of service to you?" he asked. It occurred to him belatedly to offer her his arm. "Shall we take a stroll about the gardens?"

"I should be delighted," the lady answered. She tucked her hand inside the crook of his arm—it fitted exceptionally well there, he thought—and they walked side by side along the path. She had the faintest aroma of lily of the valley about her.

He cleared his throat and expounded upon the various varieties of tulips that they passed. Mrs. Forsyth listened gravely until he had listed all the flowers before them and even explained how the word *tulip* came from the Turkish word for *turban,* when he fell silent, suddenly aware that he had done it again.

"I am boring you, I know," he said. "Please forgive me."

"Heavens, no." His petite companion smiled up at him. "It delights me to see someone with a genuine enjoyment of such beautiful things. And your knowledge of their Latin names, not to say all the scientific terms they seem to require, is quite amazing."

Was she roasting him, as the boys at school used to? No, she seemed sincere. In fact—he gazed at her intently for a moment—he did not think there was a cruel bone in Mrs. Forsyth's whole pleasingly proportioned body. Her husband must have been a most happy man.

"You must wonder why I took the liberty of asking for this meeting," she said, breaking the short silence.

He nodded before he could stop himself. "Yes, that is—"

"No, it is quite understandable." She paused to stare at a small shrub; Sir John opened his lips to inform her of its genus and family, then restrained himself. *This must be something delicate,* he thought, alarmed. Why she should come to him, however, he couldn't imagine. He had never been the one to consult about social matters, and he hardly fancied she had a dying daylily in her garden for him to revive.

Sally pursed her lips. How on earth could she tell him that he needed instruction in courtship, she wondered, suddenly close to panic. Her plan had seemed simple enough in her boudoir, and she had dressed with no anxiety over this meeting. But now, gazing at his creased forehead as he looked back at her with obvious concern, she worried that she might wound his feelings. This man had more sensibilities than most, she suspected, for all his sometimes prosy manner. And he had a good heart; she had known that at once. She must be most careful how she went about her mission.

"I noted last evening at the ball that you—you will forgive me for noting that you seemed to have an interest in Miss Circe Hill," she said.

The baronet flushed and looked away, but then turned back to meet her anxious gaze. "Yes, I found the lady in question most pleasing," he agreed, his tone steady. "But why . . ."

He paused, and Sally hurried on. "I am not looking for snippets of gossip, I promise you. I only thought—I am an old friend of Circe's sister, and perhaps I would be able to bring you into her company now and then."

"Why would you wish to help me?" he asked. The simplicity of his manner averted any suggestion of uncivility about his query. She smiled.

"As I chatted with the other guests last night, your name did come up once or twice. I found that you have a reputation as a man of sterling character, just the kind of gentleman I would wish to see spending time with our dear Circe."

He grinned ruefully.

She would not, of course, add that she had also learned that he had a most comfortable income and was widely reported to have been very kind to his widowed mother until she had died three years ago. Both tidbits, while telling enough, might embarrass him.

Then Sir John looked down at a blossoming bush and frowned. Did the shrub grow out of place?

"I appreciate your kindness," he told her, choosing his words with obvious care. "But I fear your efforts would come to naught."

"Why is that?" Sally pushed her free hand deeper into her soft muff; the wind was still most chill. She was glad to have him on one side of her, sheltering her from the freshened breeze.

"It pains me to say it, but I have no skill with the ladies," Sir John informed her, his tone now matter-of-fact. "I may be able to induce an orange tree to grow in a conservatory despite the cold winds outside, but my efforts with the fairer sex have been far less productive."

"Why should that be?" Sally opened her eyes wider. "You are a man of pleasing aspect, of good family and fortune. Why should ladies not enjoy your company?"

Oh, dear, she had made him blush again. Sir John stared

hard at a tall tree across the park. Happily, he did not attempt to tell her its species.

"The fact is that I am no—I am not very—oh, I just don't know what to say with ladies," he confessed in a rush. "I am not good on the dance floor—I'm so sorry about your gown, by the way—and while I can be perfectly sensible in male company, when a young lady comes into the room, I seem to turn into an unversed boy again, with that feeling that my hands and feet have grown two sizes too big, and my tongue has grafted to the top of my mouth."

Sally regarded the tree with equal gravity; she would not smile, no matter how much she wished to; he would take it as derision instead of sympathy. "I think perhaps you are simply somewhat shy, Sir John, if you would allow me to say so. Have you spent much time in the company of ladies?"

He shook his head. "Not really. I was the only surviving child of my parents, and of course at school there were only boys, and at university, men. And since then, I just— I just never seemed to pick up the knack of pleasing a gently born female."

He grimaced, and she patted his arm. He did not pull away.

There was some advantage to having left her girlhood behind, Sally thought. She could assume the soothing tone of a kindly aunt. "Sir John, I am certain that you have qualities deep inside that would please any woman. All you need is a little polish, and perhaps someone who could give you a chance to practice your social skills."

He gazed at her, his expression perplexed, but he did not seem offended. "I'm afraid I do not see—"

"Perhaps if you and I were to spend some time together, now and then, and you would allow me to offer a little advice, it would be to your advantage the next time you approach Circe—Miss Hill."

He brightened. "Do you think—would you really be so kind? I don't wish to be a bother."

"Of course I would," she agreed. "And it will not be a bother. In fact, it will help me as well. If I have the pleasure of your escort now and then, I can escape the somewhat tedious attentions of a certain gentleman whom I would much like to discourage."

He smiled, easier at once, she could tell, in the role of benefactor than as the one in need of assistance. Good, she had no qualms about sacrificing Mr. Elliston's feelings, if the old leech had any, to ease Sir John's.

"Then we are agreed," she told him, her tone now more brisk. "Perhaps you would come and have tea with me tomorrow at four, and we shall begin."

"I should be most happy," Sir John agreed. "Although I do hope your teacups are not irreplaceable."

She laughed. "You are too hard on yourself, Sir John," she said. "It is only on the dance floor that you become dangerous."

The anxious set of his lips eased, and they finished their turn around the park in the comfort of shared laughter.

⁂

Circe rose early and went straight to the schoolroom to pick up her paintbrush. As she stirred a small vial of paint to the right consistency, she drew a deep breath, relishing the smells of paint and linseed oil.

What a relief to be back with her paints and canvas, her brushes and paint-spattered cloths. And the loose-fitting smock she had donned to protect her morning dress was also an old friend. Here, she knew her skills and could test her limitations, and she could forget all her worries about gowns and dances and perplexing males who might or might not be admirers. She put down the paint and turned to her easel.

There was nothing so exciting as an empty canvas! She gazed at it happily, and slowly in the back of her mind, an image formed. She should sketch a few preliminary studies of her idea and see how it developed. She put down her brush and picked up a sketch pad, moving close to the window with its clear morning light.

She made a quick sketch of the image in her mind, then while she paused to consider the placement of the figures, movement in the back courtyard just below her window distracted her. She glanced through the windowpane.

Was that not Luciana? But who was the man speaking with her?

Circe frowned, hoping her protégée had not fallen into bad company. The man wore rough clothes, and his face, what she could see of it from this angle, was shadowed with several days' growth of beard that did not totally obscure the scar on his cheek.

But Luciana had the right to make her own friends, Circe told herself, pulling her attention back to her drawing. She moved the pencil across the paper, with deft lines added here, there, then could not keep herself from once more glancing out the window.

The two were still there, and why did Luciana look so perturbed? The girl might struggle to keep her expression bland, but Circe could clearly see the way her eyes widened, and how, beneath her apron, she continued to wring her hands together.

Luciana said something to the stranger that Circe, from inside the house, could not hear. Whatever his answer was, it seemed to distress the girl, because Luciana lifted her hands to her face and covered her mouth. But although she hid the lower part of her face, her eyes were round with fear or some other strong emotion.

If someone was threatening the girl, or trying to take advantage of her lack of familiarity with English customs, Circe could not allow it. With the same ferocity that always led her to champion those in distress, Circe threw aside her sketch pad and hurried out of the schoolroom and down the hall, almost racing down the several flights of steps till she could slip across the front hall and through the baize-covered door that led to the back hall and the kitchen and pantries. It also led to the servants' entrance.

As she hastened her steps through the narrow passageway, Circe met only a startled scullery maid, who almost dropped a large copper pan as she made her curtsy.

"Good morning, Mollie," Circe called as she passed, and had a brief glimpse of the girl's grin.

When Circe opened the outer door, she saw only Luciana, standing alone, while one of the grooms led Gabriel's favorite mount along the yard. The large gray horse twitched its tail and rolled its eyes.

Gabriel must be going for an early-morning ride. Even as she thought it, Circe saw her brother-in-law, in riding dress, striding around the corner of the house.

"Luciana?" Circe turned back to regard her lady's maid. "Is everything all right?"

"Of course, signorina," Luciana said, her voice thin. "Excuse me, I must press your gown for tea this afternoon."

"Good morning, Circe." Gabriel had reached them, and as he greeted Circe, Luciana curtsied and slipped away. Circe smothered a sigh. The girl was obviously not going to confide in her. Why did the Italian not trust Circe more, after all her help?

"Would you like to join me for a jaunt in the park?" Gabriel went on. "I will have Psyche's mare saddled for you."

"No," Circe said, a bit absently. "I must get back to my sketching. But thank you for asking. How is Psyche?"

"Holding her own." He grinned. "I left her making a game effort with a bit of toast and a coddled egg."

"I'm glad to hear it." Circe watched as, with a leg up from the groom, Gabriel mounted the horse in one smooth motion. As he settled into his saddle, she reflected that she must draw him on horseback one day. The horse shook its sleek head, cocked its ears as Gabriel spoke soothingly to it, and then broke into a well-mannered trot. Gabriel left the yard, and Circe turned back toward the house.

Marking the height of the sun's passage, Circe grimaced. The morning was flying by, and she had accomplished very little. Annoyed with herself for wasting time on what was likely nothing of importance—Luciana had recovered her composure quickly, after all—Circe went back inside. She had turned toward the main staircase when she noticed one of the footmen coming inside with a large armful of flowers.

"What on earth?" she said. "Did Psyche order more flowers for the drawing room?"

"Um, these came with a card, miss," the servant said. He held it out for her, and Circe was startled to see her own name on the paper.

Miss Circe Hill. She turned over the heavy sheet and saw on the back a short note: *You light up any room you enter. I shall live in perpetual shadow until our next meeting.* It was signed *Count von Freistadt.*

Good heavens. Circe gazed at the extravagant bunch of roses, hothouse grown and shamefully expensive. Had she ever received flowers before, except from her own family? This was what coming out meant. She really was a young lady of fashion!

She realized that the footman was watching her with obvious interest. "Where would you like me to put them, miss? And the others?"

"Others?" Circe was surprised again. "What—how many, that is—"

"I set them in the morning room until you could tell us where you would like them placed," the butler announced from behind them.

Circe turned and found Jowers gazing at the footman with lifted brows. The censure in his expression was apparent, and the younger servant carried off the lush red roses without any more conversation.

Circe followed him into the morning room and found a vase full of fragrant lilacs arranged in a pleasing fashion and accented with some unusual greenery. With it was a polite and noncommittal note from a Sir John Templeton.

Sir John? Circe narrowed her eyes, trying to remember.

Oh, yes, the pleasant young man who was interested in plants. And there was one more, too, a small vase of just-opening rosebuds, delicately pink and lightly scented. She looked for the card and felt a small shock of recognition when she saw the seal: the heavily embossed *W* edged by laurel wreaths was the mark of the earl of Westbury.

David?

Seven

*D*avid was sending her flowers? Did this mean he had acknowledged his attraction, that she had not imagined his reaction to her? The thrill that she felt faded quickly as another, more sobering thought interrupted. Or was this another "family friend's" obligation he was observing all too punctiliously?

Circe put one paint-stained hand to her mouth. How was she to know? For a moment, she longed to be back in Italy. She could almost smell the hot summer breeze, heavy with the scent of growing things, and see golden meadows. . . .

No, she was here. She had promised Psyche, and she would not let her sister down. Circe looked around at the flowers, her first rush of surprised joy tempered by a realization of the different sentiments these flowers could signify. Courtship or duty?

What did it matter? She had no plans for marriage. She would waste no more time considering the question, she told herself. But she would arrange the lovely blossoms; it would be a crime to leave them bunched up so unprepossessingly. Sir John's gift was a pleasure to the eye just as they were, but the other two bunches could be displayed to better advantage. She told the footman to fetch her some vases to choose from, and half an hour later she was able to direct the placement of all three sets of flowers around the drawing room. At least, she left two sets of flowers in the drawing room. David's rosebuds she carried herself up to her bedroom and set on the table nearest her bed—just in case they had not been sent out of duty.

Then at last she climbed the stairs until she reached the schoolroom. The best light was gone. She would have to do better than this, she scolded herself. At least she did have an idea about the next painting. She found the sketch pad she had tossed aside when she'd hurried downstairs and studied what she had done so far.

A man and a woman waltzed in a ballroom, their bodies a study in arrested motion. She had only sketched in their outlines, but she knew already that the woman's face, currently a blank, would later show an expression of delighted surprise that such grace and beauty could be found in the movement of the dance. And the man's face—should it be stern and bearded, even arrogant, with a guarded look about the dark eyes? Or should it show a studiously proper expression, which could not completely hide the humor and intelligence that glinted in the blue-gray eyes?

Her barely sketched gentleman dancer had suddenly taken on David's face, and she knew from experience just how hard it was to put aside a mental image that had implanted itself in her mind's eye. David would laugh indeed if he thought Circe had put him into a painting!

Annoyed, Circe was about to put down the sketch pad when she noticed a smaller figure at the edge of the sheet. It was only a few lines, hastily drawn, but the face jumped out at her, its identify obvious at once. It was the roughly dressed man who had spoken to Luciana in the courtyard. Without realizing it, she had drawn his face into her sketch, and the piercing eyes, the scar across the cheek, the hard mouth stared back at her now.

Circe felt her heart beat a little faster. This was not a face that would be easily forgotten.

⌐⌐⌐

David stood very still. Half hidden in the shadow of an
elm tree, he leaned against the low fence that surrounded
the park in the middle of the west London square where
Count von Freistadt made his residence. David had found
this spot handy when he had observed the count's comings and goings in his previous bouts of espionage. True,
his legs tended to ache after a while, and it was damned
annoying the way that pesky horsefly buzzed about his
head, but for love of country, for the commitment he had
given his uncle, a gentleman had to endure these hard-
ships.

He was reasonably sure he had not been observed by
the count or his household; it was important not to put
them on their guard. This morning, the count's house had
been quiet, with only a couple of footmen approaching
the front door, likely bearing invitations.

Ridiculous the way the Austrian was invited to all the
best parties. David frowned, remembering the count's
presence at Circe's ball. Just because he cut a good figure
in his evening coat and could dance, just because he had
a title and a foreign accent, why should that make him so
desirable? Women were silly creatures, for the most part.
Annabelle had had little enough taste, going off with a
rich merchant when she could have had David's continued
favor. Although, strange as it seemed, he found he could
muster little excitement at the thought of seeing Annabelle
again. Perhaps that Cit had done them both a favor.

But Circe, now, he was surprised that Circe should be
taken in by this Austrian fellow. Circe should see beyond
the man's so-called air of distinction, or did artists pay
too much attention to what met the eye? Perhaps David
should have another talk with Circe and try to alert her
to the perils of any further association with the count.

The rumble of wheels reminded him where his attention
should be. David peered toward the servants' entrance of

the count's large house. He was particularly interested in people who went around to the back entrance, and though he could barely glimpse it from this angle, he tried to keep up with comings and goings there. At the moment he saw only a butcher's cart. The man carried in a large side of beef, two hams, and two freshly killed geese, then pushed his cart off again toward the next house. Earlier there had been a delivery of coal, which also seemed perfectly legitimate. David sighed, wondering if the dodgy chap with the shaggy dark hair would make a reappearance; he had turned up three days ago and slipped into the house, not to reappear for some time.

The horsefly buzzed close to his face, and David waved it away. But as he craned his head to observe the rear of the house, the insect lit on a piece of exposed skin. David slapped at his ear, but too late. He felt the sharp bite and swore angrily—angrily, and too loudly.

Someone was passing in the street. It was the count's butler, a dark-complected man with narrow eyes and a perpetual scowl. David had observed him several times at the front door of the mansion. And he was coming closer.

Hell, he'd made a cake of it now.

"Can I help you, sir?" the man asked, his expression suspicious.

"No, no, all's well," David answered, trying to sound off-hand, trying to ignore the stinging bump on his ear.

"It, ah, is not usual for well-dressed gentlemen to linger in the park," the servant pointed out. "I thought there might be some problem?"

And as David was about to remark that he was merely strolling past, the man added, "I believe I glimpsed you here two hours ago, sir."

Damnation! So much for his hiding place. David lifted his brows and stared down at the shorter man. "I, uh, had an appointment, with, uh, a certain female who shall remain nameless."

Some of the suspicion in the man's face eased. "I see.

It does not seem that the female is going to appear, if you don't mind me saying so, sir."

"I fear you must be right," David agreed, pulling out his gold pocket watch and making a show of consulting it. "No point in wasting my time any longer." And trying not to look as if he understood the butler's barely disguised sneer toward a man of good family who spent his time having assignations with ladies' maids, David adjusted his hat and ambled away.

And now how was he to watch the count's comings and goings? Not only had he lost his partly obscured hiding place, his face was now known to the count's butler. What now? Go back to his uncle and admit that David was still the nitwit that everyone had once supposed him to be?

Dammed if he would.

The butler walked briskly away. David ambled in the other direction, and once he was out of sight of the Austrian's residence, he paused and tried to think. A carriage carrying two older ladies rolled past him, followed by a thin gentleman in an ostentatious habit riding a roan with a tendency to shy. When a small ball rolled too near to the horse, it tried to rear. The rider pulled at the reins, his expression alarmed.

"Here, lad, stay out of my path. Settle down, Cicero."

" 'Enry! Don't you get yourself killed by no 'orse; what would the mistress say? Come along if you please." The little boy who had pitched the ball stopped at this call to order by his nursemaid, who also carried a younger child well wrapped in shawls. The boy scooped up the ball and ran back to her side. They walked on through the gate and into the park.

David considered borrowing a child, but decided he would still stand out if he loitered in the park. He could hardly pretend to be some brat's governess.

Then he realized that his glance had slid over a street vendor without conscious thought. With the glimmering of an idea, David considered the man. He was dressed in a rough coat and trousers and his face was partly hidden by a soft cap. He was handing out roasted chestnuts to a pair of giggling housemaids, who chatted with him for another minute, then handed over their coins and headed back to their chores.

A street vendor. Indeed.

David walked closer, and the man looked up. "Hot roasted chestnuts, sir? Only tuppence a scoop."

David nodded. "Do you come here every day?"

"I ain't caused no problem, sir." The man looked suddenly anxious.

"No, no, nothing like that," David assured him. "I just wondered. Have a bet with a friend, you see."

The vendor obviously didn't, but he accepted the coin that David handed over, and answered readily. "I'm 'ere for a good part of the morning, sir, then I goes on to the next square and spends the top of the afternoon there, then on to the next square for teatime, like, and then one more for the early evenin', and one last till it gets too late and I 'ead for me bed."

"I see. How much do you make on a good day?"

The man blinked, but after a minute named a modest sum.

"How would you like to earn double that for the next few days?"

The vendor gaped at him. "Uh, what—?"

"I want to, um, rent your pushcart, and, ah, your clothes as well. Especially the cap."

"Me clothes?" The vendor's mouth dropped even wider. " 'Ere, what kind of unnatural monster are you? You want to see me naked in the street? I don't 'ave no more!"

"No, no," David said. "Never mind, I'll find my own clothes. I'll settle for the cart."

The vendor shook his head at the madness of wealthy young gentlemen who had no more to do than kick up a lark, but the jingle of the coins that David shook in one loosely cupped hand drew his gaze. "You can't do nothing rude to me regular customers, like," he cautioned, though he already reached for the money.

"I promise to be the most polite hot chestnut vendor in the west of London," David assured the man. He wanted badly to laugh, but this was serious business, even with hot nuts added.

It turned out that the man truly owned only the one set of outer clothes, but he was willing to tell David where to find more, so they had to push the cart to another neighborhood to locate a shop selling used clothing. There, David spent a few shillings for a set of raiment more suited to his new occupation, and after digging through a basket of dilapidated headware, located a loose cloth cap similar to the vendor's. First, someone along the man's route might remember and note the lack of it when David appeared. Second, though it was overlarge and tended to slip over his eyes, it would hide much of his face if he kept his head down.

The man gave him instructions about his route and times and showed him the small iron pot of charcoal inside the cart, which heated the nuts. "Got to add a piece of coal one at a time, like," the man explained. "Not too much at once; it's h'easy to burn down the 'ole cart if you're not careful." From his accessing glance at David, he seem to be having second thoughts about risking David with hot coals.

David sighed and added a guinea to the money he had already given the man. The vendor's eyes widened at such largess, then he stuffed the coin into his pocket before anyone else in the almost empty shop should glimpse it.

"Just to put your mind at ease," David told him, "about any damage to your cart."

"Thank'ee, sir. No offense taken, I 'ope." The man gaped at him, then drew a deep breath. "But I 'ave to look out for my cart, you see. Got four children to feed, I do, and me wife, of course."

"Of course, commendable of you, I'm sure," David assured him, trying not to grin. He changed his own clothes behind a curtain in the shop, probably doing irreparable damage to his snowy cravat, then bundled his tailor-made clothes and left them in the shopowner's care. Hopefully, they would be here when he got back, and if not—he'd never liked that coat much, anyhow, not quite up to Weston's usual standards, and the mustard-colored waistcoat had definitely been a mistake—then slipped out the back way and met the vendor at the corner of the next street for the switch. Soon, the chestnut man was on his way, though, David suspected, perhaps not to his loving wife and children, but instead toward the nearest alehouse to celebrate the acquisition of his unexpected wealth.

For his part, David pushed the cart back to the count's square and set up shop again. He was a little off the vendor's usual schedule, but not enough, he hoped, to excite comment. The cart was a trial. By the time he got the heavy, clumsy thing back to the corner of von Freistadt's house, David's arms were sore and his back ached from bending forward to push its long handles. And he had often prided himself on going a dozen rounds with the best amateur boxer in London!

He would advise his Corinthian friends to try a pushcart if they wanted to build up their stamina. Wiping his forehead, David bent low over the cart and lifted the small door on top to add just one piece of coal, as instructed, and to stir his chestnuts with a long-handled wooden spoon. From the corner of his eye, he tried to watch both the front and the rear entrances of the Austrian's home.

The next hour passed slowly. David slipped his gold watch out of the pocket of his roughly cut trousers to check the time. The small fire was surprisingly hard to keep going. Either it threatened to die altogether, or it grew too hot and the chestnuts came near to scorching. While he labored, two maids came out to buy chestnuts, and David bantered with them, remembering to affect an accent similar to the real vendor.

"Guess you ladies have an exciting life, living 'ere with all the noble folk coming and going, parties and all that."

They giggled at being called "ladies," and the shorter one said, "La, my lady's past sixty. Don't have no parties, she don't."

"And the other houses in the square?" David asked, adding an extra chestnut to each of their handfuls. "That one there, with the 'eavy iron grills on the windows?" He nodded toward the count's residence.

"Sober as a church mouse, 'e is," the other maid answered. "Goes out a lot, mind you, but no big parties at home."

"I suspect he has his lady friends in, though?" David suggested, winking suggestively.

The two women glanced at each other and giggled again, but the shorter one said, "They don't talk much at that 'ouse. Master tells 'em h'all to 'old their tongues, or they're h'out on their h'ears."

"Really?" David asked, his interest not in the least feigned. "How singular—-er, odd."

"Yeah, real Cossack about gossip, 'e is," the other agreed. "Glad I don't work for 'im."

David tried a few more questions, but learned nothing else of note.

"Lawd, look at that sun. Morning's flying, and I got a basket of turnips to peel, I do." The two servants hurried back to their own household.

David went back to his tedious observation. After another quarter hour, the count's carriage was brought to the front of the house, and von Freistadt himself came out and took his seat inside. The coachman flicked his reins, the four well-matched roans picked up their feet, and the vehicle rolled away.

David kept his head down until the carriage was safely down the street, but he glowered toward the back as it departed. If von Freistadt was off to make social calls, it better not be to the Sinclair residence.

Then, just as a plain-faced kitchen maid came up from the other corner of the square to buy some chestnuts, David saw movement at the rear of the count's house. Yes, it was the man he had observed three days ago! Now this was more like it.

"I only got ha'penny today," she said.

Absently, David nodded and scooped up warm nuts for the servant girl, watching for the man to exit the house. The servants inside always let him in without question. This time, David was determined not to be left behind when he departed. During the last visit, the dark-haired man had stayed for half an hour at least, but this afternoon the count was not at home. That might affect—yes, the man was leaving already. David couldn't lose him!

He picked up the handles of his cart, as the startled maid said, " 'Ere, I ain't given you your ha'penny yet."

"It's all right, my dear," he said, anxious to get away.

The woman sniffed. "Cheeky! I ain't that type o' gel!" She tossed the coin onto his cart.

David blinked in surprise, but hurried on. He followed the man, studying his back with its dark, badly cut coat and burly shoulders; he had to keep him within view. Trying to keep up with the man's rapid pace, David cursed the awkward, heavy cart beneath his breath. Pushing hard, David shoved the cart down two more blocks, so it wouldn't be found suspiciously in front of the Austrian's dwelling, then left it at the corner of another small park. It would be there when he got back, or it wouldn't. The vendor had been given money enough to replace it.

Now David could make better time, and as he hurried after his prey, he found the man was leading him into the heart of the City itself. This man didn't seem to belong in courtyards devoted to barristers and businessmen and prosperous bankers. What was he about?

The streets were busy now, and one man harder to keep within his gaze. When they reached the busy corner by the Royal Exchange, the broad-shouldered man slipped into a group of well-fed merchants congregated at the edge of the street. David looked quickly to the left and right. Where was he? The businessmen blocked his vision.

David hurried out into the street, avoiding a large

wagon pulled by thick-necked drayhorses. As he evaded the wagon, which was piled high with fragrant onions, he almost stepped into the path of a faster vehicle. A high-perch phaeton flew by him, the sporty carriage's large wheels coming so close that he felt the skirts of his loosely hanging coat lift.

"Mind your step," the driver called rudely.

David ignored the admonition. He had lost his prey again! Where could the man have gone?

～⊷～

Circe spent the morning with her sister in her boudoir while Aunt Sophie indulged in a lie-in. Psyche was having a good day, and they laughed and chatted as they had done when Circe was only a little girl and had loved to sit on Psyche's chaise and feel grown up. Once, their mother had been there, too, to read to them from books of poetry and travel and history, to play silly word games, and to beat them soundly at chess. But the accident had changed all that, taking her parents away, and only the two sisters had been left.

Now there was Gabriel, of course, and he had always treated Circe like a true sister. But still, Psyche's health was very important to her. Circe could not bear to lose Psyche, too. And though Psyche disliked being coddled, both Circe and Gabriel were still forcing her to rest most of the day.

"You're missing nothing of any importance," Circe assured her sister. "I was invited to two teas this afternoon, but I knew they would be most tedious. I have excused myself from both."

"Circe," Psyche protested. "If you would just make an effort! I wanted you to get out and enjoy yourself, make friends. Sally would have accompanied you."

"I didn't ask her," Circe said. "I'm going out to see the new exhibit of Italian oils and forget all about balls and teas and society itself. I want to lose myself in a beautiful landscape or an artful portrait, and remember who I really am."

Psyche shook her head. "Circe, I am not trying to change who you are! I'm just trying to help you."

Circe felt a pang of remorse. Had she sounded totally ungrateful? But before she could speak, her sister leaned forward and held out her hand. Circe took it and squeezed back with affection and apology.

"I simply want to expand your interests, just a little," Psyche explained.

Circe gave her a quick hug. "Oh, my interests will be expanded nicely when you give me a niece or nephew to dote upon."

After a light luncheon, Circe changed into a walking dress to enjoy some precious hours of freedom. At the last moment, just as Circe was about to start down the stair-well, Psyche looked out from her room and called, "Circe, don't forget to take your parasol. The sun is bright today."

Circe grimaced. She knew her complexion was too brown to be fashionable, but a parasol was such a nuisance. However, she didn't wish to irk her sister, so she accepted the parasol that Simpson hurried to offer her.

"You are taking your maid, of course?" Psyche asked.

"Yes, of course, she's already downstairs," Circe said. Oh dear, now she was stuck with Luciana, too. The girl was a sweet thing, but although she didn't complain, she did have a tendency to dawdle, falling behind the fast pace Circe always set, and to profess a need to sit every hundred yards or so. Circe, who had been accustomed to climbing hill and dale in search of the perfect aspect to paint, had to occasionally clench her teeth and restrain herself from dragging the younger girl along.

However, the Italian did not demur today when Circe located her in the laundry room, pressing one of Circe's fine muslin gowns. She soon reappeared as instructed in the front hall with her hat and gloves, also carrying, to Circe's surprise, a plain medium-sized basket.

"Do you have some errands to do?" Circe asked.

Luciana blushed. "Only one small chore, a favor for Simpson, if you don't mind, signorina. She asked me to stop at the greengrocer's and bring home some fresh grapes for Lady Gabriel."

"Of course."

Strange, Simpson hadn't mentioned it abovestairs. Still, Circe was happy to bring her sister a treat. Just now, the fresh air drew her, and with the added happy prospect of new paintings to study and admire, she almost skipped down the front steps and didn't mind in the least that the footman who held open the heavy front door stared after them.

A bird trilled from a bush, and a horseman in a blue coat rode by at a smart trot. What a glorious day! Circe strode off with unfashionable enthusiasm, and Luciana hurried to catch up. But Circe's serenity was short-lived. They had not yet reached the end of their own block when a man in rough clothes, a dark kerchief wrapped around most of his face, jumped out of the bushes.

Circe gasped in surprise. A thief in their own sedate square? Circe instinctively pulled her reticule, which contained only a modest amount of coin, back to her chest. But the man reached past her and lunged for Luciana's basket.

Luciana screamed.

He grasped the basket. Luciana looked as if she would faint, but she clung to the wicker handle. They struggled for a moment, then the man took one hand away to clout the maid heavily upon her shoulder.

Luciana shrieked again and almost lost her hold. Circe, who had felt too stunned for an instant to react, snapped, "How dare you!" and whacked the unopened parasol over his head. The ribs of the fragile thing cracked. The stranger turned, more surprised than impeded, so Circe kicked the thief hard in the ankle and then stomped on the sensitive instep of his foot.

Swearing, the man stumbled, and his grip on the basket's handle wavered. Another man in rough clothes started toward them from the other side of the square, and Circe felt a moment of real fear. How many of them were there?

She glanced back toward their own house and, to her relief and frustration, saw the footman still standing on the steps, gaping at them.

"You fool, come to our aid!" she called.

The servant ran toward them. Their attacker let go of the basket and bolted for the next house, disappearing around its side into the back alley and out of sight.

"You all right, miss?" the footman panted as he came up to them.

"There was another one," Circe said, wary of further assault. But looking around, she saw no one but a startled kitchenmaid at the corner of the opposite house, her hands to her mouth. The potatoes she had been carrying in her apron were scattered about the gravel. The second man had vanished, too.

Luciana, Circe noticed suddenly, was sobbing.

"Oh, dear, did he frighten you?" She patted the young maid's hand. "Here, you are safe now. I hope you are not badly hurt?"

The girl had been struck, Circe remembered. And indeed, the shoulder of the girl's dress was torn, although Circe saw no trace of blood. Luciana put one hand up to touch the rent in her gown, but she shook her head. "No, signorina, only, only—"

"Only badly shaken and your nerves disordered." Circe nodded. "The footman will take you back to the house; tell Simpson I said you are to have the remainder of the day to rest, and some hot tea would not be amiss, either. I shall check on you when I return."

"I'll escort you both back to the house, miss," the footman said.

What, and give up her much anticipated excursion? Circe shook her head decisively. "No, indeed. You look after Luciana; she is the one who has been assaulted. I am quite all right."

"But, miss," the footman said, sounding more upset than Circe. At the same time Luciana shook her head, looking alarmed. "You can't go off alone."

Oh, dear, that "proper young lady" business again. She could take one of the other footmen with her, but Circe was impatient to be on her way. She had already lost valuable time that she could have spent at the exhibit, and she was not sure of the gallery's closing hour. Anyhow, a little freedom would be most enjoyable; how long had it been since she had been alone with her own thoughts?

"I shall be fine," she told them, her tone brisk. "It's most unlikely that I should be attacked twice in one day. This is London, after all, not Sicily."

"Signorina, if you please . . ." Luciana still seemed disposed to argue, but Circe refused to waste any more time.

She slipped the basket out of the maid's hand and turned to go. "I will pick up the grapes as you planned," she told her.

"Miss!" Luciana shrieked. "You cannot go off with a plain basket on your arm like any servant. I cannot allow you to do my errand!"

"It's nothing," Circe said, and added to the footman, "Support her back to the house and get her aid at once. But do not tell my sister about the attempted theft; it might alarm her, and you know her health is uncertain just now. I will tell her the story when I return." She fixed him with a firm stare, and the man nodded.

Luciana babbled something, but Circe gave her a comforting smile and turned on her heel. She would not give up her first chance at escape from all the obligations that society had pressed upon her. Today was her day, and she would have it!

Circe could not hold back a sigh. Perhaps she should be having hysterics. Circe supposed she was getting even this aspect of being a lady wrong. But Circe had faced down bigger perils in her unconventional travels across Europe. There had been that pockfaced highwayman who had stopped their coach on the road to Verona, and—

anyhow, just as well that Psyche and Gabriel didn't know about some of her adventures. Her faithful Telly had been sworn to silence many times over.

Circe grinned—she missed her usual companion. A couple of weeks ago, Telly had departed for a long and well-deserved repairing visit to her married sister in Brighton. From the letters Circe received from her old friend, Telly was reacquainting herself with a large family of nieces and nephews.

With the same determination that had kept her at her painting when most females would have given up, Circe set off for the row of shops on Timmons Street, the basket light on her arm and her heart even lighter. She would take care of the errand for Psyche, and then spend the rest of the afternoon at the exhibition.

The streets were full on this pleasant day, and she passed other well-dressed women, either strolling in groups or trailed by maids or footmen. Sometimes they stared in surprise to see her walking unattended, sometimes they nodded politely to her, perhaps acquaintances from her ball. Circe smiled and nodded back, but did not slow her pace. Mostly her thoughts were on paintings, wondering just which artists' work she would see today.

Carriages rumbled by on the street, and when she reached the next intersection, an urchin rushed forward to sweep the crossing before she stepped off the pavement. He pushed his dirty broom briskly, removing the odorous evidence of the horses that had passed recently along the avenue, and she shifted the basket on her arm and found a coin in her reticule to give him.

When she reached Timmons Street, Circe located the greengrocer's that Psyche patronized. A strong smell of onions and fresh garlic met her as she entered, but the small shop looked well tended, and the floor was clean and well swept. Garlands of braided onions hung from hooks, and she saw a basket of rosy apples next to bins of potatoes and turnips, the root vegetables still dusty with clumps of dirt from the farmers' fields.

The owner stared at her when she explained what she wanted. "You see, miss, Simpson got the best of the grapes when she was 'ere this morning, but I'll see what's left."

"Oh," Circe said, startled. Psyche was certainly eating a lot of grapes. On the other hand . . .

The man seemed to have the same thought as he returned with a small bunch to put into her basket. "Still, ladies in a certain, ahem, condition do tend to get their hearts set on particular foods, don't they, miss? We got the best fruit in London, believe you me, always fresh. We got a crate of lemons and tamarinds just in from the docks this morning, if you care for any of those, miss?"

"Ah, just the grapes for now, if you please." Circe paid him, hiding her grin. Just as well that Psyche didn't know that her pregnancy was being discussed by the shopkeepers. She pulled a clean cloth lying inside the basket over the fruit to protect it from the street's dust, then turned back toward the door.

Happy that the errand was accomplished, she came out of the shop, eager to reach her real destination. The street was still full of carriages; Circe allowed an elegant chaise to pass, then set out again across the street.

She had paused at a corner to consider her direction—she was still reacquainting herself with London after her long stay abroad—when a shadow darted from the alley behind the shops. A rough hand reached for the basket.

Too startled to scream, Circe instinctively tightened her grip on the handle.

She struggled with the man. It must have been the same one—he wore dark clothing and he still had the scarf obscuring his face. Near them, a woman shrieked and a portly man shouted, "Here, stop that!" but did nothing to assist her.

The rest of the well-dressed crowd on the pavement seemed too stunned to come to her aid. The man would be gone with her basket—his grip was stronger, and Circe knew that in another minute she would lose her grip and—

A second roughly dressed man darted forward. She was lost!

But instead of overpowering her, the second man grabbed the first assailant by the throat and wrestled him away from Circe. In the struggle, the scarf fell away, and Circe saw his face. This was the man from the courtyard, the man she had sketched talking to Luciana.

Circe stared at them both in shock. What on earth was going on? She watched the two men roll around on the ground, pummeling each other with fierce abandon, then the second man got in a good hit to the chin, which left the first thief momentarily stunned. The scarf that had hidden his face had fallen away. As the latecomer pushed himself erect, the first thief scrambled up, hooked the other man's feet out from under him, causing his head to hit the stones with a solid *thwack*, and took off down the alley. In a moment, the first thief was out of sight.

The second man, who against all probability seemed to have come to her aid, lay still. Was he dead? Circe held her breath, then let it out with a sigh when she heard him groan.

Slowly, the man lifted his torso off the ground. He leaned on one elbow, breathing hard from the impact of his fall, and carefully touched his head, wincing a little. Then he checked his ribs matter-of-factly, as if this were not the first rough-and-tumble he had lost. His loose cap had fallen to the pavement, and she glanced at his face for the first time.

No, it wasn't possible!

Her voice sounded shrill to her own ears. "David?"

Eight

David Lydford, earl of Westbury, pushed himself up from the dusty ground. Reaching past her feet, he retrieved the soft cloth cap. As he stood, he shoved it back on his head and gave her a caricature of a bow. "H'at your service, miss," he said in a Cockney accent.

"Have you lost your wits?" Circe couldn't believe her eyes. "What are you doing here, dressed like—like that?"

"Saving you from a dangerous attack," he said. His cultured drawl had returned, but his tone sounded a little short. Perhaps he had been hit harder than she'd realized.

"And for that it was necessary for you to lose both your decorum and your trousers?" She looked him up and down, staring at his strange rough costume. She saw him swallow a shout of laughter.

"My ladies usually prefer that I lose both at the same time," he said, a mischievous glint in his eyes.

Gasps rose from the bystanders who had collected around them. "I never!" a stout matron in puce exclaimed, fanning herself to allay the shock.

Dismissing his comment—which she was fairly certain she understood—Circe was about to continue her questions when he held up one hand.

"Explanations in a moment." David lowered his voice.

"I think we need a more private place to chat—we seem to be drawing a crowd."

Now that the real villain had fled, several of the gentlemen in the group hurried to her aid. "Is this rascal bothering you, miss?" a ruddy-faced man in a loud waistcoat asked, his tone belligerent.

"No, no, *he* came to my assistance," Circe said, trying not to make her answer too obvious a reproach. "But thank you for inquiring."

The man looked perplexed. Several of the women nearby still wore shocked expressions, and one sniffed at a vial of smelling salts. "I shall speak to my husband," the matron said loudly. "A woman of good birth accosted in broad daylight, inexcusable! I am most distressed!"

She was distressed? Circe shook her head. At this rate, all of London would know about the attack, and Circe did not want any more gossip. What if Psyche heard the tale before Circe could soften the impact of the news? Her sister might be seriously agitated and, in her condition, this could not be allowed.

"Would you not like a sniff of my vinaigrette?" a second lady asked, more timidly, reaching inside her reticule.

"No, I'm all right." Circe tried not to sound impatient.

"I don't think you quite comprehend what you've been through." The woman sounded anxious. "Here, my dear, take it with you, just in case your nerves do become overset."

At least this woman spoke kindly, and her faded blue eyes and softly lined face displayed an expression of genuine concern. Circe felt a flicker of guilt at her abrupt refusal.

"I'm sure I shall be quite all right. But thank you, you're very kind." Circe reluctantly accepted the small vial and dropped it into her reticule. She turned to David and said loudly, "Here, my good man, you may come with me to the next block where my footman is waiting for me at the, er, dress shop. You will be amply rewarded for your bravery."

David took his cue and followed her along the walk-way. To Circe's relief, the spectators did not try to follow, and she had a moment to think.

Why was the man from the courtyard trying to rob her? Or, he had gone for Luciana the first time. No, he had gone for the basket, which looked much the worse for wear, having been the object of not one but two tugs-of-war in the last hour. Why on earth would he desire such a paltry object? Circe frowned as she mulled over that thought, which led inescapably to the next. Why had the thief not reached for her reticule? By all reason, any money or valuables would have been carried there, not in a plain shopping basket.

David still walked a couple of steps behind her; in his present garb, he could hardly take her arm, though she found herself wishing for it. A little friendly support right now would not be such a bad thing. When they had passed a block lined with shops, she heard him say, in a low tone, "Turn into the next alley."

She complied, walking into the shadows without fear, then paused a couple of feet inside so that he could catch up. As she waited, she glanced inside the basket, but saw nothing except the slightly crushed grapes, their dark juice staining the cloth beneath them. Why had the thief—then David joined her, and she lifted her gaze to stare at him. The absurd spectacle he made reminded her of earlier un-answered questions, and she spoke first.

"What on earth are you doing clad in such unsuitable attire?" Circe demanded.

David pushed the cloth cap back in order to meet her eyes. "My usual garments await me in a secondhand clothing shop, not that far from here. You're the one, I'm told, who has been accustomed to sitting in meadows and painting half-naked peasants."

"True, but you, my lord"—Circe kept her tone cool—"are no peasant."

He shrugged. "Despite my rustic garb? Perhaps I

donned this humble costume in hopes of drawing your artist's eye."

Circe frowned. "If you are making sport of me . . ."

"How could I poke fun at anyone else, dressed like this?"

He chuckled, and his blue-gray eyes twinkled, like the David she remembered. She found her anger ebbing as swiftly as it had come.

"I would never make sport of you, Miss Hill. Why should I be so unkind?"

She couldn't think why he would. David had never laughed at her for being different. Perhaps that was why he had captured her heart when she was a schoolgirl, long before she knew what love really was, or what love might be. To be honest, she was still not sure. She pulled her thoughts back to the matter at hand. If he was trying to distract her, this effort was most successful.

"If you are going to 'Miss Hill' me, you force me back to 'my lord,' " she warned him.

"You began it, but very well." He nodded to concede defeat. "Since we are alone—most improperly, I might add—we will be candid."

"Then tell me why you wear those clothes," Circe repeated before the obvious thought occurred. "David, you're not taking part in some silly wager?"

"Of course not!" He looked hurt, and she regretted her question at once.

"Then what?"

"I have been doing a chore for . . . someone," he said slowly.

"What kind of chore would require you to dress like a ragman?" Circe gazed at him, trying to read his face.

"I've been watching someone we do not trust."

"Oh, yes, thank you. It is now as clear as a Waterford goblet." Circe drew a deep breath, trying not to lose her temper.

"I'm afraid this is a matter about which I cannot speak."

David sounded unusually serious. "In all truth, Circe, it is not my secret, and it is a most weighty affair. You will have to trust me on that."

Circe stared back at him, a little surprised at the somber look in his eyes. "Of course I trust you," she said slowly. "But, David—"

"Never mind me," he interrupted. "How came you to be accosted on the street, twice in one day?"

"How should I know?" Circe shrugged. Then she paused. "Who told you I have been attacked twice?"

"I witnessed both assaults."

She remembered the first attack, and the other man who had started toward them. "That was you, in front of our house!" Circe exclaimed, suddenly putting it all together. She had believed the second man to be another thief, but it had been David, in disguise. "You were coming to my aid, then, too."

"I could hardly stand by and do nothing while the villain assailed you and your maid," David said shortly. "Even though interceding would have disclosed my ruse. But you stood up to him like a little Napoleon, and then the footman arrived, so I slipped away, in order not to lose him again."

"But why? And how did you come to be there?"

"I had been following this man," David told her, his tone grim. "Unhappily, he has the knack of evading pursuit. He eluded me in the city, but I located him again several blocks away and followed him here. However, in rescuing you this time, I have lost him again."

"And worse, now he knows you are after him?"

David nodded. Circe bit her lip. "I am sorry."

"Then help me figure out who he is and what he wants," David urged her. "It might assist me. Do you have any idea about his identity or his purpose? Why is he hanging about Gabriel and Psyche's town house?"

Circe considered. "I don't know his name. But I know the man." The memory came flashing back. When his scarf had been pushed aside in the fight, she had glimpsed the telltale scar. "Or at least, I have seen him before."

"Where?"

"In our back courtyard." Circe tried to think how much she could safely explain. She did not want David going to Gabriel, who might order Luciana discharged at once if he thought the girl was consorting with thieves. Perhaps David had his secrets, but then, so did she.

Looking alarmed, David seized her upper arm, his grip almost painful, but loosened his hold a moment later. "In your own yard? What was he doing there?"

She would not mention Luciana—she would not abandon the young woman whom she had rescued. "Perhaps waiting for me to emerge? I don't know."

"And why would he be after you to start with? No, I realize you don't know that." David took a deep breath. "I will escort you home."

"No, you will not see me home," Circe said firmly. "I was going to see an exhibit!" But then she sighed and shook her head. "Oh, very well, the afternoon is too far advanced anyway. I shall try again tomorrow."

"With a footman to accompany you," David suggested, scowling. "The biggest, brawniest you have."

Circe frowned at him. "I believe I did more damage to him today than my slow-moving footman did!"

"You might not be so lucky next time."

"Lucky? I think not, my lord." Circe considered taking offense. He might at least acknowledge that she had kept her wits about her. Brute force was not everything.

His warm fingers still gripped her arm. Circe jumped when he lightly stroked the sensitive skin on its underside. The thin fabric of her muslin gown did nothing to dull the sensation; his touch tickled a bit, but more than anything, it tantalized. What was he about? She considered removing herself from his hold. No, she wanted very much to stay where she was and see what happened next.

David tilted his head toward her, a disheveled lock of chestnut hair just brushing Circe's forehead. When he spoke, his breath was warm against her face.

"Wasn't it you who just said no more 'my lord'-ing?"

"Yes," Circe almost whispered as she gazed up into David's face. His eyes had taken on a heavy, slumberous look that she recognized from study but with which she had no personal experience . . . until now.

Perhaps longing made one's vision hazy, she thought as she looked up into David's magnificent eyes, the blue-gray irises being swallowed by his dilating pupils. Yes, this too had been explained, but to have it actually happen to her . . . to have the one man she desired, desire her in return. Circe parted her lips and leaned closer, eager to touch his firm lips. *Kiss me, please, just kiss me. . . .*

She waited. Despite her longing, she felt a flicker of doubt intrude. She had inclined her head and pursed her lips in preparation; now she opened her eyes to stare at him. David, most oddly, hesitated.

His forehead now pressing heavily into hers, he spoke against her cheek. "Circe, have I told you how lovely you both look today?"

Both of her? Oh, dear. On further reflection, Circe wasn't sure that a lover's pupils were supposed to get *quite* so large.

She barely had time to lift her arms to catch him as David sagged against her, pinning her against the coarse brick wall. He was too heavy to hold. Carefully, she slid herself and David down the rough surface to the ground. Leaving him slumped against her, she reached around his inert body for her reticule, which she had let fall before the kiss that failed to materialize. Rummaging through the embroidered bag, she searched for the recently donated bottle of smelling salts.

Circe's gloved fingers closed around the small vial. "Oh, thank you, thank you," she whispered to her un-named benefactor. With the awkward movements of a woman who has an unconscious man reclining against her person, Circe pulled the stopper out of the bottle and tipped David's head back from her bosom.

"I hope this vile stuff does the trick," she muttered.

With a wince of apology, Circe shoved the bottle under David's nose.

David jerked to wakefulness with the rage of a wounded bear. Recoiling from the noxious smell, he rolled off Circe and onto the filthy ground.

"What the hell are you doing to me?" he roared.

"Administering smelling salts," Circe replied calmly.

"Why in damnation would you do such a mean-spirited thing?"

Circe frowned at his ingratitude. "You men have been sticking it up the nostrils of women for a hundred years, so it can't be all bad."

Looking grumpier than ever, David blinked and rubbed his watering eyes.

"Besides, it worked!" she added.

David jumped on that remark. "It most certainly did not!"

Circe stared at him. "It most certainly did. You swooned, now you are awake. I'd say the outcome should be fairly obvious."

Still weaving a bit, David braced one hand against the wall and struggled to his feet. He glared down at Circe. "A gentleman does not swoon, Circe. He might be dazed after a round with Gentleman Jackson, or bemused after a fall from the saddle when his horse has refused a jump. But he never, ever swoons. And he never, ever requires smelling salts."

Circe gazed back at him and marveled at the monstrous vanity of the English gentleman. The alley could hardly contain it.

"So you were only 'dazed' from your fisticuffs?" she repeated.

David rolled his eyes. "You weren't paying attention. I might be dazed after boxing with a master, not as a result of a tussle with a common thief. You wish to make me a laughingstock?"

Circe still struggled to comprehend the complexities.

"If you weren't in a swoon or a daze, then what were you?"

David thought for a moment. "Resting from my exertions."

Circe sighed. "Of course you were. It's perfectly clear now. I suppose you would never live down such a disgrace. Do not fear, no one shall hear it from me." She put the offending vinaigrette away in her reticule, and added beneath her breath, "My lord vanity."

"How long was I, uh, resting?" he demanded. "Has anyone passed the alley and seen you like that?"

Circe looked down and saw that she still sat with legs splayed and skirts hitched up from her slide down the wall. Her bodice had been pushed low and she was fairly certain by the hair hanging over one eye that Luciana's delicate creation had come loose from its pins yet again.

"I'm certain that no one walked past." She had no idea, but if it would make him feel better . . .

David's shoulders relaxed. "Good." Reaching out a hand, he helped Circe to her feet. "If any of the Ton had seen you lying in an alley with a man between your thighs"—David paused briefly and then continued—"in such a position, rather—"

Her hands in her hair as she redid her twist and thrust some of the hated hairpins back into place, Circe paused to interrupt. "I've heard the word *thighs* before, you know."

David, who had averted his eyes, turned back and surveyed her from head to toe. His gaze lingered on the delicate swells of her breasts, the subtle curve of her slender neck, the lushness of her lower lip. Then his glance dropped to the body part that she had so boldly mentioned. She felt as well as saw him skim the long length of her thighs before he once more turned away.

Circe had never been so aware of herself as a woman in her life—not even when she had taken her turn to pose for her fellow art students, wearing a simple muslin gown and holding an urn. But David looked at her in a way that made her feel completely feminine and completely exposed. She found that she rather liked it. No, she liked it very much.

His voice was thick when he spoke. "You are unlike any young woman I have ever known."

Circe smiled, just a little. "You have said that before. I do not think it was meant as a compliment."

"Imp!" David retorted, then he lowered his voice with obvious effort. He seemed in control of himself once more. "Just promise me you will not venture out again without a footman."

There was genuine worry in David's tone this time, and a look about his eyes she had not seen there before. Circe decided not to argue. "Yes, indeed," she said meekly.

He gazed at her, his frown suspicious. "I mean it!"

"I'm sure you do," she agreed. "Now what about a change of apparel?"

"Yes." He scratched absently beneath his arms. "I weary of this pose. Come with me, it's only a few blocks, and then I will see you safely home. After that I have to check on a hot chestnut cart."

"A what?" Circe thought she could not have heard him properly.

"Never mind." David waved her back toward the street. "It's just that the fellow who owns it seemed quite attached to the clumsy awkward thing. I want to see it returned in one piece."

They walked, slowly because he was most unsteady on his feet, with Circe again in the forefront, feeling as if she were leading a parade. At the shop where David had left his own clothes, Circe waited while David disappeared behind a ragged curtain. At first she was quite interested in the baskets of discarded clothing that filled the tiny shop; they suggested all sorts of picture ideas. But he seemed to take a very long time, and finally she spoke to the curtain.

"I need to be home before dinner, you know."

David pushed back the curtain, and she saw that he was properly dressed, though he still labored to tie a very rumpled neckcloth.

"Hard to do without a proper looking glass," he explained. A sliver of glass was propped up on the rough board behind him, but the reflection it sent back was splintered and hard to decipher.

"Here," she said. "Let me help."

"And what do you know about tying a cravat?" he retorted, his expression quizzical.

"Let's just say that it was a—a costume ball," she said. Yes, it was as well that Psyche and Gabriel did not know *all* the details of her painting excursions across the Continent.

She stepped in front of him, set her basket on the cluttered floor, and smoothed the crumpled cloth as best she could, before retying it yet again.

She had nimble hands, David thought, looking down at the intent set of her mouth as she concentrated on the task at hand. They were standing very close; he could smell her faint scent of apple blossom beneath a heavier odor of turpentine—and see the effect of the sun's rays on her glowing cheeks. She had arched her brows just a little as she struggled to make the neckcloth conform to her wishes, and one lock of soft brown hair still curled over her temple from their misadventure.

He wanted to reach out and pull her hard against him, he wanted to bend down and press his lips against her soft, slightly parted mouth. . . . David took a deep breath.

"You needn't fret," she said absently. "I couldn't make a worse job of it than you were doing."

"No, indeed," David managed to say. He must not think like this about Circe, who had been just a schoolgirl when David had begun his debauchery. He had roamed the underbelly of London for too many years, gambling and drinking and, yes, whoring, until even Gabriel had spoken to him sternly.

Because he cared very much about being Gabriel's

friend, and because he had realized he was following a too familiar pattern, David had abated his excesses. He had vowed to become a respectable gentleman, and to seek out a very proper young lady to be his wife. Perhaps that way, he could avoid the angry turmoil of his own childhood, the wretched chaos of his parents' marriage.

And Circe was not the prim maiden he had promised himself to find. He would not reenact his parents' drawing room farces, nor subject Circe to the risk of being tied to someone who, after all, was ill suited to make her happy.

Circe looked at him, as if realizing how close he stood, and there was a pause that seemed to stretch on for a small eternity. He could see her chest rising and falling beneath the thin muslin of her dress. He yearned to stroke those small, sweet arching breasts and, *oh, Circe, if only—*

He stepped back. He was still dizzy, that must be what was weakening his self-control. His sore head bumped the rough wall and almost cracked the already fractured bit of glass even further. "Let's get you home before your sister becomes anxious about you," he suggested.

As he knew it would, the mention of Psyche distracted Circe from whatever thoughts she had been having.

"Yes," she agreed. "Let us make haste."

"Besides," David added as they left the second-hand shop, and he scratched, as discreetly as possible, at his elbow, "I think I could use a hot bath. And these clothes are going to wend their way promptly back to this shop, with my blessings, along with whatever denizens they and I have accidently acquired."

Circe bit back a trill of laughter, but he saw that she walked just a few more inches away from him. And that was by design, too, though it made his hunger for her even keener. He wanted her closer, not more distant. But what he wanted didn't matter. What was best for Circe did.

They walked out of the shop together, David stubbornly carrying the battered basket. But he was still so obviously unwell that Circe insisted they hail a hansom. She gave the driver the direction and they climbed into the shabby vehicle and sat for several minutes in silence, both apparently deep in thought.

When they neared the Sinclair town house, he repeated his warning about going out alone.

"You said that already," Circe noted, her tone dry.

"Yes, but I'm not sure you were listening," he said. "Circe, for one thing, this is London. You must show some evidence of decorum."

"Oh, yes, those lovely rules again," she muttered, making a face.

"Yes, those rules. What are your plans for tomorrow?"

Circe thought. "I don't think there are any social engagements I can't get out of. I mean to try the exhibition again. Oh, no, I believe I have promised to speak to Sir John's horticulture club before tea. Perhaps if I leave early for the exhibition . . ."

"Just remember to take along an escort." He ignored her rebellious expression. "Circe, this is imperative. Someone means you harm, though why I don't know. Are you carrying anything valuable?"

"Only a few shillings," she said. "If I purchased anything more dear, it would be charged to Psyche, you know that."

He nodded absently.

"I did wonder, earlier, why the thief went for the basket instead of my reticule," she said.

"Yes," David agreed. "What is in this pathetic-looking basket, Circe?" He gave the inoffensive basket a shake.

"Only some grapes for Psyche," she explained.

He shook it again. "Really. And why are your grapes jingling?"

Nine

Circe started. She had been too disturbed by David's close presence to notice the small sound. Reaching for the basket, she pushed aside the cloth that covered the fruit, then picked up the small bunch of battered grapes. This time she dug deeper, beneath the second cloth that covered the bottom of the basket. What she saw made her eyes widen. It had been carefully enfolded in the beginning, perhaps, but all the jolting had knocked it free of the confining wrap. She pulled up the glittering object, and David whistled.

"Just a little something for the fruit bowl, eh?" He took the necklace from her. The choker was of an old-fashioned design, and although it was fairly modest in size, surely those gems were real? The flashing rubies, set off by an occasional pearl and some modest diamonds, would have made any thief quite happy with his haul.

But how would the scar-faced man have known that she would be carrying a basket with such an unlikely object concealed at the bottom? And why was it concealed at the bottom?

It all came back to Luciana. Luciana had been speaking to the ruffian before the theft ever occurred; Luciana had prepared the basket and brought it along to fetch the grapes—grapes that neither Psyche nor Simpson had likely requested. Circe pressed her lips tightly together, annoyed at her naivete. How could Luciana repay her generous assistance with such subterfuge?

Circe realized that David had spoken, and she pulled her attention back. "You were saying?"

"I was asking if this trinket belongs to you."

"I—no—that is, yes." It would be hard to explain the necklace's presence if it were Circe's own, but even harder if she claimed to have never seen it before. Circe tried to think quickly, but David was ahead of her.

"Not thinking of trying a moneylender, were you, Circe? Those are dangerous chaps, my dear. I would really advise against it. If you have the hounds on your scent—"

"What?" She wrinkled her brow in bewilderment.

"If you've overspent your allowance and you do not wish to ask Psyche for more, at least come to me. I can help you with a loan."

Circe frowned. "David, I am not lacking for funds." Her personal fortune was large, and Psyche and Gabriel had never stinted her for spending money.

"You are carrying an expensive bit of jewelry around in a basket as if it were a hot cross bun!" David looked at her, and she found she could not meet his eyes. She had to speak to Luciana, find out what this was about, before she could speak candidly to anyone, even David, about this matter.

"I think we should get you home," she said. "From the way your forehead is creased, I am sure that your blow is still troubling you. Does your head hurt?"

"Abominably, but Circe, you are changing the subject. What about this necklace?"

"I will explain later," she told him, devoutly hoping that she would indeed have something to explain. Just now, she felt truly at sea. "But you need to rest."

"You first," he insisted. "Then I will go straight home, I give you my word."

She regarded him steadily, and he put his hand on his heart, though his expression was mocking. "Truly, I will."

"And no late hours tonight?" she suggested. "I think you should see a surgeon."

"Lord, no," he protested. "I will have my valet bathe the wound—he has seen worse."

"I'm sure of it," she agreed, "considering the low places you once frequented." But she made no more fuss, to David's relief.

He knew she was hiding something, but it was true that his head ached like the devil, and the pummeling he had received had left him as sore as though an ox had stomped its path over David's prone body. He still felt a little dizzy from the blow to the head, and his shoulders and back ached from his labors in propelling that damned pushcart across the greater part of London. Reminded of the cart, he groaned.

"What is it, are you worse?" Circe sounded alarmed.

"No, no, it's nothing," he told her. "Here, we are approaching your house. Let us get you and this doomed basket inside. But I shall call on you tomorrow, and I expect a full detailing of your reasons for carting valuable property hither and yon and getting us both knocked about."

"I'm going out tomorrow," Circe protested.

"Your art display can wait," he said.

"David!" Circe looked offended. Arms crossed, she seemed ready to argue the point.

"Yes, I know. The paintings matter. I did not mean— I just don't want you wandering about alone, Circe. I will come and escort you to the exhibition, how is that?"

"Very well," Circe agreed, relaxing her stance. "But come early. I want plenty of time to study the paintings, and I have to speak to Sir John's horticulture salon at four."

The hansom rolled to a stop, and David got out to help her down. "Until tomorrow, Miss Hill," he said, his tone as formal as his words.

"I am obliged to you, Lord Westbury," Circe answered, her tone equally reserved and noncommittal. But the gleam of laughter in her eyes told him she was beginning to find her way in this game of social manners. Her formality lasted until she paused in front of the doorway. As a footman hurried to open the front door, she glanced demurely up at David.

"But next time, do remember your trousers!"

The footman gaped at them. David managed not to laugh. "I will," he promised.

Trust Circe to have the last—and most improper— word.

When Sir John presented himself at Sally's house for tea as arranged, he was smiling. It had been a splendid day. The morning had dawned mildly and with a light rain— perfect for transplanting outside all the seedlings he had started in early winter. Sir John had spent the morning on his knees, ignoring the damage to his trousers as he moved the tiny plants to their new homes. As protective as a mother with her babe, he had spread the delicate roots, surrounded them with his own specially mixed potting mixture, patted the soil around the plants careful to eliminate any dangerous air pockets that could threaten their growth, and watered them one by one.

Sir John knew that many people considered his passion a bit extreme, for passion it certainly was. Even some of his fellow horticulturists thought his enthusiasm overdone. But to him, the scent of freshly turned soil and the sight of a neat row of flourishing perennials were heady stuff. It never occurred to him to wonder why he lavished so much of himself on his plants. He just knew that from the very first time he had begged to hold a spade, and the family's gardener had permitted him to work beside him in the flower beds, John had made green things sprout, flower, and flourish.

But yes, he knew that he tended to get carried away. Instead of stopping well before teatime, as he had told himself he would, he had instead worked through his luncheon and right up to an hour before his appointment.

His staff, while accustomed to him missing meals in his absorption, were not used to their master leaving to make social calls. His valet had been stunned when Sir John, contrite when he had at last noted the booming of the clock in the hall, had rushed upstairs and demanded a new set of clothing suitable for attending tea. He had made a quick wash and change, picked up his hat and gloves and the gift he had prepared, then hurried out, barely aware that the butler, valet, and at least one of the footmen were all staring after him from the main hall.

When he was admitted to Mrs. Forsyth's house, the elderly butler accepted what he held out with a nod of understanding, then led Sir John into a salon of dazzling color. No pale rose or blue for this lady, apparently. The furniture was covered in shades of vivid turquoise and teal with bright touches of yellow, like a formal garden where irises and chrysanthemums bloomed all at once, instead of in their proper season. He would like to escort her to the gardens at Vauxhall, he thought absently. She would appreciate their variety.

Sir John supposed the effect of all the bright colors should have been garish, but instead he found it rather charming and . . . stimulating to the senses. Rather like the woman who presently appeared in the doorway.

A bit startled by that unbidden thought, he pulled his attention away from the furnishings to rise and bow politely. Mrs. Forsyth stood with one small hand on the door frame, the other grasping at her waist the nosegay he had brought her. He was pleased to note that the simple arrangement of scarlet Oriental poppies and butter-colored peonies flattered the gown she wore and confirmed her apparent love of vibrant color.

"The flowers are beautiful and a very nice touch," Sally said. "Thank you."

Sir John tried not to blush—a ridiculous habit that always made him feel awkward and insecure. The old discomfort, the feeling of being unsure about himself, resurfaced like a too familiar tune.

"I thought you might enjoy them. At least, I hoped you might enjoy them. . . ." Sir John found himself floundering and despised himself for it. It didn't help that Mrs. Forsyth lifted her lashes and her big brown eyes regarded him steadily. "They seem to match your, um, frock quite nicely," he ended lamely.

To his relief, Sally grinned and came into the room. "What you should have said, Sir John, is that you chose the flowers because you knew they would complement my beauty and good taste."

Sir John nodded, mentally berating himself for not seeing this.

"And then," Sally continued as she sank gracefully onto the settee, "while I blushed in confusion, you could have finished me off entirely with your vast knowledge by comparing my own virtues with the virtues that mythology has bestowed on the flowers." She arranged her filmy skirts to her satisfaction and patted the seat next to her. "No other gentleman in the Ton has the advantage of your particular skill."

Sir John hesitated, then sat down where she indicated. He had never thought of his botanical knowledge as a skill that would attract a lady. He tried to absorb this novel idea.

"And lastly"—Sally's honey-colored eyes sparkled up at him—"my 'frock,' which my dressmaker would explain to you is a carefully crafted tea gown, matches so nicely because the moment you handed the flowers to my butler, he passed them to my housekeeper, who passed them to my lady's maid, who passed them to me. I directed her as to which dress would showcase both your thoughtfulness and my beauty. Having made that decision, Betsy frantically helped me to change my clothing and my jewelry."

He was struck by her brilliance. "Why, of course." It seemed so simple once she had explained it all. How had he expected that his flowers would match her dress so perfectly?

Sally stopped for a moment as if struck by a thought. "My goodness," she said. "I didn't realize that by tutoring you, I would reveal so many of a lady's little ruses." She shrugged. "So be it. It is for a good cause. If I can help you to understand women better, I think you will be more at ease in their company."

Sir John's expression must have given him away, because Sally arched her brows. "Are you so pessimistic, Sir John? You do not expect our little experiment to succeed?"

"It's not—it's not your own skill I doubt," he tried to explain, so as not to wound her feelings. "And it's very kind of you to make the effort to help me. It's my own lack of social grace. I do all right with men, you know. At my club, at the horticulture salons, I'm quite at ease, and I don't stumble over my words or go red at the most inopportune times. It's only with females . . ."

"Yes, I understand." Sally patted his arm. She pretended not to see how he jumped at her touch. Mercy, the poor man was as jumpy as a fox with a pack of hounds baying in the next field. "But I still believe that with a little practice, you shall become more at ease and then more adept in your attempts to please the ladies. And with one lady, especially."

"She is very nice, isn't she?" Sir John said shyly. "Miss Hill, I mean. Such a wonderful talent and very kind, although I don't think she noticed me, really. It was gracious of her to agree to join us for our weekly salon tomorrow afternoon."

"Yes, well, that is why we must have a little practice," Sally told him, pleased by the honest admiration for Circe that he did not attempt to conceal. Not that the poor man would have known how to conceal it if he'd wished to. Really, he should have been brought out more as a lad, Sally thought. What had his mother been thinking?

Her butler appeared in the doorway with a silver tray filled with tea things, and Sally nodded for it to be placed on the table in front of them. She poured a cup of steaming liquid and passed it to Sir John. He accepted it with anxious care.

"I assume you serve tea at your salons," she ventured. "Since they are in the afternoon?"

"Oh, yes," Sir John replied. "After the lecture, of course."

"Then let us take tea together, and you will pretend I am Circe and think of what you would like to tell her—"

Her guest had been about to sip the tea, but now he took too big a gulp, and then sputtered, droplets of tea flying across the tray. "Oh, so sorry. I didn't—it's just— when you said—"

Sally sighed. This could be a long lesson.

When the door shut behind Circe, David shook his head at her impudence, then wished he had not. Groaning, he tried to make the pavement stop its rising and falling. He drew a deep breath and returned to the hired carriage. His head pained him still, and the sway of the badly sprung vehicle made his stomach lurch.

When he reached his own home, he paid off the driver and just managed to walk through the front door with a reasonably steady gait. First, he sent a footman with directions to find the pushcart, if it was still where he had left it, and see that it was safely reclaimed by its owner. The servant opened his eyes wide at his instructions, but he nodded and set out promptly.

"And tell the kitchen to send up hot water for a bath," David told the butler, who had hovered in the background as the footman received his instructions. The man's expression was a bit strained. Surely it was not about the footman; David had done stranger things in his misbegotten youth than borrow a vendor's pushcart, and his servants were accustomed to unusual errands.

"Yes, your lordship," Richards agreed. "I shall attend to it. But, my lord, you need to know—"

"Later," David cut the man short. "I am in need of a large brandy, and then the bath, and then a good dinner."

"Ah, dinner is about to be announced, my lord," the elderly servant said, looking distinctly nervous.

"At this hour?" David pulled out his pocket watch. "Has the whole household run amok? It's barely past six. I never dine so early."

"Yes, my lord, but—"

"Who in blazes took it upon themselves to countermand my orders?" David demanded. This was somehow the last straw in a large haystack of grievances. His head pounded, and the hall swayed, and now his dinner was to be shoved down his throat before he had even washed or savored a glass of wine? "I shall have them discharged! Who was it?"

"The countess, my lord," the butler said, keeping his voice soft.

David thought he had misheard.

"You don't mean—"

The butler's usually bland expression revealed a hint of sympathy. "Yes, your lordship. The countess arrived in her carriage at just past noon, having journeyed up from Bath."

David shut his eyes for a moment and leaned against the elaborately carved newel post. His mother—in London. Hellfire, this was all he needed. "Can we send her back again?" he muttered beneath his breath.

Richards blinked, but he kept his expression suitably impassive. And now a high-pitched voice could be heard from the large sitting room one floor up. "David, is that you, darling boy?"

David considered feigning deafness, but he knew his mother—she never gave up. And indeed, her voice came again. "Come up at once, I wish to see you. We have so much to discuss."

With one hand on the banister, he climbed the staircase slowly, pausing to look back at the butler. "Tell the cook to put dinner off as long as he can."

The butler's expression gave some hint of the turmoil that must be ensuing in his kitchen; the cook had already been ordered to push the dinner ahead by two hours, and now—David only hoped the excellent chef did not resign his post before morning.

When David reached the landing, he heard his mother call again. "David, I am waiting."

"Yes, Mother," he said, though he had to restrain himself from adding a few more choice words. "I'm afraid I need to change before I greet you properly. I'm, ah, a bit the worse for wear."

"Nonsense, you could never—" She had bestirred herself at last from her favorite chaise and now stood in the double doorway, her expression taut with disapproval as she looked him up and down. "David! Your neckcloth is wrinkled, your coat is covered in dust, and—oh, my—you have a rip in your coat sleeve! How can you go out in such a state of disrepair, my darling? Did I teach you nothing about what is due your station?"

"Yes, indeed. I assure you I set out looking much more up to snuff than I do now. But I had a rather fatiguing day," he said with a straight face.

His mother frowned, then swayed a little.

David grimaced.

"I feel a swoon coming on." She clutched at her chest. "I fear that my poor heart is having one of its spasms. Oh, dear, oh, dear. If you would assist me . . ."

He hurried forward to support her before she sank gracefully all the way to the floor. His mother was well practiced in her swooning. She shut her eyes as he deposited her efficiently if somewhat abruptly into the nearest chair.

He was still weak enough himself that he almost fell

with her, but caught himself by grabbing the chair's cherry frame. The delicate-looking chair, a fine model by Mr. Sheraton, creaked a little, but it withstood this double burden of weight.

"Here, Mother, sit down. Do not distress yourself. I was just on my way to my chamber to bathe and change my clothes for dinner. I will be more presentable directly."

"But dinner is about to be announced—you cannot be late." Her voice sounded weak, but David recognized, from long experience, the veiled iron in her tone.

"I have already sent a message to the cook," he said.

She opened one eye, and her expression altered subtly from ailing to just plain annoyed. "You countermanded my orders?"

"As you did mine," he agreed. "I'm afraid I was not expecting an early dinner, Mother."

Before she could protest further, he looked around. "You need your vinaigrette. Where is Cousin Thomasina?"

"She is still in Bath. She has a lingering pleurisy that has much distressed her, and she feared to leave the healing waters of the pump fountain." His mother's tone, however, revealed her exasperation.

David swallowed a groan. Not only was his mother here, but she had no one to press her hand and hover about her, as she liked. He really was in trouble. She and her favorite cousin both enjoyed their ill health enormously, and just who was ailing the most on any given day was impossible to predict. This time, it seemed that Cousin Thomasina had trumped the countess's weak heart and frequent swoons with her own ailments. The fact that his mother had nursed her ailing heart for the last twenty years with remarkable success was impossible to comment upon.

However, dealing with his mother without her companion by her side would be even more difficult. He wove his way across the room to find her reticule, then pulled a bell rope. Fortunately, his mother had shut her eyes again and did not note his lack of stability. He gave her the bejeweled vinaigrette—she had a collection of them and changed them to suit her costume—and his mother thanked him in a long-suffering tone.

When a footman arrived, David thought quickly.

"Fetch the housekeeper," he said. "My mother is in need of assistance." The woman had been with them for years; she would know how to deal with his mother and soothe her agitations.

When Mrs. Milburn arrived, pausing in the doorway to give the countess a dignified curtsy, David handed his mother over to her with a sigh of relief, then excused himself quickly before his mother could demur. He made his way up to his own bedchamber, where, miracle of blessed miracles, a hip bath stood full of steaming water.

David shed his dusty clothing. "Take these straight out to the back court and burn them," he told his valet.

His manservant blinked. "Your lordship?"

"I fear my coat and I have picked up some unwanted visitors."

"Ah, I see. I shall be back presently." His man picked up the offending bundle of clothing, holding it at arm's length, and disappeared into the hallway.

David stepped into the tub and leaned back against its copper rim, sighing as he allowed his sore muscles to relax in the liquid caress of the warm water. What a day. And while he longed to do nothing more than fall into bed and sleep for a week, he still had too much on his plate to contemplate any such well-earned respite. He had to keep his word to his uncle and maintain his watch on von Freistadt, and even more urgently, he had to find out about this dodgy fellow who had caused so much trouble today, assailing Circe and putting her in peril.

David frowned, remembering the shock of alarm he had felt when he had seen Circe in danger. His stomach had gone hollow, and his heart had jumped almost out of his chest. He could not recall ever being so frightened. Circe could not be harmed. He would not allow it, not one smooth brown hair on her head, not one inch of sun-kissed skin. If anything happened to Circe . . . He pushed the thought away as intolerable even to contemplate.

But that made his Foreign Office mission only more imperative, and somehow, he was not at all sure why, Circe had become entangled in its complicated coils. Did this go back to von Freistadt?

David stretched his legs as far as they would go in the too-short tub and remembered how Circe had looked, sprawled in the alley. It should have been a comical sight, but, Lord, not with legs as long and shapely as hers. The delicate curve of her calf and the lush smoothness of her thighs—he had lain across them for a few brief moments. He cursed the lack of consciousness that had denied him an awareness of his good fortune. The next time he was granted the privilege of—

Then, angry at the direction of his thoughts, David slipped down to dunk his head into the water and reached for the soap. Wincing when his fingers touched the rising bump on his head, and his still swollen ear, he scrubbed his whole body with unwonted vigor, as if to wash away not only his outer soil, but the inner thoughts he could not indulge. There would be no next time. He could not take his pleasure with Circe; she was no loose woman. Neither was she the proper, reticent type of maiden he had vowed to marry. And anyhow, she seemed to have little awareness of him as a man.

Although he would damned well like to change that. . . .

When the valet returned, he poured a ewer of warm water over David's head. Still lost in his thoughts, David sputtered and had to rub the water out of his eyes. Then his man brought in heavy towels that had been warmed by the fire, and David reluctantly stepped out of the bath. Rubbing himself dry, he donned an immaculate set of evening clothes, then arranged a new neckcloth to even the most exacting standards—his mother's, in other words— ran a silver-backed comb through his unruly chestnut hair, wincing as he hit the lump, still remarkably sore, then strode forcefully down the hallway. He felt more himself since the bath, and his steps were more steady.

His mother awaited him in the drawing room, with the housekeeper and her own lady's maid hovering nearby. Mrs. Milburn had a slight crease in her forehead. David glanced at the woman and made a mental note to raise her pay, at once.

His mother sighed audibly when he appeared. He braced himself for the lecture, or the haranguing, that was forthcoming, but it was postponed by the appearance of the butler in the doorway. Had the man been listening for his step on the stairs? Obviously, Richards needed a raise, too.

"Dinner is served, my lord, my lady."

David offered his mother his arm, she accepted his support, although in his present state, he suspected she steadied him as much as he did her, and they made a sedate procession into the dining room. He saw her seated at one end of the table, then took his own chair at the other end. The fact that they were separated by several feet of polished wood made conversation difficult, but his mother liked the stately formality. David just liked the distance.

The profusion of dishes that crowded the table top showed that David's staff remembered well the demanding tastes of their former mistress, and perhaps was also trying to offer support for David's current plight. At any rate the poulet sauté and the jellied eels kept the countess occupied for some minutes, while David was able to chew his beef and boiled lobster and spear a healthy portion of potatoes and stewed apricots in peace.

It was not, of course, to last.

"David," his mother said, her fork pausing with a morsel of creamed shrimp at its tip. "I was most displeased by your appearance when you returned home today."

"I'm sure you were." David kept his tone light. "It was, as I said, an unusual day. I don't generally walk about in soiled neckcloths. I assure you, my valet would not permit it."

"As long as you are not falling back into the low habits of your youth?" His mother lifted her limpid blue eyes to gaze at him, her expression one of practiced martyrdom. "Far be it from me to scold you, dearest, but your old practices of frequenting gaming hells and drinking copiously and—well, consorting with low companions, it cannot bring you any happiness. You know I only think of your health, dear boy."

"Yes, indeed," David agreed, ignoring the first part of the sentence.

"In fact," she continued. "A nice hand of whist, a good book, a quiet social evening with friends, I'm sure this would bring you much contentment if only you tried."

David had to consciously unclench his jaw. "I appreciate the suggestions, Mother. I assure you I am no more licentious than the average gentleman."

She sniffed. "Darling, you must never be average."

"I'll keep that in mind." He sipped his wine, wishing the dull ache in his head would pass. "As it happens, I have amended much of my most foolish ways, though for my reasons, not for yours. However, gentlemen do go to gaming clubs, Mother. I am not a vicar. Gentlemen go out at night, and often keep late hours."

"I'm all too aware of that." She broke off a piece of bread with unnecessary emphasis, sending a shower of crumbs across the table. "Your father—"

Any sentence that began with "Your father" did not bode well. David tried to change the subject. "I hope the weather was fair in Bath?"

His mother plowed ahead. "Your father followed a precipitous path leading to our family's near ruination, and he caused me deep vexation and grief, dear boy. I do not wish to see you fall into the same trap."

"Would you like an accounting of my days, Mother? As you once enjoyed?"

David found that his voice had an edge to it. He took a deep breath and pulled himself back from the acrimony that could easily follow. When he was younger, his mother had hired bodyguards to follow him all over London—at least, they followed him when he could not shake them off. The humiliating practice had continued until he was four-and-twenty and finally issued a tersely worded ultimatum: she would cease the practice, or he would send them all back to her on a stretcher. That was also the year she had given up shouting at him and had taken to swooning instead.

She ignored his provocation. "Don't be ungrateful, David. It was for your own protection. But it's most important for you to confirm yourself as a man of character, especially considering the wonderful news that brought me back from Bath."

Puzzled, David answered cautiously as he accepted a serving of almond cake from the footman. "New dressmaker in town, is there?"

"David, this is nothing to jest about."

"New milliner?"

She had dipped her spoon into a creamy trifle, but now she put down her utensil. "David, I am quite serious. I am really overjoyed." She actually smiled at him. "However, if you mean to make a success of this most important venture, you really must be careful to maintain respectable habits."

David felt a hint of unease. "Habits for . . . ?"

"For your married state, of course." Now she was beaming.

He felt as if he were mired in a bog. "Mother, what in hell—I mean, what in blazes are you talking about?"

"That *on-dit* on page four of the *Times* about a young reformed rake being stricken by Cupid's arrow and enchanted by the sincere love of a young lady of good family in her first Season."

David felt a wave of nausea. "You must be jesting, indeed. What on earth made you think that such a ridiculous and sentimental bit of pap should apply to me?"

She hardly seemed to hear. "And then when I met Sophia Hill's bosom friend at the Pump Room, and she told me about your kind attentions to Miss Circe Hill, which Sophia had conveyed to her in a letter, well, I must tell you—"

"Oh, Lord," David muttered. His exclamation could have well been mistaken for a prayer, he thought wildly. His tone was deep enough, and his expression must have shown dismay. But his mother was regarding a silver candelabra with a blissful expression that suggested to him she was already contemplating the imminent arrival of her first grandchild. Despite his words to Circe, David had never so much as hinted to his mother that he was courting a potentially marriageable miss.

"I'm surprised you are not spending the evening with the young lady tonight. You have not quarreled?"

"Mother, you are jumping to conclusions." He tried to keep his expression serene. "I barely know Miss Hill, and I have no plans for the evening—"

"Then you have engagements for the morrow?"

"Um, I imagine so, Mother," he answered, stalling for time.

"Perhaps even a soiree I might wish to share?"

"Why are you suddenly so desirous of my company, Mother?" As if he didn't know. David frowned at her.

She avoided meeting his eyes. "I have been long away from London, dear boy. Of course I should enjoy your companionship. So what are your plans for tomorrow night?"

"I believe there is a small musical evening I have promised to look in upon." He tried to sound offhand, but his mother sat up straighter, picking up the scent like a seasoned hound.

"You have never been interested in music, David. Who will be there?"

"I don't know the entire guest list, Mother." He felt tension in his jaw as he bit down on a nutmeat, and he had to remind himself to maintain his even tone. He was no longer a child—he would not shout at his mother, whatever the provocation.

"Perhaps Miss Hill will be there?"

"Perhaps."

His mother almost purred. "Ah, I thought so. So the newspaper was correct. What a pleasure it is, dear boy, to see you at last considering a proper alliance."

"Mother, I have not said . . ."

His words were wasted. She sailed on. "The Hills have a distinguished lineage, although there is no title, which is a pity. And I hear she has a most respectable fortune, which is never a bad thing, not that you have any need to marry for money, now that your father is dead and done wasting the family fortune on wine and cards and immoral women."

"Indeed." He took a spoonful of the pears in port sauce and refused to show any emotion.

"But one would be a fool not to admit that a healthy settlement is always to be esteemed. And mind you, it's not that you couldn't have aimed higher, you are a Westbury, and despite your father's many failings, the family itself goes back for hundreds of years, to the time of Henry Tudor, at least. And my family, well, their roots can be traced back to . . ."

Nodding, David applied himself to his dessert. He had heard all this before, many times. But the listing of forebears was at least better than his mother planning his wedding. For one mad moment, he imagined Circe sitting at the end of the table instead of his mother, smiling at him in that way she had, so open and unaffected. But then his vision blurred, and recollections of his parents' loud and bitter combats intruded. He almost choked on a nut, and he shook away the moment of wistful illusion.

When the countess's conversation returned to the highly valued Miss Hill, he tried once more to change her mind. "Mother, it is not what you—I don't want you to think—"

"Oh, certainly you should have apprised me of your choice much earlier, dear boy. But this time, as her fortune and family are most exceptional, I cannot fault you. As for the lady herself, I understand she can be a trifle eccentric. But I'm sure a word from an older and wiser lady—her mother is dead, after all, and I shall be happy to stand in her stead—will not be amiss."

David put one hand up to rub his brow. His mother was going to give Circe lessons in propriety? Because of her connection to David?

He was done for.

Ten

Circe had hoped to go upstairs and change her dress before seeing anyone except the footman who had let her in. The servants' hall would be buzzing with gossip before she reached the second landing, but that was nothing if she could escape her sister's attention. However, today her luck was out, indeed. Psyche was just emerging from her bedchamber when Circe reached the landing.

"Oh, good, you are home. Dinner will be announced very shortly—Circe! My heavens, what happened to you? You did not have a carriage accident?"

Sounding genuinely overset, Psyche put one hand to her mouth.

"No, no, I'm quite all right, truly. Just a little dusty, that is all." Circe tried to hurry past, but her sister reached out, with the prerogative of an elder sibling who has played the role of a parent for years, and gripped her arm.

"Circe, what are you keeping from me? You look as if you have been assaulted!"

This came too close for comfort. Conscious of her duplicity, Circe blinked and avoided meeting her sister's startled gaze. She glanced instead toward Psyche and Gabriel's bedchamber, and a handsome pier glass inside the room showed her an appalling sight. Lord, no wonder

Psyche sounded alarmed. Circe's hair straggled in long dusty locks around her face, her skirt was ripped at the hem and covered in mud, and her neck revealed a very suggestive streak of dirt that led straight into the bosom of her dress—no doubt where David had collapsed on top of her in the alley.

When she did not answer, Psyche spoke again, her voice sharper. "Circe? Tell me at once what has happened! And why are you carrying that coarse basket?"

Circe put her hands, with her reticule and the basket, behind her like a small child caught with a purloined sweet. "It did not happen precisely like that, only—"

"You were attacked?"

Psyche paled, and Circe felt even worse. She was going to make her sister ill—*think, think,* she told herself.

"Someone tried to steal my—my reticule, but it was nothing. Only I got knocked down, but I am unhurt. It's only my dress that suffered."

"Good heavens! Are you sure you're not injured?" Psyche's grip on her sister's arm tightened till it was almost painful.

"No, really—" Circe tried to explain, but her sister rushed on and did not pause to listen.

"Tell me you did not go out unaccompanied, Circe. If you have ignored my repeated requests, I swear, I will have you locked in your room for the rest of the Season!"

Psyche had never been harsh with her younger sister, but she was so emotional now with motherhood impending that she sometimes seemed a stranger. And the genuine concern that sparked her anger only increased Circe's burden of guilt.

"No, no, I went out with Luciana, but—"

"Luciana has been here in the servants' hall; Simpson mentioned she was not feeling well. I thought you must have had a footman with you. Oh, Circe, you went out alone! I can't believe you broke your word to me." Psyche sounded both shocked and hurt.

"I was not alone! David was with me," Circe blurted.

She had not meant to mention David, but she couldn't bear to wound her sister so.

Psyche took a deep breath and fixed Circe with an unwavering gaze.

"It's the truth," Circe assured her sister. "And I am perfectly all right, I promise you, not a scratch upon me."

"But the shock to your nerves," Psyche murmured. "You may not realize it yet, but you will be most unsettled."

Circe wanted to laugh, but she didn't dare.

"You can have your dinner on a tray," her sister suggested. "Lie down, and I will send Simpson to you."

"No." This time Circe's amusement faded. "I wish for Luciana. I have no doubt she is feeling better by now. And I will be down for dinner after I bathe and change. Please do not be anxious about me, Psyche. I promise you I am not hurt."

She touched her sister's hand gently. Psyche sighed. "It's only—you are very dear to me, you know." Tears glistened in Psyche's eyes.

Circe winced—she was an ungrateful wretch to distress her sister so. "I know, as you are to me," she answered. "I will be most careful when I go out again, I promise you. David says he is coming tomorrow to escort me to the exhibition."

"Good, good." Psyche took a deep breath. "I'm going down to the drawing room and will have a cup of tea until dinner is announced. I shall see you shortly. Ring for your maid before the whole staff is scandalized."

They already were, but Circe knew better than to point that out. "I shall," she promised. She waited only to see Psyche descend the stairwell, then hurried into her own bedchamber, dropped the basket and her reticule on a small table beside her bed, and pulled the bell rope. She looked into her own looking glass and made a face. She was brushing a twig out of her hair when one of the housemaids appeared. Circe asked her to bring up hot water, and added, "Would you inform Luciana that I wish to see her, please."

"Um, your maid is sitting in the servants' hall, miss," the little maid told her, her voice timid. "She says you instructed her to rest."

"I did and if she is still unwell, I will be happy to come down and speak to her there." Circe did not intend to put this off any longer, even though they would have no privacy in the servants' common room. "But I suspect she will wish to come up. You may tell her it is about the grapes."

The servant gaped, but nodded. "Yes, miss."

Sure enough, Luciana came into the room only minutes later. She was breathing quickly—she must have run up the back stairs. Or perhaps there was another reason for her agitation. When she looked at her employer, she gasped. "Signorina! What has happened?"

"I will explain in a moment. First, I have procured the grapes that my sister wished." Circe nodded toward the basket on the table. "Strange, she did not mention desiring them when I spoke to her just now."

Luciana dropped her gaze, and her hands twisted beneath her apron. "Perhaps she has forgotten, signorina. Ladies in her condition are subject to sudden fancies."

"True," Circe agreed. "You may take the basket."

Luciana had averted her eyes from the battered article, but now she moved quickly to snatch it up. "I will take the grapes down to the cook and return at once." She seemed ready to rush away, but as she made for the door, she put one hand inside the cloth that covered the basket's contents. She stopped abruptly.

"I have it here—what you're looking for," Circe said, her tone cool. "After I left you, I was attacked yet again by the man who struck you as we left the house, thus my disheveled appearance. I think you have something you need to tell me?"

Luciana stood still, her shoulders as rigid as if she had been constructed of brick and mortar. After a long pause, she turned slowly, revealing an expression of such panic that Circe might have been holding a saber pointed at the girl's heart. Some of Circe's anger eased, seeing the genuine fear on her maid's face.

"Luciana, why have you not been honest with me? I have tried to help you."

"I know, and I am most grateful, truly I am."

Circe ignored the protestation and held up the choker. "Where did this necklace come from?"

"It was my grandmother's, signorina. I hoped to sell it to raise a little money," Luciana almost whispered. She still didn't quite meet Circe's gaze, but her hands had relaxed, and her voice sounded sincere.

Circe regarded her thoughtfully. It was not such an unlikely story. If Circe herself had been about to flee her native country, she would have chosen portable valuables to take with her so that she could convert them later into cash. Decades earlier, the many refugees from the French Revolution had brought an amazing array of family heirlooms into England; she had heard Aunt Sophie tell stories of the lace and jewels and miniatures and sometimes even small pieces of furniture that had been seen in the London shops after the infusion of émigrés.

And she had never thought that the girl came from a peasant family. Indeed, Luciana had had to be taught how to do her new mistress's hair. She had known about sewing and mending, but any girl of all but the most wealthy families would have been taught those skills.

"Of what estate was your parents, and your grandparents?" Circe asked slowly.

Luciana lifted her head in an instinctive gesture of pride. "My father owned—owns—a shop in Genoa, signorina. My grandfather was a man of property and owned the shop and a mill as well. But the mill was destroyed in one of the battles."

Europe had been through great turmoil in the last generations; it was not impossible, Circe thought. But there was another question to be answered. "And how did you come to know that dark-haired man with the mark on his cheek? The one who attacked us, me twice, today."

The maid hesitated, and Circe lifted her brows. "Don't lie to me, Luciana," she said quietly.

Luciana sighed. "I heard, by chance, that he would know where to find a buyer for the necklace, one who would not question a poor girl who has no friends in this country to vouch for her. I was afraid to walk into a shop, signorina."

Circe felt hurt. "You do have a friend here, Luciana. If you needed anything more, you should have come to me." She didn't add that without her aid, Luciana would never have made it to England at all, but the other girl blushed to the roots of her dark hair.

"But I did not think it seemly to ask you to do such an errand for your maid."

It could be true, all of it. But she had the feeling that Luciana was hiding something, that some part of this story was not quite right. Circe glanced at the clock. Heavens, she had only a few minutes left until dinner would be announced.

"Are you feeling better?" she asked Luciana.

The girl nodded. "Yes, and I am so sorry that you should have been attacked. . . . I never thought . . . That man is not to be trusted. He is a scoundrel!"

"Yes, I have deduced that," Circe agreed drily. "We will talk more about this later. Just now, I need to get cleaned up and downstairs in time for dinner. I do not wish Lord Gabriel to be asking questions, too."

Luciana's eyes widened at the thought. She seemed to wholeheartedly agree, and with her help, Circe made a fast toilette and was able to descend the stairs in a spotless yellow gown just as the butler entered the drawing room to announce dinner. She went in with Psyche and Gabriel, glad they had no company tonight, and took her accustomed place at the dinner table.

She had to endure another scolding from Gabriel, who sounded even more insistent than Psyche that Circe remember not to walk alone in London. Only after she had promised one more time that she would faithfully follow their instructions did her sister and brother-in-law change the subject. At least Aunt Sophie had missed the contretemps; she was having a tray in her room.

For the rest of the meal, Circe ate quietly while the other two chatted. Circe was happy to observe that tonight Psyche managed to eat a decent dinner, applying herself to the excellent roast pork. The cook, who was devoted to her mistress, was putting herself out to concoct the most appealing dishes to tempt a mother-to-be's capricious appetite. But although she enjoyed the excellent dinner, too, the truth was Circe still had a great deal to mull over.

❧

Sir John was unusually tense the next morning. Ordinarily, on the days that the horticulture salon met at his house, he was excited and pleased. Most of those who attended were men he'd known for years, and he had no reason to feel the anxiety that always afflicted him when he had to walk into a group of strangers. But this week, knowing that Miss Circe Hill would grace them with her presence, his disquiet had returned in full force.

Mrs. Forsyth had suggested that he might be a little shy. Sir John grimaced as he recalled her gentle words. She would scorn him if she knew the truth. The fact was, he suffered intense discomfort in large groups, always had, since he was a boy.

Knowing the salon was to have a special guest, a feminine guest, he had tossed and turned all night, and when he slept, he'd dreamed he was a gawky lad sitting once more in the schoolroom.

He had found himself at his old desk, his stomach clenching as the instructor tapped his long rod on the desk and gazed about the room, selecting one of the squirming pupils for the next interrogation. When the schoolmaster's stern gaze settled upon young John, John experienced once more the usual agonies of panic, and every fact he had crammed into his head by diligent study, every Latin verb, every European capital, every name of long-dead English kings, seemed to instantly fly out again.

When the teacher barked a question, and all the other boys turned to stare at John, he could feel his face burn with his too-ready flush and hear the other students tittering beneath their breath. The whispers only added to his confusion.

"So, Master Templeton, dare I ask *you* a question?" The sarcastic tone of the schoolmaster made young John's shoulders hunch as he longed to duck beneath the desk and disappear from view.

"Y-yes, sir," he stuttered.

"So you can tell us the date of Caesar's first invasion of England?"

"Yes, sir. I mean, I knew it a minute ago, sir," John blurted, hearing that dreadful rustle of laughter go round the schoolroom again.

"I seem to ask you too late; a pity your wits run out like sand in the hourglass," the teacher mocked him. "You will write out the list of dates for today's lesson a hundred times before you are excused for tea, is that clear?"

"Yes, sir," John answered miserably, knowing that he had failed again.

When he woke at last from the familiar nightmare, he found his brow damp with sweat and his sheets tangled into knots. He lay sprawled across the bed, clutching a handful of bed linen as if it were the schoolmaster's neck, wishing he could wring it instead of the wrinkled covers. Damn the man, and damn himself for being such a miserable failure. If only he could be as smooth and polished as the darlings of the Ton, those men who could spout sweet words, dance gracefully, and charm the ladies with less noticeable effort than it took to tie their cravats.

It would be a wonder if Miss Hill should ever deign to smile upon him.

Groaning to himself, Sir John pushed himself up and went to pour water from the ewer into the china bowl. Splashing his face, he gazed into the small looking glass above the basin and remembered Mrs. Forsyth's patient coaching. She had a wonderfully kind heart, that lady. She was as beautiful on the inside as she was to the eye, and she seemed to trust that he could be helped. If only he could believe the same. . . .

After he dressed, he had a light breakfast and then went down at once into his conservatory. Here, amid the lush greenery, with the fragrant smells of flowers and growing things, the air heavy with moisture, he always became calmer. Here, touching lightly a hollyhock leaf, checking the newest buds opening on the nasturtiums, he could forget about himself and treasure the serenity that growing things induced in him. Here, for once, he was the benefactor, the gentle giant who coaxed these lovely things into health and full growth, and no one ever laughed. . . .

He managed to forget the time till his butler appeared in the doorway to announce his luncheon.

"I'll just have a tray in here," Sir John said absently.

"Yes, Sir John," his man responded without surprise. "I have checked on the drawing room, sir, and the chairs have been positioned as usual for your salon."

"Thank you." Sir John felt a flicker of nervousness that he tried to push away. It was hours yet before his guests would arrive; he was still considering which potted plants to bring out to use as examples for the discussion that would ensue after Miss Hill spoke. Later, the other amateur botanists would visit his conservatory, of course, but there was not enough room to allow them all to sit here and talk, so they would begin in the drawing room.

And he wanted to show Miss Hill the utmost courtesy; he would certainly not crowd her into the small space in the center of his glass-sided greenhouse, even if it was his favorite spot in the whole spacious house.

When a footman brought the luncheon tray, Sir John had his fingers deep in potting soil, and though he wiped one hand so he could sip his tea, he never got around to eating the sliced meat and fruit arranged pleasingly on the gold-bordered plate. And when the servant returned to remind him that it was time to change before his guests arrived, it seemed hardly an hour had passed. Yet, from the slanting rays of the sun, he could tell the afternoon had flown as it always did when he was absorbed in his favorite pastime.

Sir John carefully replaced one last pot of verbena and went upstairs to wash and change his clothes. He would not be seen in trousers spotted with dirt, or a shirt whose cuff might have become soiled as he worked, and besides, he was trying out a new tailor. When he and his long-suffering valet were satisfied with his appearance (the valet actually smiled) Sir John hurried back downstairs. He entered the drawing room and saw his great-uncle seated in one of the neatly aligned chairs meant to accommodate the dozen or so men who usually attended. With the rush of affection that he always felt for his favorite relative, Sir John smiled broadly.

"You came after all." Bending so that his uncle would not have to exert himself to stand, Sir John shook hands with Mr. Bircham.

"When I heard that Miss Hill would be attending, I thought perhaps her aunt . . ." The older man shrugged with boyish charm.

"Uncle, your persistence amazes me."

"Ah, well. I'm wearing her down, John. I can feel it!" Mr. Bircham chuckled, his eyes shining with humorous mischief. "Sophie Hill will have me yet!"

Sir John shook his head and grinned along with his uncle. He had a feeling that the elderly pair enjoyed their familiar game: Arthur chasing and Sophie eluding. Even if, Sir John thought as he looked at his uncle's frail legs, Arthur wasn't as fleet as he used to be.

Shaking his head to clear his thoughts and focus on the important meeting ahead, Sir John studied the drawing room. The big room itself was as neat as always, but it seemed bland to his eyes. The straw-colored upholstery and pale yellow wallpaper lacked the zest of Mrs. Forsyth's drawing room, though he had not really noticed the banality until he had visited her home. True, he spent little time in this room as, aside from his salons, he seldom entertained, but still, the room now seemed vaguely unsatisfying. Perhaps he could ask Mrs. Forsyth . . .

He was pulled from his reverie by the sound of the knocker pounding on the front door, and he turned to await more guests.

Two men entered, a stout fellow puffing a little from the climb up the flight of stairs and a thinner, spindly-shanked gentleman, both old acquaintances.

"Afternoon, Sir John, Mr. Bircham," the first man said when he got his breath. "Lovely day, eh? How are those nasturtiums coming along?"

"Splendidly, Lankley," Sir John answered. "I believe that new mixture of crushed shell and loam that we discussed last time has been just the tonic the plants needed."

"Excellent," the other man agreed, and they slipped easily into a stimulating discussion of the kinds of fertilizer best applied to sun-loving Tropaeolaceae.

More men arrived, and when he saw, from the corner of his eye as he stood chatting in the midst of a group of fellow botanists, the flutter of soft skirts and a brightly colored bonnet, Sir John stiffened and turned quickly. But it was not Miss Hill.

"Mrs. Forsyth," he said with real delight, hurrying over to take her hand. "Thank you for coming."

She smiled up at him. "It's my pleasure," she told him. "When you became worried that Circe might be uncomfortable in the company of so many males—not that any rational female would, mind you—I was happy to join the group." Her honey-colored eyes twinkled, and he relaxed enough to smile back. He did not think that Mrs. Forsyth would be uneasy anywhere, but Miss Hill was younger, and it had seemed a good idea to provide her with some feminine companionship.

And he was happy to see Mrs. Forsyth; her scarlet bonnet and matching pelisse seemed to brighten his whole drawing room. "You will be a flower amid the drab male shrubbery," he assured her. "Just what we need to enliven our staid bunch."

"Oh, very good." His guest smiled back. "You are making excellent progress, Sir John. Say something as graceful to Circe, and I'm sure you will attract her notice."

He was not at all as sure, but he nodded and escorted Mrs. Forsyth to a comfortable chair.

Sally looked around her; nearby, an aged man sat with his walking stick near at hand; he beamed at her as Sir John made introductions.

"Delighted to meet you." Sally allowed him to lift her hand to his lips with old-fashioned gallantry.

"You're the young lady who has advised my nephew to seek a new tailor and new hairdresser," Mr. Bircham declared as Sir John moved away to greet another arrival. "Been telling him that for years, but somehow, he has paid more attention to you. It shows, too."

Sally dimpled at being called "young lady," then glanced toward Sir John. It was true, his new jacket fitted his shoulders much more smoothly, and his fair hair looked more ordered, the cut more even. She had wanted to tell him that he looked exceptionally well today, but was afraid it would only make him self-conscious.

"Not sure it will do much good, in the long run," his uncle added, to Sally's surprise. "He's not much of a hand with the ladies."

"I'm sure you are mistaken," Sally argued, lowering her voice so that the other gentlemen would not overhear. "Sir John is all that is good and honorable and pleasing; he only needs a little outer polish to reflect his inner worth."

Mr. Bircham regarded her intently. "Indeed?" he murmured. He looked thoughtful, then his solemn expression relaxed into another grin.

But Sally turned her head; she detected the lighter sound of a feminine voice in the hallway. Sir John had heard it, too. She saw him excuse himself and hurry through the doorway. She sighed, then remembered to smile and listen attentively to the gentleman on her other side.

Sir John hastened to check on the arrival of their honored speaker. This time, it was indeed Miss Hill. She was saying farewell to Lord Westbury. "I had a wonderful afternoon, David," she told the elegant gentleman. "The paintings were so marvelous—thank you for taking me."

"I wanted to keep an eye on you" was the reply. "At least we had no unwanted excitement today."

"No, indeed, the artwork was excitement enough," Miss Hill answered. "Are you sure you don't wish to stay and attend the discussion here?"

Sir John had descended the stairs and he added his invitation to hers. "Delighted to have you join us, Westbury."

"A bit above my touch, I'm afraid," David replied. "I'm sure your flowers and plants and such stuff are most intriguing, but I have something to check on while Circe—Miss Hill—is safely occupied."

She gave Westbury a look that Sir John could not interpret, but for himself, he couldn't mind that such a good-looking chap chose to absent himself from the group. Already, Sir John could feel the tension building inside him as he drank in the lovely lines of Miss Hill's form, the delicate coloring of her lightly browned cheeks and clear green eyes. So unusual, those eyes; they made him think of the first buds of elm trees, unfurling in the spring. . . .

Westbury made his farewells and departed, and Sir John tried to pull himself together.

"We are—that is"—he cleared his throat and tried again—"I am so honored that you could come."

She held a small portfolio, and he reached to carry it for her, then offered her his arm. To his inner delight, she laid her hand lightly upon it and allowed him to escort her up the flight of steps to the drawing room. He felt a thrill run through him that had nothing to do with potted plants.

In the drawing room, he performed introductions, then led her to a seat beside Mrs. Forsyth. As the two women greeted each other, and Circe leaned across Sally to smile at Mr. Bircham, Sir John walked to the front of the room to address the whole group.

First he described briefly the arrangement of flowers and greenery at the ball for the benefit of those who had not attended, then added, "When I saw such a tasteful display, such a sensitivity to the hues and shapes of the plants, I knew that you would wish to hear more from such a talented lady." He bowed to their guest. "Miss Hill."

Everyone else turned to regard her.

Circe blinked; she was not accustomed to so many people staring at her with obvious interest. However, she reflected, it was better than facing all the matronly gossips at the ball, and after all, she had taken part in painting classes with groups of young men, and occasionally even been the model. This was not so very different.

"I fear that Sir John is too generous," she told them, smiling. "I did look to the shapes of the plants for a pleasing symmetry, balanced by that graceful dishevel that Nature often provides, but it was not an unusual choice, I assure you."

"Then you agree with Repton's view of the rustic style," one of the men suggested. "I have always said that his views upon the picturesque are the most enlightened of the day!"

"Ah, well," Circe tried to play for time. "I regret that I'm not really familiar with—"

"Indeed," another one of the group interrupted. "We will be most happy to instruct you. As an artist, yourself, you must know that light and shade play most important roles in—"

"Oh, yes," Circe agreed, but another member was also eager to educate her.

"My favorite," he said, waving his plump fingers in his enthusiasm. "is a rustic colonnade, upon which roses are trained to grow—"

"No, no, roses are so overdone. Honeysuckle and jasmine, that's the ticket," another man suggested.

The discussion grew heated, and flora were tossed, metaphorically, back and forth through the crowd until Circe felt almost dizzy. While she hesitated, the door to the hall opened again, and she saw a latecomer, two latecomers, enter the drawing room. She detected Sir John's frown.

One of the men was apparently known to Sir John; they spoke quietly together. Circe heard him say, "Brought along a guest, knew you wouldn't mind."

"Of course, glad to have you," Sir John was forced to say, nodding to the second man. Good heavens, it was Count von Freistadt, the last person she had expected to see this afternoon. Circe pulled her attention back to the discussion.

"A rural cottage," one man offered. "The only proper spot for Nature's beauty to grow, untouched by man's artifice. My cottage in Hampstead—"

"Humph," another member retorted. "Your cottage has ten rooms, James. I'm not sure that is the kind of 'cottage' your farm laborers are accustomed to."

"He started it for his pig man and grew so enamored of the garden's design that he enlarged and finished it for himself," the stout man sitting just past Sally whispered. Sally giggled behind her hand, and Circe tried not to laugh.

"Would you enjoy a cottage, do you think?" Sir John asked Circe quietly in his usual calm tone.

Circe gave this serious consideration. "Perhaps. I stayed in one during my time in Italy. It, too, had been built for a pig farmer. Unfortunately, when he left, some of his pigs decided to remain."

Sally tried to turn her strangled laugh into a cough, but to Circe's relief, Sir John nodded, taking her comment seriously. "I do not think that a pig would make a convenient housemate," he agreed, though his eyes twinkled.

He really was a nice man, she thought, but a new voice cut in and shattered their moment of rapport.

"And I cannot think that such a lovely lady should be discussing pigs," a deep voice announced. "Come, Miss Hill, there is a particularly nice specimen of lilacs at the side of the room that you will wish to inspect more closely." Count von Freistadt bowed to the ladies, then offered Circe his arm.

Circe found herself somehow on her feet and escorted away from the group. She saw Sir John's expression of chagrin and wished she had not followed the count's suggestion so quickly. How did the man always seem to addle her thoughts?

She stepped a little farther away from him and kept her tone cool. "I had not expected to see you here. Are you interested in lilacs, my lord?"

"Not particularly," he told her. "But I am most interested in one lady whose presence drew me like a butterfly to a fragrant rose. That is why you see me here with these, ah, dedicated horticulturists." The glance he sent toward the group behind them was openly scornful.

"I admire their passion," she retorted, irritated by the condescension he did not bother to hide.

"I have passion," von Freistadt told her, moving closer and reaching boldly for her hand. "It simply is devoted to a more worthy object."

She felt her heart pound and her knees go curiously weak. She retrieved her hand on the guise of reaching down to touch the lilac's delicate flower. "I found their interest most admirable."

The Austrian bent, as well, and his larger hand covered her own, his index finger stroking her palm. "Your skin is even softer than the petal."

She wished she had not removed her gloves; she felt trapped. "I don't think . . ."

"And your fragrance is even sweeter." The count's fingers curled around her smaller ones. She had to swallow hard.

"I believe Miss Hill wishes to present her drawings," a voice behind them interrupted. "The salon is most anxious to see her work."

Circe turned toward him with some relief. It was Sir John, and his expression seemed tight; Circe could detect the rigidness of his mouth.

"Miss Hill is more pleasingly occupied," the Austrian retorted, not releasing her hand. "The plant lovers can wait."

Sir John reddened, and he stuttered. "I th-think—that is, I do not think—Miss Hill is—isn't —"

His confusion made the count's smile broaden. Circe was so annoyed by the older man's cruelty that she pulled her hand from his grasp and stepped back. "Of course," she said. "I brought some studies of the Italian hills that I think will interest your friends in the salon."

She turned and accompanied Sir John back to the group, but the baronet was silent, and she felt his tenseness. Was he angry at her?

She took out the sketches and watercolors that she had chosen to bring, being lighter and smaller than her oils, and the other members responded with enthusiasm. Answering their questions, or as many as possible when some of the flowers' names eluded her, she had little opportunity to observe Sir John. But she thought that his expression was dark, and once she caught Sally watching their host with an expression of concern.

Von Freistadt stood a little apart from the group with a condescending smile that vexed Circe.

When Sir John's butler brought in the tea tray at last, Circe found a moment to speak quietly to Sally. "I don't know why he perturbs me so," she muttered under cover of the clatter of teacups.

"Sir John?" Sally sounded hopeful.

"No, no, he's a nice man. Von Freistadt," Circe explained, keeping a wary eye on the Austrian. He had made no more moves toward her, but she often felt his gaze upon her.

Sally rolled her eyes. "My dear girl," she said. "He enjoys your apprehension. Why do you think he devotes his attention to young girls just out?"

Circe felt indignant. Outrage stirred inside her, and suddenly the curious mixture of attraction and fear that the older man evoked in her vanished like a mist dissipated by a strong shaft of sunlight. "Are you serious?" she demanded, turning on Sally with such intensity that the other lady lifted her brows.

"Of course. I think he finds that response in his chosen *chère amie* quite, ah, stimulating." There was a wealth of experience in Sally's tone.

Circe drew a deep breath. "I am not his *chère amie,*" she snapped. "And I find it horrid that he enjoys intimidating younger women who have little practice with men."

"I agree," Sally said calmly. "I also think—" She paused at a particularly loud burst of conversation from a group of men nearby, then continued, "I fancy that this time he has chosen the wrong person to play his games upon."

Circe's indignation faded a little, and she smiled. Sally's faith warmed her and renewed her conviction. "Yes, I trust you are right," she said.

Sally's lighthearted laughter rang out, causing several of the men to glance at her with appreciation. "Will you give him the cut direct?" she inquired.

"Not yet," Circe answered, considering. "Though if he continues to press his attentions, I may consider it."

Sally looked curious, but Circe turned the conversation to an anecdote about her watercolors. She needed time to think.

When von Freistadt approached her again, Circe was able to meet his gaze without blushing. Smiling confidently, he suggested, "Shall I take you away from this tedious group of plant devotees, Miss Hill? We could take

a turn through the park in my phaeton and have a modi-
cum of privacy." He leaned forward as he spoke, and
although she still felt the force of his strong personality,
Circe was able to keep her tone level.

"No, thank you, I am looking forward to the tour of
Sir John's conservatory."

To her disappointment, the diplomat did not seem
crushed at her putdown. His dark brows lifted in an even
more sardonic expression than usual, and his smile faded
into a skeptical grin. "Your good manners do you credit,"
he noted. "Play the attentive guest if you must. For me, I
think I will make my excuses."

"It's not merely good manners," Circe retorted. "I think
their remarks are most interesting."

"If you say so," the count said, his disbelief and amusement obvious. "But do not worry, my sweet, we shall
meet again very soon."

Before Circe could respond that she had no concerns
at all about their next meeting, he had turned to say a few
words of farewell to his host, and then he swept out the
door as imperiously as he had entered. All that was
needed was a line of bowing peasants, thought Circe.
Really!

To make up for the count's arrogance, she applied herself to the conversation and then to the plants that Sir John
had brought out to show them. When the baronet led them
into his conservatory, she joined Sally in oohs and ahs
over the lush greenery and the pleasing arrangement of
plants. While the men tossed Latin plant names about,
inspected plant leaves for signs of blight, and speculated
over drainage and fertilizer, Circe gazed about her, seeing
how the lovely, artfully arranged potted plants would appear to best advantage in a painting or sketch. She became
so absorbed that she forgot to make polite conversation
with Sir John, and when she said her good-byes, she
thought he seemed somewhat subdued.

"Thank you for joining us," he said, his tone polite.

"Your paintings are a delight to the eye, pleasing in both form and color."

"As is your conservatory," she told him. "You have a creative genius of your own, Sir John."

He smiled briefly, but the wistfulness in his eyes belied his quiet manner, and as she walked out with Sally, Circe noticed that her friend frowned.

"He is a most pleasant young man," Sally suggested as they were handed into Sally's carriage, and Circe's portfolio placed carefully at her feet.

"Yes, indeed," Circe agreed. "Most pleasing."

"And one can learn to be more skilled at flirtation, you know," Sally pointed out.

Oh, dear, had she been woefully inadequate as a guest? Circe sighed. How did the other young ladies master such a tricky art? Perhaps she needed someone to practice upon.

"I will do better next time," she promised.

Sally looked at her strangely, but Circe had no time to wonder why. Her thoughts were taken up with more urgent matters: the annoying yet still somewhat disturbing presence of von Freistadt, David's mysterious masquerades, Luciana's possible duplicity, the man who had attacked her in the street, the thrill she had felt every time David leaned closer to her to comment on a painting at the exhibition earlier in the day. . . .

Surely David was escorting her only out of a sense of duty, after yesterday's attacks. But still, their time together today had been very enjoyable. Even surrounded by wonderful landscapes and portraits and still lifes, she had been aware of David's presence, of the tingle that ran through her when she touched his arm or when he stood close amid the crush of exhibition visitors. But she dared not presume that his attentions were more than that of any family friend . . . unless she could find some way to change his perception of her?

Deep in thought, Circe gazed out the small window as the carriage bounced over a loose stone in the road. Instead of chattering away as usual, Sally also sat silently by her side.

When they reached the Sinclair town house, Circe stepped out of the carriage. "Would you like to come in?" she asked Sally.

The other woman shook her head. "I think not today. Give my regards to Psyche."

"Of course," Circe said. "Thank you for accompanying me to the salon."

Sally had a curious expression on her face. Circe could not determine exactly what it signified. "For all the good it did," her friend murmured.

The footman closed the carriage door before Circe could question the remark. Frowning, she entered the house.

She had some time before dinner, and although the best light had long fled, she could make a few sketches. The conservatory had suggested ideas to her, and she wished to get them down before the images faded from her mind. She climbed the steps to the schoolroom and set to work.

When a maid came to summon her for dinner, Circe stopped in her room long enough to quickly change her dress and push an errant brown lock back into place. Luciana was very quiet and tended not to meet her eye.

When Circe joined her sister and her husband and Aunt Sophie, leaning on her walking stick, as they went into the dining room, Psyche smiled in relief. "No adventures today, I see," she said.

Circe grinned. "No. David escorted me to the exhibition, and I saw some wonderful studies in landscape by de Valenciennes and Hodges. Then David drove me to Sir John's horticulture salon, and I showed the members some watercolors and sketches of Italian hillsides."

Psyche took her seat at the long table. "How nice. Sir John seemed like a very pleasant young man. Was it all males at the salon, my dear?"

Aunt Sophie sat straighter in her chair, her sharp gaze on Circe. "*Most* improper," she said severely.

"Sir John is very polite," Circe agreed and then turned her head to address Aunt Sophie. "It was mostly men, yes, but Sally came to lend me company."

Aunt Sophie sniffed. "I suppose that is meant to be reassuring."

Gabriel laughed aloud and to her credit, Psyche kept her expression even, though she lifted her brows.

"Sally must have been in her element, then," Gabriel suggested, taking a serving of beef from the footman who leaned forward with a silver dish. "Surrounded by men."

Circe accepted a slice of roasted chicken. "She was rather quiet, I thought. Perhaps she was bored by the discussion of plants and their arrangement."

"Bored by horticulture, perhaps, surely not by all the gentlemen." Gabriel's deep blue eyes twinkled. "Or were they all too elderly, or too boyish, to tempt her?" The look he sent his wife was both teasing and provocative.

"I doubt that Sally would find any man totally unpleasing." Aunt Sophie motioned to the footman for more sauce on her chicken.

"Really, Gabriel, Aunt," Psyche scolded them both. "Sally possesses a fine character. You make her sound like—like—"

"Like a delightful lady with a zest for male companionship," her husband finished, his tone soothing. "Try some of these stewed peaches, my love, they are most tasty."

Psyche eyed the fruit dish with obvious misgivings. "Just a spoonful, if you would."

The conversation became more general, and Circe gave some thought to Sally. Was their old friend finding her chaperonage more irksome, or more tedious, than she had imagined? Circe did not wish to be a nuisance.

And really, she herself would be happy to turn down almost all the social invitations that presently crowded her mantel, except that Psyche would scold. Circe had two more balls, three dinners, and the obligatory visit to Almack's lined up for the next week, and the thought made her sigh.

Tonight she and her sister had promised to attend a musical evening—Aunt Sophie had declared she was too tired, and Gabriel had made some excuse—if Psyche's constitution allowed. But David had hinted he might be there.

Circe took another bite of tender pork and allowed her mind to retreat to the pleasure of the exhibition they had visited, and the joy of David's company.

Eleven

When Sally left Circe at the Sinclair town house, she watched her young friend climb the steps. When the door closed behind the slender figure, she sat there, unmoving.

She heard the coachman call down to her. "Home, madam?"

She should have agreed, of course, she should. Instead, Sally felt the urge that had been pulling at her ever since they had left Sir John's residence, Sir John himself looking so desolate and defeated, suddenly rise up and overwhelm all common sense.

"No," she said, to her own surprise. Then she cleared her throat and said more loudly, "Back to Sir John's, if you please. I, ah, left my handkerchief at the salon."

Not that she needed to explain her actions to her servants, but she had no business returning, unaccompanied, to that lonely young man's comfortable manse.

But the look in his eyes when they had taken their leave, it haunted her, that intensity of emotion. And the count had been his usual insolent self, putting Sir John in a bad light. It was not that the baronet was truly indecisive, Sally argued fiercely inside her head. His feelings for Circe, understandable feelings for so lovely and unique a young lady, left him handicapped, and his habitual shyness rendered him mute when he should have spoken, still when he should have taken action. There was strength inside him, she was sure of it, more resolve than the rest of the world had a chance to see. And she was going to help him see it, realize it, believe in it, and then, once Sir John understood how much of his true nature he was stifling, it would be easy enough for everyone else to see it, too.

Fired with new resolve, Sally was prepared when her carriage pulled up once more in front of the big house. When she rapped on the door and it opened, she stared down the butler, who gazed at her in surprise.

"Is Sir John still here?" she asked, keeping her tone polite and disinterested. "We have some business from the salon still unsettled."

The butler gazed at her as if she were one of the vases in the hallway suddenly come to life and spouting speech instead of greenery. "Ah, yes, that is, I believe—I will inquire, ma'am."

He showed her to the drawing room, still filled with chairs from the salon, vacant chairs now, and indeed the room held a sense of emptiness and disarray that she had noticed through most of the house, except for the conservatory, which was where Sir John's heart lay. As for the rest—well, a house needed a mistress, and despite reasonably good staff, the slight air of neglect was obvious. This room needed a complete turnout, some new cushions for the settee, and a few artful touches of color to brighten its blandness. She wondered that Sir John did not see it. But he was a man, bless him, and not many had an eye for decor. As good as he was with plants, if you took away the greenery, he seemed as oblivious as the next gentleman.

She heard a footstep outside, and the door opened. Sir John gazed at her in surprise.

For a moment, she wondered if she had been foolish to return. He came forward quickly, his smile polite, and she was about to make some excuse and go. Then she looked into his hazel eyes, which were desolate with loneliness and something worse, a hint of the self-reproach that must gnaw at him, and she knew she had made the right decision.

"I told your butler that we had unfinished business. I told my coachman that I left a handkerchief behind," she began.

He looked around at the empty chairs. "Ah, I regret that I have not seen it, Mrs. Forsyth, but I will inquire of the servants—"

She put out her hand, then caught herself and pulled it back before he noticed. "No, Sir John. That was only a pretext."

"Oh?" He looked at her in genuine surprise. His innocence always moved her, and she blinked, not sure if she should go on. "I was afraid that you felt badly," she said slowly, "that—that you might think—"

"That I had made a complete ass of myself, as usual?" he suggested, his tone wry, the humor deflecting the self-pity that she knew he would despise. "I fear that was quite obvious to everyone at the salon."

She shook her head, but he plunged forward and did not wait for her to answer.

"I am afraid that I am not cut out for wooing, Mrs. Forsyth, as kind as your attempts to tutor me in the finer points of courtship have been."

"No, no," she said, and this time her hand moved, unbidden, to tenderly touch his cheek and linger there. "It is I who have failed. It was too soon. You simply need more practice!"

He stood very still, and she could feel his breath tickle her wrist; his skin was warm and supple. And the expression of his face was arrested—oh, dear, what was she doing?

She was about to withdraw her hand, when, to her surprise, he took it and turned it, lifting it to his lips to very gently kiss the palm.

She shivered with the delicious sensation, then tried to compose herself.

"I only m-meant . . ." she stammered.

This time it was Sir John who seemed to take on the role of comforter. "You meant only to reassure me, out of the great goodness of your heart and from the depths of your generous spirit," he said.

She was aware of how close together they stood, and was he breathing quickly, too?

"I should go," she said, her voice sounding strange to her ears. "But tomorrow, we will try again, yes?"

"I will try, if you wish it," he told her. "If you are willing to waste your time on me—"

"It is never a waste!" she cried, forgetting her embarrassment.

Sir John kissed her hand again before relinquishing it. "If you say so, dearest lady."

She made her curtsy, then turned away before she could discredit herself entirely and allow him to see how much he affected her. But she felt his gaze on her back as she walked, in as dignified a pace as she could manage, to the front door. What on earth must he think of her?

And he had never called her "dearest lady" before.

～

*Psyche seemed to have temporarily conquered her mal-*aise. After dinner, she and Circe set off in one of the family's carriages. During the brief ride, Psyche chatted, and Circe tried to hide her own abstraction. But when she stepped out of the carriage, she found her heart beating faster. David would be here tonight. Perhaps they would steal a few minutes alone. . . .

When Circe and her sister sat among the other guests, she found that she cared little how well or ill their hostess and her daughters sang or played; she was more interested in keeping a covert watch for a wide pair of shoulders and a sleek dark head. Where was David?

Circe looked around Lady Bryson's large salon, which was filled almost to capacity with debutantes and their mothers. As a most eligible earl, David would be much in demand, but she intended to be sure she managed some time with him. He needed someone to bring him down to earth, when the other more decorous young ladies simpered and giggled and gazed soulfully at his least change of expression.

Circe chuckled at the thought, and Psyche, who was seated next to her on another of the delicate cane chairs, elbowed her discreetly.

"The musical hasn't even begun, Circe," Psyche whispered with a mock frown. "If you must make sport, at least wait until it can be drowned out by the missed notes."

Circe leaned close to her sister and whispered into her ear. "You do not seem to have much confidence in the musical talents of Lady Bryson's daughters."

"Those two can't even laugh in tune. I have very little hope that they can do better accompanying a pianoforte."

Circe laughed aloud this time, and several heads turned to look at her in surprise. She composed her expression and leaned toward Psyche.

"I have rarely heard you say anything so cutting about another woman, Psyche. Are the Misses Bryson so very terrible?"

Psyche sighed and smoothed the skirt of her sky blue gown. "No, indeed they are not. I just can't seem to control my feelings lately. Every little thought—pleasing or not—flies out of my mouth with no discretion at all. One moment I'm happy as can be, and the next I'm ready to either weep my eyes out or scratch out someone else's."

Circe was careful not to smile. "All this time I thought I had an artistic temperament. Now I realize I've been pregnant from birth."

Psyche's slightly frantic giggle echoed through the room like the pop of a champagne cork. Hastily, she covered her mouth with the back of her hand. "Stop it, Circe!

Don't be so outrageous. You know better than to speak of such things in public."

Circe looked around at the other ladies and shrugged. "No one heard me, and why should being with child be so taboo a subject? It's the most natural thing in the world, is it not?"

Psyche actually blushed. "Of course it is, but young ladies are not supposed to talk so freely about such intimate matters, or know about them, either. Maidens might begin to wonder about other details of the process as well."

Circe studied Psyche's lovely face closely. "Are you teasing me?"

Psyche's eyes widened in surprise. "Why, no. Why would you think I am?"

"Psyche, I've known how a baby is conceived for . . . forever."

The flattering blush faded from Psyche's cheeks. Turning in her chair, she looked directly into her sister's eyes. "Circe, who has been telling you such personal things?"

"Ah . . ." Circe shifted a bit in her seat as she avoided Psyche's piercing blue gaze. "I might have persuaded Telly to answer a few harmless questions, and I have read quite a lot." And there had been the gypsy couple she had surprised beneath an oak tree once when she had been walking back to the village carrying her paints and canvas, but she certainly would not mention that. Fortunately, the couple had been too involved in their . . . pursuits to even notice her, and Circe, red-faced, had tiptoed away at once. But it had left her with quite a clear picture of what a man and a woman did when they made love. And pictures were, for Circe, the clearest explanation of all.

Psyche turned back to face the front of the room. "I should never have permitted you to reside on the Continent alone. Gabriel was certain you would be all right. But what does a man know?"

"I had Telly," Circe reassured her sister.

"Who obviously wasn't enough!" Psyche faced her

again, and this time her expression was determined. "Listen to me, Circe. I don't know what sort of books you've read or what an unmarried old woman, dear as Telly may be, has told you about"—Psyche ducked close to Circe and whispered in her ear—"the marriage bed, but I feel sure that you haven't heard the right information."

"The book explained it quite well, really. There were even a few engravings, but they were difficult to make out. It was a very old book, you see," Circe said calmly.

Psyche cut her off with a look that Circe remembered all too well from her youth. It was Psyche's I'm-the-big-sister-and-if-you-don't-listen-I-will-sit-on-you-until-you-do look.

Circe listened.

"We will discuss this later, Circe."

Circe believed her. Few who looked at her delicate, golden sister would suppose she had that thread of steel within her, but those who knew her well never doubted it. The noise and movement of the other guests crowding into the room provided a welcome distraction, for which even Psyche appeared glad.

Circe looked around her at all the other ladies and admired the charming picture they made. Gowns of every hue were pressed together in the close-packed room. Circe would have liked to sketch the scene. She remembered her ballroom sketches . . . she had had entirely too many interruptions, and her artwork was suffering for it. If Psyche thought Circe could marry and maintain her painting—no, it would not work. Circe shook her head.

Psyche leaned close so that no one could overhear. "Would that the Misses Bryson's musical gifts were as developed as their mother's cunning." Her tone was calm again; perhaps she was trying to make her peace with her sister.

Circe raised her brows.

"Practically no one attended the last two musicals that Lady Bryson hosted for her daughters. And those who were here were so embarrassed for her . . . well, she's made certain this won't happen again by inviting professional musicians to perform after her daughters. Spanish, I have heard, though I am not certain."

Genuinely delighted, Circe smiled. "How wonderful!"

Just then, Sally hurried to join them. "Psyche, how lovely to see you out. You look quite—"

"Don't you dare say blooming," Psyche snapped, then softened her words with a quick smile. "I've heard that word until I am quite nauseated by it."

Sally giggled. "Then I will not add to your woes, but you do look charming," she said, adding, "Circe, my dear, you look delightful, too, with that silver trim. How are you?"

"Very well, thank you," Circe said. The two older women fell into a discussion of Sally's newest ball gown and Psyche's dressmaker's attempts to hide the increasing bulk of her client's belly, and Circe was free to look about her.

David had entered the room, his gait dignified, his expression studiously proper, and on his arm, oh, good Lord, it was the countess.

Circe had heard much of David's mother, though this was the first time she had actually seen her. Circe had been too young to go into society, of course, before she left for her studies abroad. She studied the older woman with interest, wondering if even half of what she had heard was true.

The countess was a slim woman who dressed with slightly too ostentatious detail; her purple gown would have been more pleasing without the gold trim at the hem and the overly large medallions that adorned the bodice. Her turban was large and embellished by three ostrich plumes, which moved every time she nodded or turned her head, making Circe think of some very tall bird. She stifled a laugh just as David glanced about the room, catching her eye.

He gave her a brief but expressive grimace, a sort of "just you wait" signal that seemed, oddly, very personal, as if only she would understand his feelings, and only she was allowed to be privy to them.

The encouraging smile she had flashed him faltered, and she looked down, feeling color stain her cheeks. She was reading too much into a simple gesture. The whole room must know of David's constant troubles with his too controlling, too solicitous mother. No, that wasn't fair. David only spoke of his mother to close friends; she had never heard him mention the countess in a larger group; he was too well mannered to do such a thing.

But it did not mean she and David had a special understanding—she must not allow herself to think in that direction. The dangers they had shared together, the awkward accident in the alley—they were friends, yes, but she could not swear to any clear indication of a closer regard. She knew that she was too different, too odd, to attract any gentleman's serious admiration, and David had certainly turned himself into the most proper of gentlemen.

The tinkling sound of a pianoforte signaled the beginning of the musical program, and Circe pulled her gaze back to the front of the room. A thin young lady rose to take her place beside the instrument, and another even more gawky girl, obviously her sister—they shared the same pattern for their long thin noses—joined her. The pianist moved her hands across the keys, and the smooth flow of notes made Circe nod in appreciation, at least until the two young ladies added their voices to the melody.

Circe winced. Oh, dear. Psyche was quite right. This evening would be an exercise in endurance. In front of her, a matron coughed and pulled out a scented handkerchief to cover her face.

Circe steeled her expression to one of polite approval, then glanced covertly about the room. What on earth must David think of this performance? She saw his expression—the slightly horrified one of a man expecting champagne and tasting bathwater instead—and then his recovery. Trying not to giggle, she observed him from the corner of her eye. He and his mother had sat down at the edge of the audience.

Circe saw the countess cough, too. David bent close to whisper something into her ear, then when his mother nodded, he rose and slipped out of the room.

Whatever excuse he had made, she would bet her best sable brush that David would not reappear until the last note had been played. No wonder Gabriel had bowed out of this engagement. Several interminable songs later, Circe found that she had been correct in her surmise. Not until the sisters gave their last bow, and the audience applauded heartily—in relief?—did David return to join his mother, bearing a glass of wine.

That rogue! Circe wanted to laugh, but she turned it into a cough. Too bad she hadn't thought of that ruse herself.

Psyche stood and rubbed her back. "Are you all right?" Circe turned to her sister, anxious for her comfort.

"Just a little cramped. I think I shall take a turn about the room," Psyche said.

"Certainly," Circe agreed. Sally had been waylaid by a matron in a garishly trimmed rose gown, but Circe and her sister circled along the side of the salon, and Circe directed their progress so that they headed toward David and his mother.

The countess sipped her wine, and David had been thronged by several women, both young and old, who seemed entranced by his charm. A ripple of laughter ran through the group as Circe and her sister approached, but David stopped his latest story in midstream and bowed to them.

"Lady Gabriel and Miss Hill, how good to see you," David said. "You know my mother, Countess of Westbury. She has recently returned from Bath."

The older woman gave them a condescending nod, but Psyche, obviously in no mood for top-lofty matrons, dipped only a brief curtsy. "So pleased to see you again,

Countess," Psyche said. "You have tired of the delights of Bath?"

David's mother answered, and while she and Psyche chatted, Circe tried to hide her grin until she had the opportunity to speak quietly, for David's ear alone.

"I saw you slip out," she said. "Shame on you—those poor girls must feel terribly slighted."

"I had an excellent excuse," he said, his tone dignified. "My mother was in urgent need of refreshment to ease her dry throat."

"So urgent that it took you a half hour to return? The household must guard their wine with vigor," Circe suggested.

He caught the smile she tried hard to hide and returned it. "They should. We'll all be driven to drink if we have to hear more from those two."

"Shhh." Circe glanced guiltily at the two young ladies chatting merrily on the other side of the room. "I only wish I had thought of such a good pretext," Circe admitted, remembering to keep her voice low. "That display of, ah, talent was a trial for any person of average hearing. It was good of you to come tonight."

"For you—" he began, then paused.

Psyche had turned away to greet a friend, and now the countess regarded both Circe and her son with a steely eye. "My dear, I have long waited to meet you," she told Circe.

Circe tried to conceal her surprise. She couldn't imagine that the countess, until recently, had any conception that she existed. "Really? You're too kind."

"Of course, any young lady that would induce my son to at last turn his attention to purer thoughts . . ."

Circe gazed at the woman, awestruck, then glanced toward David. He was actually turning red; she couldn't believe it. Served him right! She had warned him not to say too much to his mother.

"I'm sure David has always had pure thoughts," she couldn't resist commenting.

David made a strangled sound, but his mother surged on. "No, I regret to say that his earlier conduct was not the most admirable—I will not lie to you, dear girl, considering how close you are about to become to my son and me."

Oh, dear, Circe thought faintly. He *had* said too much.

". . . But I'm sure that you will be the one to change all of that."

"Mother—" David tried to interrupt, but the countess charged ahead with all the tact of the African rhinoceros Circe had once seen displayed at a French circus.

"What I mean is, the love of a good woman, you know, is the surest cure for the most wayward of men, or most of them, at any rate. It didn't do much for his late father, but I believe that David is not beyond help."

The expression on David's face was enough to make even the countess take note. "David, dear boy, do you have a spasm of indigestion?"

"A habitual problem," David muttered. "Ah, I see one of your friends, Mother, allow me to escort you to her side." He took his mother's arm in a firm grip and steered her toward the other side of the room.

"We shall talk again later," the countess called to Circe. "I have much good advice for your ear, dear girl, and long experience with the proper conduct—"

What? Circe saw David wince as he hastened his steps and almost pulled his mother along beside him.

Circe chatted for a few moments with two young ladies she recognized from her own coming-out ball until a deep familiar voice met her ears.

"My dear Miss Hill."

"Count von Freistadt." Circe gazed at the Austrian and did not bother to smile. "I didn't observe you earlier."

"No, indeed, I have only just arrived. So sad that I missed the first session. But then, as with Sir John's tedious salon, it was other allurements that drew me here." His tone was smooth, as always. "Perhaps we could take a turn about the room?" He reached for her hand and placed it on his arm.

She tried to draw back, but his grip tightened. "My lord, you forget yourself!" she snapped.

He mocked her with his deep dark eyes, although his full lips lifted only slightly. One part of her mind noted that she would have to remember his expression for some future picture, while the rest of her seethed with anger.

"On the contrary, I remember very well how much I admire that angry sparkle in your eyes," he said, as coolly as if they chatted only about the music.

"You enjoy making women angry?" Circe tried to match his savoir faire, tried to keep her voice icy and controlled.

"I enjoy making women—or one special woman—experience passion."

"It is not passion that I am feeling!" Circe retorted. Despite her efforts, she could not remain as cool as he; the man was too annoying. She was still aware of his vaunting masculinity, but this time she felt barely stirred by its lure.

"Anger, passion, they are a hair breadth apart, did you not know?" His voice was low and husky.

"And fear?" Circe asked. "Is that a heartbeat away from passion, too?"

"Of course." His wide lips twisted into a grin. "But you are not afraid of me, little flower?" He tightened his grip on her hand, and she could feel the strength of his fingers. Circe met his gaze squarely, without blinking. "Never."

He threw back his head and laughed, but somehow the harsh sound did not lend itself to shared mirth. Did he truly enjoy her unease? What kind of man was he, beneath his suave exterior? "Then perhaps I must try harder," he said, his tone teasing but his eyes curiously hard.

Circe drew a deep breath. Glancing about the room, she was happy to see Sally coming her way. "Excuse me, I must speak to Mrs. Forsyth."

"Perhaps your old friend can wait a moment," the count answered. Was there a subtle emphasis on the word *old*? Circe frowned.

"Circe, dear." Sally had arrived at her side. "I believe you promised to introduce me to the Misses Bryson. I know I must say something polite about their unique performance before I take my leave."

Sally beamed with her usual good-humored smile, as if she suspected nothing at all amiss. But her brown eyes glinted with shrewdness, and she showed no inclination to leave them alone. Circe breathed a quiet sigh of relief.

"Mrs. Forsyth, Miss Hill, allow me to escort you into the dining room to congratulate our hostesses on their performance." It was Sir John, and Circe had never heard him speak so firmly. She gazed at him in surprise, and von Freistadt scowled. Sir John met his gaze squarely; the tension between the two men seemed to vibrate in the air.

Beneath her hand, Circe felt the Austrian stiffen, but this time, the count did not try to prevent her from stepping away. His glance at the other man was coldly angry. "I see that my presence is unnecessary," he said, giving them all a slight bow.

No one contradicted him, and his dark eyes were hard as he raised his head. "Another time, perhaps." He walked away, the line of his back very stiff.

Sally's face looked a little flushed. "Sir John, that was so gallant of you," she said. "But I hope you have not made an enemy. Austrians are noted for their devotion to dueling, you know."

"Do not distress yourself, Mrs. Forsyth," Sir John answered, his tone calm. "Dueling is illegal in England. Besides, I hardly think the man will remark on such a slight encounter."

Circe hoped he was right. She tried not to waste any more reflection on the count. The three of them strolled into the dining room together, and Sally delivered polite comments on the two sisters' musical performance.

"You're too kind," the eldest Miss Bryson said, looking complacent.

Circe thought so, too, but she smiled and nodded lest she hurt the girl's feelings.

Fortunately, her train of thought was diverted when the younger sister added, "We have more surprises to come. The Spanish musicians we hired are visiting from the Continent, and they are said to be most unusual."

"How lovely," Circe exclaimed. "I became fond of Spanish music while I was studying abroad."

They spoke briefly, then retraced their steps to check on Psyche. Circe found her sister seated at a table, enjoying a light repast and chatting with a friend. Sally and Sir John joined them, but Circe felt too restless to sit, and she was not hungry.

It was very warm in the big room; she glanced longingly toward the tall windows. And indeed, she saw numerous guests strolling at the edge of the garden.

"I think I will get some air," she told her sister.

Psyche reached into her reticule and pulled out a delicate fan. "If you are overwarm, take this," she offered. "And don't stay too long."

Circe nodded. Unfurling the fan, a delicate thing of gold and white, she headed toward an open door that led into the garden. On the way, she caught sight of a familiar silhouette; David stood just outside the door. Was he overheated, too, or simply escaping his mother's company?

He looked up as she came out the door. "You, too?"

Circe smiled back at him. "It's much too warm inside. Come farther out," she suggested. "I want to see the garden."

He hesitated, and Circe raised her brows. "Grandfather," she teased.

He frowned at her, but he stepped away from the door.

Impulsively, Circe grasped David by the hand and pulled him down the wide marble steps, past other strolling couples, and into the garden. The shadowy paths were dimly lit by torches as well as the blue-tinged light of the full moon.

Sir John would approve. It was no formal garden of straight paths but rather a delightfully wild garden where flowering shrubs, full-leaved trees, and vines heavy with blossom were left to grow and entwine. She could smell the heady scent of wild roses and feel a slight gust of air touch her cheek. The shadows wavered around them as shrubbery whispered in the breeze. It was as if they had stepped into a fantasy world; Circe was enthralled by the intricate patterns of light and darkness. And with David beside her—the night seemed enchanted.

"Wait, Circe," David said. "We should not go so far from the house."

"Only a little more," Circe said. "It's so lovely amid the shadows."

Still holding his hand, she led him down a curving path until they were hidden from the other party guests milling about on the terrace. But she could still hear the occasional snatch of whispered conversation, or a clandestine giggle and answering chuckle carried on the breeze. And most importantly, she could still hear the musicians clearly. They had begun their program; she heard the full chord of a guitar, and the deeper answer of a viola. The tune was not at all like classical English music, but rich and heavy with its Spanish rhythm—the sounds took her back to her years abroad.

Circe stopped and turned, laughing up into David's face. He wore the slightly disapproving frown she was heartily tired of seeing. She found that her breathing seemed too rapid, as if the pulsating beat of the music had slipped inside her. She was here, alone with David in a beautiful garden, and the music evoked thoughts of . . . of many things her sister would have considered improper . . . of caressing David's cheek and slipping her hand inside his tight-fitting jacket to touch the hard muscles beneath.

As if feeling her gaze, David crossed his arms across

his chest and regarded her seriously. "If Gabriel knew we were out here alone, he'd have my head on a pike."

"Why? He trusts you. Besides, I've never known you to be afraid of Gabriel."

David shrugged coolly. "Call it a highly developed appreciation for my good health."

Was he so unaffected by her presence, as they stood alone together in the sweet-scented darkness? How could he be talking about Gabriel?

David continued. "I thought you were too warm."

Circe nodded. "Yes, it was much too close inside."

"I thought you wanted to stroll the terrace and the garden's edge," he continued drily, "not play jungle explorer."

Circe laughed. "We're hardly out of view, David. My, you've gotten old and staid."

"Staid?" David repeated, then added in disgust, "Old?"

Circe flashed a quick smile. "Yes, terribly old and fussy. In fact, you've lately reminded me of my fusty cousin Percy or even one of my elderly aunts."

"That cold fish?"

Circe bristled. "You'd best be speaking of Percy."

"I am, of course. How could you compare me to that horse's ass?"

"You've been most disapproving, and so like Percy that I can hardly see the difference."

"Oh, can't you?" David asked darkly. "Coming it much too strong, Circe."

Circe pretended to consider. "I suppose you do dress more elegantly."

"Thank you for that high praise." His eyes narrowed.

"And your shoulders are broader." She ran her hand lightly over his right shoulder, enjoying the smooth texture of his well-cut evening jacket, and the firm muscled body beneath it. "And your chest is—"

He caught her hand, holding it still beneath his strong fingers. "Circe, what are you up to?"

The music played behind them; how could he ignore its beat?

"I know that Percy would never come out into a dim garden with a woman. In fact, Percy hardly considers me respectable."

David stiffened. "Why would he think such an absurd thing?"

Circe laughed. "You know perfectly well why, David. I've been places no woman should go and seen things no woman should see. And I know things no woman should ever know—according to Percy, of course."

"Of course," David said, his voice dropping.

"For instance," Circe added, "this music."

David paused to listen. "Spanish, I believe. A welcome diversion from the usual party fare."

Circe was impressed. "That's correct. And the dance which is performed to this music—"

David's brows lifted in surprise. "The fandango?"

Circe smiled. "You've seen it?"

"I've heard of it, a gypsy dance. How would you know of . . . hell, Circe! Were you never properly chaperoned? Did your abigail do nothing while you were observing gypsies?"

Circe laughed beneath her breath. "Telly is a very heavy sleeper. Besides, how could I have resisted? The gypsy women were so beautiful with their bright, ruffled skirts and their long golden limbs." Circe raised her own slim arms in example. "So exotic and so, so"—Circe shut her eyes and allowed the music to flow through her whole body—"so sensual." Her hips swayed to the beat of the music.

When she glanced at him, something dark had sparked to life in David's eyes at her provocative comments. Or perhaps it was the way Circe moved to the haunting rhythm set by the guitar's strings, her arms sweeping out and above her head, then down to her waist, curving gently to the fluid melody.

David opened his mouth to speak but stopped as Circe raised her palm.

"Shhh, don't speak. Only listen to the rhythm." She flicked open the fan her sister had given her and held it to her face, glancing over it toward him, allowing only her eyes to laugh up at his, and then her whole body arched, as graceful as a swan.

David tried to keep his expression stern. This was highly improper, this was—then the first sharp click of her low heels against the brick path startled him. He'd heard of this shocking dance but had never thought to see it firsthand. Certainly not in London or performed by a debutante!

Circe's slim hips undulated as her heels struck the pavement. Faster and faster went the clicking of her heels and the stamping of her feet. How could she produce such an enticing staccato sound?

As though she heard his thoughts, she scooped up one side of her skirt, clutching the soft pale silk so that her movements would not be impeded, and though it did not seem possible, her feet moved even more quickly. But now he could see her feet flashing in rapid motion as well as—scandalously—her ankles, calves, and even her knees. Never had he seen this much of a woman without also sharing her bed.

He was growing entirely too fond of seeing Circe's curvy legs and delicate ankles. He knew damn well he should look away from the tantalizing sight, but he could not. Instead, he watched the flex of her muscles, the delicious sway of her hips. Her other arm was held high above her head, her back arched gracefully, thrusting her breasts forward, and her head was thrown back in sheer delight at the dance. Nothing could compare. Certainly not the restrained country dances of England with their stately processions and stiff, precise movements—more like military maneuvers than Circe's artless, free-flowing swirling.

And she was magnificent. He had never seen anything

more beautiful than Circe at this moment. She seemed part
of the garden, part of the moonlit darkness, a silver-white
nymph come to lure him too far into madness, away from
the safety of civilized behavior. Her joy was infectious,
exuberant. It was more even than that. It was a celebra-
tion, pagan and wild. His heart seemed to beat in time to
the music, and his breathing was too fast.

He tried to step away, but he seemed immobile. The
music and the darkness and Circe—most of all, Circe—
had cast a spell over him. He meant to ease away, but
instead, he found that he moved closer.

Now she widened eyes that had been half-shut, a smile
playing mysteriously across her lips. Circe had no right
to look at him that way, so seductive, so knowing. Moving
tantalizingly closer, her swaying hips brushed against him,
and he could not have stopped his body's reaction if the
archbishop of Canterbury himself had stood beside them.

Hellfire, he wanted her, wanted her here and now,
wanted to throw her down in the shadowy grass, delve
beneath her hiked-up skirts, and stroke the satiny smooth
skin he knew was above her garters. He wanted to share
in her abandon, join their two bodies with a ferocity that
he'd never dared to imagine . . . but then he'd never before known a woman like Circe.

Suddenly, through accident or design, she tossed one
slim white shoe into the air. Without thinking, he reached
out and caught it.

Circe laughed. "Well done!"

"Imp," David exclaimed, and he found that his voice
sounded hoarse. "Would you go barefoot back into the
party? Here."

And without thinking, he bent to replace the errant slipper onto her silk-stockinged foot. He encircled her ankle
with trembling fingers and stroked a path up the strong
curve of her calf. Her flesh seemed to burn his skin, even
through the gossamer covering. His gaze followed the
long elegant line of her leg, past her slim hips and small
breasts to her face. Circe's eyes met his evenly, without

shame or evasion. Passion surged inside him, and he felt his breath catch in his throat.

Damnation, they could not! He stood up too quickly, almost losing his balance, and she reached to steady him. Or to incite him even more, who could say, on this shadow-crossed path where the bounds of civility seemed to slip further and further away.

Circe looked up, missing the loss of his touch as keenly as if he had always been hers. She had watched him replace the lost shoe, felt the thrill of his touch run over her whole body. The last dramatic chords of the music were fading, but now she had forgotten even the music.

Why did David look so still, so arrested? She put one hand to his cheek and heard the sharp intake of his breath. "You do not always have to be so proper, David," she murmured. "I don't believe that is the real you, not at all the man I once knew.... Have you really changed so much?"

He lowered his head and pulled her abruptly closer. His mouth captured hers, the touch of his lips and tongue with their hungry urgency making Circe's pulse jump. She returned his kiss eagerly, delighting in the firmness of his lips, the masculine scent of him, the strength of the arms that pulled her closer. She pressed her whole body against his, nestling against him with voluptuous delight.

Then some unreadable emotion flickered across his face, and he hesitated. She could feel his whole body go rigid with his inner struggle. He stepped back.

"I will not make love to an innocent girl in the shadows of my hostess's garden!" he exclaimed, his voice constricted. "I have a regard for the proprieties, dammit! I am not my father."

Turning, he strode heavily toward the house.

Circe stood still; she had never felt so alone, so abandoned. She had reached out to David, sure that he would share her delight in the natural spontaneity of their embrace. But he could not let go of his inhibitions.

Or perhaps he simply didn't want her. Perhaps what

she had always suspected was true. She was beyond the pale, too different, too unconventional to be loved.

She lingered a few minutes more, wiping the few tears off her cheeks, pushing the hurt inside, composing her expression. Then she walked inside, slipping back into the main room to listen to the end of the musical performance. When the musicians took their last bow, Circe located her sister, and they said their farewells.

On the ride home, Circe said little, watching the glow of streetlamps as the carriage rocked and swayed over the cobblestones. And when Gabriel came into the hall to greet them, kissing his wife and listening to her pointed critique of the first part of the musical evening, which made him shout with laughter, Circe forced a smile.

"I'm sorry to have put you through such a tedious evening." Psyche turned to her sister and patted her arm. "I hope it was not a total bore; the Spanish music was lovely. Besides, several young men did ask about you, while you were hiding yourself out in the shrubbery, and told me they were hoping to see you again."

"That's nice," Circe said absently, thinking only of how she had felt in David's arms, how wonderful it had been—until he had rejected her. The pain threatened to swell up again, and she pushed it back.

Psyche made a face and said to Gabriel, "She's not even going to ask me who inquired about her! Circe, have you no maidenly curiosity about your possible admirers?"

Circe started. "I'm sorry, what did you say?"

Gabriel laughed. "It's what you did not say, Circe. I fear she has something else on her mind," he told his wife, kissing her again. "You might as well have done, my love. Circe will follow her own path."

"I know, I know, she thinks only of her next painting," Psyche said, her tone wry. "Oh, well, I shall have tried."

Circe tried to smile, then said good night and made her way up to her bedchamber and pulled the bell rope absently.

But Luciana did not appear. Presently, one of the

housemaids came in with a pitcher of warm water. The servant curtsied and poured the water into the china basin on her dressing table.

"Pardon, miss, but your own maid is indisposed, so she sent me instead."

"I see," Circe said, sighing. She would have to confront Luciana again tomorrow. Why did the girl not want to face her? Was Luciana still hiding something? But she would not seek her out tonight. Circe was tired and unsettled, and she had too much already to think about.

She made a quick toilette and then climbed into bed, blowing out her candle and pulling the covers up to her chin. She fell asleep almost at once, and dreamed confused dreams of classical paintings with nymphs and satyrs and Cupids—grinning satyrs with von Freistadt's dark brows and sardonic smile, and an almost naked Adonis who looked strangely like David. And the sensations that rushed through her broke the serenity of her sleep and made her toss restlessly in her bed.

Perhaps it was this almost awake state that caused her to hear the sound.

It was a small sound, really, but even in her half-dormant state, she knew it was not normal. Pulling herself out of her slumber with great effort, like a swimmer rising to the surface of murky water, Circe blinked at the darkness, trying to orient herself.

She lay in her bed, in her own bedchamber, the air cool against her bare feet, and the bed linen pushed almost off the bed by her restless slumber. But why did she lie so tensely?

Then the sound came again, a whisper of cloth as if trousers brushed together as someone moved stealthily, and then a soft clunk as if someone's foot had struck the small stool she had left slightly out of place in front of her dressing table.

There was someone in her room.

Twelve

Circe stiffened in alarm. But she did not dare move or cry out. If she screamed, the intruder would know that she was awake, and perhaps he would feel compelled to silence her before she made a prolonged outcry.

Unless that was his original intent. Why would someone break into their house, into her bedchamber? She had few valuables here, only a little jewelry that had belonged to her mother, or that were gifts from Psyche and Gabriel. Anyhow, the most valuable gems were in Psyche's bedchamber; Gabriel delighted in bringing home surprises for his wife.

Had the thief, if such it was, already visited Gabriel and Psyche's room? Was Psyche all right? Circe's fear grew; she felt more alarm for Psyche and her unborn baby than for herself. But surely Gabriel would have taken action if anyone had assaulted his wife.

The man moved so quietly, as if on cat feet, about her room. Only by the faint rustle of clothing put aside could she tell that the invisible visitor was patting her clothing in the clothes press—for what? Her eyes half-shut to avoid revealing her wakefulness, Circe nonetheless stared hard into the blackness. A shape somewhat darker than the darkness of the room was all she could make out.

Heavy draperies covered her windows, so that only the faintest shimmer from the streetlamps outside slipped past them, and no candle burned at this hour of the early morning. Dawn was still far away. Outside the house, even the avenue was quiet as honest folk slumbered, and merchant's carts had yet to begin their deliveries.

The presence, almost ghostly in its silence, moved to her bureau, and one of the drawers squeaked a little as it was pulled open.

Circe felt the hair on her neck rise. It could not be a ghost! No, no spirit that she had ever heard of moved so methodically, searching each drawer in turn, as if in search of some treasure—but what? She did not have time to consider the question. This person was corporeal, no phantom, and thus posed a real and physical threat.

Now the shape turned and came closer to her bed. Circe found it hard to breathe; her heart was thumping so loudly she thought the intruder must detect its beat. But still she hesitated. Should she scream? It would take long moments for someone to hear her voice through her heavy chamber door, longer for Gabriel to come to her aid. The bell rope was across the room, and the servants' rooms several floors up. They must be all asleep, anyhow, and no one would hear the bell clang belowstairs in the servants' hall.

And the intruder was here, now, approaching her bedside.

She heard a quick inhalation of breath—had he made out her half-opened eyes? Yes, something changed about his posture. She could almost see the heightened sense of alertness. And even in the murky dimness, she detected motion. She made out a faint sheen of metal rising over her prone body—

He had a knife!

She hesitated no longer. Drawing her knee high and pulling her nightgown up to leave her leg unfettered, she focused all her strength into a vicious kick to the intruder's groin.

A howl of pain was the gratifying response.

Not for nothing had Circe studied the human form, memorized anatomy charts at her art instructor's bequest. She knew, as few maidens did, just where a man could be hurt most precisely. And there she struck again, as hard as she was able.

The man shrieked, and Circe added her voice to his.

"Gabriel! Help! We have an intruder!"

The man was doubled over, groaning and making terrible retching noises. Circe took the opportunity to roll off the other side of the bed and dash for the door. But the intruder recovered his wits and moved as rapidly as possible—his body still hunched in pain—to stop her. She found the door standing ajar—in the dimness, she had not been able to detect that before—and she pulled it wider, but before she could slip through, a strong hand grasped her arm and pulled her back.

"Gabriel!" Circe screamed again.

The man, still just a dark blur, grappled with her, pushing his hand against her mouth. Unable now to scream, Circe struggled with all her might, biting his hand and trying to twist out of his grip.

"You damned bitch!" The man's deep voice grunted in Circe's ear. A part of her terrified mind registered the slight accent as German, or perhaps—but her speculation ended abruptly when she felt the prick of a blade against her neck. Terror threatened for an instant to overwhelm her. Then anger surged up, momentarily eclipsing her fear. She clenched her fist and hit him hard in his groin again, and the blade dropped with a clatter to the hardwood floor. She heard a sharp intake of breath.

Then the door of her bedchamber was shoved open, and she caught the glimmer of a candle's flame from the corridor. Circe was pulled away from her attacker and pushed toward the doorway, while Gabriel launched himself forward with the force of an avenging angel.

"Take care, he has a knife!" Circe shrieked, then found herself clasped by her sister's arms.

"Oh, Circe!" Psyche sobbed, almost dropping the candle.

"I'm unharmed," Circe said, though her knees felt weak, and she was glad to cling to her sister for support. She rescued the candle from her sister's trembling hold, and they both stared into the room, where sounds of crashing bodies announced the rough-and-tumble battle taking place.

"Go upstairs and summon the servants," Psyche ordered.

"And leave you here alone? No, no, you go," Circe argued.

"Oh, this is no time—" Psyche paused, gasping in shock as a dark figure plunged out of the bedchamber and barreled into them.

Both reeled from the impact and barely kept their footing. Circe dropped the candle as she tried to steady her sister; the small flame puffed out. In the same instant, their assailant rushed past them and disappeared into the darkness of the hall.

"Gabriel!" Psyche called, her voice thin with fear. "Are you hurt?"

Circe held her breath. Had her brother-in-law been murdered?

After a small eternity, the response came. "I'm here." Gabriel sounded winded, but otherwise composed, remarkable considering such an unheard-of attack while they slept in their beds.

Psyche rushed into the room, and Circe followed more slowly. She could make out the two embracing. She made her way to the table beside her bed and lit her own candle.

"Are you all right, Circe? You're trembling, Psyche, love; here, sit down," Gabriel said, his voice concerned. "Where did the villain go?"

"Toward the stairs," Circe told him, hurrying to take Psyche's hand. "Take a deep breath, Psyche. Would you like some brandy?"

Psyche shook her head, but she did sink down upon

the chair. Gabriel went into the hall, and Circe heard him summoning help from the servants by the simple expedient of putting his head into the stairwell and shouting loudly.

In a minute their butler and two footmen appeared. Gabriel informed them briefly of the invasion, which had the servants goggling and mute with shock.

"You stay with the ladies," Gabriel directed the largest footman. "You two, come with me. We must check the house and make sure that the intruder is not hiding somewhere in the darkness. And take care, he has a blade."

The servants looked less than enthused over this announcement, but they followed loyally as Gabriel headed for the stairs. Circe gave them her candle to take along. The footman who remained with the ladies soon retrieved the fallen candle from the hall and lit it, as well as the tapers on Circe's secretary and bureau.

"Thank you," Circe said, trying not to giggle as the room lightened. The poor man stood before them in his nightshirt and bare feet, though he had crammed his wig lopsidedly upon his head, his only concession to his usual meticulous livery.

Reminded of her own disarray, Circe found her dressing gown and slippers and brought a warm shawl to wrap around her sister. In the circle of light, Circe was able to see that Psyche had stopped shaking. "Are you feeling better, Psyche?"

Her sister nodded. "But I would like to see Gabriel back in one piece. How on earth did the thief get in? And what was he doing on this level? I should expect him to go for the household silver."

Circe nodded, though she had her own thoughts about his possible motivations. "Perhaps looking for the family jewelry," she suggested, taking her sister's hand.

"But in your bedchamber?" Psyche asked tartly, sounding more her normal self.

"The man would hardly know which room was which," Circe pointed out, practical as always.

"True." Psyche sighed. "I hate to wake any more of the servants at this hour, but I admit, I would love a cup of tea."

"I will go and—" Circe moved toward the doorway, but her sister grabbed her arm.

"No! Not till Gabriel says all is safe," Psyche said, her voice determined.

"Very well," Circe agreed, not willing to further perturb her sister. She came back to the bed—her stool was up-ended against the wall, and the dressing table was a shambles—and perched upon the edge. She felt a roughness in the smooth linen sheets, and her hand touched a large rent in the mattress, where feathers drifted through.

The discovery sent a chill through her. The stranger had stabbed at her bed, stabbed at Circe, and missed in the darkness. Whatever he sought in their house, he had been ready to kill for it.

"Do you hear any sounds from below, Charles?" Psyche asked the footman.

"No, my lady," the man answered, turning his head toward the doorway to listen.

Circe pulled the top sheet up to cover the damaged bed. No need for Psyche to see the evidence of her attack. She would talk to Gabriel later.

Or perhaps not. But she had to consult with someone. This was too close to home, now, to hold back her secrets, even another person's secrets.

If this strange attack had anything to do with the earlier assaults on the street, with Luciana and the secrets that Circe was increasingly sure the girl was hiding, the truth had to come out. Psyche and her unborn child had to be protected. If their home was raided, something was seriously amiss.

Circe had returned the necklace to her maid, but was that piece of jewelry enough to trigger such an invasion? Or was there more—what clandestine prize was Luciana hiding?

Tomorrow—today, Circe corrected, glancing at the

draperies, where the faint evidence of dawning light peeped past the edges—perhaps she would put aside her wounded pride and send a note to David. He alone knew the complete story about the street assaults. It was time to be completely open and acquaint him with the background that might have led to this attack.

When Gabriel returned, he announced that he and the servants had searched the house and were now certain it was empty. The intruder was not hiding out to threaten them again.

"Is anything missing?" Psyche asked.

Gabriel shook his head. "I took a quick look at the silver," he told them. "All the plateware seems to be accounted for. And no one entered our room. Your jewelry box is untouched."

"I cannot think why he came upstairs," Psyche pondered.

Circe tried not to look guilty. She was not, after all, absolutely certain of the intruder's intent.

Fortunately, her sister and her brother-in-law had their minds on other things. "Did you see how he might have gotten into the house?" Psyche continued.

"We found a study window broken," Gabriel answered, frowning. "I think it is how he came in, and how he departed, as well."

"And no one heard him." Psyche grimaced.

"No, the whole household was asleep, and no one of course was on the ground floor," Gabriel agreed. "I think I shall have to look into getting a dog, a large dog."

Apparently awakened by all the commotion, Simpson hurried into the room. "Oh, my lady, what is it? Are you ill?"

"No, but she could use a strong cup of tea," Circe told her. The lady's maid fussed over her mistress, and between her and Gabriel, Circe was content to leave her sister in their competent hands. Psyche went back to her room with her husband, and Circe pulled open the draperies to gaze out into the street.

All seemed quiet. Yet somewhere a threat existed, and she must find out what it was and what drew it to their home.

She didn't bother to go back to bed. She knew she would never be able to fall back to sleep. Without bothering to ring for a servant, Circe washed her face in cool water and dressed quickly, pulling her hair back into a simple twist. She wanted to face Luciana only when she was prepared. There was much to discuss.

But to do it alone . . . Circe hesitated, then made up her mind. She went to her small corner desk and penned a short note to David. Despite the hurt she felt over last night, despite the awkwardness that might linger between them, she needed his help. He might think it unusual to receive such a summons—she had never written to him before—but she knew, somehow, that he would come.

She went downstairs and located a yawning footman, now completely clothed, though a little less neatly than usual, and sent the note off. She asked a housemaid to fetch tea and toast, then climbed the stairs again and sought the comfort of art. Sketching preliminary plans for possible artwork soothed her, and she paused in her drawing only long enough to sip the tea and eat the toast when a servant brought up a tray.

She had worked for over an hour when she heard a firm step outside the schoolroom door. She looked up in time to see David, in riding dress, his neckcloth artfully arranged but his expression less composed than normal, hurry into the room.

"Circe, what's amiss?"

"Thank you for coming so early," she told him, her tone stiff. "I am sorry to pull you out of bed at such an hour. Would you like a cup of tea? You have likely not broken your fast."

"Of course I didn't linger to eat," David said, but the rigid set of his shoulders relaxed. "Not when you send me a note saying 'Come at once.' What's this all about,

Circe? You didn't call me at the break of dawn because
of a sudden urge to share your porridge."

She smiled, and much of her tension drained away; today they seemed almost back to normal. David appeared
to have put aside his proper ways, and his natural—and
quick—response warmed her. "I will explain, but I
thought you might be hungry."

"I am, but if you think that constitutes a decent breakfast . . ." He gazed, affronted, at the plate of toast, then
walked across to the bellrope and pulled hard.

When a maid answered the summons, Circe instructed
the girl to bring David a tray with an abundance of food,
enough to satisfy a male appetite. David nodded, but when
they were alone again, he regarded her with a stern gaze.

"Very well, what is this all about? Gabriel had gone
out when I arrived, and the butler said something about
him searching for a bulldog, but that can't be right."

"Oh, it is," Circe told him, pulling up a chair so that
David would sit down, too. "Someone broke into our
house last night."

"What?" David blinked in surprise. "You must be jok-
ing."

Circe shook her head. "Not at all. I woke up and found
an intruder in my room, David. It was most unnerving."

He made an impulsive gesture, as if to clasp her arm,
then dropped his hand and swore heartily. Circe jumped—
he was usually more circumspect in her presence.

"Sorry," he said. "But, Circe, curse it, that's the third
time you've been attacked. What in bloody hell is going
on?"

"Ah, well, as to that . . ." She couldn't help feeling a
twinge of guilt, and he leaned forward to grip her shoulder.

"Circe! Out with it; what have you been keeping from
me?"

"I think perhaps it is connected with Luciana," she told
him, lowering her voice in case the servant should return
with the food.

"Who is Luciana?" David blinked, but he did not release his grip on her shoulder. She found his touch comforting, so unlike the effect that von Freistadt had upon her. What had made her remember the obnoxious Austrian?

"Circe, explain!" David commanded, his tone impatient.

"Luciana is my new lady's maid. She comes from Piedmont, at the top of the Italian peninsula," Circe explained. "I made her acquaintance in somewhat unusual circumstances." She told him the whole story of how she had encountered the girl. Before she had finished, David leapt to his feet and paced up and down.

"Circe, I hardly believe this, even of you."

"Excuse me?" She tried to sound offended, but found herself biting her lip instead.

"You should have been open with me when the attacks occurred. You take a complete stranger into your home, with no knowledge of her background or her motives in fleeing her native country—Lord, Circe, it's a wonder you weren't murdered in your own bed!"

"My art teacher sent her to me," Circe protested. "I did have some reference for her character."

"Really? He advised you of her character? In person?" David turned to regard her, his expression still grim.

"No, not precisely."

"But you sent him a letter to confirm his support of your protégée?"

"Well, no. I knew that Signor DuPree had already departed to visit a hot springs, in the hope of assuaging his gout, and I did not have his direction. But Luciana told me—" Circe paused, and he nodded.

"Just so."

It had never occurred to her that Luciana might have made up the whole story. "But she knew his habits," Circe said slowly. "We have discussed him once or twice since. She is familiar with his views on art and—"

"She could have acquired that knowledge in other

ways," David said. "But I think you are right that she must be involved in this attack. What about the jewelry we found in the basket? Could it be stolen?"

It was hard to think that Luciana, with her sweet face, could be a thief. "I do not see greed in her," Circe argued.

"You think she is being honest with you?"

"Not completely," Circe admitted, sighing. "I was going to question her again today."

"Most certainly, you will," David agreed, emphasis in his tone. "We will. I will add my inquiries to yours."

The maidservant entered the room with a tray of food, and they paused while she sat the array of potables upon the schoolroom table.

"Thank you, you may leave; I will pour out the tea," Circe told her. And after they were alone, she added to David, "Eat first, then we will summon Luciana."

Circe found herself suddenly dreading the coming interview. She did not like to think that Luciana could have lied to her or used Circe's well-intentioned aid to some evil purpose.

David's expression relaxed for the first time. He seemed to follow her thoughts. "I do not fault you," he told her quietly. "But it must be done, you know."

"I blame myself, if I have brought danger to Psyche and Gabriel," Circe answered, her voice very soft.

David made quick work of the ham and kippers, coddled eggs, and brown bread and jam, then Circe rang again. This time, when the housemaid appeared, she said, "Send Luciana to me, please."

The maid curtsied and left, and Circe felt herself grow tense once more. Would Luciana be truthful, at last? Dare Circe hope that there was an innocent explanation for all of this commotion and danger?

She walked across to her easel, still covered with a cloth, and peered unseeing out the window behind it. She heard David's footsteps; he had come up behind her. He put one hand on her shoulder.

"Don't be hard on yourself, Circe."

"No, you were right. It was a foolhardy thing to do." Circe swallowed against the lump in her throat. "I only wanted to save her from the secret police—she was genuinely afraid. And there are terrible stories about what they do to their victims, guilty or innocent."

"I know—my uncle works under the Foreign Secretary," David said. "I'm sorry that you have heard the stories, too."

Most young Englishwomen knew little of the Continent, he thought, little of its convoluted history and complicated politics. As absorbed as Circe had been in her art during her years abroad, she seemed also aware of the currents of intrigue and the power struggles which still plagued so many countries. Trust Circe to feel for the underdog, for anyone who was mistreated.

He allowed his hand to rest lightly on her shoulder, allowed himself the luxury of touching her, imagined slipping her dress down and delving into the treasures that were so modestly covered with muslin and ribbon. His fingertips tingled with the thought of stroking her glowing skin, so different from the pale London misses.

She was so unlike any woman he had ever dallied with, so different in every way. Just for a moment, David could feel the energy that seemed to course through her body, relish the smoothness of her skin, smell the light scent of apple blossoms, for once unmixed with smells of paint and linseed oil.

Circe was a delectable and forbidden sweet, and he must curb his appetite. He would not harm her, nor sacrifice his own hard-won respectability and glimmerings of self-respect. Grimacing, David heard a step outside the door, and he lifted his hand quickly.

Circe sighed, glad that David could not see her face. The moment of compassion had been a balm to her unease. And more, it had stirred the old ache inside her, the particular longing that only David induced. But how could she risk being spurned once more?

She wished he would never leave. She wished she

could leave, right now, end this silly season of courtship, and go back to the Continent to paint. There was no point in meeting young men when only one man would ever move her passions. Yet David didn't want her, he had made that plain enough. David had other plans for his future, and he had stipulated what type of woman he sought. . . . Circe tried to pull her thoughts together; they had a serious interview to conduct, and she was dreading that, too.

Luciana came into the room and looked at her mistress, her expression hard to read. "You wished to see me, signorina? I have your walking dress ready if you wish to go out. Or did you wish to go riding with the gentleman?"

"Not just yet," Circe said. "Luciana, we need to talk."

"Signorina?" But the girl seemed more tense at once. "I do not understand."

"You have heard that we had an intruder last night?" Circe asked slowly. "I'm sure they were talking about it belowstairs."

The servant lowered her head. "I—I heard the footmen say that someone was trying to steal the silver. A terrible thing, but not unheard of, signorina, even in England."

"Perhaps," Circe said. "Or perhaps the man was not after the silver. The silver is, in fact, untouched, is it not?"

"Perhaps the robber lost his way?"

"Up two flights of stairs?" Circe would have liked to think that Luciana was only naive, but even she could not help but doubt the girl's lowered eyes and hesitant tone.

"He was upstairs?" The maid raised her gaze for a moment and appeared genuinely frightened.

"Indeed he was," Circe said. "He stabbed my mattress. You will find the feathers all over the floor. Did you not wonder about it?"

Luciana had gone very pale. "Signorina, I—I—"

"He cut your bed? With you in it! Circe, damn it all, you didn't tell me that!" David interrupted. He walked across to the other side of the room and then back, as if unable to be still while he listened to Circe's interrogation.

Circe kept her attention on the other girl. "Luciana, this is a very dangerous man, and I need to know if he is connected to the attacks on your basket. Is this the same man who tried to steal your necklace?"

"How can I know that, signorina?" the girl whispered.

"I think this is more than just a random theft," Circe persisted. "What have you not told me?"

"Nothing, signorina, I swear it!" But Luciana would not meet her gaze. She glanced nervously from Circe to David and back again, then stared down at the floor.

"You are lying," David said. He had been pacing up and down, but now he whirled to face the younger girl. "I demand the truth."

"Please, my lord!" Luciana's voice squeaked with tension.

"Are there other valuables that you have brought out of Piedmont with you, and which some robber would know about?" David demanded.

"No, no, I—I don't know, my lord."

"I think we must take a look in your room, Luciana." David's gaze was steely.

The girl gasped. "No, please!"

Circe felt a moment of contrition. "We cannot, David, surely."

"You are risking your safety," David reminded her, his tone grim. "Not to mention Psyche's. And I do not believe she is telling us the whole story."

Nor did Circe, but it seemed so wrong to go through the young woman's personal possessions. But to protect Psyche's well-being—they did not seem to have a choice.

They went together up the rear stairs. Fortunately, Psyche was lying down, still tired after the disturbances in the night, and as far as Circe knew, Gabriel had not yet returned. She would just as soon not admit the whole story to her brother-in-law, not yet. They climbed the narrow stairs until they reached the servants' floor with its rows of small bedrooms.

Luciana led the way silently down the hall and pointed

out her bedchamber. When she opened the door of the small room, David took hold of the girl's arm.

"Stay here," he told her.

Luciana stood by the door as he bade her, but her face was very white. Circe bit her lip, torn between sympathy for the girl and an increasing distrust of her true motives.

The room held only a few pieces of furniture: a narrow bed with an extra blanket folded across its foot, a small chest of drawers, a straight chair, and a plain table that held a china bowl and ewer. Pegs on the wall held Luciana's street clothes and a clean apron. A small window looked down upon the street, and simple muslin curtains framed its glass panes. It was simple and clean and painfully neat, a decent enough room for a servant, but it offered few hiding places where anything could have been concealed.

David patted the blankets on the bed, knelt to peer under the bed frame, glanced quickly through the chest of drawers and even into the water pitcher. Nothing.

Circe felt a great wave of relief. "You see," she said. "It must be something else."

David paused and looked around the room. The floorboards were bare except for one small rug that sat beside the bed. He lifted it, and Circe saw, from the corner of her eye, how Luciana stiffened.

Oh, dear.

David ran his finger along the floorboards. "Wonderfully clean, your floor, not a speck of dust," he muttered. "But I do believe there is a loose board here."

He took a pocket knife from his buckskin trousers and pried the edge of the board; it seemed to come up very easily. Circe sighed. Hidden beneath the loose board was a space, and in it lay a brown cylinder.

"God, could this be it?" David exclaimed. "What everyone is searching for?"

Circe was not sure what he meant. David pressed his lips together and fell abruptly silent. Now the room was very quiet as David lifted the cylinder out of its hiding place. Circe felt as if she could hardly breathe.

"What does it hold?" she asked, her voice low.

David did not answer, but he removed the end cap and Circe had a glimpse of a well-padded interior containing—what? David tilted the cylinder and dumped the contents onto the bed. A cloth slipped out, lumpy and heavier than it should have been. David unfolded it slowly, and in-side—inside gold glinted, and gems flashed brightly in the sunlight from the window.

Circe took a deep breath. She looked at Luciana, who was pressing her hands to her face.

"Please," the girl whispered. "Do not take it from me."

It was not what Circe had expected, and she saw from David's raised brows that he was surprised, too.

"What do you mean?" Circe asked.

David demanded, at almost the same moment, "Where did you get this jewelry, Luciana? Is it stolen?"

The Italian lifted her head, and for a moment, her fear seemed to be surpassed by anger. "This is mine! It is from my family, my mother's eardrops, my grandmother's necklace!"

Circe came forward to inspect the tangle of jewelry more closely. She touched it gently with one finger, sep-arating the chains and earrings so that she could make out what was there. In fact, the jewelry was nothing like the gems that inhabited her sister's jewel box, or even the few pieces that Circe held dear. They were valuable, certainly, but most of the jewels were small, and that broach held only topaz, she was sure, and that necklace was most likely composed of coral. These trinkets would bring a few pounds, but the necklace that had ridden about in the bottom of the basket yesterday was the most valuable of the lot. And even with that combined, this whole cache could not be worth a hundred pounds. A large sum for a servant, but Luciana had not always been a servant. This was not that much for a family of property to have ac-cumulated over several generations.

"I believe her," Circe said to David. "I don't believe this is stolen."

David raised his brows, but he seemed less intense as he gazed at Luciana. "We will still have to inform Gabriel about all this, Circe. It's only fair."

"No," Circe said, even as Luciana sobbed, pleading, "Signorina, you must not!"

"I'm afraid he will send her away," Circe confessed.

"Bloody well ought to," David retorted. "Attracting thieves to the house."

"I did not mean to," Luciana cried, her voice desperate. "I did not know that villain would break in, I swear it. I cannot lose my jewelry, signorina. It is the only hope for my parents."

"What do you mean?" David asked.

"My mother and father, they are in great danger," Luciana blurted. "I wanted to raise enough money to bring them out of Piedmont. My father, he was part of the rebellion—the Austrians want him dead. Oh, please, signorina. Do not send me away, and do not take away my only funds. I must send money to my parents, or they will be killed, and I will have no one left!"

This time, Circe did not doubt the girl's sincerity. Luciana's brown eyes were wide with entreaty, and her lips trembled.

"We shall have to inform Gabriel," David insisted, but the anger in his voice had faded.

Circe hesitated. Gabriel might agree to aiding Luciana, but what if he did not? He had his wife and unborn child to protect. "Please, David. I cannot see Luciana's parents killed because we were too precipitous in our judgment."

"Precipitous? The thief tried to stab you, Circe!"

"But I am all right, and surely he will not dare to come back to the house after he was discovered."

Luciana sobbed again, and her voice sounded husky with tears. "Please do not destroy all my plans, signorina."

Circe felt her throat close up for a moment. She had lost her own parents when she was very small, and she still ached over their loss. How could she blame Luciana for trying to save her family? It was not Luciana's fault that her bungling attempts at selling her valuables had led them all into peril.

"I will go with you to a reputable jeweler," she decided suddenly. "Gabriel visits a shop in Bond Street. I have seen the box often enough when he brings home gifts for Psyche. If I speak to the owner myself, I am sure he will give us an honest price for your family's gems. Then you can arrange to send the money back, and surely there will be no more problems with petty criminals."

"I'm not so sure they are petty," David argued, but Circe saw the hope brighten Luciana's expression, and she would not be swayed.

"Let us go back downstairs and discuss it," she said, handing the cloth full of jewelry back to Luciana. "We shall go out this afternoon, Luciana, directly after lunch. Keep these safe until then."

Luciana beamed, but David was scowling as she almost dragged him back into the hallway.

"Dammit, Circe—"

"Hush, just a moment," Circe entreated. "Let us have more privacy before we talk about the matter."

He was silent as they descended the steps, but when they reached the level that held the family's bedrooms, he drew her onto the landing. "I wish to see your mattress, Circe."

"Why on earth?" Circe said in surprise.

"I want to see that 'small slit' that the intruder made."

"I cannot see how that will help us," she argued, but David met her rebellious gaze firmly. "Oh, very well."

She led the way to her own bedchamber, motioning for silence. She did not wish to wake Psyche or cause a scandal in their own house. David should not be here at all, of course—they would only linger a moment.

But when she opened the door, someone was already in her bedchamber.

"Oh, miss!" The little housemaid jumped. "Such a fright you gave me. I'm just finishing your room, miss. A right mess it was, with His Lordship jumping that horrid man."

"Indeed it was," Circe agreed. Her dressing table had been put back to rights, she saw, and the bed was now neatly made. "I just, ah, forgot something. Did you see the damage to the mattress?"

"Oh, yes, miss, such a terrible thing." The housemaid blinked, her ruddy cheeks blanching a little. "Could have been killed in our beds, we could!"

"Yes, I'm sure." Circe moved to pull back the bed linen and inspected the damage herself for the first time in full daylight. "The mattress will have to be stitched up."

"Yes, miss," the housemaid agreed.

David had come up behind her; she heard him stifle an oath.

"It's not so very bad," she said quickly, but she saw by his expression that he did not seem to agree.

"Take care of this as soon as you can," she told the servant. "And mind you, not a word to Lady Gabriel. I do not wish her to be worried any further."

"Yes, miss," the housemaid replied. "And I'll see to your nightgown, as well, when I bring up my sewing basket."

"My nightgown?" Circe asked. "I had no tears in my gown."

"But I found this beside the bed." The servant held up a dark scrap of material.

Circe took it, fingering the soft cloth. "It is a shard of black silk," she said. "I have no nightgowns in black."

David reached to examine it. "Did it come from some other, uh, garment?" he demanded delicately.

Circe shook her head. "Everything I was wearing last night was white," she said. "And I'm sure this was not here yesterday, nor do I have any black frocks—we are not in mourning, thank goodness."

The maid simply looked confused, but David frowned.

"I think—" He paused. "We need to go downstairs."

Circe nodded, though she would have liked to point out the absurdity of such rules in light of the break-in. She watched as David looked down at the bed where it was bleeding feathers. He swallowed hard, then turned away from the sight. "I will be in the drawing room."

He bowed and took himself off. Circe stayed only long enough to repeat her instructions to the housemaid forbidding any casual chatter with the other servants, then she followed David down the stairwell and into the formal rooms.

He had poured himself a glass of wine from the decanter, she noted. And he still held the scrap of black silk.

"You think it is important?" she asked, going straight to the point as usual. She took the small piece of silk and gave it closer attention. "It has not been cut, David; it seems to be ripped. You don't suppose . . ."

Circe had been studying the scrap of fabric intently; now she realized that the silence had dragged on for too long. David was standing very still, so still that even the wine in his glass did not move. His blue-gray eyes were grave beneath his lowered brows, his mouth set in a straight line. She had rarely seen him so serious.

"Would you like some tea? It's early for wine." She spoke softly and nodded toward the glass in his hand.

David looked down at the wine as if surprised to find it there. A look of distaste crossed his handsome face. "An automatic—and familial—reaction." His expression hardened. "And one that I am done with."

Spinning so quickly and unexpectedly that Circe jumped, David flung the contents of his goblet into the fireplace. The flames sizzled and leapt to devour the alcohol, yellow pinpoints glimmering amid the scarlet.

Calm once more, David placed the glass softly on the mantel. In the silence, the fire still hissed. Circe watched the light of the blaze play across David's face. Because she could not allow herself to feel what she wanted to feel, she tried to stay detached and think only as an artist would think. The flickering light made David look by turns angelic and demonic. It was an interesting illusion, one that would require oils to show to best effect and . . .

Without turning to look at her, David spoke. "How can you do that now?"

Circe blinked, startled by both the sound of his voice and the question itself. "Do what?"

He turned, a lock of chestnut hair falling in disarray over his brow. "How can you be thinking so calmly about your painting when a madman just tried to use you as a pincushion? Do you not realize that you could have been killed and taken from m—" He stopped, color rising to his cheeks. ". . . From your family forever?"

"David." Circe took a deep breath. He must feel something for her; it was too obvious. But he refused to admit it; that would not be *proper*. God, how she hated that word.

Then neither would she confess her feelings, not when he refused to return them. And as for the rest—"I was afraid when he held a knife to my throat; I was terrified. But I don't want to remember that, now. I don't wish to relive it, and I certainly can't upset Psyche by falling into hysterics myself. And my art brings order to my life. It always did, even as a child when I lost my beloved parents. It is my greatest pleasure. It gives me joy and no surprises." She grimaced. "At least, only pleasant surprises."

He frowned, and she wondered if he read her statement as a rebuke. "Your painting is your greatest pleasure? You make your art sound as entrancing as a lover."

She felt the hurt inside her, stilled it. Pride kept her voice level, even defiant. She lifted her chin. "Yes, you could say it is my greatest passion."

David walked toward her slowly, as if drawn despite his best intentions. He came so near that she almost stepped back, but she realized she had no wish to flee.

They stood so close that the clean starchy scent of his shirt and neckcloth tickled her nose. She thought wildly that she would disgrace herself with a sneeze, but then he leaned forward, his face so near that sneezing, even breathing, was forgotten. . . .

Thick spiky lashes fringed his fabulous eyes, eyes now inches from her own. They held such a heat in their blue-gray depths that she was sure the fire must be jealous. She felt it warm her; surely her cheeks had flushed. But still, one corner of her mind was framing him in tones of blue and ivory and brown, and even as she felt the thrill of his closeness, hungered for him to continue, she whispered, "I have to paint you."

For once, his smile seemed real. "Whenever you get that faraway gaze, I know that you are thinking of your work and not of what is right under your pert little nose. You have no idea how challenging that is to a man."

Circe's breaths came short and quick. "Challenging?"

"Oh, yes," he drawled. "It makes a man want to refocus all that creative energy on himself, upon less cerebral and more carnal passions."

"You did not think so last evening in the garden." As soon as the words escaped her lips, she wished she could take them back.

David stiffened, and she saw him pull his society face back into place. Once more, he refused to be honest with her, to be the man she still believed lingered beneath the mask.

Circe bit back a few choice Italian curses. Why could she not change his mind? How could he ignore the feelings that surged between them? They were drawn together, but always, he pulled away.

David drew a deep breath, then turned. Staring into the fire, he cleared his throat. "The black silk—I believe it may have been part of a mask."

She looked up at him. "What?"

"The fabric." He gestured to the black scrap that she still clutched in her hand, but had almost forgotten.

With effort, Circe answered, "Like a masquerade, you mean?"

"Not exactly. A mask made to hide his countenance, or simply a silk scarf tied around the man's face, so that he was harder to see in the dark."

She bit her lip, trying to think. "It's true that it was very hard to make out his form, and a pale face should have stood out against the general dimness. That might be it, David."

"And the mask may have been torn in the fight with Gabriel," David continued. "The only other motivation for covering his face would be if it were someone you knew."

Circe considered his comments. "I have seen the man who was hired to steal the basket," she agreed. "And he covered his face the last time, too. David, the intruder spoke once, and I believe his accent was foreign."

"Ah!" David said, his expression intent.

To her frustration, he did not share his thoughts. "What? And what did you mean, upstairs," she pressed, "when you said it might be what 'everyone' was searching for. Who is everyone?"

"It doesn't signify," David said, his tone closed. He stared into the fire instead of meeting her gaze.

Circe folded her arms. "You demanded that I should be open with you and cease concealing any secrets! I can certainly ask the same of you."

"It is not my secret," David told her.

"Nor was Luciana's secret mine! What are you keeping from me, and what does it have to do with Luciana's jewelry?" Circe felt a wave of anxiety that took precedence over her personal concerns. She could tell from the stiffness of David's stance that whatever information he was holding back was significant.

David looked stern. "My uncle—we know that something important, really important, has been smuggled out of the Continent. I thought for a moment, when I saw the jewelry, it might be what we sought. But that cannot be the case—the jewelry she has is of slight value, really, certainly nothing that would stir up rumors through all of Europe."

"That makes sense," Circe agreed. "Besides, I believe Luciana's concern for her parents is genuine. I don't think we should risk seeing her turned out over an attack that was not her fault. Gabriel is a kind man, but his concern for Psyche's safety will outweigh everything else. Even if the thief came here to steal Luciana's little bit of valuables, he must have been scared off by the resulting uproar."

"But—"

"It's just not reasonable, you know," Circe added, warming to her argument. "Any house on this square would hold more valuable jewelry than Luciana's little cache. Psyche's box certainly has ten times, a hundred times more gems than Luciana owns. I do not believe that Luciana can have anything to do with the robbery attempt at all."

"It is all coincidence?" David asked her, his tone skeptical. "What of the attacks on the street?"

"That did seem connected to her basket. But I will see that she is able to sell her property safely, and we will have nothing more to fear."

David stared at her. "My—Circe, I fear that you are listening to your heart much more than your head."

Circe met his gaze defiantly. "David, if I could bring my parents back, if I could have protected them before their deaths, I would have sold the clothing off my back!"

He frowned. "I know that. But I still think Gabriel should be informed. If he knew you were keeping such secrets—"

"They are only little secrets," Circe argued. "We have agreed that Luciana played no part in the robber's intrusion."

"You have agreed," David said drily. "I have merely listened."

"Very well, we will tell Gabriel, but allow me a little more time, first, to eliminate the lure that led the thief here," Circe urged. She forgot her determination to match his reserve and took an impulsive step forward, clasping his hand. "David, please."

The contact they shared seemed almost electric, like the experiments in her father's laboratory that had shocked the small Circe when she'd put her fingers on a copper wire. But she did not feel at all like a child, touching David. She took a deep breath, not sure if he were aware of how her heart leapt, how her body responded to the merest brush of his hand. They were again standing very close; energy seemed to vibrate between them.

David's lips parted, and his lids dipped lower over his eyes. He leaned forward, and brushed her lips with his own. She did not draw back, drinking in the feel of him, the smell of starched linen and musky clean male flesh.

"Oh, damn me for a fool," he whispered against her mouth before pulling her to him. His mouth was strong and his touch sure; Circe felt as if she were sinking into a warm and languorous whirlpool, and she had no urge to fight its pull. She put her hands about his neck and returned his embrace with hearty abandon, and for an instant, new and powerful feelings surged between them, making the whole world fade.

He moved one hand up from her waist to touch the curve of her breast. Circe felt her passion leap, and she could barely breathe. She wanted him to continue, wanted him to push aside the thin muslin and touch the skin that yearned to share his warmth. She wanted—

She heard Gabriel speaking on the floor below them, and the deep barking of what was undoubtedly a very large dog. Her brother-in-law did not climb the steps, and his voice sank, but they both startled, and David moved back, almost stumbling.

"I must go."

Circe blinked, the awakened longing inside her protesting his absence from her arms. She ached for him, wanted to pull him back, wanted to feed the fire they had ignited together, not extinguish it, but he had already retreated into his usual damnable correctness. When she spoke, her voice sounded somehow too high in pitch; she tried to steady it. "Must you?"

"Yes, overdue for, um, an appointment. We'll discuss this again later," he said, looking about him as if dazed.

"But you won't tell Gabriel just yet?" she insisted, trying to hang on to rational thought when she still felt giddy herself.

"Good God, no!" he said, then seemed to steady himself. "Oh, about Luciana—no, not yet. But we will talk more about this."

Then he left the room with such dispatch that she felt once more abandoned. And the memory of his hands and lips still lingered, and her heart seemed to take such a long time to return to its normal beat.

Thirteen

*D*avid spent the next day watching von Freistadt's house. As the hours passed slowly, he tried not to remember the near disastrous slip he had made with Circe. Damn it, he had to have more self-control! But it was hard not to dwell on the smooth lips and generous mouth, the soft skin of her throat, and the long legs that enticed his eye up into the more private, even more alluring . . . dammit! He pulled his attention back to the house.

Late in the afternoon, David witnessed the Austrian's return, but no other mysterious visitors showed themselves. When the sun dropped low in the sky, David rubbed his aching back—he had rented the hot chestnut cart again—and decided enough was enough.

When he met the cart's owner at the pub where they had arranged to rendezvous, David noticed a half-grown lad lingering at the man's elbow. The boy had shaggy hair and patched clothing, but his eyes were bright with intelligence, and he watched David with obvious curiosity.

"Your son?" David asked as he reached into his grimy second-hand coat to pull out a handful of coins.

The chestnut seller, accepting the money eagerly, gave a hoarse guffaw. " 'At's what 'is mum says."

The boy paid little attention to this old jest; he watched David instead.

A likely-looking boy, David observed, thinking quickly. His back ached and his whole body longed for a bath and decent clothes. And anyhow, he was going to become conspicuous, disguise or not, if he lingered in the square every day. It was time for reinforcements.

"How'd you like to earn some blunt, too?" David suggested, looking at the lad.

The boy blinked. "Oo, for real?"

His loving father scowled. " 'Ow come you want 'im?"

"Because he's small and young and will be less likely to attract attention," David explained. To the boy, he added, "Have you ever been on your father's route?"

The lad nodded. "When 'e was too 'eavy-'eaded from the rum," he elaborated. "Bloody 'eavy, that cart is."

" 'Ere, watch your mouth." His father gave him a good-natured clout on the arm, which the lad ignored.

"Do you know the large redbrick house with the iron grill on the windows in Devon Square?"

The boy nodded again. "Got a grumpy butler and a good-looking parlor maid," he offered.

David grinned. "Good lad. What's your name?"

"Timothy."

"Can you follow orders, Timothy? Keep your mouth shut? Do you have a good memory?"

Timothy nodded earnestly to each question.

"I want you to observe that house and remember who comes and goes, but especially anyone who seems out of place, anyone who is not a merchant or a servant of the house. I want you to remember it all; can you do that?"

Timothy's eyes sparkled with eagerness. "Cor, aye!"

"I'll meet you here after sunset every day, and I'll want a full report. And I'll make it worth your while," David promised. He took out a coin from his pocket and flipped it toward the boy, who snatched it out of the air with commendable speed.

When he left the pub, David considered the new arrangement. He couldn't watch the house day in and day out; his absence from his usual haunts was becoming noticeable. And he needed to be at the social events that the count patronized, not only to watch the Austrian's contacts but even more important, to keep an eye on Circe. If the chit would only listen to him and avoid von Freistadt. But then, when had she ever listened to him?

He made his change of clothes at the used clothing shop—he was definitely raising the income of the inhabitants in this part of London, he thought wryly—and hurried home. This time, he was able to slip in the house and upstairs into his bath without encountering his mother. She was showing an unusual disposition to linger in London, although every day he hoped privately that she would announce her return to Bath.

When he came downstairs for dinner, which had been moved back to its normal London hour, he was immaculately groomed and dressed. Nonetheless, his mother looked him up and down.

"I hope you approve, Mother?" he noted, his tone polite but guarded.

"Yes, I suppose."

"My tailor will be relieved to hear it."

She never took note of his irony, and anyhow, she was not finished. "Although a gold waistcoat would be more indicative of your rank, you know, and a few pieces of jewelry. What about that ruby ring that belonged to your grandfather?"

David winced at the thought of the gaudy gem. "As I recall, it is nothing like my measure. Grandfather had broad hands."

"Surely it could be resized. And that opal stickpin of your father's?"

"I believe he gave that away," David said vaguely, and his mother sniffed again.

"To one of his petticoat fancies, no doubt! To think that some harlot is parading about London flaunting a family heirloom that should have remained in our line for many more generations . . ."

She continued her harangue as he escorted her in to dinner. David sighed. It was true that his father's behavior had been inexcusable, his sinning often drunken and ostentatious, but David had moments of sympathy for his late sire when his mother began one of her too frequent bouts of castigation. That she was bitter about her wretched marriage was understandable, but her bile often spilled over to include David in its acid touch, even if she did manage nowadays to avoid throwing the china. But it reminded him, as usual, why he had never been eager to subject himself to the risks of matrimony.

By the second course he was able to turn his mother's thoughts with a question about the lineage of her family.

She paused, giving the matter some thought, then answered, "I'm sure it was my great-great-aunt Clarissa who married the earl, not her sister, no matter what Cousin Thomasina says. If my brother William ever comes to tea, as I requested, I will question him about it."

She meandered on, tracing their genealogy to her own satisfaction, while David, feeling the weight of his family upon his shoulders in more ways than one, pushed back his plate and waved aside the footman who offered the next course.

He had lost all appetite.

≈≈

The next morning, David rose early and made another breakfast visit to his uncle, so that they could discuss the ongoing surveillance.

His uncle approved of hiring the chestnut vendor's son. "Although I would have given much to have seen you in such a getup," he added, chuckling.

David smiled ruefully and touched his immaculate neckcloth. "I am most happy to have my own costume back, I promise you." He took another bite of ham. When he swallowed, he added, "Do we know any more about the mysterious treasure the Austrians are seeking?"

"Treasure?" His uncle took a sip of tea.

"Jewelry, document, person, whatever it is," David said.

"Unfortunately, no. But I still believe that von Freistadt is involved, and if we are patient and persistent, I believe we, or you, will discover a vital clue," Uncle William answered, his voice serene. "Diplomacy is ninety percent patience, my boy."

David wished he could summon patience so easily. "There is one possibility I am pursuing," he said, "though I am not yet sure if it is connected." Then he glanced at the clock on the wall and pushed back his chair.

"I must go," he said. "My mother is expecting a drive in the park."

His uncle made an expression of sympathy. "Give her my best."

David grinned. "I'll tell her you will call one afternoon soon."

"Ah, I've a most busy week," his mother's brother answered, looking quite unregretful. "I'm really not sure when I will get there."

David returned home and was able to greet his mother when she at last came downstairs, half an hour past the time she had asked him to be ready. Fortunately, he knew her habits and had not yet called for his carriage. He did not wish his horses to stand in such a fresh breeze.

She did not realize he had already been out, and he saw no need to bring it up and endure more interrogations. His carriage was called for, and he helped his mother up, then took the reins from the groom.

It was a lovely brisk spring morning, with a light breeze that fluttered the roses on his mother's bonnet. He tried to enjoy the weather, but otherwise, he simply endured the drive, holding his horses to the sedate trot that his mother preferred, while the countess commented on the other ladies' outfits, the other men's carriages, the posture of the grooms who clung to the back of some of the carriages, the coolness of the air, the shabby notions some people had about riding habits trimmed with too many epaulets and gold lace, and the like.

Finally, after his mother had eyed every other lady making the circuit of the park and nodded to her friends, she turned to regard him with a steely gaze. "Tell me about the Season so far," she demanded in her usual imperious style. "What delights have I missed by rusticating in Bath?"

"Precious little," he said, then softened the impulsive comment with a smile. "The parties are too crowded, the luncheons are boring, the chances to ride are, as you see, much circumscribed. I find that I tire of polite society—it is too tedious."

Too late, he saw the ditch that he had galloped so unwittingly toward, metaphorically speaking, of course.

"Then why—" His mother tugged her bonnet back from a capricious gust of wind and tied it more firmly beneath her chin—"did you venture out the other night to hear that pair of shrill-voiced singers, dear boy?"

David kept his gaze on his team, trotting with utmost decorum down the lane. "It was a momentary impulse, no more."

"No, indeed, you wished to see the lovely Miss Hill," the countess said, her tone encouraging. "I cannot blame you; indeed, she is quite a beauty, in a refreshingly novel kind of way."

If Circe were less wealthy and her family less distinguished, David thought cynically, his mother would have been horrified by her "refreshing" ways. And he refused to be manipulated.

"Of course," he agreed. "Although there are many other lovely young ladies out this Season."

"David Lydford, do not suggest that you are still eyeing every young woman you meet, just when you have a prime catch interested in your imminent proposal! You must not imitate your father's immoral ways! When I think of all the women he ogled and fondled and made such an ass of himself over—Lord, the time he brought home that trollop with the hennaed hair and tried to tell me she was a teacher of French when I surprised them in the study, heavens preserve us . . ." She was off again, and one distasteful memory always led to another.

The carriage lurched, and David pulled the horses back into line. He found that he had inadvertently tightened his grip on the reins. *Take a deep breath,* he told himself. *Smile.*

But the tenseness in his lips made that hard to do, and he kept a tight check on both his own rebellious thoughts and his horses until the drive was, mercifully, finally ended.

When they returned to the Westbury mansion, he saw his mother off to her luncheon engagement, then enjoyed a light meal and took himself off, as well. He had promised Circe he would accompany her to a jewelry shop, though he would never have let on to his mother that he was going about London with the young lady she was yearning for him to spend more time with.

When he pulled up in front of the house, the door opened—she must have been watching from the window—and Circe regarded his curricle, and the groom who stood very straight at its back, with surprise.

"We are driving?"

David nodded. "If there are any more thieves waiting to pounce on us as we walk, I want to make it as difficult as possible. Besides, I wished to keep you from strolling absentmindedly down St. James's Street again."

"David, you promised not to mention that. I was simply thinking of a painting that I might—oh, you wretch!" She saw that he was teasing her and allowed the groom to help her into the vehicle as David held the pair of well-matched chestnuts steady, then settled herself gracefully beside him. She wore a simple walking outfit of dark green, which made her eyes seem even greener; he wished he could forget his mother, his uncle, all his duties, and lose himself in her lucid gaze.

Circe raised her brows. "David?"

He realized he had not been attending. "Sorry, you said?"

"I said, how would anyone know that today I was carrying all of Luciana's jewels in my reticule?"

"Other than the fact that it sags like a sack of potatoes?" he asked politely.

She giggled. "No, really."

"Just erring on the judicious side," he suggested and pulled his team back into the traffic. In a moment, he added, "Circe, I don't mean to depress your hopes, but you do realize that top-flight shops do not generally *buy* trinkets such as these; they sell them."

"Yes, but why should that prevent me from selling these to the jeweler? He will know they are authentic, and some are almost antiques, which should lend a certain interest to them. Remember all the jewelry the émigrés brought into England years ago after the French Revolution?"

David was too young to remember, and he wasn't so sure about the validity of her logic, but he didn't argue that point. "At any rate, there is no profit for them in buying at the same price as they might later sell the stuff for, so you must not be distressed if the gems do not fetch what you had hoped for."

"It is not for me, but for Luciana," she pointed out. "Though yes, I would be anxious for her sake—it is essential for her to be able to buy her parents' safe passage out of Piedmont."

He knew how much this quest touched Circe's sympathies and stirred her still deep mourning for her own lost parents, so he did not argue, but he retained his doubts about the success their outing was likely to enjoy.

They rolled very shortly into Bond Street, and Circe directed him to the elegant establishment where Gabriel bought gifts for Psyche. He held the heavy door open for her, and they entered the tastefully decorated shop with its glass cases holding gleaming diamond tiaras and cunningly wrought necklaces sparkling with colored gems.

Circe walked up to the young man who bowed to her. "May I help you, ma'am?"

"Good afternoon." She smiled at him. "I have some jewelry to sell, if you please."

His welcoming expression faded. "We do not buy jewelry, ma'am. Perhaps you are looking for a moneylender? We are not such an establishment."

Hell, he had warned her, David thought.

She raised her brows. "I believe my business would best be conducted with the owner of the shop. If you would summon him, please."

· The man hesitated a moment, but he was no match for Circe's calm, assured gaze. "Just a moment, miss," he said, and vanished through a rear door.

David hid a grin; he should have had more faith in Circe. She looked unperturbed as they waited. At last, footsteps announced the return of the clerk, along with a stout older man whose look of self-assurance suggested a short interview.

"May I assist you, ma'am? My assistant says you are perhaps in search of a different sort of enterprise?"

"Not in the least," Circe assured him, her tone pleasant. "I am Miss Circe Hill, sister of Lady Gabriel Sinclair. I believe Lord Gabriel Sinclair is a valued customer of long standing? And we assume he will continue to be a regular visitor to your shop."

The man's expression melted like clotted cream on a hot scone into an obsequious smile. "Of course! And how may I help you, Miss Hill?"

"Perhaps we should discuss this in your office," Circe suggested.

"I was just about to propose it," the man agreed, bowing and leading the way. Circe followed, with David just behind her.

"Blackmail, Circe?" he leaned forward to whisper into

her ear. He saw that her jaw trembled with suppressed laughter, though she did not answer.

Thirty minutes later they were bowed with utmost courtesy out of the shop, and the bulge in Circe's reticule had been replaced by an even heavier burden of coin.

"How will Luciana get this safely to her parents on the other side of the Continent?" David asked. "I do not wish it to be stolen after all the trouble you have gone through to assist her."

"I assumed you would have the answer to that," Circe said blithely.

"Me?"

"You do have an uncle in the Foreign Office; he must have couriers." She smiled up at him.

"Yes." David sighed with resignation. "I suppose he does." He offered his hand as she stepped back into the carriage. The light touch of her fingers made him wish to linger on the pavement, but he pushed such weaknesses aside.

"Luciana has agreed that you are a trustworthy person to take charge of her money, and as soon as she has word of their condition, we will have the money changed and you will arrange to send it to her parents," Circe told him.

"Then I shall take this to my bank straightaway," David suggested. Circe agreed, and they made a detour into the more masculine haunts of the City. Ladies did not generally frequent banking establishments, so Circe decided for once to be proper and wait for David in the carriage while he went inside the large stone building.

She was sitting in the open curricle, enjoying the fresh breeze that tugged at her bonnet and staring at the building across the street, which had interesting angles, when a sudden noise made her start.

David's groom, who had hopped down to the pavement to hold the reins of the horses while David was inside, now doubled over, as if he had been taken suddenly ill. The horses snorted and tossed their heads in alarm as the groom fell to his knees.

"Are you all right?" Circe called out. She bent forward to grab the suddenly slack reins herself before the horses took fright, but she could not reach the traces. Suddenly a man scrambled up into the carriage beside her.

"What are you doing?" Circe demanded, remembering to moderate her tone. If she shouted for David, the horses would surely bolt. Then she looked more closely, and she had to put one hand to her mouth to stop from crying out.

It was the man with the scar on his cheek, the same villain who had attacked her before.

"Where is it?" he demanded, his voice hoarse and threatening.

"The jewelry has been sold," Circe said as calmly as she could. "And the money is safely inside the bank vault by now. You have nothing to gain by lingering here."

The man shook his head. "Not the trinkets, nor the little coin she got for them. I'm after bigger game, as you well know."

She gazed at him, at a loss to follow his meaning. "I don't know what you mean."

"You know what I want!" The man's eyes narrowed. "If you don't tell me where to find it, someone will pay—"

A muffled shout from the doorway of the bank made the team jump and the carriage tremble. David lunged for the carriage. But the sudden movement, and the shudder as the would-be robber jumped unceremoniously from the curricle to the pavement and took to his heels, was too much for the untended horses. They broke into a run.

Circe clutched the edge of her seat and felt her heart pound. A runaway team was dangerous in any circumstance, but on a busy London street—

Then she saw that David had stepped onto the splashing board and in a moment was clinging to the side of the carriage for dear life, one foot dragging the pavement as he tried to pull himself into the carriage. Now he was precariously balanced between the large wheel and the horses' pounding hooves.

Shouts rose from the spectators around them, and a lumber coach caused the horses to shy and change their direction slightly, but this only sent them heading straight for a wagon piled high with corn.

David was going to lose his grip and fall beneath the heavy wheel—they would both die here! Circe set her jaw with grim resolve. Not if she could help it. She reached to grab his wrists. Throwing her weight back into the curricle, she pulled him a few inches inside, until he could lever the rest of his body into the driver's seat.

But he still could not reach the reins, which dragged along the cobblestones behind the horses' iron-clad hooves. David pushed her back into the seat. "Hold on!" he shouted.

She saw what he was about to do and bit back a protest. The trailing traces could trip up the horses at any moment and add to their certain doom.

David stood, balanced himself for a moment while the curricle lurched and bounced across the rough stones, then threw himself forward. He landed atop the back of the first horse, but slightly off balance, and for a horrified instant, she was sure he would slip beneath the horses' hooves, to be pummeled and kicked to death.

"David!" This time, she did scream, but her voice went unheard amid the shouts and the whistles around them, and the sound of the horses' snorts and the dog that barked at them from the walkway.

But David had caught himself and, clinging to the horse's harness and dragging himself back, tugged on the horse's head until the team began to slow, pulling abruptly to the left and almost hauling the curricle into the front window of a bookshop, until two men in rough dress leapt to grab the horses's manes and help draw them to a stop.

"David!" Circe called again. "Are you hurt?"

Jumping down from the horse, he waved to her almost carelessly, then turned to inspect his team.

Circe found that her heart was beating so fast she was

almost faint. David was not dead. For a moment she had thought—she had thought she would lose him forever. She'd thought she had reconciled herself to a life without David, but not like this, oh, dear God, never like this!

David was too dear to her, too—Circe inhaled sharply, and for a moment, everything else faded. She loved him. . . . David had captured her heart, not just her curiosity or her artist's eye. The perception left her feeling as shocked as their near escape from disaster.

Dazed, she found it hard to focus her thoughts. This time it was not merely a schoolgirl's crush; this time, she had seen David at his best and his worst, and she loved him still. But what that would mean for all her plans . . .

Presently, she found that the team seemed to be uninjured, though both horses tossed their heads and snorted. They were lathered in sweat. David was thanking the men who had helped stop the team and rewarding them generously.

When he pulled himself back into the driver's seat, with the reins carefully in his hands, he looked at her. "You're very pale, Circe. Are you injured?"

"No, only frightened," Circe said, but she found that her voice still trembled. She did not want to meet his eye. "I think—"

"Let me check on my groom," David told her. "Then I will see you home. Perhaps you should rest for—"

"David," Circe interrupted. "You don't understand, it was the same man!"

"Yes, I saw." David had turned the curricle carefully to get out of the traffic snarl they had unwittingly caused. The horses were held to a careful trot. "He must have hoped to find the money from—"

"No, no. I told him it was in the bank. There's something else he wants!"

He raised his brows, but by then they had arrived back in front of the bank. David gave her the reins to hold and jumped down to see about his servant. The man was sitting on the curb, holding his head, but after speaking to

David, he nodded and seemed able to take his place again behind the carriage.

David resumed his seat and directed their carriage back into the stream of vehicles, then could meet her worried gaze. This danger must be dealt with; any other troubling emotions would have to wait, Circe told herself.

"Now, what do you mean?"

"There's something else Luciana has not told us," Circe said, her tone grim. She had been feeling so sorry for the girl—"Some other treasure she must have in her keeping."

"Indeed?" David's brows rose. "Then I think we are due for another talk with your too-ingenious protégée."

When they reached the Sinclair town house, Circe bade David inspect her carefully and tuck in any stray locks, which he did with a lingering touch that made her pulse jump. But she could not risk her sister seeing her disheveled once again. She dusted her skirts and made sure her gown was neat before they entered the house. Psyche was nowhere to be seen, and they made their way to the schoolroom without meeting anyone but the footman who had opened the door. Circe pulled the bell rope and told the housemaid who appeared shortly after, "Please send Luciana to me."

The maid nodded and slipped out. Circe paced up and down, while David stood with folded arms. When the door to the schoolroom opened again, Luciana stood on the threshold. She took two steps inside, then hesitated, glancing at David's implacable expression.

"Signorina?"

Circe took a deep breath. "Luciana, something happened today when I took your valuables to the jeweler's shop to sell for you—there was another assault."

The young maid paled. "But you are allright, signorina? Oh, my jewelry—"

"No, it is safe. I have sold the jewelry as you wished, and the money is secure until you wish to send it to Piedmont. But the thief wants something more."

"No!" Luciana blurted, her face very white against the

dark of her hair, pulled neatly back into a small bun at the nape of her neck. "No, no, I do not . . ."

"Do not . . . ?" David prompted. He took a step forward, and Luciana stared up at him with widened eyes.

"I do not have it."

"Have what?" David took another step and thought for a moment that the girl would break and run. He walked around her and shut the door firmly, leaning against it. Luciana gave a little sob deep in her throat.

Circe looked almost as anguished as the Italian, but David was resolute that this time, they would have the whole truth. Circe had been put in danger enough—he could not allow it to continue.

"The thief seemed to think that you have something else in your possession, something even more valuable than your family jewelry."

Silence.

David spoke again. "Tell us what else you brought out of the kingdom of Piedmont, Luciana, that has set the whole Austrian Empire abuzz with rumors."

She shook her head, but her eyes were dark with emotion, and perhaps, thought David, guilt? "How can you say such a thing, signore? An innocent girl . . ."

"Sometimes the most innocent travelers make the best couriers," David suggested. Circe threw him a puzzled glance.

"But I—I—" Luciana fell silent again, twisting her apron between her fingers until the carefully ironed cotton was creased and wrinkled.

"Tell us, please. We will help you all that we can," Circe put in. "But you must be honest with us, Luciana."

Still, the girl was silent.

David took a deep breath. He would rather she had been open with them, but if they must . . . "Then we must search your room again," he said.

"No!" Luciana blurted, but her agitation only made David more certain about the necessity of their action.

"Come," he said, feeling judge and executioner at once

as the girl's gaze flew about the room as if searching for a way out. But when David opened the door, he put one hand on the girl's shoulder until all three were out of the room. He was taking no chances of Luciana bolting this time.

They climbed the servants' stair and made their way to the small room they had seen once before. David shut the door against any curious eyes. While the two women stood stiffly against the wall, he made a quick inventory of the small bedchamber. At first, he could see nothing at all that they had not seen already. The space under the floorboard was still there, but the only thing occupying the narrow space was the same padded cylinder, now silent when he shook it to check for any gems that Luciana might have been holding back.

Nothing. He dropped it back into the hollow. What were they missing? Then he sensed that Luciana had relaxed subtly when he turned away from the bed. He twisted back to check the bed linen once more. No, the wool blankets, the sheets, all were clean and neat but quite devoid of anything unusual. He went back to the loose floorboard beneath the rug and lifted it again. Nothing except the padded cylinder, which was empty of . . . the padded cylinder.

The back of his neck prickled, and he could almost feel the increased tension in the room as Luciana's panic returned. He took the cardboard cylinder into his hand and slid out the padding.

It was not simply folded cloth, as he had assumed, put there to muffle the sound of the jewelry. It was stiffer, canvas that had been carefully rolled, and it had the musty scent of very old fabric.

He heard Circe gasp as she realized what the cylinder had held, and Luciana gave a small groan. He unrolled it slowly upon the bed as the women watched. A stunned silence filled the little room, then Circe spoke, too loudly.

"How dare you!"

Fourteen

Circe rounded upon Luciana, and her expression must have been fierce, indeed, because the other girl cowered and turned her face away.

"How dare you treat such a painting so, stuffed into a tube like this, subjected to sea air and damage and, good Lord, what if the boat had sunk?"

"Here, now," David put in, not following this at all. "What's this got to do with—"

"But to take it away from Italy where—and how did you get it to start with? You must have stolen it! Oh, my God, I can't believe this, and I have helped you! How could you, Luciana?"

The girl burst into tears. Her mouth twisted, and she pulled her apron up to hide her face.

David stared at them both, his expression perplexed. Circe realized that he had no clue about what was going on.

"Circe?"

She tried to control herself, lowering her voice as she spoke again. They would have the whole household here if she were not more circumspect. "David, don't you know what this is?"

"A painting, obviously. Looks a bit antiquated." David

stared down as Circe touched its aged canvas with reverent fingers. "A couple of naked people, like those Greek fellows on some of the canvases in the British Museum. Didn't believe in clothes much, did they? Are you saying this is valuable?"

"Valuable? It's absolutely priceless! Look at the artwork, the typically Venetian use of color and free brushwork, the earthy and sensuous solidity of the figures. . . ."

She realized that David was lost again. "What I mean is," Circe said as patiently as she was able, "I believe this is one of Titian's works."

"Titian?"

"Oh, for pity's sake, he was a contemporary of Michelangelo and Raphael," Circe said, frowning. "One of the great artists of the Italian Renaissance."

"Oh, yes." David nodded, his expression clearing as if he finally connected the oil and canvas before him with names that even he recognized. "As important as that?"

"I don't know for sure who the figures are, but it looks similar to his *Bacchus and Ariadne;* he often used classical stories as a basis for his works. This must be worth—oh, I don't know, but it has to be invaluable. I can't believe we haven't heard that it is missing." Circe took a deep breath. "How is it that there has been no uproar about its theft?"

"I can explain that," David said. He nodded as if many things were becoming clear to him at last. With a glance at the near-hysterical maid, he pulled Circe aside and whispered into her ear. "They don't want to admit that it's been taken; it would be a scandal of prime proportions, you know, and a major embarrassment for the Empire if a small band of rebels in Piedmont were able to spirit away a prize such as this from beneath their noses. But this must be the source of the rumors my uncle has ferreted out—we did not know what it was about, that was all. The whole Austrian Empire is straining its resources to find the painting. And this chit"—his glance toward the still-sobbing Luciana was tinged with admiration, Circe was irked to see—"this girl did it all by herself?"

"Oh, no, she got it out of Europe with my help," Circe told him, her tone short and too loud. "I can't believe I was so duped. I thought Luciana was telling the truth—"

"I was, I was," the girl interrupted, her accent heavier than usual in her agitation. "I only wanted to save my parents. They are being held by the Austrians, and—"

Another thought struck Circe. "My instructor, Signor DuPree, is he imprisoned, too?" she demanded of Luciana.

The other girl shook her head. "No, signorina, he was able to get away before the agents arrived. He is in hiding, I think in France."

"Thank goodness for that, at least." Circe sighed. But Luciana watched with an anxious expression on her face.

"But my parents—if you take this away, I will never see them alive again. A little money is not enough. I had to have something truly valuable to trade for their lives." She sobbed once more, and this time her voice was overwhelmed by a torrent of tears that made Circe's anger fade.

If she could have saved her parents from their accidental death, would she have stolen, lied, used every connivance she could devise?

She had no doubt of the answer.

Her indignation waning, Circe walked closer and put her arms around Luciana. The girl's slender frame shook as if she wept for months of terror and grief. How much pain had she witnessed already, how much fear? The last of Circe's anger dissipated. Patting the girl on the back, Circe looked over at David.

He frowned. "We have to return this," he said. "You know we do, Circe."

Luciana's tears returned in full force, and her thin body shook.

Circe hugged her more tightly. "We do, of course, but

not just yet," she said. "Do you believe that the Austrian secret police are capable of murder?"

David hesitated, then nodded. "Yes, I'm afraid there is no doubt."

"Then we cannot abandon her parents to such a fate," Circe told him, hearing the firmness in her own voice. Luciana must have heard it, too, because the girl lifted her tear-streaked face. Her eyes were swollen and red. "Do you mean it, signorina? I will work for you the rest of my life, for nothing, I swear it!"

"We are not the secret police, and we will not trade abductees for slaves," Circe told the other girl. "All I want is for you to be reunited with your family, Luciana. We will see them safely to England, somehow. You have my word on it."

"Circe!" David raised his brows, but she met his gaze and did not flinch.

"We will," she repeated. "And then the painting will be returned—we cannot keep this hidden for very long. It must go back to its rightful owners, of course, and be preserved for future admirers of great art. But not just yet."

David groaned, but she ignored him, patting Luciana's back as the girl rubbed her damp face with an even damper handkerchief.

"All in good time," Circe said, adding, almost to herself. "We just have to figure out how."

David tried to argue with her, but he soon saw that Circe's stubborn streak had reasserted itself. They left Luciana in her room to compose herself. Circe took the painting away from the servant's room for safekeeping, but when they paused on the next landing, she refused to allow him to take charge of it. "If you give it to your uncle, he will send it back right away, don't you think?"

"He might," David admitted. "It shouldn't be in England at all. But, see here, Circe—"

"Then what will happen to Luciana's parents?" she demanded. "I will not allow them to be sacrificed just to avoid a diplomatic incident and to soothe the Austrian Empire's wounded pride!"

He thought that he had seldom seen her look so beautiful, with fire in her eyes as she defended two strangers she had never set eyes upon. But that was Circe, passionate about injustice, as stubborn as she was warmhearted. Luciana could not have chosen a more determined champion if she had looked over half of Europe.

It did not make his task any easier, however. David folded his arms, but Circe looked up at him, switching suddenly from defiance to earnest supplication. She put one hand on his arm, and he felt her touch run through his whole body, potent as strong wine. It was his turn to take a deep breath, trying to clear his head.

This was no sultry courtesan, teasing him with her practiced touch, this was Circe, sweet innocent little Circe. He must not forget that. But her eyes were big with entreaty, luminous with trust, and he hesitated.

"I have to tell him, Circe. He is counting on me."

"You will tell him, we will, but not just yet," Circe pleaded. "I need some time to think, please, David."

"I don't see how waiting will change anything."

"There has to be a way to do both, to return the painting and avoid an international scandal, but also to save Luciana's parents."

He saw the old pain that always lay beneath her surface calm, and he found that he couldn't say no to her. "Very well," he said slowly. "I will leave the painting in your charge. But you will make no disposition of it without consulting me first?"

"Of course not," Circe agreed.

"I have your word?"

"Absolutely." Her expression had lightened already, and David tried to push down his own guilt about deceiving his uncle, by omission if not commission.

"It has to go back, Circe," he was compelled to say again. "And soon. I believe this is the treasure that von Freistadt and his spies are seeking. Every day we wait is another opportunity for von Freistadt to find out where the painting is, and if the authorities discover we knew where it was and did not send it back—England doesn't need that kind of embarrassment."

"Von Freistadt?" Circe blinked. "Is that why he has been plaguing me? Oh, damn the man. I will most certainly not play into his hand; we will think of something," she repeated, her tone stubborn.

He knew that note from years past. He gave her a brief bow and then hurried out before he could regret leaving her with such a valuable hostage, for such it was, really.

How could they trade it for those other hostages, if Luciana was speaking the truth? David frowned, and he walked out of the house deep in thought.

After David took his leave, Circe took the painting to her bedchamber and locked it into a travel chest. Then she heard the clock chime from the landing below and realized she had little time to change before dinner and the theater engagement she had promised Psyche she would attend. She washed her face and tried to pin up her hair again, hesitating to ring for Luciana, but the girl must have also noticed the hour, because she hurried into the room, her face still red but looking more composed.

"Thank you a thousand times, signorina. You have been so kind!"

Circe sighed. She had no idea how she would resolve this tangle, but she would try her best. With Luciana's help, she changed her gown, then picked up her shawl and fan and hurried down to dinner, for once glad that they would leave directly after the last course. She did not want Psyche asking too many questions about her day.

The next afternoon, Sally returned to Sir John's home— this time by prior invitation—and he met her at the door. Right away she could tell that something was different; there was a sparkle in his eye and an animation to his features that she had never witnessed before. She thought it became him amazingly.

He pressed her hand, then led her into the big formal sitting room, and the footman brought tea. Sally poured for them, and they sipped and chatted, but although she encouraged Sir John to talk about his beloved flowers, his enthusiasm suddenly seemed to fade, and he sighed.

"What's wrong?" Sally put down her cup.

He stood and paced up and down, as she had noticed he did when he was agitated.

"You know the old adage about making a silk purse out of a sow's ear," he argued. "I don't believe that this is going to work. I think that we should simply agree—"

She laughed, surprising them both, and he paused and turned to regard her. His expression seemed startled and a little guarded, as if he suspected mockery from her as well.

She hastened to reassure him. "Sir John, that is ridiculous. You are not—by any flight of fancy—a pig part!"

He chuckled, too, this time, and she did not stop to think how absurd a statement that was. If she had made him laugh, it was worth tangling her metaphors. She rushed on, trying to explain. "You are a most gentle man, which is only to your credit, but you have strength, too, the deep strength of goodness and conviction, and I know it is there. I have always sensed it is there."

He gazed at her, and this time she could not read his expression at all. "Mrs. Forsyth, you do me more honor than you know. But I still think—"

"No, you must allow me the courtesy of winning this dispute," she told him, feeling more assured as she sensed his moment of discouragement abate. "I must not be disgraced as a tutor; we shall spend more time practicing your courtship, and the next time you attempt to spend time with Miss Hill, you will feel more assured. You were very smooth the other night, were you not?"

"Ah, I was thinking only of your—of both your comfort, dealing with that Austrian," Sir John confessed.

Sally felt her cheeks warm. What a dear man he was! "But you see, that only proves my point. With practice, you become more at ease."

He smiled, perhaps more rueful than convinced, but his air of hopelessness had faded. "I'm afraid I will never be anything but, if not the sow's ear, at least a very plain clump of moor grass, and nothing, not even your delightful tutoring, will change me into a delicate flower."

"Heaven forbid," she said before she thought. Sir John laughed again. "Even though your metaphors may be more apt than mine, I do not, by any stretch of the imagination, wish to turn you into a delicate flower!"

"I agree," he said, his hazel eyes almost merry. "I retract the statement entirely."

"Good," she said, glad to see that his mood had altered. She had been right to continue; all that was needed was the right friend to fortify his self-esteem and give him some practical advice. "Come and sit by me."

He hesitated, glancing around at the big empty room. Sally suddenly knew, intuitively, that the drawing room was the wrong setting. Not here, where a few days ago he had been outmaneuvered by a foe, where he felt out of place. Even though the chairs had been put away, the room was still too vivid a reminder of the horticultural salon. No, they needed to go to a room where he was at ease, comfortable, most himself.

"The conservatory," she said, inspired. "If you would kindly allow me another look at that beautiful place?"

"Of course," he said, his tone puzzled but also pleased. He offered his arm, and she tucked her gloved hand into its crook, delighted that this lesson was beginning so well. He opened the door, and a footman who seemed to be loitering in the hall straightened suddenly and pretended to dust a small table.

Sir John ignored the man, but Sally was aware of the servant's barely disguised curiosity. When they reached the conservatory, Sir John held the door for her and she swept inside, then paused, gazing at the rich array of plant life.

"Your servants will not interrupt us, will they?" she asked, doubtfully.

He shook his head. "They have orders never to disturb me while I am in the conservatory unless I specifically bid them enter." His tone was unusually firm, and Sally felt reassured. She did not wish to be caught with Sir John's lips on her wrists or throat or—She pulled her mind back from that path. No, no, they would certainly not go that far; why did such a thought come unbidden to her mind?

She allowed Sir John to escort her about the paths that lay between the heavy rows of plants until they came to the heart of the conservatory. An ornamental iron bench sat in the middle of a small open space, and lush flowers bloomed all around, a riot of color and scent that was quite intoxicating. Tall ferns shaded the more delicate blooms, and the potted plants were so dense she could not see the glass walls of the conservatory itself, though the golden light that slanted across the large open space above them revealed that the afternoon was fading to a close.

"What a beautiful spot." She seated herself on the bench. "Pray, do join me, Sir John."

He sat, but he looked suddenly tense, just as he had done when Circe had been present yesterday. Good, he was putting himself in the mood, imagining her to be Circe. He must get over this awkward shyness in order to put himself forward to best effect. How else would Circe ever see the sterling man who lay beneath the slightly awkward exterior?

Sally thought hard about how she should proceed. "Very well, I am a lady that you think you might have feelings for. You have brought me here to show me the splendors of your plants," she said. "It would be only natural for you to bring me one perfect blossom, yes?"

"Of course," he said, amusement glinting in his eyes. He stood, and after a short inspection, reached up to break off a small white flower. Bringing it back to where she waited, he sat beside her once more.

The flower was exquisite, slight yet graceful, its form perfectly symmetrical, one drop of moisture christening a velvety petal.

Sally slowly removed her gloves, stripping them off one by one. It was only natural to want to touch the flower, relish the soft downiness of its surface.

"It's so beautiful," she said, almost whispering. "What is it? I am not familiar with the plant."

"An orchid from South America," he told her, his tone also hushed. "It lives off the air itself. Brought here by a sea captain who knows that I love unusual varieties of plants."

She gazed at it, not just at the flower but the care with which he held it. What a gentle person he was, how perceptive, how easily moved. Sally found that she had to blink back the tears swelling in her eyes.

"Did I say something to distress you?" he said at once, his tone concerned.

Sally blinked again and touched his hand. The flower quivered for a moment, and she knew she should have restrained herself. But the feel of his hand made her shiver, and she had to disguise her reaction with a slight nervous laugh. Gracious, now she was the one who felt like a schoolgirl!

"Sometimes," she said, trying to make the moment less intense, "sometimes it is good to surprise your companion. Touch is a form of communication in itself. Just as we instinctively wish to stroke the soft petal of a flower, reaching out to someone we care for—" she found that her voice had gone husky, and she had to clear her throat—"is—is a natural reaction and should not be restrained. Within the bounds of propriety . . ."

She paused again; her thoughts were harder and harder

to keep in check. Instead of falling in line like a disciplined team of horses, they were racing about like excited cattle. She tried to think what she had meant to say.

Sir John gazed at her small hand as if he had never seen it before. Touching his bare skin sent shivers of delight through her. Oh, dear, oh, dear. She would disgust him and he would think—Sally drew back her hand, but he reached to take it, dropping the blossom into her lap as if he had forgotten its existence.

"No, no, I mean, I agree," he told her, and his voice, too, seemed not quite normal. He cleared his throat, flushing just a little, but he still gripped her fingers. And without a glove, too. Oh, folly.

Did he sense the thrill of sensation that traveled through her, coursing over her body like a wave of hot air? In fact, Sir John kept this conservatory much too warm, Sally thought wildly. Perhaps the plants need it, but just now, she found that she was breathing much too quickly.

He seemed affected, too. "Then, it seems to me, Mrs. Forsyth—"

"I believe you should call me Sally," she interrupted, "for the purpose of our pretense, I mean."

"Yes," he agreed. He shifted a little closer and put one hand around the back of her shoulders. "Then it seems to me, Sally . . ."

Her name had never sounded so sweet, and she had almost forgotten how lovely it felt to have a man's hand on her back. Not just any man, of course, not the bumbling Mr. Elliston, not any of the gallants who had tried to become too intimate with her since the death of her husband, but a special man, a man who moved her heart and stirred her blood like—

This was madness, she must not think of such—but his arm moved to pull her even closer, and she found that she could not think at all. His fingers were smooth against the bare skin of her back above the neckline of her gown, and she leaned her head onto his shoulder.

Just for one moment, to pretend again that she was

loved, to enjoy the physical closeness and emotional intimacy blended into that perfect harmony, which offered love's greatest bounty. Oh, God, she had missed it, missed it all.

Sir John put his hand against her cheek, stroking the skin, and she heard him murmur, "Oh, Sally. I thought of you last night. . . ."

It seemed like the purest poetry, much more lyrical than the best of Mr. Elliston's silly verses. She opened her suddenly damp eyes and smiled up at him. It seemed only natural that Sir John should lower his head and touch his lips to hers.

The shock of that contact stirred long-dormant desire inside her; she clung to him, returning his kiss with a fervor that seemed to surprise him. Sir John hesitated only a moment, then his kiss became firmer, more demanding, and she gave herself to his demands with delighted abandon. She had never been a prim miss, often bringing down upon herself the censure of her prudish aunts when she had danced too gaily, laughed too loudly, smiled too often.

But true passion had never been placed quite within her grasp. Even her sweet Andrew, her late husband, had been a considerate but not exuberant lover. She had never lain with a man her own age, much less one younger. . . . There was something about that thought that she knew should hold her back, but coherent thought was fleeing with every second that Sir John's kiss lingered. And now he was kissing her neck, and the soft expanse of breast that lay above her gown, pushing her neckline lower to taste the forbidden swells of her breast, the dusky areola, which ached for his mouth upon it.

He pushed harder against the dress's neckline and she felt a hook snap and the gown slip lower, in earnest. As if startled, he pulled back, but she lifted her hands and touched his face, caressing it, holding it, pulling him back gently to her. Without a word, she smiled into his eyes and told him what she wished.

Sir John kissed her again, his embrace tightened, and he pushed the dress down, and the thin linen chemise after it, till he could caress the soft rounded curves of her breasts, slip his mouth over their peaks, delighting her with an intensity of feeling that left her moaning and calling his name.

"Oh, John," she whispered. "Yes, my love."

"My dearest," he said, "Dearest Sally, sweet as the most fragrant rose . . ." Then his lips were again pressed against the fullness of her breast, and Sally forgot her renewed delight in hearing her Christian name on his lips. Sensation ran through her like warm water pouring over her skin, and she shivered and pulled him even closer.

Somehow they had slipped off the hard bench and were lying on the softer floor of the conservatory, where wood chips cushioned their bodies and held them as if in some sylvan nest. Around them, the bright reds and pinks and purples of the flowers blended together into a rainbow of sensation, almost as vivid as the emotions that throbbed through her body, too long hungry for a man's touch.

Now he had tugged her gown totally down to her feet, and he put one hand lightly on her thighs. She moved instinctively, and his hand slipped into the right place, the deep secret place where ecstasy waited. Sally moaned softly, and he made a soft hungry sound of his own.

Then he pulled away, and before she could protest, she saw from eyes glazed with desire that he was stripping off his tight pantaloons. Already she could see his own desire obvious through the thin cloth. His neckcloth and jacket and other apparel followed, then he sank down again to press his hard, male body against hers. She pressed forward to meet him, delighting in the firmness of his torso, the hardness of his legs and arms, the muscles built up by years of lifting heavy earth and plants. . . . She should thank his devotion to his art, she thought, bubbling with secret laughter.

Then he positioned himself above her and she felt him hesitate, for an instant, then push inside her. She was ripe, ready for his jointure, and the sensation that rippled through her whole body made her call out, once, then she tried to stifle her instinctive cries of joy.

John kissed her heartily, then lifted his head to concentrate on the rhythmic pace of their union. He needed no instruction in this, she was delighted to see, and his careful timing made her passion surge with his, as she matched him wave for wave of sensation, of passion, of joy both physical and emotional. He was as strong and sure as she had always known he could be. . . .

Thought melted into a symphony of sensation, the flowers' heavy scent, the rainbow of colors backed by lush greenery, the rosy rays of light that spoke of sunset. All were only a glorious backdrop to the swirling pleasures of his touch, the rhythmic ecstasy of their coupling, which led her to higher and higher peaks of delight until she could no longer keep silent, but called out each time he surged deeper and deeper inside her. Her spirit soared to the very apex of perfection.

When at last she cried out in total release, he covered her lips with his and kissed her to smother the sound. She returned his kiss with all the exhausted fervor inside her, and then he rolled her to her side so they could lie, legs still entwined, her head cushioned on his shoulder, still in perfect harmony and, at least for Sally, unalloyed happiness.

After a few minutes, John's breathing slowed and his eyes closed, but Sally stared up at the last waning light of a smoky London sunset. The glory of their lovemaking faded slowly; she would never lose it entirely, she thought. It had been too incredibly perfect. But reality began to intrude, as much as she tried to push it back.

This had been the most marvelous day of her entire existence.

And she had made her biggest and most unforgivable mistake.

Fifteen

*T*he next day, as usual, David went to check on the chestnut vendor's son. Just after sunset, David made his way to the pub where he met his young spy and found Timothy devouring a large meat pie.

" 'E said you would pay for it," the stout barmaid be hind the counter said. Her belligerence was mostly assumed; in truth she was clearly a soft touch, for the youngster had already talked her into extending credit.

"And so I will," David agreed, tossing the woman a coin. "What happened to the blunt I gave you earlier in the week?" David asked the boy.

Timothy shrugged. "Me dad took it off me," he said with more resignation than anger. "And I got 'ungry, 'anging around the square all day."

"Not now," David warned. Timothy obligingly filled his mouth with pie, and David called for a mug of ale and some cider for the boy. After the barmaid brought the heavy mugs, she turned to tend to other customers, and David retired with the stripling to a quiet table in the corner, walking around two men, stable lads, judging by their leather aprons and faint smell of horses, drinking at a table nearby.

"Anything interesting today?" he asked young Timothy when they were seated again.

"Naw," the boy said, biting into the remnants of the pie. " 'Cept the tailor sent over the count's latest order."

"I don't suppose you know what that was?" David asked, idly.

The boy surprised him, as he often did. "Aye, two heavy pairs of trousers, one new riding coat, and a wool cape," the boy said, licking the last bit of grease off his fingers. "I 'eard the tailor griping to the butler about the bills 'at ain't been paid yet."

"Good work, lad." Impressed, David pulled another coin from his pocket.

The boy scooped it up.

"That sounds to me as if a journey is imminent; I wonder if he fancies his prize is almost within reach," David said more to himself than to the boy.

"Dunno, grumpy he is," Timothy commented. "He's been after the servants right and left; I 'eard the stable boy talking to the second footman."

"Then perhaps his superiors are getting impatient." David grinned a little; it was almost worth holding on to the painting if it caused problems for the arrogant Austrian.

David gave the boy a few last instructions and rose from the table. Reaching into his pocket, he handed over a healthy amount of blunt. Timothy scooped up the money and grinned his thanks.

Smiling, David said, "Keep that well hidden so that your father can't commandeer it, Timothy. There's no sense in punishing the son for the father's . . ." David faltered, as the words seemed to echo in his own heart. "Sins," he finished weakly.

Leaving the inn, he walked back to his own home. He had been trying so hard to break the pattern, to escape the drunken and senseless debauchery that had marked his father's inglorious career. Could it be that Circe was right, that he had gone too far in the other direction?

He tensed as he entered the large front door and handed

his hat and gloves to the footman. Automatically, he waited for the piercing tone, the commanding words.

"David, is that you? Come up at once!"

"Yes, Mother," he said, and with an effort managed not to grit his teeth. If at any time he was tempted to lower his guard against the thought of imminent matrimony, an hour with his mother was enough to remind him . . . of the loud arguments, the broken china, the shouted insults that had marked the infrequent episodes when his mother and father had actually been in the same room together.

No, he would have to marry someday, but not now, not for some years yet. And when he did, he would be forced to choose a very proper lady, one who would never remotely resemble his mother or imitate her habit of leaning out an upper window and shouting angrily into the street when his father stumbled off for another round of drinking or gaming or whoring. Once she had slashed all his father's undergarments and hung the tattered cloths on the trees in the square. . . .

David shuddered. He had been ten years old, and on holiday from school. Some holiday that had been.

Better a lonely life than the kind of imbroglio which a bad marriage could entail. And although he had witnessed the occasional miracle, a union such as the one between Gabriel and Psyche, his only hope of achieving anything like his friend's happiness was to choose a well-bred lady who was the antithesis of his mother, one who was proper, decorous, conventional in every way.

And this did not describe Circe, as much as she stirred his blood and, of late, seemed too often to monopolize his thoughts.

"David? I'm waiting, dear boy."

Sighing, he braced his shoulders and ascended the steps slowly, prepared for the daily interrogation.

❧

That night there was a theater party planned, but Psyche felt unwell, and it was obvious that Gabriel really wanted to stay with his wife, though he offered to escort Circe and Sally to the theater as planned.

Circe looked from one to the other as Gabriel held his wife's hand tenderly, kissing the slender wrist with such love that it made Circe ache inside, wishing for that look from a lover of her own, someone she could trust so implicitly. Psyche gazed up at her husband with her whole heart in her glance, then groaned and turned her head again as a wave of nausea threatened to overcome her.

Circe said, "Oh, poor Psyche! Is there anything I can do?"

Her sister started to shake her head, then had to stop, the motion obviously not what she needed just now. She was very pale. "Go on to the theater and have a good time, both of you."

Gabriel's expression was determined. "Yes, I will see to Circe," he agreed. "Do not worry, my love."

"I would rather stay in tonight," Circe said. "Really."

Gabriel's aspect brightened despite his best efforts, but he offered a civil protest. "I will be happy to escort you and Sally."

"I would prefer to stay home, truly I would. I will send a note to Sally; she won't mind being free to make her own plans for once, and then you can stay with Psyche."

"Are you sure, Circe?" her sister demanded, her handkerchief still at her lips. "I do not mean to limit your amusement."

"And what a terrible thing that would be, to lose an evening of frivolity over such a minor object as the health of my sister and my soon-to-be niece or nephew?" Circe answered, her tone gently mocking. "No, I'd like to. It has been a fatiguing week."

"Very well," Psyche said. "Be sure to let Sally know."

"I will," Circe agreed. She slipped out of the room, leaving Psyche and Gabriel still holding hands, with a look passing between them that must surely alleviate some of her sister's distress.

To have such love around you, every day, every night . . . to have a husband who was willing, eager to *be* a husband . . . Circe sighed and walked down the hall to her own chamber. She sat down at her small desk and penned a short note to Sally, explaining the change of plans. Then she pulled the bell rope and summoned a housemaid, bidding her give the note to a footman to deliver.

Then the whole evening stretched ahead of her. The darkness that had fallen outside made it too dim inside, candles or not, to paint, but she could read or sketch or just . . . she knew what she really wanted to do. Circe rose and went to her travel chest, unlocking it and reaching inside to pull out the carefully rolled canvas.

She wanted to feast her eyes upon the painting again, admire the classical figures, the artwork, the genius that had inspired such a work. Would she ever produce something even a tenth as splendid?

It didn't matter, as long as she had the opportunity to spend her life trying. This was better than stubborn men who would not acknowledge affections that lay beneath their own noses. This was safer than risking a problematic marriage, which could alter or deter the goals she had dreamed of since childhood. She spread the piece of art across her bed and, sinking down into a chair, lost herself in its magnificence.

⁂

David slept only in snatches, dreading the morning's interview with his uncle. He woke when the first flush of light pooled over the trees in the square. The darkness in his bedchamber lightened, also; he had not pulled his drapes shut since he knew he planned to rise early. Blinking as he pulled himself out of a chaotic dream, he tried to locate the source of the unease that hung over him, then grimaced as he remembered.

Circe. His uncle. The painting.

Damn it all, he had hoped to go to his uncle in triumph, having found the missing object that was causing such an intense, if undercover, diplomatic fervor. David could have demonstrated to his uncle that the man's faith in David had not been misplaced. He wanted to do that, wanted badly to take the painting and hand it over and receive his accolades. He sat up and reached for his dressing gown, glancing toward the rosy sky outside his window.

But how could he be so selfish? He could never blame Circe for her soft heart. She knew the pain of losing two beloved parents. David had never had parents such as that, ones who offered love and support and comfort . . . how could he understand? No, in a way, he did; the difficult years of his childhood were easy enough to recall, though he tried to blot out those memories. If he had had a mother who was kind and a father who was dependable, he would have felt the same way.

So how could he blame Circe, and how could he condemn Luciana to such a loss? Luciana wished to save her parents. Were her hopes based in reality? He wasn't at all sure; Luciana's parents could be already dead. Tyrants and their instruments of torture seldom played fair.

Yet he worried about Circe's safety, and Psyche's and Gabriel's and the rest of their household. If von Freistadt put two and two together and realized that it was Circe who now had the painting . . . he obviously had suspicions already. The man was bold and arrogant to a fault; David had no doubt he was behind the earlier break-in at Gabriel and Psyche's town house, and what the count would do if he were sure of the location of the object he sought— they had to resolve this dilemma, and soon.

David dressed quickly and was sipping a cup of tea when a footman brought in a note sealed with his uncle's signet ring. David opened it quickly and scanned the few lines inside. His uncle had been called into the Foreign Office early, and their meeting would have to be postponed. David felt a surge of relief; he would not have to prevaricate then or, at least, stall for time.

David decided to return to speak to Circe; they must act quickly, though he was damned if he knew the way out of this mess. When he reached the Sinclair residence, he was still frowning, and the footman who admitted him did not seem disposed to argue about his early arrival. David suspected the whole household had become accustomed to the unconventional times of his comings and goings.

"Lord Gabriel is out, my lord," the servant told him. "And Lady Gabriel is still abed. Miss Circe has not yet come down, either." The man's tone was more resigned than censorious.

"She's probably in the schoolroom, painting," David suggested, giving up his hat and gloves. "I'll run up and see."

He climbed the stairs easily and continued past the sitting room, past the level with the family bedchambers, onto the landing that led to the schoolroom. But to his surprise, when he knocked on the door and then pushed it open, the room was empty. He looked around, noting absently the large scratched table where he had sipped tea with Circe, the empty rocking chair in the corner where Telly, when she was in residence, always rocked and knit and dozed.

Had Circe gone out? No, surely the footman would have known. Though perhaps if she had slipped out for an early-morning walk, no one would have seen her.

But where would Circe have wanted to go so urgently that she would have given up the best light of the day? She would never put aside her painting for a simple errand, or even for a sudden urge for fresh air. No, he didn't believe it.

He came back to the landing and hesitated, a little worried. Then he caught a whiff of a familiar scent—oil paint and the sharper odor of turpentine. Grinning, he turned and went up the narrow steps instead of down. He climbed two flights, past the servants' rooms; he must be at the attic level now; the roof was slanting above his head and the stairs were narrow and cramped. Yes, there was a door, firmly shut. He turned the handle, but it didn't budge. Locked.

Perhaps he had been wrong. . . . No, Circe would tell him to trust his instincts. David knocked lightly at the door, then waited, and in a moment, he heard soft footsteps inside and the rustle of skirts.

"Who is it?"

"It's me, David. Circe, what are you doing?"

She opened the door just a crack and peered out at him; she had a smear of ocher on the tip of her nose. "What do you want?"

"To see you. What on earth are you up to, hidden away up here?"

She opened the door somewhat reluctantly, he thought, and allowed him to enter the small attic room, though she locked the door again behind them.

"Why are you being so secretive?"

"You told me no one must know that I had the painting," Circe reminded him, lifting her brows. "It's not that I don't trust our servants, mind you, but you were so emphatic about it that I thought I should be extra careful."

David gazed about him. It was not as dark as he would have expected an attic to be; a window at the east end of the house let in the early light, which shone upon the easel set up nearby. And a few feet away, he saw, carefully held in place by a gilt frame—

"The Titian? I had more in mind that you would lock it away somewhere secure."

Circe looked guilty. "I did, at first. But it's a crime to shut such a beautiful painting out of sight. And besides, as long as I had it, I thought I might as well take advantage of the opportunity to practice a master's techniques."

David crossed the dusty bare floorboards so that he could see what the fresh canvas held, and saw that she had begun a copy. Circe's canvas showed only the out-

lines of two figures, but he could see that she was following the example of the older painting.

"It's what art students do, you know, imitate more accomplished painters to learn technique. Sir Joshua Reynolds said that students must view the works of great
masters as 'perfect and infallible guides.' I've rarely had
the good fortune to study such a masterpiece at close
range. I couldn't pass up the chance."

He nodded slowly, though something in his expression
must have worried her.

"What?" she asked, studying his face.

He could never hide anything from Circe. "It's just, this
man is—well, quite naked, Circe."

She smiled in genuine amusement. "That troubles
you?"

"What troubles me is that it doesn't trouble you!" he
retorted, rubbing his hand along the edge of her canvas.

"Careful, that isn't dry," she said. "Why should a naked
man reduce me to anxious hysterics?"

"Circe, for pity's sake," he exploded. "You're unmarried."

"And likely to remain so," she agreed, her voice calm.
"But I'm also an artist. Do you think I could paint a convincing portrait if I had no idea of the anatomy of a fellow
human, whether male or female?"

"Anatomy is one thing," he argued, knowing this was
a waste of time. "But such personal—I mean—"

This time she did look peeved. Frowning, Circe put
down her brush. "I don't think 'personal' is the right term,
David. It's not like I have a naked man in front of me."

"I should bloody well hope not!" David exclaimed.

"Though the models we had in my art class—"

David swore; he couldn't help it. "Are you telling me
that you had real men, unclothed men, standing in front
of you?"

This time she grinned, quite unrepentant. "Don't you
remember the conversation at my coming-out ball, where

you rescued me from my own rash tongue and a group of censorious matrons?"

"Forget it, no. But I didn't quite believe you," he admitted, looking from her clear-eyed gaze back to the painting, with those unapologetic gamboling pagans wearing only a few wispy strands of mist to cover their, well, those regions that should be quite unknown to maiden sensibilities.

Circe raised her brows. "The human body is a beautiful thing, David. Don't you think so?"

It was hard to converse with little Circe about such a topic. Yes, he knew she was no child any longer, but she was hardly a woman of the world just yet. At least, she'd better not be! David felt the usual mixture of irritation and suppressed desire that she elicited in him all too often.

She watched him through eyes that held a devilish glint. "David, darling, surely you have seen naked people before?"

"Very amusing, Circe. What I have done is not the point," he said, hearing the exasperation in his own voice. "The point is—"

"I know, you told me not to discuss such a topic in public, and I have remembered your advice. But surely I can be candid with you?"

Her gaze was so open; how could he possibly explain? David ran one hand through his dark hair. As the silence stretched, her green eyes widened.

"Are you saying that you do not wish me to be honest?" She sounded hurt, and he couldn't bear that, either.

"I'm only looking out for your welfare, Circe," David tried to tell her. "It's just not seemly that you should be so at ease with naked bodies. And if you say as much to me, you might forget and—"

"I am no fool," Circe told him, and this time she looked away, as if withdrawing inside herself. "If I have learned anything from my first Season, it's to know when to hold my tongue!" She picked up the brush she had left on the small table near her painting. He saw her take a deep breath, as if reassured by the brush in her hand.

"I never said you were a fool," he argued. "Only—"

"And why you should think that I must be as abashed as a timid miss who has never left the schoolroom, shocked by the sight of a couple of unclothed bodies— well, really, David. How do you think I could ever pursue my painting with that kind of provincial attitude?"

The fact that her logic made perfect sense was not the issue; his increasing annoyance at the coolness of her tone and her perfect control made him rise too readily to the bait.

"I suppose that if I pulled off my clothing, you wouldn't blink an eye?" he snapped, feeling compelled to ruffle her unnatural composure by fair means or foul.

She stared at her canvas as if achieving the proper brush stroke alone occupied her attention. "I did say once that I would love to paint you, did I not?"

The challenge she threw back at him took his breath with its audacity. Did the chit seriously propose—David found his ready temper rising past the point of no return. "Perhaps I should accede to your wishes, then," he suggested. He shrugged himself out of his close-fitting blue coat and tossed it toward a wooden chair with a broken slat in its back.

"As you like," Circe said, not looking up. She would not act like some missish schoolgirl, just to satisfy David's obsession with propriety! If David thought to unnerve her by such childish pranks, he would see she was made of sterner stuff.

David pulled at his carefully tied white stock till the long neckcloth unwound in his hand. "I would not wish to put any obstacles in the path of your study of the human body," he said with heavy sarcasm.

Circe concentrated on her palette, but she found that the colors on her board seemed to run together. Surely he would not go through with it!

His shirt came next, pulled off with such force that she heard a seam rip. Circe found it hard to breathe; she glanced at him from the corner of her eye, then tried to focus on the Titian. She wished she knew its name. She wished she knew David's game. If she commented on the well-muscled upper arm she could now covertly admire, would he go all scolding and proper again? Heavens, he was beautifully made! He was also naked now from the waist up. He put her canvas models to shame, there was no doubt of it.

The figures Titian had portrayed were fleshy and round compared to David's hard, muscled body. His shoulders were so wide she suspected her arms would not completely wrap around him. Her eyes dropped to stomach muscles that were taut and tightly ridged. Intriguingly, his chest held a sprinkling of dark hair. She found herself wishing to touch it, and stroke the flat, copper-hued nipples that nestled there.

She was an artist, yes, but she was also a woman. If David's body moved her in a way no model's ever had ... No, his only motive seemed to taunt her; this was no time to admit her attraction. She did not wish to be rejected once again.

And she would certainly not blush or simper, since that was what he wished, that she should look distressed by his boldness. She was no witless ninny! If she could not be a woman with David, she was still an artist, and she would show him how calm and disinterested she could be. He did not have to know how fast her heart was beating. . . .

She put down the brush—she had been clutching it much too tightly—and picked up her sketch pad and charcoal. "Since you wish to model for me, I shall not squander the opportunity." She forced her tone to remain cool.

She kept her expression grave with an effort, pleased to see that he was now the one to draw a deep breath. Had he seriously thought she would run screaming from the room, like some silly twit who knew only the boring rules of London's elite?

David bit back an oath; she was going to do it, the little

devil! She was seriously going to sketch him, and he now wore nothing but his trousers and underclothes, and his shoes, of course. He bent to pull off his shoes and tossed them aside. Fine, in for a farthing, in for a crown. He had never quelled before a challenge, though this hardly compared to horse races across a windy heath or silly drinking contests between two striplings newly on the town.

"Shall I remove these, too?" God, it was hard to stand still and pretend indifference as she came closer. He could smell the hint of apple blossom beneath the surface aroma of paint and turpentine, and as her hand moved across the pad, he gazed at her face. She kept her eyes focused on the paper in her hands, but he could see how she breathed too quickly—ha, so she was not totally calm, he told himself, trying to ignore the fact that he was also finding it hard to control his breath.

He saw a heavy strand of brown hair that had escaped the severe twist at the back of her head. In these last few weeks, she too often pulled her hair back, but he remembered the first time he had seen her, painting then, too, after her return to England. Her thick hair had been a glorious affair, wild and tumbled. He had liked it, he realized, that was the real Circe, genuine, free, honest to a fault. Who would wish to change her into a simpering society miss mouthing empty phrases? Why were they— why was anyone trying to change her?

Why was he provoking her with such juvenile taunts, such mad posturing? He must have lost his mind.

"Circe," he said, speaking to her this time without a hint of provocation, only his naked longing coloring his voice. "Circe, I must tell you—"

And then he paused. What could he say?

Circe heard the difference in his tone, and his apparent sincerity almost melted the control she maintained with such effort. He paused, and she felt an urgent need to hear the rest of his sentence.

"What?" she said, lowering her pad and tucking it into the large pocket on the front of her smock. Making her first great mistake, she looked up and met his gaze. Smoky blue-gray eyes looked into clear green ones.

She realized how close together they stood. She could see the faintest sheen of perspiration on his upper lip. Strange, it was not overwarm in the attic, especially not for him in his present unclothed condition, the artist part of her mind said. But that part of her thoughts, Circe realized, was retreating further and further away.

She was fully aware of his body, its exquisite hollows and curves, the firmness of his arms and upper chest, the enticing line of his hard belly. . . . She had sketched men before, almost nude men, but they had seldom been so delightfully shaped. And she had never touched a model's skin, discovered if those ridges of muscle felt as she imagined they would.

Circe put out her hand. She touched his chest very lightly, but David sucked in air as sharply as if she had struck him. Circe hesitated, pulling her hand away. "Did I hurt you?"

God, she had no idea what her touch did to him, David thought. Though if she looked further down, the effect would be all too obvious. She was such an unusual mixture of openness and innocence that he felt at a loss. He had no experience with anyone like Circe. . . . What was he thinking? This could not continue, he could not even dream of it going further.

But she ran her fingers very lightly across his chest, and he shivered. She looked up at him, still concerned, but he shook his head.

He had to clear his throat before he could speak, keeping his tone gentle and unalarming. "You do not hurt me," he said, "but you most certainly affect me."

"So it seems," she murmured.

The minx! She had indeed observed the changes in his body; how could he think she would not?

"Should I stop?" she went on, her voice very low.

"Yes," he said, hearing how husky his own voice had

become. "Yes, you must absolutely stop, at once."

But he made no move to put aside her hand, and she continued to stroke him lightly across his chest and upper arms, his shoulders, his neck, as if memorizing through her touch the contours of his body.

A lowering thought struck him; was this only for her artistic education? Did she wish to know more about how a male body was shaped, for the sake of her painting and its accuracy?

No, he didn't believe she was unaffected. Her softly flushed cheeks and quickened breath showed him that she, too, could not avoid taking this encounter personally.

Thank God. He put his hand on top of hers, holding it immobile on his chest. He had to end this madness, now.

"Enough, Circe," he told her. "I think you have more than ample resources for your next painting."

She looked up, startled at his words, then shook her head. "I wasn't thinking of my painting," she said, her tone as low as his own.

The answer sent waves of longing through him.

"You weren't?" And before he realized just what a precipitous step he was taking, he bent to touch her lips.

The memory of their brief kisses had lain in the back of his mind, tempting him often. At last he was able to repeat them, measure the depth of their charm. But it was all true what he had recalled, her mouth was as sweet as he remembered, her lips as smooth, luscious as a peach newly ripened. Of all the women he had kissed, trifled with, acted the fool over, nothing came close to the anticipation he felt at this moment. Circe was intoxicating, one simple kiss leaving him as exhilarated as the best champagne. Skillfully, he separated her lips and reveled in her receptive warmth.

Circe did not move away, did not draw back in alarm. Instead, she formed her lips to his. Desire lanced through him as she returned his embrace without the slightest hint of coquetry. She rose to her tiptoes to press against him, and her dawning passion was both honest and endearing. David had never admired her more.

Oh, Circe, he thought, and for her sake, he tried to break their kiss. But she followed his movement of retreat, putting her arms about his neck and drawing him back.

"Circe, we can't," he mumbled against her smooth mouth, but she ignored his protest. "You are—you are a maiden, and it would be your ruin—"

"Hush," she whispered, and he saw in the pale attic light that her eyes were clear and unafraid. "I will never be a normal marriageable miss, David, you know that. If I cannot have marriage, surely I can at least taste the delights of passion—with a man I choose freely. I've waited my whole life for this, to touch your lips, to lie in your arms. We can't stop now! I want you to teach me, please, David."

Did she have any idea what she was saying? She couldn't, she—David felt her hand slide down his chest and into the forbidden area of his trousers, where his body was already rigid and aching with need. His whole body arched with the shock of her touch.

"I always wondered what a man was like, when he was full of desire," she whispered. "Our models never looked like this."

"Circe, tell me again you aren't doing this just to learn more about your precious anatomy." Then he saw the laughter in her eyes and the curve of her lips and knew that she was gulling him, teasing him with his preconceived notions. Circe would never be anything but honest. And he saw her smile up at him, now, calm and unafraid, waiting.

It was wrong, he knew it was wrong, and he mustn't—but her touch made the sane, cautionary reflections vanish into the mists that seemed more and more to cloud his brain. He pulled her against him, forming his whole body against her slim shape, feeling the softness of her curves incite his senses even further.

He tugged the smock over her head and tossed it aside, then unfastened her bodice and pushed the rounded neckline of her muslin gown off the edge of her shoulders, allowing himself the luxury of tracing the line of her neck, moving his hand slowly over the slender lines of her shoulder, down, down, as she gasped, until he could stroke the smooth hollow between her breasts. She was not the only one who had had dreams, dreams of feeling satiny skin now open to his touch.

He swallowed a sudden desire to laugh with pure delight. She had indeed grown a bosom during her sojourn on the Continent, small but well shaped, lovely swelling curves that quivered beneath his hand. If this was what French and Italian cuisine conferred, every young girl should go abroad.

She met his eyes and lifted her slender brows in inquiry. He shook his head, "Later," he murmured, and then he dropped his head to kiss the curves he had just caressed.

He heard Circe take a deep breath. Then he moved the bodice lower until he could gently kiss a rosy nipple and then cover it with his mouth. Circe jerked in shock.

Good, she had not conceived of that, at least. He continued his caresses till she moaned and pressed even more closely against him. Again he hesitated; they were at the point of no return, and he knew better than Circe what social downfall this could entail for a young woman of good birth. It behooved him to be the saner partner, to pull back, to—

She touched him again, there, and he thought he might lose all control. Without a doubt, his powers of conscious reflection were slipping away. There seemed nothing to do but to free her from the confines of her clinging dress and thin shift, then lay her gently back against the bare dusty floorboards. With worshiping hands, he stroked the long lines of her legs, from the tips of her dainty toes to the lean length of her thighs. He dipped his head down and pressed hot kisses up the same path that his fingers had just taken. She was every bit as exquisite as he knew she would be.

Circe gazed up at him with eyes glistening with eagerness and something else—something he couldn't identify, not now. He shed his trousers and underclothes and dropped to lie beside her on the cool wood floor.

She reached for him, pulling him closer as if she had some instinctive knowledge of how pleasingly their bodies could fit together.

"Circe, are you sure—"

She covered his moment of indecision with her mouth, her sweet lips and questing tongue, and all thought fled. He only knew, at some deep level of instinct and emotion, that this was right, this was more than right, this was fate, this was his most profound and fervent desire. . . .

He moved his own hand down, too, running his fingers lightly over her taut, smooth belly till he touched the curly soft hair. Circe moved beneath his hand, her first startled stir of surprise turning quickly into a sensuous wave of appreciation. The natural way her body moved beneath his—God, he could barely hold himself back.

She never quelled, Circe, his Circe, dear and innocent and wise beyond her years. He could only try to give her the best, the deepest delight, the highest ecstasy. . . .

David bent his head to kiss her once more, then poised himself over her. "Be easy," he whispered. "It might hurt for a moment, but it should be only a little pain."

She nodded, her eyes still eager, her lips smiling. He thought she was sweetness itself.

He pushed himself inside her; the resistance of her body seemed slight. Circe stiffened for a moment, then relaxed against him once more.

He began to move, gently at first, then with stronger force. He found Circe adapting quickly to his rhythm, pushing back against him with instinctive pacing that only heightened his desire.

Circe felt as if she could barely breathe. Such sensations, no one had ever told her she could feel sensations such as this. The cold lines of lovers entwined, which she had sometimes drawn upon her sketch pad, the soft colors of the painting itself, they were light and shadow and delicate hue, but they were only for the eye.

This was more, the feelings of pleasure so intense that they were almost impossible to contain, the intensity that grew inside her belly and rose up, up to consume her from head to toe. She had never imagined such scathing heat and icy cold that immersed her as David pushed closer and closer to the apex of desire. She gasped and moved with him, rising toward a completion she could not envisage, had never experienced, yet which her body longed for with its own instinctive wisdom.

When they touched the heights together, David unexpectedly withdrew and slipped his fingers into the sudden emptiness of her body, massaging her almost unbearably sensitive flesh and maintaining her cresting passion. Circe reached for him and clasped his damp body to hers.

She'd lost all knowledge of the bare dusty attic, forgotten even the masterpiece of art that watched them with mute irony just a few feet away. This was real, this was genuine, and suddenly even the most masterful depiction was only a pale reflection of the glory she experienced. The waves of delight that ran through her, the melting joy that seemed to pull her into a whirlpool of repletion, it was all totally unknown and yet it felt as right and wonderful as the most familiar ritual.

Dear God, what wonders he had saved for men and women to create together!

She gasped for breath, feeling weak as a newborn babe. She felt newly made, newly created with fresh insights that had up to now been closed to her. What if she had lived her whole life and never known this joy? What a tragedy that would have been.

What if she had never joined with David? He had been the object of her first schoolgirl adoration, and she had never found anyone else who moved her so, despite his silly insistence on propriety and rules and restraint. She loved him now as a woman, had loved him all her life, almost, though he refused to see it. She could tell from the line of worry and concern that only the heights of passion had finally wiped from his brow. But she would never regret this joining, this initiation of love and passion drawn together by her feelings for this man. She laid her head against his chest, hearing the pounding of his heart slowing gradually from its tumultuous beat, and she stopped thinking altogether.

David watched her eyes close, the too-knowing eyes that always read his reflections too clearly from his face, he who thought himself so circumspect in cards and love and similar games of chance. He had known enough not to spill his seed inside her, and he hoped that would be sufficient to prevent the making of a baby. Gabriel had instructed him about that some time ago, that and much more as the two of them had talked together over wine late one night, though his old friend surely had never thought that he would use such knowledge on Circe. . . .

Guilt surged inside him, again. Even if no child were conceived, even without visible evidence of their passion, he had still taken a great chance, altered Circe, given her knowledge that maidens were not supposed to embrace. Had he done her irretrievable harm?

And if so, how could he live with himself?

Sixteen

He must have dozed, too, because when he opened his eyes again, David saw with alarm that the light had shifted. How long had they lain here together?

Circe still lay curled against him, her head on his chest, her thick shining brown hair in disarray, her long lashes touching her cheek. He allowed himself the luxury of gazing at her for a lengthy moment with no need to try to cloak his thoughts.

She was so beautiful, so unique, so utterly wonderful . . . and he had dealt her a most underhanded blow. Circe deserved better. It was bad enough to compromise a young lady of virtue, but to do it knowing perfectly well that he was the poorest potential husband she could hope to find—how could he risk trapping Circe in the kind of marriage made in hell that his parents had endured? Dare he risk her happiness by such an action?

And if not, could he bear to live without her? To never know again the uncommon bliss they had shared—the natural open responses that Circe had given him. She was a priceless treasure; he could search the rest of his life and never find any woman to measure up to her. But that led straight back to his wretched conundrum. She deserved so much better.

They could not tarry here. Or he could not, at any rate. He shook her gently, and when her eyes slowly opened, steeled himself against the dazzling smile that she bestowed upon him.

"Hello," she said, sounding a little shy.

He kissed her lightly, and then offered his arm to move her to a sitting position. "I must go, Circe," he said, and tried to pretend he did not see her grimace of disappointment. "We cannot stir the servants' imagination too much"—*or, God forbid, Gabriel's or Psyche's,* he thought—"being shut away together with no chaperone."

"I suppose," she agreed, reaching for her shift. "Do you really have to leave? Would you like—tea?"

He grinned despite himself. "My dear, I am replete with my taste of you," he whispered. "Tea would be woefully anticlimactic." He kissed her lips quickly again before she laughed. She pulled on her shift and he reached for his own garments. When they were both clothed again, he helped her pull her hair back into some semblance of order, delighting in the silky touch of the thick mane. Before they left the attic, he glanced back at the Titian, reminded of other responsibilities.

"Will it be safe, here?"

"Oh, yes, I'm careful to always lock the door," she promised, taking a key from her pocket. She turned it in the lock, then they went down the narrow stairs together.

On the second landing, he paused and pressed her hand briefly. "I should be off," he said, his gaze lingering on her face, still a little flushed. "It was—beyond words."

"Even beyond art," she agreed, flashing her brilliant wide smile.

David felt his heart contract. To hide his confused emotions, he bowed over her hand, kissing it lightly, paint stains and all.

Her answering smile was unalloyed by regret, yet it only heightened his feelings of culpability. He had to get away, try to sort out the maelstrom of emotion that swirled inside him, try to think what was the best course to take now to protect Circe.

He descended the last flight of stairs and nodded absently to the footman who let him out. Circe was a delight beyond description; even her own wonderful artwork could not express the marvel of honesty and warmth and passion that made up her dazzling beauty. As he walked slowly along, he became aware that the sunlight seemed brighter, the air sweeter, and his step lighter than ever before.

He loved her.

Of course he did, how long had he adored her, without having the sense—or the courage—to admit it to himself? Was it possible—was it even remotely likely—that he could marry Circe, assuming she would have him, and make a better union than his parents' miserable example? Was it?

Crossing a street still lost in thought, he stepped out almost under the hooves of a matched set of chestnuts that pulled a flashy phaeton. The coachman shouted, and David jumped back, just in time.

He was so bemused that he barely recognized the handsome woman who laughed at his close escape from death, then batted her lashes and pushed a stray hennaed lock beneath her daring bonnet.

"David, darling, take care. Don't risk that gorgeous body!" She smirked again at her own risqué wit.

It was Annabelle, his one-time mistress. David looked at her lush curves, her slightly too revealing neckline, her brassy hair and overly decorated hat. This was the woman whose loss he had lamented? What had he been thinking? Compared to Circe, she was dross before purest gold.

"I appreciate your solicitude, madam," he said, lifting his hat politely, but he did not pause to chat as she seemed to wish. She had moved on to her rich new keeper, and he—he would never desire her again. He walked on, still musing.

He had been a fool, to throw away so much of his younger years over women such as that. And all the while,

Circe had been growing up beneath his nose—well, not exactly, after she went off to the Continent. But that was no excuse for his miserable lack of perception. And now, these prim young ladies among whom he meant to find his future countess . . . how could any one of them measure up to Circe? Each would be a pale imitation of her glowing beauty, unable to compare.

He was so lost in thought that he found himself at his own residence before he was aware of walking so far. He rapped on the door and walked inside, barely acknowledging the footman, though he was usually polite to his staff.

If only . . . if only . . .

"David, is that you? I need you, dear boy. Where have you been for so long?"

His mother's shrill voice evoked a rush of memory. David came of bad blood, tainted, doomed—he had always believed—to reenact such sordid melodramas if he should dare to contract matrimony. Finding an utterly proper, entirely prim bride had been his only hope. And whatever wonderful attributes marked Circe, she was not prim and proper. . . .

"David, I believe I am having a sinking fit!" The countess leaned against the door frame, gazing down at him from the first landing, her voice heavy with reproach.

David felt his gut tighten with revulsion. "I'm so sorry, Mother. You should lie down." He managed to keep an even tone, but only with the greatest effort. "Elias, see to my mother; help her to her chamber and call for her maid."

The footman moved at once toward the stairs, but the countess frowned. "David, I want you, not a servant!"

"I have an appointment, Mother," he told her.

"But—"

"An urgent appointment." He was already turning back toward the door as she called after him.

"But my heart—I believe it is palpitating—"

"Elias will call your physician, Mother, who will prescribe a soothing draught, no doubt. I'm sure you will be fine." As she always was once her whims were catered to. But this time he did not slow his steps, and in a moment, he was outside again, feeling like a mouse who has escaped a particularly tenacious cat. Free, for the moment, but reminded once again how unlikely he was to make half of a decent marriage. And even if he could make a fit husband, which he doubted, how could he give Circe a mother-in-law from hell?

Sick at heart, he walked quietly through London's most pleasant streets, at last turning toward St. James's Street and White's. He craved the calm of his most sedate club, the only one his father had never been a member of, and most especially the reserve and respite of exclusively male companionship.

No parent here to suck up his very essence and drown him with her demands. No woman to harass and scold and pose and posture and wheedle her way. No women at all.

He went into the club, leaving his hat and gloves, and called for a stiff brandy. Perhaps he should just get drunk and lose all thought in the kind of drunken stupor that he had once enjoyed—or endured—all too often.

He thought of the first time he had seen Gabriel after his friend had returned to England after a long absence, and the idiotic scene he, David, had created, the sodden fool he had been. As if the painful memory conjured up his closest friend, David heard a familiar voice call his name.

"Morning, David. You're looking uncommonly glum." Gabriel was seated in a comfortable leather club chair, and he nodded toward the next chair.

Oh, hell. The one person he did not want to see. Was his sudden flash of guilt visible in his face? What would Gabriel say to him if he knew what harm he had done to innocent, trusting Circe? Tell him never to show his face in the Sinclair home again? Call him out, strike him dead in a duel?

He deserved every stricture that Gabriel should inflict

upon him. Feeling as heavy with shame as a condemned man taking his last steps toward the gallows, David walked across the dimly lit, smoky room, past other men reading newspapers, chatting quietly, drinking wine, or dozing openly in their chairs.

He sat down next to Gabriel, but did not relax into the soft cushion. He was about to lose his most cherished friend, the man who had helped him see himself with new eyes. Perhaps before their friendship was severed beyond hope of repair, David could tell him that, at least.

"Do you know," David spoke abruptly, "that is, do you remember that first night in the gaming hell in the East End, the night you redeemed my vowels from that villain who had won a small fortune from me?"

"Too well," Gabriel replied, his voice dry. "Not the most pleasant memory, though we did both survive the night."

"It was unconscionable behavior, since my estate was on the brink of insolvency, mired in my father's endless debts. But I was too drunk and too stupid to consider any type of behavior but the one my illustrious sire had modeled."

Gabriel watched him, folding the newspaper he had been reading and laying it aside. But he did not interrupt, and David was grateful.

"That night, I fell in the muck on the way home—not really aware that I'd never have lived to get home, if not for you. And later, when I saw myself in the looking glass in my hallway, covered in filth, it seemed an apt metaphor for my life, and I wondered why you had bothered."

"I knew there was more to you than that, David," Gabriel said quietly.

David refused to accept the offered balm. "Something changed in me, that night. I knew I had to repay you, and I tried my best."

"Yes, I remember that," Gabriel agreed, a suspicion of amusement glinting in his deep lapis eyes, though he kept his tone solemn.

"Even more, I had to change my behavior, alter the pattern of my existence. It took me years, but I feel that I have finally achieved a level of propriety that is as opposite to my father's life as I can manage."

"Yes, I have observed you do it, and that you perhaps go a bit too far. You are allowed to be human still, David," Gabriel noted, his gaze keen. "Not that I didn't admire you for abandoning your more lascivious habits, giving up heavy drinking and gaming, and for spending time and effort on your estate, watching your expenditures, and slowly paying off your father's debts."

David grimaced. "Not easy, with my mother accustomed to a singular lack of economy, but yes, I have pretty well gotten my estate back in order."

"So why this sudden need to acknowledge all of your early sins?"

David swallowed and found his mouth very dry. It was the moment of truth, and there was one very recent and indisputable transgression that he did not need to confess.

He took a sip of the brandy, letting the fiery wine burn its way into his empty belly. "I may not be as foolish as I was in my salad days, but Gabriel, the fact remains, I am not very good husband material. I have been postponing any real commitment for years; I don't want to cause or endure the kind of anguish that my parents suffered. But now, with Circe, she is so different—I somehow lost my resolve."

"And this was a mistake?" Gabriel lifted his brows.

"Circe doesn't deserve—that I—I should not have—" The words slipped away from him, and he waited, his whole body tense, for Gabriel to react with anger, with repudiation.

Instead, Gabriel gazed at him with seemingly undisturbed calm. "I see."

David could tell by Gabriel's serious, steady gaze that he did.

"And being such a hardened reprobate, you immediately rush to admit an indiscretion to me? What do you expect, a horsewhipping? An invitation to swords at dawn?" His tone was wry.

Indiscretion? How could he—

But Gabriel held up one hand. "David, I think enough has been said. If Circe comes to me and tells me she feels compromised by some unwise action, then I would certainly have words with you."

"But—"

"I know, an unmarried girl deserves every protection. Since I married her sister, I have been her legal guardian; aside from that, I adore Circe, always have. I have tried to act like the most doting brother-in-law, concerned only with her best interests. But Circe is not a typical ingenue; you know that, and I know that. Circe makes her own rules, and anyone who loves her has to understand as much. If Circe tells me she thinks she has been deceived or abused, I should most certainly listen. Until then, I think you should allow Circe to decide what she wishes."

It was such an unexpected reaction that David gazed at his friend, still incredulous that Gabriel had not grabbed him by the throat and thrown him bodily from the club's august setting, proclaiming to the world that he was no gentleman. Wasn't that what he deserved?

Gabriel took out his pocket watch. "I am due to meet my man of business, David. Do you wish me to put off the appointment?"

"No, no," David said. "Of course not."

"Then I will speak to you again soon. In the meantime, try to think this through, rationally."

Gabriel rose and put one hand on his shoulder in a fatherly gesture. "I don't think your halo has slipped all that far, David."

As David watched the other man depart, he tried to take a deep breath. Yet all he could think was that Gabriel did not understand, not really. He had not lived the life that David had lived. He would not return to the London house where David's mother seemed to have taken up permanent residence. She would await him, like a patient spider, probing for details of his supposed courtship. Oh God, if she knew about his tryst this morning with Circe what a to-do there would be! David thought of his mother daring to reproach Circe and shuddered. He sipped the brandy and stared into the fire, and despite Gabriel's well-meaning words, he felt lost in his own private purgatory.

At last he pulled himself together. He would have to speak to Circe, do the right thing, even though he worried that marriage to a Westbury might leave her unhappy in the long run. He could not bear to hurt Circe, but their unplanned lovemaking had left him with no choice.

He left the club and retraced his steps to the Sinclair mansion, rapping lightly on the door. The footman who opened it stared at him with polite resignation.

"Yes, it's me again," David agreed. "Is Miss Circe in?"

"I believe so, my lord," the servant said, shutting the door behind him as David walked inside.

"Would you ask her to come down, please?" David said. He did not wish to risk meeting Circe in the familiar confines of the schoolroom, much less the attic. If he were given the opportunity to touch her smooth skin, trace her plump lower lip with his thumb—he might succumb to temptation all over again. He could not continue to risk Circe's reputation.

The servant looked curious, but he answered, "I will inquire." He took David's hat and gloves and put them on the hall table, then disappeared up the stairs.

David paced up and down the wide hallway, trying to marshal his thoughts and his words, thinking how to persuade Circe that marriage was now their only option. Any normal well-bred young lady would understand, would be in agonies of guilt and anxiety, but Circe—probably not.

"David!" she called from the staircase, her tone mellow and happy.

For a moment he was pulled back in time, looking up and expecting to see the child that Circe had once been, leaning over the banister. But when he raised his eyes, he saw a vision not at all childlike. Circe had removed her painting smock and had changed her dress; she now wore a white muslin gown sprigged with green, and her hair was pulled back loosely, as she had used to wear it, when she bothered with it at all. Her clear eyes glowed with happiness, and her smile flashed wide.

He felt sick with fear. What if he failed her as a husband? She was so lovely, so innocent, so trusting. What if he ruined it all?

She came rapidly down the stairs, holding out her hands. He took them and lifted them to kiss lightly, while Circe beamed at him.

"You missed Aunt Sophie's departure; she has returned to Bath, saying we have exhausted her with our 'mad rounds of gaiety.' And I hear that dear Mr. Bircham has developed a sudden thirst for the spa's famed mineral waters." He heard her infectious laugh, but could not share it.

"I wish I could send my mother back with her," he muttered beneath his breath. David became aware of the footman staring, and the rustle of sound from a housemaid crossing the landing above. "Let us go into the morning room," he suggested.

Circe's eyes twinkled. "Whatever you say, my lord," she agreed demurely, an attitude he knew to be totally assumed. She led the way into the chamber, which was empty of other occupants, and shut the door firmly behind them.

David glanced uneasily at the door—they should not really be alone together, but it was a bit late to start worrying about the proprieties now. Still, that was exactly what must concern him.

Circe rushed across the room to him and wrapped her arms around his neck, her soft lips waiting for his kiss. David felt desire leap as he gazed down into her face, her expression relaxed, her incomparable green eyes animated. He kissed her lightly on the forehead.

Circe blinked at him in surprise. "What's wrong, David?" She lowered her arms and stared at him, her expression suddenly anxious.

His nervousness made him put off the all-important question. While he tried to find the right words, he backed away and glanced across at an unusually large and extravagant arrangement of flowers.

"Nice," he said vaguely. "Hothouse flowers in the morning room?"

She nodded in resignation. "We're running out of places to put them, between Sir John's offerings and now the count's."

"Von Freistadt? What's that scoundrel up to now?" David demanded, more sharply than he had intended.

Circe dimpled. "Ah, he desires the pleasure of my company."

David's jaw dropped. "For what?"

"Drives, balls, dinner parties, theater, opera, al fresco outings, you name it," she told him cheerfully.

"You know he's up to no good, Circe! Trying to wheedle out of you if you know about the painting, if you know its whereabouts. We'll have more hired thugs after us. Don't trust him, and don't allow him to hang over you," David warned her.

"Have some faith in my intelligence, David," Circe retorted. "I think I am up to scratch enough not to blurt out secrets which must be kept hidden."

He blinked at the cant expression, but she continued.

"Of course I don't intend to allow him to hang over me. Especially now—" She paused, as if waiting for him to confirm their new status of intimacy. David swallowed.

"About that, Circe . . ."

She waited, while he struggled to find the words, and slowly her expression darkened. "What, David?" She moved closer and put one hand lightly on his arm. "You don't regret what we did?"

Regret the most wonderful joining he had ever experienced? He had never before known how special such intimacy could be, bringing together both love and passion, cresting into undreamed-of bliss.

"Of course not, Circe," he said, feeling tongue-tied and

clumsy from the fear that had lived inside him for too long. "But we must not do it again. It's too great a risk, for you, I mean. Your reputation, your standing in society—"

She lifted her chin, her smile fading. "Don't you think I have anything to say about it? Don't try to play the lordly and proper gentleman, David. It's a bit late for that."

Stung by her reminder, he spoke more sharply than he intended. "I was wrong, I know it. I should never have taken advantage of your innocence—"

"Oh, posh, you didn't seduce me, you didn't tie me to a tree in the forest and ravish me," she snapped back. "I made a decision just as you did. And I am not cowardly enough to regret it scarcely two hours later!"

One part of his mind and heart rejoiced that she did not regret their union, but the other, saner side rued her rashness, her unflagging sincerity, her unwillingness to consider what harm she could suffer. But if she did not think of it, he must. He was older, a man of the world, and he knew how fragile a lady's reputation really was.

"I can't allow it," he repeated, his voice low. "We cannot make such a mis—we cannot," he ended forcefully. "We must—"

David found that he was sweating—it was so hard to say the words. Not because he doubted his love for Circe, only because he feared for her. Would marriage to David condemn Circe to a painful and endless farce like the one his parents had enacted? Of course he did not intend to repeat his father's sins, but he was afraid to trust himself. . . . The sins of the fathers . . . what if he slipped, what if he could not control the base instincts he had inherited? To risk Circe's happiness, to see her injured as his mother had been, to see her changed into a bitter harridan . . . not Circe, whose lilting free spirit and unfettered soul had never known such despair. . . .

The thoughts left his tone heavy, and his expression bleak. He took a deep breath and spat out the words. "We must marry!"

Seventeen

"Marry me, Circe," he repeated.
Circe stared at him for an endless moment. "You're proposing?"

"We must marry," David said again, still almost sick with anxiety. "It's the only proper thing to do, now that—"

Circe gazed at him, and he could not read her expression.

"The proper thing to do?" she repeated, her tone dull.

"Yes, that's right." Good, at least she was going to listen to reason.

Circe felt her heart contract. He said nothing of love, not even of passion, only of propriety. What had happened to the David she had loved? How had he transformed once more into this cultivated ass whose only motivation was the rules of decorum? She would rather have had a loving and honest affair, no matter what it did to her precious reputation, than a marriage based only on David's obsession with society's mandates.

He wiped his damp brow, looking relieved, as if taking her acquiescence for granted. Did he think she was so easily swayed?

Damned if she would. If he didn't love her for herself,

did he really think she would accept a duty-bound proposal?

"Thank you for your generous offer, my lad Westbury, but you can take your rules of propriety and stuff them up your very proper ass!"

"Circe!" David said, blinking in shock. "I didn't mean that. Wait!"

But Circe was already gone, slamming the door behind her. Ignoring the footman's curious glance, she bolted up the stairs.

⤳

*The next hour was one that Circe would shudder to re-*member as long as she lived. David did not love her. David had sampled the most generous and passionate response she could give him, and it had failed to move him. Her love meant nothing to him.

She felt as if her heart had been ripped out and her body left an empty shell. After her precipitous leave-taking, she flung herself across the bed and wept.

The tears seemed endless. At last, when her throat ached from trying to smother her loud sobs, and her cheeks were warm, and her eyelids swollen, at last she closed her eyes and drifted into an uneasy sleep.

The oblivion was a welcome release, at first, then confused figures troubled her sleep. She knew that she dreamed, but could not wake herself, though she gasped when she saw David as if from a distance, saw him climb into the basket beneath a hot air balloon and loose its tethers to drift up, up into the air.

"No, David!" she tried to call out, but her throat was closed, and she could only feel tremors of terror as she waited for him to crash, too, come to grief like her parents. But instead David floated up, up until he was out of her sight, away into the endless blue sky, leaving her alone forever.

She woke to find that she sobbed again into her pillow.

She cried heartily for another minute, then pushed herself up, rubbing her wet cheeks with the back of her hand. She would not do this, bemoan his loss like some village maiden whose life centered around the farmer's good-looking son. . . . She had more. She had her family, she had her art. She would survive without David and his empty offer.

She would not, could not settle merely for form and ceremony, for the artificial joining that many of the Ton considered normal. She understood too much about real intimacy, real passion. She had discovered passion in her art, and David had taught her even more, apparently despite his own inclinations, in the one exquisite hour of lovemaking they had shared. . . . All she had ever required from David was honesty, and he had offered her false coin, a blank canvas.

But she had loved him since she was twelve years old, one side of her mind lamented. *You were a child,* she told that part of herself coldly. *What did you know about love?* No, David could pursue some empty headed, conventional maiden. What's more, he would not see her languish because of the lack of his company! She had more respect for herself than that. Even if all she really wanted was to shut herself away and paint . . . after one wistful moment, she had to put that dream aside as well.

She had to finish out this accursed Season. It would make Psyche unhappy if Circe withdrew, and it might cause David to think she was hiding from him if she stayed at home.

She would not give him so much satisfaction! He thought he was the only one whose caresses might somehow corrupt her, that she was such an innocent that she would give away a love affair that she knew society considered improper. He felt forced into marriage with her? Damn him for climbing on his wretched high horse and making such a magnanimous, noble gesture.

She went to the china basin on her dressing table and stared into the looking glass above it. Her face was red, her eyelids swollen, her hair a tangle of snarls. She looked a mess.

Pressing her lips firmly together, Circe washed her face and combed her hair back into something more presentable. She could ring for Luciana to help, of course, but right now, she didn't want to see anyone, even her maid. Thinking of her dresser brought back the whole equally tangled quagmire of the painting and its theft.

Circe sighed. But the stolen masterpiece called to her troubled spirit, and she gave herself up to the temptation. Until it was returned, which it must be, she might as well enjoy its presence. The light would be wretched in the afternoon, but no matter. Picking up a paint brush would soothe her troubled spirit like nothing else. She tucked the attic key into her pocket and headed for the stairs. In the attic, she pulled on her smock and picked up her brush and palette. Even the familiar smells comforted her. Despite the poor light, she painted until it was time to change for dinner.

At least Psyche was well enough to come down to dinner, and she talked with Circe and Gabriel with considerable animation. Circe smiled to see her sister's improved spirits, and as she toyed with her roast beef, she thought for a moment of confiding in Psyche about David, about their stolen morning of love. But even though she and her older sister had always been close, for once, her courage failed her. Glancing at her lovely sister, with her cool blue eyes and serene smile and her always faultless decorum—at her very *proper* sister—Circe could not imagine Psyche being tempted by illicit lovemaking. How could she possibly understand Circe's plight, much less Circe's heartbreak over David's lack of a genuine response? And Circe was in no mood for a scolding, nor did she wish to upset her sister's good spirits and perhaps temporarily improved health.

"Aren't you going out tonight?" Psyche interrupted Circe's musing. "I believe Sally will be here shortly to escort you to Almack's."

Oh, Lord, Circe thought, trying to conceal her dismay. Of all the places she was most uninspired by, the Ton's favorite "marriage mart" was high on the list. It was good that she had dressed up for dinner in an effort to cheer herself and try to hide her melancholy.

She had chosen one of her favorites: a deceptively simple, brightly hued aquamarine silk that draped beautifully. Its skirt was pulled tautly across her hips with the bulk of the rich material gathered behind her. At first, Psyche had been unsure about the low, snug square neckline but she had finally agreed with Circe and the modiste that it was very becoming to Circe's slender neck and shoulders. Her mother's pearls were the finishing touch and provided Circe with a reminder of the strength of her convictions.

Still, she hoped David would have the decency to stay away from Almack's; she did not wish to spend time with him while her feelings were still raw.

She lifted her chin and gave the best smile she could manage. "Oh, yes, I had forgotten."

In fact, Sally arrived by the time dinner ended. Sally was gaily dressed in a crimson gown with scallops around the hem, and sported handsome ruby earrings and a matching jeweled choker. But she seemed somehow out of spirits, too, and Circe reflected that they would make a dismal pair tonight. But then, for such a tepid group as they would find at Almack's, what did it matter? After a little conversation—Sally wanted to hear how Psyche was faring and she had a new recipe for chicken fricassee she was sure the mother-to-be would enjoy—Circe accepted her evening cloak and they said their good-byes and were handed up into the carriage. Gabriel did the honors, and he gazed into Circe's face as he offered his arm.

"Cheer up, little sister," he suggested. "The ratafia will lift your spirits, I'm sure, if the scintillating surroundings do not." His blue eyes twinkled, and Circe smiled in answer. Gabriel understood her feelings, but yes, she would try, for Psyche's sake, if nothing else.

Sally was unusually quiet in the carriage, but when they

reached the private club, she seemed to rouse herself and chatted with Princess Esterhazy. While Sally visited with other matrons, Circe hesitated. One quick glance about the room had told her what she really wanted to know.

No David, thank goodness. She wondered idly what he would tell his mother. He would have to sacrifice some other marriageable young lady to soothe his parent's tantrums. And as for lovemaking, no doubt he would return to the arms of his *chère amie*. Circe stifled a sigh.

"You look about as cheerful as Marie Antoinette on her way to the guillotine," a deep voice said.

Circe stiffened, then nodded to Count von Freistadt as he made his bow. The man had incredible gall, to greet her so calmly after he had behaved like a bully and a boor the last time they had met.

She could cut him totally. But he might put her rejection down to fear or timidity. And she would not allow him to think she might be afraid. So she kept her tone cool but composed. "A novel comparison; I trust I am in no danger of losing my head."

"Certainly not," he agreed, a gleam of laughter appearing in his dark eyes. "I only meant to suggest a certain lack of enthusiasm for this august assembly."

He was smooth, she would give him that. Circe gazed about the huge ballroom, decorated with gilt columns, classic medallions, and enormous mirrors, the cut-glass lusters bright with modern gas lighting. The rooms were elegant, if uninspired—the artist in her longed to add a few fresh touches to the decor—and the food was bland and the drinks insipid. As for the company, she glanced over the assembled hopeful mamas and nervous daughters, the scattering of callow youth who made up the bulk of the guests, and said, keeping her tone demure, "I can't imagine why you would think such a thing."

He raised one thick brow. "Because I know you, Miss Hill, and this is not your idea of an exciting evening."

And he could offer something more pleasing? Hardly,

Circe thought, but she tried to keep her thoughts from showing.

Von Freistadt chuckled. "You will never have a face suitable for hiding secrets, my lovely young friend. Your countenance reveals too much."

Irked, Circe allowed herself to frown. "If so, it is hardly kind of you to tell me as much," she pointed out.

He stroked his neatly trimmed beard and did not attempt to hide his smile. "But I only meant to imply that I know you have other, more intellectual interests. Art, for example, paintings of genius and beauty."

Her pulse leapt as she recalled the stolen Titian, but she tried to keep her tone steady. "What makes you say that?"

He quirked a brow again. "Why, Miss Hill, everyone knows of your artistic talents and ambitions."

"Oh," she said, feeling foolish. He was teasing her, like a predator with his prey.

"Of course, being a lovely young woman has many advantages"—he glanced over her well-cut gown in a way that made her long to tug at its neckline—"but it does hamper your artistic career, I fear."

She thought of the stolen interlude in the attic and felt her heart ache. He was right, of course, in ways he could not conceive of. Still, she felt constrained to argue. "But it does not make one impossible," she said as the count signaled to a passing servant and procured two glasses of ratafia. He held out one to Circe, with the same elegant grace with which he would have offered vintage champagne.

She took it, but refused to be distracted. "Even if the Royal Academy will not offer me the privilege of membership, I can still attract private patrons. You mentioned Marie Antoinette, the late queen of France; her favorite painter was a woman, Elizabeth Vigée-Lebrun."

"Indeed. And did the lady in question survive the Revolution?" He sipped his own libation and grimaced briefly at the taste.

Circe smiled. "Yes, indeed, although I fear the experience left her somewhat embittered. I traveled to Vienna to meet her while I was abroad; she is still painting. She was kind enough to give me several lessons before I returned to—"

She broke off, annoyed with herself. She did not wish to bring up Piedmont, which might lead to the subject of the upheaval that had taken place there. It would only link her more closely to the stolen painting and its current whereabouts.

Looking about for a reason to excuse an abrupt change of topic, Circe put down her glass and waved toward a young man with such tall shirt collars and high neckcloth that he could barely turn his head. "Ah, I believe I have promised this dance to Mr. Murak."

The gentleman in question moved forward eagerly, though they had no such previous agreement. But it was a good excuse to break off her present conversation, which was becoming too sensitive for her liking, and she was sure no gentleman would question her declaration.

Unfortunately, she had forgotten that von Freistadt was not a gentleman, despite his long line of distinguished Austrian ancestors. "No, I fear your memory fails you. I believe this dance is mine," he said.

And beneath the offended gaze of the young Mr. Murak, who gazed at them like a befuddled turkey cock, the count tucked Circe's hand into the crook of his arm and led her onto the dance floor.

Circe bit her lip; she had long ago wearied of the Austrian's imperious manners. And to her alarm, she recognized the beginning notes of a waltz. It was true, she was now allowed to waltz, but—"I do not believe we are well suited for this dance," she said. "I did not care for our last waltz. I think I should prefer to sit this one out."

He put one hand on her waist and held her just a little too close. "Miss Hill, do not let that awkward encounter mislead you. The setting is quite proper, this time, and I think we are well suited, indeed."

He led her into the rhythm of the dance, and she had

to follow his lead or look totally gauche. She was aware of other ladies around the room glancing at their passage across the floor; the count was always the subject of veiled feminine attention. He knew it, too, which annoyed her even further. But though he might pride himself on his military carriage and knowledge of dance, he lacked David's elegant grace.

Still, she waited to experience her usual awareness of his too overtly masculine bearing. But Circe was no inexperienced maiden, not any longer. After her first moment of alarm, she found that her response to the Austrian had changed. Loving David, being with David, had altered her forever. She felt armored, somehow, against the count's predatory advances.

She knew what love could be, now. She had an understanding of the nature of genuine passion between two adults who chose each other freely. And it did not resemble the nervous agitation that the count loved to induce in young ladies he "honored" with his attentions. No, not in the least!

So this time she could look up at him without the old fluttering of her pulse and answer calmly when he whispered, "Miss Hill, you grace the dance with your beauty."

"Far more beautiful women than I have danced here." She met his gaze without having to look away.

To her annoyance, he did not show any sign of chagrin at her lack of trepidation. If anything, he seemed to redouble his efforts to agitate her, pulling her even closer and bending to whisper into her ear, "You bring out the best in me, dear Miss Hill; I can barely contain my admiration."

Circe's palm itched to slap the dark saturnine face held so close to her own. Creating a scandal in the middle of the ball would not help, however. She stiffened, her whole body rigid with anger, and looked pointedly away.

Her woodenness made the dance more awkward, because she did not care to follow his lead as easily as she would had she been dancing with Dav—with any partner more sympathetic. But she didn't care; looking clumsy on the dance floor was the least of her worries.

The dance seemed endless, but at last the music faded, and she could step back.

He raised his brows. "Must you hurry away so soon?"

"Yes," she said, giving him a brief curtsy and turning aside, not in the least perturbed by his expression of annoyance. A pox on arrogant men, men who thought they could rule your life, direct your conversation, establish your morals by their own decision. . . . Why did every thought lead back to David?

Where was Sally? She was supposed to be Circe's chaperone, after all. Circe looked about for her companion and found her conversing, her expression animated, with Sir John. He seemed to be trying to lead her away from the other ladies standing nearby, but Sally was resisting, which again seemed very strange.

Had Sir John offended her?

Sally's expression was hard to read, but Circe could detect the tension in her body; she looked almost as stiff as Circe had felt when confronting von Freistadt. Then Sally turned, and the despondency on Sir John's face was easy enough to see. He made his bow and walked away, almost colliding with a waiter balancing a full tray.

Circe was moved to forget her own woes. She crossed the room to join him.

"Are you enjoying the evening, Sir John?" she asked politely, trying to keep the curiosity out of her voice. "I don't believe I have seen you at Almack's before."

"No, I—it—it is my first—" the young man stammered. "How are you, Miss Hill?"

He was ill at ease once more, and his hazel eyes looked so forlorn that she felt her heart go out to him. Here was another sufferer, though she didn't know how or why his heart was troubled. But she felt for him, as one heartsick wretch to another.

"I am well," she said, trying hard to make her tone fit

the words. "And you? What has your horticulture group discussed this week?"

As she had hoped, the introduction of his favorite topic caused the baronet to relax and speak in livelier tones as he regaled her with accounts of garden plans and fierce debates over the question of follies and circular rosariums.

She was so pleased to see the unhappiness in his eyes fade that she encouraged him to continue and listened with every appearance of interest to his explanation of Repton's views on specialized gardens.

"You have to separate them, of course, for the most pleasing aesthetic appearance," Sir John explained earnestly. "One could not have a Chinese garden side by side with an English rosarium without hedges in between to screen the boundaries."

"Of course not." Circe nodded and took Sir John's arm. She could see, from the corner of her eye, von Freistadt frowning at them from across the room. If she could cheer the baronet a little and avoid the Austrian at the same time, everyone would benefit. So she and Sir John continued to chat, and she even induced the shy young man to lead her in a country dance.

From the side of the room, Sally watched them, trying to keep her wistfulness from showing on her face, while she listened to an acquaintance tell her outrageous gossip that Sally already knew. There, Circe was dancing with Sir John, which was just what Sally had always meant to happen. The two young people were spending time together, and in that way Circe might have the chance to discover all the worthy qualities that the somewhat gawky baronet did not always reveal at first glance.

Despite his occasional awkwardness, despite his obsession with flowers and plants and garden designs, he was the most delightful man, tender and thoughtful and good. . . . And these thoughts were not conducive to lifting the black cloud of loneliness, which his absence had left behind. The brief dazzling hour of passion and mutual regard they had shared had been snatched away too soon, and the shadow of its absence chilled her to the core.

But he had not cared about her, not really, Sally tried to remind herself. He was in love with Circe, and Sally was honor bound to do all that she could to further that much desired relationship. Circe would be happy with such a sensitive young man, and their mutual interests, art and horticulture, should complement each other nicely. It was all very logical and pleasing, so why did Sally feel so wretched and miserable and certain that the sun would never shine again?

Sally plied her favorite ivory-handled fan so hard that one of the delicate ribs cracked under the strain, and she tried to smile at Lady Seton, as if she had really been listening to the long story of a certain duke and his latest amour. It was too warm in these crowded rooms, the food was wretched, and Sally wished she were dead.

"Did you ever hear of such a ridiculous pose?" Lady Seton demanded.

"Never," Sally agreed, hearing the dullness in her own voice. She should give up this attempt to maintain a normal social life. As soon as Circe's Season was safely over——and perhaps Circe and Sir John would have announced their engagement by then—Sally would retire to some sedate watering place like Bath, where the dowagers congregated to sip healing mineral waters and ride out in their antiquated coaches, sure to be back home and in bed by eight. Or perhaps she would jump off a cliff and get it over with, she thought, frowning so fiercely that a waiter, about to offer her more orgeat, withdrew hastily.

Circe thought it was the longest evening she could remember. Sir John tried to amuse her, and she kept her expression as alert as she could manage, but all she wanted was to retreat to the safety of her own rooms, perhaps to gaze on the Titian again, perhaps to look over the rough sketches she had made of David before they had lain together on the attic floor . . . no, it didn't do to remember that glorious hour. Curse the man. . . .

Her thoughts ran round and round in the same monotonous rut until she could barely keep her countenance composed. And although she kept Sir John at her side longer than was proper, she could not avoid coming face to face with von Freistadt again before the interminable evening drew to a close.

"Miss Hill," he said, "I hoped that you might allow me the pleasure of your company tomorrow afternoon."

"I'm afraid I have other plans," she answered automatically.

"What a shame." The count's smile did not falter; he seemed to have anticipated her excuse. "Lady Bessington"—this was a name Circe did not know—"is holding a salon for Alexander Nasmyth, and I thought sure you would enjoy meeting him."

"Nasmyth? The Scottish painter?" Circe blurted, idiotically. "You know him?"

"My friend does, and since his visit to London is brief, I thought you might wish to take advantage of the chance to meet such a distinguished artist. I fear he is returning to Edinburgh on Friday."

"Oh." Circe tried to think. "Perhaps I could excuse myself from my earlier engagement."

What was worse, having to spend more time with the count, or giving up a chance to meet and speak to such a respected artist? Circe found her longing to meet the great man outweighing her caution. And hadn't she told David that she could handle the count? Why should she cower in fear of the Austrian? He was only a man, and she was not a child to be alarmed by verbal innuendos. He would not draw out any secrets that she wished to hide, despite David's worries—and why did every thought lead back to David!

"I will go," Circe said abruptly. "That is, I thank you for your kind invitation."

The count's dark eyes gleamed, and she tried to ignore the triumph that he did not bother to hide. "I am so happy to hear it," he murmured. "I shall pick you up at four o'clock."

Circe pushed back her misgivings. "Yes, I look forward to it."

And finally the clock struck twelve. Circe located Sally, and they said their good-byes. Both women collected their cloaks, and Sally called for her carriage. They rode home in silence; Sally again was uncharacteristically quiet, and Circe so exhausted by the strain of pretending to enjoy the whole wretched evening that she, too, had little to say.

She did think to ask Sally for the favor of her company, and chaperonage, for the visit to the salon on Thursday with von Freistadt. Sally argued briefly over the wisdom of encouraging the count, but eventually agreed.

At home, Circe climbed the stairs to her own chamber. Psyche was likely already in bed, and Circe had no wish to make conversation.

The world was a lonely place. Even the thought of meeting Nasmyth did little to raise her spirits. Without David, life stretched bleakly ahead of her, as barren as Nasmyth's Scottish moors.

Eighteen

Circe awaited the visit to Lady Bessington's salon with some trepidation. She very much wanted to meet Alexander Nasmyth, but the thought of enduring von Freistadt's company made her grimace with distaste. In the end, her desire to meet the renowned painter triumphed, and she decided to honor the invitation.

Sally arrived well before the count on Thursday, and if von Freistadt frowned when he saw that Circe had arranged a chaperone, he made no comment. He escorted the two ladies out of the house and into an open phaeton for the excursion; they would not even be shut away for the short ride. Had he gauged her distrust so precisely? Circe glanced at him and caught the gleam of laughter in his dark eyes.

"Such a lovely day," he murmured as he helped her in. "I thought you ladies would enjoy the sunshine."

Circe took her seat with more composure than she had expected; the count even had a groom riding very properly just behind them. Sally took her seat between them—they were a little crowded; the vehicle was really built for two passengers, but Circe ignored that fact. All very proper, but it would take more than that to make Circe change her mind about the Austrian. Even the devil could have a sense of decorum, she told herself.

Lady Bessington was charming, and the salon was everything Circe had hoped for. Although the guests seemed to be mostly men, she met painters and writers and diplomats, a distinguished list that had even Circe somewhat dazzled.

While Sally chatted with a young French diplomat, Circe was introduced to Nasmyth, as promised, and was able to converse with him and listen to his views on both painting and engineering, his twin passions.

When he learned that she had lately been abroad, he was eager to question her about the Continent's most recent artistic trends. It was an enjoyable conversation, except for one moment of alarm when Nasmyth observed, "I understand that many local artists feel some sympathy for the stirrings of Italian nationalism?"

"Ah," Circe murmured, aware of von Freistadt's eyes upon her. "I know very little about the politics of the region. However, artists certainly must study the customs and habits of each area. My own art instructor bade us read de Valenciennes's 'Advice to a Student on Painting, Particularly on Landscape.' I'm sure you're familiar with the work. He counsels close attention to local styles of building and costume to give every painting a sense of place."

"Indeed," Nasmyth agreed. "Very wise. We cannot allow the noble Arcadian cultures to die unlamented and unrecorded. My own *Destruction of the Old Tollbooth* demonstrates . . ."

And he was back to his own keen interest in Scottish rural landscapes, leaving behind the dangerous topic of politics as it could intertwine with art.

Circe took a deep breath and tried not to show her relief. She was able to steer the conversation away from any more questions about Europe. Later, she also chatted with Sir Thomas Lawrence and received an invitation to view the paintings in his private studio, which delighted her.

Von Freistadt showed a tendency to hover nearby, so silent that she could have forgotten he was present, but she was aware of his keen attention to her conversations. Still, he did not interfere with her, and she had the chance to talk at length with the artists and writers who filled the salon; it was an intoxicating few hours. When they said their farewells, Circe thanked her hostess with real gratitude. The Austrian was equally circumspect on their ride home, and this time, she felt more at ease in his company.

When he said good-bye to Circe and Sally at the door of the Sinclair town house, he bowed over Circe's hand with his usual Continental élan. "Perhaps you will honor me with your company again, Miss Hill," he suggested.

And even though his query held, as usual, a hint of command below its surface level of polite supplication, Circe was blissful enough over her delightful afternoon to nod. "Perhaps," she agreed.

The only wrinkle came later, at dinner, when Psyche heard the name of her hostess. Circe had mentioned the salon, but not at whose home it was conducted. "Bessington? Good heavens, Circe, what was von Freistadt thinking? That woman is not received by most of the Ton!"

Circe raised her brows. "Really, why not? She's not part of the demimonde, surely? She seemed very nice and was quite proper in her manner."

Psyche's expression was a strange one. "She may seem proper, but she ran away from her husband with another man and had two illegitimate children by him! It was only later that she married Mountjoy, who became the earl of Bessington."

Gabriel paused, a spoonful of turtle soup halfway to his mouth. "Yes, but you know the story, my love; she was very young, and her parents forced her into marriage with an elderly sot twice her age."

Psyche exchanged a speaking glance with her husband.

"That's as may be. Not everyone allows herself to be forced!"

"Not everyone has your strength of mind, my love," Gabriel answered, grinning.

Circe knew that Psyche herself had been much pressured to marry another man, a quite odious cousin, in fact; thank heavens she had resisted! Circe glanced at Gabriel with genuine affection, then turned back to her sister. "May I really not visit her? I think she may be somewhat lonely."

Psyche looked torn. "I wish the woman no harm, Circe, but I must think about your own reputation, especially as you are yet unmarried."

Must everyone harp on her priceless reputation? And as for that—unmarried and cavorting with David in the attic . . . the memory of their illicit lovemaking flooded back, and Circe had to stare hard at the Wedgwood plate in front of her to quell the warmth that threatened to flood her cheeks. Thank goodness her sister did not know about that episode.

"If you wish to enjoy a notable and quite unexceptional salon, as soon as I am well enough I shall take you to meet the Misses Berry, in North Audley Street. Sally does not know them, but I have met the sisters. Although not fashionable, they are most respectable, and in their salons you will meet esteemed literary and artistic figures. Also, it is all very informal, just what you would like."

"Thank you, I shall look forward to it," Circe agreed politely as she stabbed her fork into a stalk of asparagus. However, she made no promise not to visit the scandalous Lady Bessington again.

During the following days, von Freistadt insisted on escorting her and Sally to 24 Bond Street where she enjoyed chatting with Sir Thomas Lawrence, a soft-spoken man whose portraits were said to flatter their subjects, often members of society as prominent as the former Prince Regent himself, but nonetheless revealed masterful brush techniques which incited Circe's admiration. Later they visited Queen Anne's Street to meet with Joseph Turner, another remarkable artist whose oils and water-colors Circe had long admired.

The count was circumspect enough; still, she felt al-ways on her guard. Despite his new reserve, she could not bring herself to trust him. She missed the ease of David's company, his lack of surprise when she said something shocking, the humorous grace with which he greeted her occasional absentminded social solecism. She missed Da-vid . . . but she was still too furious with him to see him.

Every day since his insulting proposal, he had pounded on the heavy doors of the Sinclair town house. And every day, per Circe's instructions, Jowers had repeated her re-fusal to grant him the pleasure of her company. And the flowers David sent—armloads of beautiful roses and lilacs and every other blossom the garden or the hothouse could offer up. And every day, she sent them back, decorated with the shreds of his unread notes.

And as for the count, even if she had not had David's information about his covert diplomatic mission to put her on guard, something in the man's bearing, the arrogance he could never quite hide, made it impossible for her to feel at ease with him. Plus, the knowledge of the stolen painting was always at the back of her mind; the more she tried to push it aside, the more it seemed to loom too often on the tip of her tongue, and in her many conver-sations on artistic topics, references to Titian and his style, his history, his renown, were always having to be snatched back at the last moment.

She missed David. . . .

❧

David looked up from his desk to regard the lovely flow-ers, wilting in their assorted boxes, with loathing. "I don't care what you do with them," he snapped. "Just get them out of my sight."

The footman looked bewildered, but the butler, standing just behind, cleared his throat and motioned to the younger servant.

David took a stronger rein on his temper. It was contemptible to take out his ill humor on the servants; he had sworn he would never do that.

"I'm sorry," he muttered, running one hand through his already disordered hair. "It's just—please don't bring me the flowers. Just dispose of them if she returns the next batch."

As Circe surely would, David thought in near despair. How many more days must he covertly observe her departing in von Freistadt's carriage, looking all too calm and pleasant as if she actually enjoyed that blackguard's company, while David's heart ached with the loss of her companionship—worse, of her love. How could he persuade her to feel differently if she refused to see him, refused to read his long letters and notes?

"Yes, my lord," the footman agreed.

David scowled down at his littered desk, wondering why he had been such a fool as to totally offend the only woman he had ever cared about.

The butler cleared his throat once more. "A letter for you, my lord."

He held out the silver tray. David snatched up the missive it held, ripping open the wax seal. Could Circe have relented, at last?

But it was only a message from his uncle, warning of more activity at the Austrian embassy. Von Freistadt must be watched even more carefully.

Damn! David swallowed his disappointment. At least his uncle was keeping him busy, but nothing could ease the pain inside him. How could he make Circe see reason?

And what if this were not simply wounded pride, or Circe's usual stubborn independence asserting itself? What if she truly didn't love him—how could he bear it?

David almost groaned aloud, then remembered the butler, hovering at his elbow. "I will send a reply directly," he said, and motioned the man away.

So no one was there to see when David dropped his head into his hands and groaned again, this time, most audibly. Would he end up like the ancient gentleman who shadowed Aunt Sophie everywhere she went? So be it, by God. If he must, he must.

He would never give up. Someday, Circe must listen!

~~~~~~

The days crawled by, and the only sister who seemed at all happy was Psyche, who was having longer periods free of the overpowering nausea that had kept her confined to her couch. She had come close enough to her normal spirits to become worried about Circe, who seemed to alternate between long periods spent alone in the upper regions of the house and occasional jaunts out with the middle-aged Austrian diplomat, whom Psyche could not consider an appealing suitor.

"You know he has no designs for marriage," Psyche confided in Gabriel one night as they prepared for bed. "He flirts with a different young lady every Season."

Unlike many fashionable couples, they still shared the same large bedchamber. To Psyche's mind, one of the most pleasant times of the day was the hour when they retired. She could lie next to her husband, curl into the circle of his arm, and find all her troubles eased by the sharing. And when they made love—when she was not fighting overpowering bouts of nausea—it was bliss, indeed.

"He doesn't seem the type for matrimony, no." Gabriel pulled her closer.

"And even if he did, would we wish for such a union? Can you imagine Circe happy married to such a man? His reputation is horrendous."

"Deservedly so, I'm afraid," Gabriel agreed. "And I do know a bit about dissolute behavior."

Psyche smiled up at him from inside the curve of his

arm. "In your worst hour, you were nothing like the man he is."

"As if you would know." He kissed her lightly on the forehead.

Psyche smiled as she savored the caress, but her thoughts soon returned to Circe. "I don't know why she continues to go about with him; I can't believe she enjoys his company. Circe is too canny to be taken in by his unctuous charm, surely."

"He has found all the right inducements," Gabriel pointed out. "Private showings of paintings she has longed to see, artists she yearns to meet and converse with."

"Why is he trying so hard?" Psyche stared up at her husband. When he hesitated, she nodded. "Yes, for no good end. I had the same thought, and it worries me greatly."

"We will not allow Circe to be misused," Gabriel told her, his tone firm. "She is not unprotected."

"Thank God!" Psyche sighed, remembering the days when she had been her younger sister's only guardian, in fact if not in the letter of the law, and how hard it had been to bear the burden and responsibility all alone.

"Besides," Gabriel added, "if von Freistadt has nefarious plans for Circe, I think David will have something to say about it."

"David?" Psyche paused to consider. "I don't see how. Just now, Circe refuses to even speak to him. I can't imagine why she is so angry; they have always been friends—"

Gabriel chuckled, a deep sound that rumbled inside his muscled chest as she pressed her cheek against it. "I believe he feels much more for her than friendship, though he may not have admitted it yet, may not be able to until he stops feeling haunted by the specter of his pathetic father and gets past his deep-felt fears of marriage."

"Oh, do you think—of course, I should have seen it earlier! Does Circe know?" Psyche thought back on the small clues, the hints she had been too physically ill and emotionally overwrought to pay sufficient attention to.

"I'm sure of it," Gabriel told her.

"As for David's dread of marriage—well, his father was appalling, according to Aunt Sophie's tales, and his mother is—" Psyche paused, trying to think of a word that was sufficiently ladylike, then gave up. "She's a harridan. If it should come to marriage, poor Circe, with such a mother-in-law."

"Circe can take care of herself," Gabriel predicted, grinning. "And I believe David will rise to the challenge, too. He's taking the first steps toward letting go of the past."

Psyche, recalling Gabriel's own struggle with nightmarish childhood memories, and their less than smooth path toward love and marriage, sighed. Thank heavens that was all in the past. Even the tumultuous perfidy of her own unsettled stomach was easier to bear than that. And when she thought of the coming baby, healthy this time, please God, she was filled with such joyous anticipation. . . .

"It will be a boy," she predicted, running her fingers through the light sprinkling of hair on his chest. "And he will have your deep blue eyes."

It was a game they played, one Gabriel had begun when she was feeling nauseous and miserable.

"It will be a girl," Gabriel countered with a contented smile, "and she will have your golden hair. . . ."

❧

*The next morning, Psyche was able to eat a small break-*fast, and though Gabriel insisted that she still spend most of her time resting, she felt much more alert.

When Sally was shown into the bedroom, she beamed to see Psyche sitting up with a book in her lap. "You look much better." Sally sat down in the chair next to Psyche's chaise and tucked the shawl closer around her friend's feet.

"I feel much improved," Psyche agreed. "You look pale, however. And I thought you very quiet the last time you came to see me. Are you feeling quite the thing?"

Sally shut her eyes briefly, and Psyche was shocked to see the pain that twisted her friend's usually cheery expression.

"My dear, what is it?"

"I—I know you will be discreet, if I wish it." Sally touched a dainty handkerchief briefly to her lips, then raised large and somehow tragic brown eyes.

"Of course!" Psyche sat up straighter. What was going on?

"I—you might say that your ailment is contagious," Sally said, with a strangled sort of laugh.

"But you can't catch—I mean, you know what I suffer from—" Psyche gasped. "Sally! Are you telling me that you—you—"

Sally nodded, her expression a strange mixture of chagrin and delight. "I believe that I am with child."

"Oh, my goodness." Psyche felt herself absolutely at a loss for words. She stared at Sally, who twisted her handkerchief until it shredded. "But . . ."

"I know. All the years I was married, and there was never any sign of quickening. I was sure that I was barren, you know, and I had made up my mind that I would have to bear the disappointment."

Psyche thought of the older husband whom Sally had adored. "Andrew—"

Sally nodded. "Yes, perhaps it was not just me who couldn't—who didn't—"

At any rate, Andrew, who had been dead for years, was not involved in this! Psyche tried to pull her thoughts together. "Are you sure, my dear?"

"I think so." Sally looked away for a moment, seeing something or someone that Psyche could not begin to guess at.

"You're not planning—I mean, you wouldn't—those backstreet physics who claim to be able to end a quickening—you know it's so dangerous. You could bleed to death on some butcher's dirty pallet, and the baby—"

Sally shivered. "Oh, no, never. A baby! I thought I would never be so blessed, Psyche. I would never try to end this. Even if it is, um, inconvenient, to say the least."

Psyche's eyes widened despite herself. "Inconvenient" was putting it mildly. To bear a child without a husband would ruin her friend's social standing forever, and the child itself would be ostracized, too. This was a blessing, but also a catastrophe!

"What can we do?" she said aloud, trying to think.

Sally sent her a look of deep gratitude. "I knew you would stand by me."

"Of course, but there must be something. The father"— Psyche hesitated—"have you informed him?"

"I have not told him; I cannot. It would only cause him . . . difficulties."

Oh, dear. Psyche swallowed hard. The man—the fa ther—must be married. Oh, dear.

"I have pondered my options, and I believe that I will go abroad; widows sometimes do that, you know. I shall live quietly in some French village where no one knows me, and after the baby comes, in a year or two I could return home and announce that I have adopted a child since I have none of my own. When the child was old enough, I would tell him or her the truth, of course."

"I see," Psyche said, her tone quiet.

"People will gossip, I have no doubt, and some of the Ton may shun me, but they will not know for sure, and it will offer the child some protection." Sally raised her chin. "I will not abandon my baby to some orphanage, like many by-blows, or pay a farmer's wife to house it. I will not give up my child, the only child I will ever have!"

"Of course not," Psyche agreed, touching her own swollen belly despite herself. "I will do everything I can to help, Sally. And you know that whatever happens, Gabriel and I will always be your friends."

Sally blinked hard. "Thank you, Psyche. That means a great deal to me." She brushed back a tear that lingered despite her best efforts. "Oh, dear, I am so easily over-wrought just now. I'm sorry."

Psyche gave a watery laugh of her own and held out her arms. "As if I didn't know! I understand completely. Just carry a clean handkerchief at all times, and keep a basin handy."

Laughing, Sally leaned forward to share the hug. She accepted the handkerchief Psyche offered to replace the one she had ruined, blew her nose lustily, and they talked of baby clothes and just which quiet village would offer a pleasant setting for Sally's retreat.

When lunchtime arrived, Sally agreed to stay and share a light meal.

"Good," Psyche told her old friend. "Because I am all alone. Gabriel had to travel to our estate to confer with a tenant who is having trouble with his neighbor's cows encroaching on his fields, and Circe is out."

"Not with that odious Austrian again?" Sally asked, her tone caustic.

"No, thank heavens, today she is out with Sir John," Psyche explained. "Such an agreeable young man." She pushed herself up from her chaise very carefully, in order not to set off a spasm of nausea, and when she looked up again, she saw that Sally had averted her face. "Are you all right, dear?"

"Of course," Sally said, though her voice sounded tight. "Just a moment of queasiness."

Psyche grimaced in sympathy, and the two women went down to the dining room together.

≈

At the same moment, Sir John was holding a chair for Circe. They had spent most of the morning at Acker-mann's print shop, so that Circe could survey the heavily trafficked establishment's newest editions. Even Sir John had found several prints of famous gardens to admire and enjoy, so they were both in good humor, although hot and weary.

Sir John had offered lunch, but Circe decided she was too warm to be really hungry, so they agreed to go for ices at Gunter's, instead.

They strolled to the confectioner's in Berkeley Square. There was little breeze, and the air felt sultry and heavy. By the time they reached the sweet shop, clouds were dimming the sunlight, and in the distance a rumble of thunder could be heard. They hurried inside, and once they had a table, ordered dishes of the sweet, cool dessert.

"Thank you for your escort today," Circe said after Sir John took his seat. "I've enjoyed myself."

The morning had been an agreeable reprieve from von Freistadt. Sally had had a headache but Circe felt in no danger of impropriety with the shy young baronet.

She had found she simply couldn't bear another day of the count's company. She longed intently for David's presence, but refused to summon him. Indeed, when Sir John's note came, offering her an escort to the print shop, her first thought had been of David. He was still sending her notes, which she tore up without reading, and flowers, which she returned. Circe knew she was behaving irrationally and that she would have to confront David again soon. But not now; not while the hurt was so fresh.

When she saw whom the note was from, Circe had jumped at the invitation. She was so weary of having to be on her guard every moment. After von Freistadt, Sir John offered a welcome respite. Some of her musing must have shown in her face, because Sir John seemed to read her thoughts.

"If you'll pardon me for saying so," Sir John said, "you have been seen so often with von Freistadt that the gossips are humming a wedding march. Surely, you don't intend—"

Circe shuddered.

Sir John nodded. "I found it hard to believe. So why don't you simply tell the count that you don't wish to see him so often?"

Because that would prove that David had been right all along, Circe thought, but she would not admit to such petty reasoning. "Oh, we do have some things in common," she said vaguely. "He seems to know every prominent painter in Europe, and he's been very kind about taking me around to meet all the London artists."

The waiter arrived with their ices, and Circe was glad to change the subject. "Delicious," she said, dipping her spoon in the creamy confection. "I missed Gunter's while I was in Piedmont, although they have their own delightful Italian ices, of course."

"Of course," Sir John agreed. He looked up as two women entered the room chatting, then down again, his expression revealing disappointment for the briefest moment. Whom had he expected to see?

"You also have seemed a bit downcast of late," Circe suggested, her tone diffident. "I hope you are well?"

Sir John hesitated, then he put down his spoon and met Circe's gaze with something close to defiance. "Miss Hill, I must tell you that when we first met, I was somewhat— well, very much—drawn to you. You really are the most talented, lovely young lady."

Oh, my. Surely he was not going to make a declaration here, of all places, over ices at Gunter's? The absurdity of it mingled with Circe's instinctive dismay. She had thought they were becoming such easy friends; she really could not bear another proposal!

"And as we have spent time together, I have found that your qualities are all that I had supposed, and I do indeed value our friendship, but—" He hesitated.

Circe relaxed; his face did not reveal the earnest look of a man about to declare undying love, but rather the guilty expression of a gentleman who has mistaken the direction of his interest.

"But I must confess that in the interim I discovered that

my heart—my heart has been captured by another."

She smiled at him. "I have only the most sincere congratulations to offer you, Sir John."

He looked visibly relieved, and she had to hide the laughter that bubbled inside. Really, did he think she was wearing her heart on her sleeve for him? But then his mien darkened.

"Your good wishes are appreciated, if premature. The lady does not seem to return my regard," Sir John admitted, his tone again gloomy.

"Then you must redouble your efforts," Circe told him, trying to be encouraging. "When she comes to know you better, I'm sure she will think again. In fact, we should cancel our theater date tonight to allow you to spend time with the lady of your heart, instead."

"Oh, no," Sir John protested. "I would never be so rude as to cry off after we have already made plans. But tomorrow, I will take your excellent advice and seek out the lady once more."

"Good," Circe agreed.

After they finished the light repast, Sir John escorted her home, and Circe was glad to climb the steps and anticipate some time alone.

"I will be here with my carriage at eight o'clock," Sir John called as he bowed in farewell. "I'm sure you will enjoy the new play."

Circe nodded and waved before she went inside.

∽

The rain began before Sir John reached his own home, and he had to shake off a glistening of raindrops when the footman shut the door behind him, and then go up to change his coat. But despite the change of weather, he was in a much better mood than he had enjoyed for weeks. Perhaps Circe was right, and he should redouble his efforts to convince Sally of his sincere regard. He still felt a bit awkward about his abrupt change of heart, but surely Sally could forgive him for his mistake in his own affections? Hadn't Romeo himself been in love with another girl when he first set eyes on Juliet? Shakespeare knew all about it, by Jove.

And Sally was the woman he thought of every day as he coaxed his orchids to flourish. Sally was the one he longed to show the most perfect bloom to, Sally's was the hand he wanted to hold, Sally's was the warm and rounded body he longed to pull close to him as he lay in his lonely bed every night. To share his life with Sally—what bliss that would be! Her magnanimous spirit and bright-eyed interest to enliven his days and her enthusiastic lovemaking to thrill his nights . . .

For a moment, he regretted his theater date with Circe, then he shook his head. No, he could not forsake all good manners, but tomorrow, tomorrow he would be on Sally's doorstep before breakfast, and she would have to listen to him, despite all the notes she had returned the last few weeks.

Surely she did not despise him utterly? The warmth she had exhibited during their one brief but ecstatic hour of lovemaking could not have been feigned.

He would make her see reason. She must!

He thought of her through the rest of the afternoon, while he dressed for dinner and the theater, and while he was enjoying his solitary dinner. Early in the meal, a footman came in with a short note.

I have come down with a sudden headache and regret that I must cancel our evening's plans. Please forgive me.

It was signed *Circe Hill.*

Sir John stared at the missive in surprise, then grinned. What a card Circe was; she was simply making an acceptable excuse so that he could be free to go to Sally at once and not wait a moment longer. Bless her for her generous heart! She was a good friend, indeed.

"Shall I tell the coachman you have no need for the carriage, Sir John?" the footman inquired.

"No, indeed," his master answered. "Have it brought around at once."

"Now?" The footman looked at the unfinished dinner spread out on the long table.

"Now!" Sir John agreed, and he rose so hastily that he almost upset his half-filled glass of merlot. He felt emboldened, sure that tonight was the moment to press his suit.

The rain had stopped, though tendrils of fog were rising, shrouding the streetlamps with halos of mist. He rode straight to Sally's town house, hoping that she was not out for the evening. If she was, he would badger or bribe her butler until the man told him her whereabouts, Sir John thought recklessly. He would see her tonight, he would lay his suit before her, nothing would hold him back any longer!

As it happened, when the butler opened the door and stared at him in some surprise, Sir John found that he had no need for such drastic measures.

"I will see if Madam is at home to visitors," the servant intoned, looking disapproving at such a late and unscheduled visit.

Sir John paced up and down the wide hallway, trying to think what he should say, how he should persuade her. In a moment, he heard the sound of light footsteps on the landing and he looked up to see Sally staring down at him in surprise.

"Sir John?"

"Please, you must hear me out!" he told her, afraid she would send him away out of hand. "You have returned my notes, you have refused to grant me audience so that I may speak. I cannot allow it, Sal—Madam Forsyth. You must listen!"

Sally looked a little flushed. She glanced at the butler, who gaped at them both, and motioned toward the stairs. "Please come up to the drawing room," she said. To the servant, she nodded dismissal. Reluctantly, with one last curious glance, the man withdrew toward the back of the house.

Sally retreated into the drawing room, and Sir John bounded up the staircase, taking the steps two at a time. When he entered the large room, he found Sally seated demurely on a narrow chair, so he was forced to take the settee a few feet away.

"Sir John, I don't—"

"You must listen, Sally, please, just give me a few moments. I know I must seem the most callow lovesick swain who ever mistook his affections, but you must give me a chance to prove that this time, I do know my own heart."

Sally's face was certainly flushed, and her expression hard to read. "You—you have not been speaking with Psyche?"

He paused, confused. "Lady Gabriel? Why should I do that?"

"Oh, never mind." Sally seemed to relax a little. "But I don't—I don't understand. I thought your courtship of Circe was making progress. Were you not out with her this morning?"

"Indeed, but we are only friends. She is the one who encouraged me to pursue my heart's desire," Sir John explained, leaning forward in his earnestness. "We were going to the theater tonight, but she sent me a note just now and canceled the engagement. I am sure she meant me to come to you, and I needed to see you, desperately!"

"She knows that you, that I—" Sally put one hand to her mouth in apparent alarm.

"Oh, no," Sir John assured her. "You could not believe I would bandy your name about, nor share the tidings of such a private—and wonderful—encounter. But since then I have been able to think of nothing else, of no one else but you. I love you, Sally."

She gazed at him, her dark brown eyes liquid with tears. "My dear, you are young, and I—"

"Not so young that I do not know my feelings," he said with dignity. "And you are as young at heart as any woman I have ever met. Nothing else matters. And no one else, not even Circe, has elicited the love that I feel for you, my darling. I am a different man when you are with me. Even when we are apart, just the knowledge that you believe in me elevates me beyond my circumscribed abilities—"

"Nonsense," Sally interrupted. "You value yourself too lightly, John. You are a most talented, good-hearted, well-countenanced man, and any young woman would be honored to have your regard!"

"Then there is hope that you might learn to love me, truly?" Sir John asked, hope lightening his tone. "I do not mean to rush you—we can take all the time you need—"

This time Sally did hide her face, and he heard a small choked sound that alarmed him. Had he made her cry?

"Dearest—"

He knelt in front of her and gently moved her hands aside, hoping that the thought of loving him in return had not filled her with revulsion. But though tears sparkled on her cheeks, he found that her sweet full lips curved upward.

"Perhaps not so much time as all that," she told him, her voice throaty with laughter. "There is something I need to tell you. But first—"

He smothered the rest of her words with a kiss that left them both breathless. It was some minutes before Sally was able to finish her remark, and by that time, she was sitting on his lap, with his arms wrapped tightly around her. Nothing had ever felt so good, so right.

"First," she told him, her voice stern even as she lovingly traced the strong line of his chin, "first, I must speak to Circe, and be sure that she—that I am not—that you are quite free for another woman to love. I cannot feel that I have betrayed my friend."

"Of course," he agreed. "You will find her perfectly

agreeable to our union, I am sure of it. And my carriage is outside."

"Now?" Sally said in surprise.

"My darling, I do not intend to waste any more hours in senseless estrangement," Sir John said firmly. "Circe is at home, and I am sure her 'headache' is only a subterfuge. We will visit her, and she can give us her blessing, and then we will make wedding plans, the sooner the better."

For some reason, this made Sally laugh again, but she jumped up and called for her pelisse and gloves, and they were soon on their way.

The ride was too brief, and Sir John was so besotted with happiness—she did love him, and he should have initiated this confrontation weeks ago—that it seemed as if they flew over the cobblestones, instead of riding in his well-sprung carriage. When they reached the Sinclair residence, he helped Sally out, and they both approached the door.

Sir John knocked smartly, and when the butler opened the door, he demanded almost gaily, "We are here to see Miss Circe Hill."

The servant stared at them, his eyes very wide. Was the man dim-witted? "Uh, that is not possible, Sir John."

"I know it is late, but she will see us, I am sure of it," Sir John assured the man. "Please take our message up to her."

"I can't," the servant repeated. "Miss Circe is not at home."

"She went out after all?" Sir John said in surprise. "But we need to speak to her. Do you know with whom she made plans for the evening?"

The servant's expression was very strange. "Yes, indeed. She went out with you, sir."

Nineteen

"*What are you talking about?*" *Sir John demanded,* frowning. "How could she possibly be out with me? I am here."

The servant looked as perplexed as Sir John felt. "I don't know, sir, but that's what she said."

Sally gasped, and Sir John felt a strong wave of unease. "I think I should speak to Lord Gabriel."

"He is not at home, sir," the servant said. Hell, did the man know no other phrase?

"Then Lady Gabriel," Sir John insisted. "Something is very badly awry, and we must get to the heart of the matter."

They swept through the door, and the servant hurried up the stairs. Within a few minutes, Psyche appeared at the top of the second landing.

"Sally? And Sir John! Is something wrong? But where is Circe?"

Sir John approached the foot of the stairwell. "That is what we have come to ascertain."

"But she was going to the theater with you," Psyche pointed out. "I am sure of it; she commented on it at dinner."

"She sent me a note canceling our plans; she said she

was indisposed with a sudden headache," Sir John explained.

Psyche frowned. "Let me check her bedchamber. Please come up to the drawing room, both of you."

Psyche turned away, and Sir John offered Sally his arm as they climbed the staircase and entered the drawing room. Sally perched on the edge of a Chippendale chair, but Sir John paced up and down, his unease growing.

When Psyche returned, she looked pale. "Circe is definitely not at home; her room is empty, as are the schoolroom and the attic, where she sometimes paints. I have spoken to her maid and to the footman who saw her go out. She was going to the theater with Sir John, they both agreed, and she left in a carriage just after dark."

"Oh, dear God," Sally breathed. Her color had faded, too, and her eyes were wide with shock. "Where can she be? How can this have happened?"

"Of all times for Gabriel to be away!" Psyche moaned. "It will take hours to get him a message at our country estate, and more hours for him to return. What are we to do?"

"Think, Psyche," Sally begged her friend. "Is there any clue as to where she might have gone? She was not so unhappy that she would run away, back to the Continent and her painting?"

"Oh, I pray not." Psyche blinked hard. "If I have been so selfish, made her so miserable—I would never forgive myself! Oh, surely she would have told me!"

"She did not go unaided," Sir John pointed out. "Someone's carriage came to fetch her, remember."

Both the women turned toward him. "I'm not sure if that makes me feel better or worse," Psyche managed to say, still looking tearful. "In fact, I think it's definitely worse."

"It is not—she would not be eloping?" Sally asked, her tone diffident. "Circe is somewhat, um, unconventional at times, and—"

"She would not!" Psyche protested, but she drew a deep

breath at the suggestion. "It would be such a scandal, and anyhow, there is no one—"

She hesitated.

Sir John spoke slowly. "I know who the gossips have been coupling her with, though Circe informed me she has no interest in his suit. But perhaps he is reluctant to accept her rejection."

Psyche gasped in horror. "Von Freistadt? But surely he could not consider such a nefarious action!"

Sir John made a decision. "I will go to his home; if I find him sitting sedately in front of his own fire, that will at least eliminate one possibility, and it is better than sitting here and doing nothing. Do you know his London address?"

Psyche hesitated, and Sally said, "Perhaps the servants?"

Psyche rose at once to pull the bell rope, and when the butler appeared at the door, she told him, "We need to know where Count von Freistadt resides."

The butler looked astonished. "I will inquire of the coachman, my lady."

Sir John paced up and down, and Sally held Psyche's hand as the women talked in low tones, trying to rally their courage. At last the butler reappeared in the doorway, with, strangely, Luciana at his side.

The maid curtsied, then said quickly, her accent stronger as it always was when she was agitated, "The house—it is in Devon Square, my lady. I heard Lord Westbury and Signorina Hill discuss it once."

"Thank you, Luciana," Psyche said, her gratitude outweighing her puzzlement.

"Good." Sir John nodded his thanks to the young servant, whose face was white with distress. "In that case, I'm sure I can find it."

Psyche took a deep breath. "I shall send an express messenger to fetch Gabriel, and I will also send an urgent note to David; he would wish to aid us, too, I am sure, if he is at home at this hour. Oh, if Circe should be in danger—" She sobbed and bit her lip to hold back more tears.

Sally clasped her friend's hand. "Do not despair. We will find her!"

She turned toward Sir John, and the look Sally gave him was so full of love and trust and confidence that he felt doubly emboldened; he must not disappoint Sally, and he must aid Circe if he could. He turned toward the door.

"I shall send you word as soon as I have any news," he promised.

He hurried back to his carriage and gave his coachman directions. Wisps of fog drifted above the streets and here and there thickened into patches of opacity, deepening the darkness. The driver had to drive slowly, but at last they reached the square. Sir John jumped down from his carriage and pounded on the door of the nearest house. It was not the Austrian's residence, but the affronted butler who answered was able to point him to the correct address. Sir John hurried down the walkway to the large mansion the servant had indicated and repeated his knock.

This time, a footman opened the door cautiously.

"I wish to see von Freistadt," Sir John told him. "At once."

"I'm afraid His Lordship is not at home." The servant tried to shut the door, but Sir John put out his hand to hold it open.

"Did he have plans for the evening with a young lady?" Sir John persisted. "Is he with Miss Circe Hill?"

"Dunno," the man said, and this time he would have slammed the door shut, except—except another dark form suddenly materialized out of the dimness and joined Sir John on the doorstep. The new arrival shoved back the door with such force that the servant inside reeled in shock.

"Answer the man!" And to Sir John, the newcomer added, "Why are you inquiring about Miss Hill?"

"Westbury?" Sir John peered at him. Both the flambeaux that flanked the front door and the streetlights further away were obscured by the fog that grew denser with every passing minute. "How did you—what on earth are you doing here?"

"I'll answer that later," David told him brusquely. "Why are you looking for Miss Hill, and why here?"

Sir John explained quickly, and David cursed.

"If he has had the gall to touch one lock of her hair, I shall see him drawn and quartered, and I will wield the axe myself!"

Sir John saw that David's hands had fisted. When David turned back to the door, Sir John could not blame the servant for visibly quelling.

"We have no time to waste, nor will I be put off," David snapped. "Tell me where the count is to be found, if you value your life!"

The servant gazed at him in alarm. " 'E ain't 'ere, honest," he said, his voice rising in agitation. "And 'e don't tell us where 'e goes."

Sir John found himself actually feeling sorry for the footman. But David seemed devoid of pity, demanding, "Did the count go out on foot or in his carriage?"

" 'Is carriage," the servant answered, sounding relieved that he knew some tidbit to offer this alarming gentleman.

"What does it look like?"

"H'it's black, sir, and 'as a team of four matched sorrels," the man answered.

David allowed the man to shut the door at last. He was cursing again, low and steadily.

"Surely von Freistadt would not dare to abduct a lady of good family?" Sir John protested. "I can't imagine—it makes no sense; no man of honor would behave so."

"Who said he was a man of honor?" David's dark tone only increased Sir John's apprehension. "Come along, we shall take your carriage."

"Where are we going?" Sir John followed as David scrambled without ceremony into the chaise, pausing only long enough to give directions to the coachman.

"Von Freistadt has a hunting box an hour south of London."

Sir John hastened to join him, and the carriage lurched as it pulled rapidly away. David must have impressed his usually sedate driver with the need for speed. "How do you know that? I hadn't thought you and von Freistadt on such intimate terms."

David laughed, but the sound held more bitterness than humor. "Intimates—hardly. But I have not shadowed the man for weeks without learning a few things about him. If he has harmed Circe—"

The expression on his face, even in the dimness of the carriage, made Sir John hesitate to question him further. David drew a deep breath, and then said more quietly, "There are a few things you may need to know, but you must not repeat this to anyone."

"Of course," Sir John agreed. As the carriage made the best speed it could through the foggy night, he listened to David expound an incredible tale.

❧

Circe awoke to find her head pounding and her stomach horribly queasy. She lay on a narrow bed in a room which was quite unfamiliar. A flickering candle on a small table nearby cast a circle of thin light.

Her first thought was to look for a basin; she found a bucket on the floor near at hand, and she tugged it to her just in time, bending over the edge of the bed. When the paroxysm passed, she thought fleetingly of Psyche. She had not had nearly enough sympathy for her sister's bouts of illness, she told herself, her mind still foggy. She must remember to apologize to Psyche. . . .

Only . . . what was she doing here? And where was here? As rational thought returned, Circe pushed herself up on one elbow and looked about her. Her last memory was of preparing for an evening of theater with Sir John, then an unknown servant at the door, then herself getting into a dark carriage, wondering why Sir John, usually so polite, had not come to the door himself to greet her.

Then, the intimation of something very wrong, just before a familiar voice spoke—familiar, but not Sir John's.

"Good evening, my dear."

It had been von Freistadt.

In shock, Circe had demanded, "What is this? Why are you here?" And she had turned back toward the carriage door, ready to fling it open and demand to be put down, even though the vehicle was already rolling along the pavement. Then someone had held a small vial to her mouth and a noxious-tasting liquid was forced down her throat while she struggled against it, gagging and coughing. Then she was falling into darkness. . . .

Remembering made her retch again, and then again. When she felt a little stronger, she pushed the pail aside and managed to thrust herself to a sitting position. Her head spinning, she felt shaky and weak, but she also felt the beginnings of anger.

How dare von Freistadt do this to her! What on earth was he thinking, and how did he believe he could get away with such tactics? When she told Gabriel what had occurred—

A sudden cold came over her. Perhaps the count did not mean to allow her to tell anyone; perhaps she would not leave here alive. She must do something!

Which brought her back to her first question—where was here? She looked around the small room; it looked like a lady's boudoir, and was furnished simply but tastefully. Did the count have some love nest outside of town? He would surely not have taken her to his London residence.

Did anyone know she was here?

How could they; she had gotten into the carriage thinking it was Sir John's equipage. She frowned, feeling foolish now, but it had been dark, and her thoughts had been elsewhere. She had never expected to have such an audacious attack carried out upon her person, though goodness knew, the count was bold enough in every aspect of his character.

She had told everyone at home she was going to the theater with Sir John. Even if she did not come home the next morning—how long had she been here?—they would not have any clue as to where to find her. The thought filled her with stirrings of panic.

Stumbling a little on unsteady legs, Circe made her way to the door. Was she locked in? She cautiously tried the knob; it would not turn.

She was a prisoner.

Panic flared again, and she pushed it back. She tugged at the knob. The door felt very solid. She doubted she could break it down, and if she tried without result, it would make a great deal of noise. She did not want the count to return just yet, not when she still felt so wobbly and defenseless. Stealth, then, was her first choice. Very well, she could not get out through the door.

What about the window? She hastened to the only window and pushed aside heavy draperies. The window casing was narrow, but perhaps she could squeeze through, and she was sure she could smash the glass. But when she peered into the darkness, that was all she could see. There was no convenient tree limb that she might hope to spring to, and it was obvious that she was on an upper floor.

Circe shivered at the thought of climbing out and dangling so high above the ground. Unless she chose to shimmy out the narrow opening and jump into the blackness, risking broken limbs or even death, the window did not seem to be a good choice.

Was there anything in the room that she could use as a weapon? Circe made a quick inventory of the bed—its sheets needed airing and the feather pillows smelled musty—and of the small dressing table. There was a water pitcher on the dressing table; she could smash it over someone's head, though she doubted it would be more than an annoying inconvenience.

Next she inspected the vacant clothespress. It seemed empty, but just to be sure, she ran her hands along the shelves that were built into one side, then winced when she pricked a finger. Drawing her hand back, she put the finger briefly into her mouth to ease the pain, then examined the shelf more closely. There—lodged in the corner—a gleam of metal. With great care, she pried at it until she dislodged a long shining hat pin.

It wasn't much, but she felt a little better holding the sturdy pin. She tucked it out of sight inside the sash of her gown and continued to check out the room. But nothing else presented itself to her gaze, and then she heard a sound outside the chamber.

Quickly, she retreated to the bed where she had been lying when she woke. She arranged herself on top of the coverlet and shut her eyes. It took every ounce of willpower not to open them again when she heard the creak of the door, and then footsteps—of more than one person, she thought—approaching the bed.

"Why is she not yet awake?" The count's voice. "Did you give her too much tincture of opium?"

"No, my lord, I am sure it was a safe dosage. She should come around very soon, though her wits may be a bit addled. But the better for your purposes, like," a rougher voice said.

Safe? Circe, aware of her throbbing head and roiling stomach, fought to keep her expression blank. Hardly! And what nefarious purpose did the Austrian plan? The count's reply did not ease her fears.

"Idiot! I do not want her addled; I need her memory to work, among other things."

Other things? Circe felt fear curl itself into a cold knot in her belly. She tried to breathe slowly and evenly, and she kept her eyes closed.

"I'd like a turn when you are done with her, my lord. I've got a score to settle with the little bitch myself."

The evil in the man's voice chilled Circe to the bone. Then the sound of a blow rang out, almost causing her to open her eyes.

"She is well born, fool, and above your touch! Go and

bring me a bottle of brandy, and two glasses. When she does wake, she will need some restorative," the count ordered.

The voices had moved back toward the door; Circe dared to lift her lids the slightest bit. It was von Freistadt, of course, and his companion was the man with the scar who had twice attacked her. She fought back a shiver. She was in dangerous straits, indeed.

And no one was coming to help. She was on her own, and she must keep her wits about her.

The other man went out of the room and shut the door behind him. The count was turning. She pressed her eyelids shut tightly again.

"We are alone, my dear. You may cease the pretense."

How did he know?

As if in answer, the count's suave voice continued, "If you were able to be so neatly ill, I think you must be more alert than you wish to pretend."

Of course, the sour smell of her rebellious stomach must have alerted him at once, or almost at once, though she had pushed the pail under the bed to hide it.

Circe opened her eyes, blinking at the light. She did not have to pretend to be weak; she did strive to hide her fear. "What am I doing here?"

"My dear, I believe you have something I want." He gazed down at her, allowing his glance to follow the curves of her breasts, the rounded silhouette of her hips.

For a moment, she felt pure terror.

Then he added, smoothly, "Something valuable is missing from the kingdom of Piedmont. It departed the Italian peninsula about the same time that you returned to England with your new maid, whose actions have not been the most innocent. I believe you know something about its departure and where it is being concealed."

Relief flooded her, and for a moment, she forgot to be on her guard. "No, no, indeed. I have not seen it."

"And what *it* do you refer to, my dear?"

"What—whatever treasure you speak of, of course. Jewels, gold, how should I know?"

"I think you know very well." He leaned closer, and she saw how his dark eyes reflected the dancing candle flame, and how even more saturnine the dark beard and thick brows appeared in the room's dim light and heavy shadows.

"I'm surprised that you would countenance the theft of a national treasure," he went on. "I should have thought your own instincts as an artist, if you are indeed a real artist, would be to value such a masterpiece."

"I am a real artist!" Circe countered, her tone indignant. She pushed herself up and almost forgot to be afraid. "And of course I treasure such a work of art—" She saw the trap a fraction of a second too late. "That is—I assume you are speaking of a work of art, a painting, perhaps, since I am a painter, myself. . . ." She was babbling, and she hated herself for it, and hated him more.

"I think we should cease this game." His voice was like honey, his triumph barely cloaked. "You must tell me where the painting is stashed. I have had instructions from my superiors; they are tired of waiting, and this small victory by the nationalist rebels in Piedmont must be blotted out once and for all. Tell me where to find the Titian."

She held her breath, then released it slowly. "I believe I cannot help you."

"Ah, but I believe you must. Lives depend on it."

This time, Circe had to force herself to meet his eyes. "You mean you will kill me if I do not tell you? You will likely kill me, anyhow. Because if you let me go, if I go home, when I tell what you have done, you would be ruined."

"No, my dear." He sounded only amused, to her fury. "*You* would be ruined, an innocent young lady, trysting alone in a secluded country house with a hardened old rake like myself. That is why you will tell no one what happens tonight, and why I will not be required to do something as distasteful as to order your death."

"Then what—" She paused, trying to think.

"The ones who will die are an elderly couple you know of only at secondhand, yet I have reason to believe you have taken some pity on their situation, and that of their daughter."

"Luciana!" Circe said before she could stop herself. "You do have her parents!"

"They are safely imprisoned, yes," the count said. "Two middle-class subjects of Piedmont who had ideas above their station, visions of self-rule, hopes of throwing off their Austrian yoke. Silly people, really, no one will miss them."

"Luciana will miss them!" Circe argued, furious with his cool indifference. "The murder of her parents—how can you excuse such a thing? How can you trifle so with people's lives?"

His eyes flashed, and she almost drew back at the sudden glitter of fury that crossed his face.

"I work to sustain an ancient and glorious empire, you ignorant girl. Do you not know of the rich legacy of the Hapsburgs, of all the great families of Austria, including my own, and the might and the glory they have engendered over hundreds of years? Do you think I would allow some pitiful peasant uprising to threaten even a small part of that empire? They are ants compared to my distinguished heritage! And they will be crushed like insects if they dare to rebel—as they have done. And yes, unless I have the Titian in my hands immediately, I shall send the order that will end their lives."

"You are a coward and a murderer!" Circe threw the words at him. "I think you are despicable!"

"And I think you are most stimulating when you are angry, angry and very much frightened, despite your so brave pretense." He came closer and lifted her chin as if she were an unruly child, holding it a little too tightly for comfort. "Perhaps we shall have time for other pursuits, before you tell me about the painting."

She had been right about him all along. He was a bully,

heartlessly cruel beneath the surface veneer of cultured politeness. He enjoyed seeing her afraid, and he would enjoy hurting her.

She had not known such people existed, until tonight. Like her one blissful hour with David, this would also change her, though in a different way; it would create a pool of darkness inside her she would always shudder to contemplate . . . if she lived long enough to make that an option.

He ran his hand down her cheek, and she shivered at his touch. She stood up from the bed, still shaky, and attempted to step away, but he put out one hand and grasped her upper arm. His grip was like iron.

Unable to move, she trembled, wanting to lash out at him, but sure that he would retaliate. Still holding her close, the count laughed and moved his other hand to her breast. She shut her eyes, then refused to give him the satisfaction of seeing her retreat, even in a small way, and opened them again.

He stared at the hollow between her breasts, and his breathing seemed too fast. But he was not watching her other hand. She slipped it into the sash of her gown and found the hat pin she had secreted earlier. Holding it against her palm, out of view, she slid her hand down again and waited for the best moment.

He pushed her dress down and reached to touch her nipple; she shuddered in outrage. The count seemed engrossed, stroking her skin, and she could bear his touch no longer. Circe moved, bringing the pin up and plunging it deep into his neck.

The count jerked in shock, swearing in guttural German. He released her arm to clutch at his neck; bright red blood oozed from between his fingers. Circe shoved him back and ran for the door. No, his minion had not locked it. She pulled it open and glanced wildly down the hall, then, catching a glimpse of a staircase, ran for her life.

She half ran, half fell down the stairs, clinging to the

wooden banister to keep her balance, but she kept going until she reached the ground floor. The house was dark, with only a few candles lit along the hall, but she could make out the front door. If it were locked—

She had to risk it; she had no time to find another exit. Panting, her legs still unsteady, Circe ran for the door. She was close enough to touch the knob when hands reached out to clutch her neck.

Circe choked, unable to breathe. Two hands encircled her throat, pressing painfully, and darkness hung at the edges of her vision. She had only seconds of consciousness left—she twisted in his grip, turning to face her attacker, and saw von Freistadt's face dark with anger, a thin trickle of blood still running down his neck.

The sight somehow gave her strength. She had hurt him, she would again. Instead of trying to break his hold, she rammed her knee up into his groin.

The count grunted in pain, and his clasp on her throat slackened. She pushed his hands away and managed to slip from his hold. She grabbed at the door, but it did not open; the key was still in the lock, if she could only reach it.

The count was shouting for help even as he seized her again, this time by the arm, holding her despite the fact that he was still bent over in pain. His expression was livid.

"You will regret such an attack! I know a few ways to cause pain, you arrogant English whore."

The scar-faced man appeared at the end of the hall, a bottle of wine in one hand, his expression surprised.

"Too late, as usual, Wilhelm! I can handle this myself," the count was saying. "Go back to the kitchen, you stupid oaf."

The man shrugged and stepped once more through the doorway.

It was only Circe and von Freistadt in the narrow hall; she had never felt so alone. The Austrian met her gaze and smiled slowly.

Circe wanted to rip his face apart, but he held her too tightly. All she could do was shout. Circe screamed, "Help me, help me, anyone!" She knew it was a futile gesture, but she had to do something. The count laughed.

"You may scream all you like, and you shall, my dear, you shall."

Oh, God, she thought. Please—

There was the sound of a heavy blow, and the door flew open.

She did not know who was more astonished, she or the count. For an instant, they both gaped at the door, now hanging by one hinge.

In the doorway, barely illuminated by the flickering light of the hall candles, she saw a miraculous sight.

"David!"

Twenty

How on earth had he found her? Weak from shock and relief, for an instant Circe sagged in the count's hold.

David charged across the threshold, still holding a hefty section of log with which he had broken down the door.

"Let her go, or I swear before God I'll kill you!" David lifted the rough club, his tone one that Circe had never heard before.

Circe straightened, taking a deep breath. It was over. She tried to step toward David, but her abductor's grip tightened.

"Such melodramatics!" The count raised one brow as he pulled her even closer to his body. "I think not."

David stepped forward, and suddenly von Freistadt held a small, elegant dagger to Circe's throat. David hesitated; slowly he lowered the log.

"Craven!" Circe muttered to her captor. The knife's blade pressed harder, but the anger inside her burned more keenly than the bite of the metal against her skin.

"Rash to the end," the count said, but his tone had lost some of its urbanity. "And the end may come sooner than you imagine."

"Circe, hold your tongue!" David directed, his tone rough.

"Sage advice," the count agreed. "If you heed his command, Miss Hill, and mine, you might possibly live to tell this tale to your grandchildren."

"Command? I think not!" Circe retorted, losing her head completely. Von Freistadt held her so close that she could smell the hint of garlic on his breath. "Anyhow, who would believe a man without honor?"

In answer, the count's blade pricked her skin. Circe felt the warm trickle of blood roll down her neck and into the collar of her gown.

David swore. Von Freistadt jerked his attention back.

"I fear I still have the upper hand," he told the younger man. "And you will do as you're told, if you want to see the lady released with her throat intact."

David took another step inside the hall, angling along the wall, no closer to them, but farther from the door. What was he doing?

The count turned his body to keep David under his gaze. "No more trickery," he snapped. "You will do as I say, or—"

He never finished the sentence.

Someone else stepped through the doorway. It was Sir John, holding a long, strange-looking gun with a flaring muzzle pointed directly at the count.

"Release her," Sir John said, coolly. "And step away."

Circe blinked, almost beyond surprise. The count cursed heartily in German. For a moment, his poise seemed shattered, but then to Circe's chagrin, he drew a deep breath and laughed.

Everyone else stood silent with surprise.

"You are holding a rather ancient blunderbuss," von Freistadt pointed out. "At this distance, as close as she and I stand, you will harm the lady just as much as you will injure me. I do not think you will fire."

Sir John hesitated; Circe could easily read his uncertainty. The count spoke the truth. She was still a prisoner, even with two rescuers come to her aid.

Sir John tightened his grip on the antiquated weapon, his frustration clear on his honest face. "I think—" he began.

An explosion echoed through the hall. The acrid smell of gunpowder was almost choking in the confined space.

Circe coughed. Had Sir John fired after all? She shuddered from the shock, waiting to feel pain lance through her. But she did not seem to be injured. She looked at the count; he smiled. What—?

Then she saw, to her dismay, that it was Sir John who sagged back against the door frame, scarlet blossoming from a wound in his chest.

He was murdered! Oh, God, Circe thought. How had this happened? Then she followed von Freistadt's gaze to the end of the hall and saw the scar-faced man in the doorway, holding a pistol.

"For once, Wilhelm, your timing is impeccable," the count drawled. "Now if you would do me one more favor . . ."

The man had another pistol tucked into his waistband, Circe saw, and it was surely loaded. It was a nightmare, this could not be true, it could not. David would be next; she could not stand here and allow—

"Shoot the girl," the count said clearly. He stepped aside, leaving her positioned alone against the wall.

David gave a savage growl of pure instinctive rage and sprang toward Wilhelm, but the man had pulled his pistol—David would not reach him in time—the hall was too long and though David tried to block her with his body, the angle was wrong—

Circe found she had no wish to be shot. Ignoring the knife that the count still held, she dove toward von Freistadt and threw her arms about his neck, draping herself literally over his body.

Wilhelm hesitated; if he aimed at Circe, he would also be aiming at the count.

"You idiot girl!" the Austrian snarled, trying to push her away.

Circe hung on for dear life. She heard a muffled shout, and the sound of blows, then someone falling heavily. Oh, please—

Then David said, "You may release him, Circe. Don't even think about using that dagger, von Freistadt."

But the Austrian had already begun to lift his arm. Circe had expected just such an action; she kicked him hard in the shin. Von Freistadt grunted with pain, and she was able to slip out of his reach.

"Good girl," David said. She could look around at last and see Wilhelm lying dazed on the floor, and David holding the pistol on the two villains.

But Sir John—Circe ran to the baronet's form where he lay against the front wall. There was so much blood, but at least he still breathed. He looked up at her, his eyes glassy, and Circe cried, "Stay with us, Sir John. We will get you help!"

They must stop the bleeding. She lifted her skirt, not even noticing the startled glances of the assorted males in the hall, and ripped at the bottom of her linen shift. It was hard to tear, and she looked around at von Freistadt.

"Toss me that knife," she said. "It might as well be used for something better than cutting my throat!"

"Gently," David warned, watching the Austrian.

The man's expression was hard to read. He slid the dagger across the floor, and Circe used it to cut strips off her undergarment, then folded them into a makeshift bandage and pressed it against the wound in Sir John's chest, and another even larger one she discovered in his back. There seemed to be an alarming amount of blood.

Please don't die, she prayed, *please don't, please don't, not because of me.*

Working hard, she slowed the bleeding, but she knew he was still at risk. They had to get him to a physician. They had to get out of here, and quickly.

"David," she entreated, glancing toward him. "We must get help for Sir John."

David hesitated, glancing from von Freistadt to the man on the floor, who was showing signs of recovery.

"We do seem to be at a bit of a stalemate, do we not?" the count muttered. "If you shoot me, my man will attack you, and your gun will be empty. If you shoot my man, I will be able to overpower you."

"Not bloody likely," David snapped.

"Ah, but I stand closer to the girl than you," von Freistadt pointed out. "And you have a wounded friend to consider, wounded on your account and hers, I might add. I certainly never meant to involve the worthy baronet."

Circe winced at the truth of his words. Would her foolhardy attempt to aid Luciana's escape from the dangers of the Continent end with the death of an innocent man? And what about—

"Luciana's parents!" she said aloud. "What are you going to do about them?"

She read the truth in the count's glittering eyes. Circe felt her stomach clench. No, not two more people to die. . . .

"I will give you the painting," she said slowly. "If you will release Luciana's parents and allow us to take Sir John to safety."

"Circe, no!" David said. "You cannot trust him."

"You said we must give the painting back," she pointed out.

David grimaced. "Not like this. My uncle—"

Circe ignored the interruption. "You must release us, first, and—"

The count laughed, a harsh sound in the stillness. "I will do nothing until I have the painting in my hand."

"And then?" Circe demanded.

"If I am able to take the painting back to my superiors, I can afford to forget this awkward contretemps and be generous," the count said. His tone was mocking, but what else could they do? It was the only chance they had.

"But Sir John—" Circe looked toward David. "Can you look at his wound?"

David glanced from one villain to the other; the man Wilhelm was sitting up now and seemed inclined to get to his feet. "Stay where you are," David commanded. The man obeyed, and David slid along the wall, closer to Circe and the fallen Sir John.

"You will have to hold the gun on them," he told Circe.

She took it, grasping the silver-engraved grip of the slender pistol—more elegant and up-to-date than the blunderbuss—and pointing it steadily toward the count. He did not seem to trust her with a firearm.

"I am remaining quite still, my dear," he assured her, eyeing the pistol with obvious misgivings. "Do not succumb to a fit of hysterics and pull the trigger, if you please."

Circe bit her lip. She wished she *could* indulge in a nice bout of hysterics and shoot him!

David bent over Sir John, probing the extent of the wound gently. Their friend stifled a moan of pain. David tightened the bandages she had fashioned.

"It's not as damning as it looks, I think," he told her quietly. "The bullet went all the way out through his back, so it will not have to be removed. And it appears to have missed the lung; his breathing is unaffected. If we can keep him still and stop the bleeding, I believe he has a chance."

Circe drew a long breath. "Very well," she said to the count, making a decision. "If you have pen and paper in this place, I will write a note to my maid and tell her where to find the painting. She will hand it over to your man."

"Circe, I don't like this," David repeated.

"We have to try," Circe said, although she too hated to see the triumphant gleam in von Freistadt's eyes as he directed her into a small sitting room with a desk and inkwell. Circe wrote a short note and gave it to Wilhelm.

"Make haste," she told him. "I want to get Sir John out of this place."

Von Freistadt nodded. Wilhelm took the note from her and slipped out the back way. He might double-cross them, of course, bring more of the count's men. But there didn't seem to be much purpose to such trickery if the Austrian was getting what he wanted, and anyhow, Circe thought, Wilhelm seemed the type to take orders, not to act on his own initiative.

David frowned as he kept the pistol pointed at von Freistadt. Circe could feel his displeasure, and she steeled herself against it. She spent the next hours tending to Sir John, loosening his coat and cutting away the ruins of his shirt, heating water in the small kitchen, and bathing the wounds and making a better pad to press against them.

By the time dawn lightened the horizon, Circe heard the sound of a horse's hooves, and von Freistadt turned his head to await his henchman's return. Wilhelm came in through the front door, this time, holding the narrow cylinder aloft in one hand.

"I have it!" he said.

The count drew a deep breath. "Let me see." He took the container and drew out the rolled canvas, handling it carefully. He unfolded the stiff material and gazed at the painting, his expression heavy with satisfaction.

Circe did not move closer, but she glanced at the painting, too. Even in the dim light of guttering candles, she could make out the familiar lines and lush hues of the picture.

The count rolled the painting quickly and slipped it back into its receptacle. "Come," he said to his man. "We are departing this stupid country and taking this safely back to Vienna. See to my carriage."

"And Luciana's parents?" Circe called after von Freistadt as he headed for the door.

"You shall have to depend on my generosity." His smile chilled her.

He left the hall. Circe remained by Sir John's side. She

had covered him with a blanket and slipped a pillow under his head, and he had fallen asleep. His breathing was regular, and his pulse seemed steady. David walked to the door and watched her erstwhile captors depart; he did not speak, but she saw that he frowned.

When the sound of horses' hooves and rolling wheels faded, and Circe knew that the count was truly on his way posthaste to the coast and a prompt Channel crossing, she drew a deep breath.

"Let us see if we can move him without disturbing the wound," she told David. "Perhaps if we slid one of the bed boards beneath him? Or do you think we leave him where he is—though I fear the floor is cold—and fetch a doctor first?"

David sighed. "There is a village a few miles up the road. Let me go and see if I can get help there. At least if we can save Sir John, we can perhaps salvage one victory from this disaster. You know you cannot rely on von Freistadt to spare Luciana's parents, Circe?"

His tone was gentle. He was not going to reproach her, even though she knew he still disagreed strongly with her decision. Circe felt the prickle of tears behind her lids and blinked hard against them. She must be very tired; she never cried like this.

"That depends," she said evenly.

"On what, other than the count's villainy, of which we have ample proof?"

"On whether he gives the order for their execution before he learns that the painting he carries is a fake."

"What?" David's shout made Sir John stir, and Circe motioned him to lower his voice.

David obeyed, but he crossed the floor to reach her side and hissed, "Circe, explain!"

"You don't think I would give him the real painting, do you?" She looked up at him from where she knelt at Sir John's side. "Of course he cannot be trusted to keep his word. I gave him the copy of the Titian that I painted for practice. Neither he nor his man could tell the difference, I noted, but there will be art experts on the Continent who will know at once. And after they realize they do not have the Titian back, we will bargain for the lives of Luciana's parents, if the Austrians wish to see the genuine masterpiece again."

David gave a shout of laughter, though Circe tried to shush him. This time Sir John blinked and opened his eyes.

" 'S wrong?" he muttered.

"Nothing, we are going to get you a doctor and move you soon into a bed where you will be more comfortable," Circe told him. "David—Lord Westbury is simply overcome by the excitement of our little adventure."

David pulled her to her feet, kissing her hard for a moment before he released her. "Circe, you are the masterpiece!" he told her tenderly. "I will fetch a doctor, but later, you must listen to me. I have a lot of explaining to do!"

Circe gazed at him, but this was no time to take up their old argument over his obsessive propriety and her refusal to allow it to rule her life.

"Later," she repeated, as Sir John grinned weakly. "Lie still, Sir John."

"Hang on, man, I'll be back with help very shortly," David promised. "Circe, you keep the pistol, just in case. Although, God knows, if there are any more villains abroad, I fancy they would need more protection from you than vice versa."

Circe took a firm grip on the pistol and permitted herself a smile.

"Hurry back," she said.

Twenty-one

*I*t had all seemed so promising, Circe reflected two days later. Gabriel had had some blistering words for both Circe and David, but had ended by hugging Circe fiercely and shaking David's hand, and Psyche, though tending to embrace her sister every time she remembered the close escape, was feeling much improved.

Circe's kidnapping had not been noised about, so her reputation was still unblemished. But her relationship with David still hung undecided, like a ripe apple that could not decide to fall from the tree.

Once the wounded Sir John was returned to his own house, once Circe had rested and had time to reassure her family, David had called upon her the next afternoon.

He fidgeted with tension as he paced up and down the morning room. He still refused to come up to the schoolroom, as if she might seduce him on the spot. If he hadn't been so obviously agitated, Circe would have laughed at his too exacting scruples.

"I do love you, Circe," he told her, his tone earnest. "I love you more than any woman I have ever known; I never knew I could feel this way. I did not propose just for form's sake, no matter what you thought! It's just— it is proper for us to marry—don't take my head off again, just because I must think about your reputation and the harm you could suffer if anyone knew—if it were made public—" He ran one hand through his hair, ruining the careful arrangement of dark waves.

"David, I'm not about to paste up broadsheets on the street with sketches of our most private business," she said, keeping her tone gentle. Having faced the real danger of von Freistadt's abduction, she had lost her anger at David.

In his agitation, he tugged at his cravat, too, pulling it off center. She thought both details much improved his aspect. He looked almost like the David she remembered.

"No, of course not," he said. "But—"

"I love you, too, but I never planned to marry, you know," she pointed out. "I will never give up my art."

"I would never ask it of you," he vowed.

He gazed at her as she hesitated. He seemed sincere, and yet—

"You wanted a proper young lady," she reminded him. "I will never be that. I'm not sure you will be happy with less. Perhaps you would come to find my odd ways irksome."

"I have been lying to myself, Circe. You have shown me that I cannot be something I am not, that I might hope to be myself without slipping into my father's excesses." He paused and paced up and down for a moment, before turning to face her again.

"I think that I love you the most when you are shocking and original and direct; it reminds me what matters in life," he told her, his expression as open as she had ever seen it. "It pulls me back to the self I thought I had forsworn forever, the self that will perhaps always make up the deepest level of my being. You refresh me, Circe, you make me real. I would never ask you to change; I love you just as you are."

The tone and the countenance were sincere, but the troubled look in his smoky eyes lingered.

"What is it, David?" she demanded. "What worries you still?"

He turned away, not meeting her gaze, and his voice dropped almost to a whisper. "I still fear that I could repeat my sire's failings. I fear that I might let you down, make you unhappy."

Instinctively, she reached out her hand to him, but he stared so hard at the hearth that he did not see it.

"We should marry because I love you, and I hope you love me. . . . And we should marry because I have compromised you, and although you scoff, it is the right thing to do. But I am so frightened of what it might mean to you. . . ."

The silence lingered, and she hesitated, not because she doubted her feelings, or—this time—his, but because she did not know how to convince him that his long-held dread was unfounded, that the nightmares would not come true.

"You are not your father, David," she said into the quiet.

"I hope not." He turned away without coming to take her hand, or kiss her lips, or do any of the things she wished for to bridge the space between them. "But you are betting your future happiness, everything you hold dear. I ask you to think about it carefully, Circe. I will await your decision."

Then he walked away, the set of his shoulders tense, and he looked incredibly lonely.

Circe waited a few days, and then another. David's misgivings deserved consideration, she told herself, and so did her own ambitions. So she pondered the direction of her life, and what it would mean if she married David.

Every one else seemed happy. Sir John was recovering nicely, and he and Sally—to Circe's considerable surprise—were planning a small, intimate wedding.

The count had been forced to send a terse message from Calais when he discovered he did not have the genuine Titian after all, and after David and Circe had dictated a reply and returned it by special diplomatic pouch, Luciana's parents had embarked for England on the next packet.

David's uncle appeared smug over the Austrian's loss of face, Luciana was delirious with joy as she awaited her parents' arrival, and Circe had expected to be ecstatic, too, by now.

But marriage—love was one thing, glorious passion was one thing, but a lifetime commitment—that was quite another.

So she worked as she deliberated, because that was always how she concentrated most effectively. Then one morning, as she turned the same thoughts over and over yet again, Circe stirred a dollop of green-blue with such vigor that she spattered the paint across her whole palette. Damn it!

On top of the mess she had made, the schoolroom was too hot for painting, even at this early hour, and she had totally skewed the perspective of this vastly insipid landscape. Why had she ever started this picture? She threw her brush down and folded her arms.

Nothing was right. Without David in her life, she had a lowering feeling that nothing ever would be.

A maid knocked timidly on the door. Circe looked up; the servant carried another of the long boxes she had been receiving daily from David.

Circe sighed. More flowers? She took the box, not as heavy as she had expected it to be, and dismissed the girl. Pulling off the string which had fastened it, she lifted the lid and gazed in surprise at the contents. She felt her jaw drop and her brows raise at what lay before her.

Wrapped carefully in white paper lay—not the blossoms she had expected—but instead half a dozen of the finest sable brushes. And a note said simply:

I thought you would prefer these to roses. David.

Circe felt the corners of her mouth lift, along with the last wisps of doubt that had troubled her soul. She pulled off her smock and headed for the stairs.

~

*David had risen early—he had been unable to sleep any-*how despite the weariness that pulled at his body and lowered his spirits. Not that he could get much lower. What if she said no? What if Circe never accepted his proposal?

Life without Circe—he had not realized how much he had been missing, all these years. His casual affairs had been just that, brief and unfulfilling, and the carefully chosen young ladies of breeding he had looked over as possible brides had left him totally unaffected.

Only Circe moved his heart, drew deep vibrations of empathy from the unconventional side of himself he had tried so hard to disavow. And while he had armored himself against any attachments, Circe had been too familiar to alert him to his danger. Just because he knew her so well, knew the child she had been, the woman she had become had slipped beneath his guard. Her heart-shaped face and big green eyes, her musical voice and her way of looking at him just so—he groaned aloud, causing his valet to jump.

"My lord?" The servant peered at him, hesitating as he held out David's morning coat. "Did I step on your toe?"

"No, no." David shrugged his arms into his coat. "Hand me my hat, please."

He met his uncle for an early breakfast, as arranged, and the two men discussed the whole affair one more time. David had given his uncle a full report after von Freistadt had hied himself to the Continent, and had had the sense to rely on his uncle for advice until the transfer of hostages and painting was complete.

This morning his uncle appeared in high spirits. "Excellent," he said now. "Our spies tell us that von Freistadt has been disgraced in the eyes of his superiors, and so humiliated that he will likely never return to England. His future looks perilous. And we have rubbed the noses of the Austrian secret police in their own muck. Perhaps this will lend hope to those Italian factions who still dream of more liberty and eventual self-determination."

David tried to share his uncle's sense of satisfaction, especially when the older man clapped him on the back. "You've done a capital job, my boy. A tricky business it was, too. I hope I may call upon you again when the need is urgent?"

"Of course." David felt warmed by the respect evident in his uncle's gaze. But even that did not lift the heaviness that rode inside him, day and night.

Life without Circe . . .

When he returned to his own house, he found his mother in the drawing room, waiting as usual to pounce.

"David, I must know why you make such early morning calls. It is most improper. Tell me at once what you have been up to." She raised her handkerchief to dab at her temple.

He nodded absently. "Good morning, Mother."

"I mean it, David. Explain yourself, if you please."

"I'm afraid I can't do that," he told her. "Have you had breakfast? I believe I will have some ham and a little tea, if you care to join me."

"What do you mean, you can't?" Her voice grew shrill, as it always did when she was irked. "You don't mean to act as unkindly as your father?"

"No, I do not. The fact is, I don't believe I have ever acted quite as badly as my late sire." The statement surprised him as much as his mother, who gaped and allowed her handkerchief to slip through her fingers.

Could it be true?

Then she put her hand back to her temple and gave a theatrical moan.

"If you mean to have a spasm now, I will summon the

doctor first, and then have my breakfast," David said, matter-of-factly.

"I cannot credit such treatment!" But she looked as much surprised as angry, and now she remembered to retrieve the wispy bit of lace and dab her face. "But yes, I believe I am about to have one of my spells."

"Fine," David replied, ringing the bell. When the servant appeared, he said, "My mother's cordial, if you please, and send for her maid and her physician."

He was prepared to go down to the dining room as soon as her maid answered his summons, despite his mother's increasing fury, but the person who appeared next in the doorway was no servant.

"Circe? What are you doing here?" David jumped to his feet, and even his mother paused in midflutter to stare in surprise at the newcomer, who dipped them a brief curtsy. David bowed, returning her salute, even as he felt his heart swell; surely she would not have come in person just to reject his suit?

Although, knowing Circe, who could say? Nonetheless, hope surged inside him with an almost painful force.

"I needed to speak to you," Circe told him, her voice calm. She was attired in an elegant gray and white walking dress, her thick brown hair pulled back into a loose knot, and she seemed quite recovered from her recent ordeal. "I assume I do not have to be kidnapped regularly in order to see you?"

"What is she talking about?" his mother demanded. "Miss Hill, how do you do? Allow me to correct your solecism. It is not correct for an unmarried young lady to call upon a gentleman, even if his mother is present. You may call upon me, of course, but you should never admit to seeking his company."

Circe flashed her breathtaking smile. "I'm afraid I must."

David drew a deep breath. "Circe! Do you mean—"

His mother interrupted. "You must not contradict me, my dear. Such rudeness could signify—insanity does not run in your family, I hope? I might have to rethink my blessing of your imminent union."

Still looking at David, Circe replied, "No, my family is no odder than most, I promise you."

"But—"

Circe spoke to David as if he were the only person in the room. "Yes, my love, I have made my decision." She came closer, ignoring his mother's sniff of disapproval, and lifted one hand to his cheek. "I will marry you. You will not make me miserable, as your father did your mother, and I will not return the favor, as she did."

"Well, really!" the countess huffed. "I have heard plain speaking in my time, but—"

"But you had not yet made my acquaintance, or you would have heard much more," Circe assured her. "I know it is a sad defect, but one I fear you must learn to bear. I promise you I harbor no ill-feeling behind my words, and it's really better to be aboveboard from the beginning, don't you think?"

His mother fluttered her lashes and sank back into her chair. "I think I shall have a spasm. Or two."

"My former governess knows a wonderful tisane for spasms," Circe told her cheerfully. "I will see that your maid has the receipt. It tastes vile, of course, but it is sure to end your spell, at least for the time."

"Really!" his mother sputtered again. "I think a great deal more respect is in order—"

Unfortunately, Circe did not appear to be listening. Why had he thought Circe would be manipulated by his mother. Who on God's earth could manipulate Circe? His mother was putty in her hands.

"—or I shall return to Bath," his mother finished.

David had not heard most of the tirade; he had been observing how cunningly Circe's thick, loosely coiled hair lay against the curve of her neck, and how delightful was the swelling of her breast beneath the well-cut gown. He remembered the sheen of her sun-kissed skin; and the last dregs of his despair seemed to vanish, replaced by his rising passion.

"Yes, Mother," he said absently, reaching to take Circe's hand.

She gave it to him willingly.

"Are you certain?" he said very low, for Circe alone to hear.

"Marrying you will not ruin my life," she told him firmly. "You will ruin it quite thoroughly, however, if you do not marry me. I shall never find another man I love as much, David, nor feel such passion for, and though I thought my art would be enough, I find that I need you in my life."

"You do?" It was harder and harder, feeling the warmth of her hand, the incredible vitality of the pulse that throbbed in her delicate-looking but surprisingly strong wrist, to hide behind all the barriers he had erected, all the layers of armor with which he had imprisoned himself for so long. "But, Circe—"

"No, David," she answered. "No more doubts. We will marry, my dearest, and we shall be very happy. I will allow nothing else."

"Life is not as easy to arrange as one of your paintings," he warned. "You cannot just sketch out your life, say we shall be happy together, and make it so!"

"Why not?" she asked, leaning forward to kiss his lips so lightly that it was the barest caress, the sweetest invitation to more, so much more.

"If I am being totally ignored, I shall withdraw to my own chamber," David dimly heard his mother proclaim. "Perhaps I shall start packing, since I am so disregarded; I seem to serve little purpose here!"

"Thank you, Mother," he said absently.

Throwing up her hands, the countess stalked out of the room, leaving them blessedly alone. He gazed at Circe, hardly daring to credit her words. But—

"Why not, indeed," David said slowly. It was no use; Circe had transformed him, freed his soul. He dared for the first time to believe in happiness, to accept the possibility that the curse that his parents' discord and misery had cast over his future could be lifted. Like a dark shadow fading in the dawn's first light, the bars of his self-imposed prison were melting away.

Circe made life bright again, just like one of her paintings, fresh and colorful and clear. With her beside him, anything seemed possible.

"Are you sure?" he asked, his voice husky with emotion. "I only want you to be happy, my love."

Circe leaned nearer and this time pressed her lips hard against his. He pulled her even closer.

It was a very good thing the countess had left the room.

Epilogue

*C*irce put down *her pad and pencil and shifted her seat* on the blanket that had been spread over the grass; she could not seem to get comfortable. And as for the sketches she tried to make—it would help if her subjects would be somewhat more amenable to suggestion. Or if they would just slow down!

On the next blanket, Psyche chuckled, and Sally, who lay back against the rising hillock upon which they all sat, rose to one elbow to admonish the child who had just dumped a handful of pebbles upon his playmate's head.

"Jonathan! Mind your manners, if you please!"

The sturdy dark-haired two-year-old with Sally's big brown eyes chortled, and the other boy, a few months older, turned to chase Jonathan around the grassy meadow.

"Alexander Hill Sinclair, you do not have to be rag-mannered, as well," Psyche scolded, but her tone was so fond that her blue-eyed, blond-haired son did little to heed his mother.

He paused only long enough to throw one bewitching smile over his shoulder and then continued his pursuit. In a moment, the boys' mad chase flushed a toad out of hiding beneath a broad blade of grass. The creature hopped away, and both children paused, wide-eyed, to watch his progress.

Now! Circe grabbed her pad and pencil. She could capture the delicate curve of Alexander's cheek, and the way Jonathan's eyes crinkled when he laughed. But she was already too late; the tots were jumping up and down, emulating the toad. She sighed.

Psyche watched her. "It's so good of you to offer to paint the boys," her sister said. "I know you have a long list of mothers clamoring for portraits, ever since you did that painting of the countess of Stonesbury and her children. Everyone is commenting on how exquisite it is."

"They grow so fast," Sally put in. "It will be wonderful to have this memory of their tender years. And no one could capture their beauty better than you."

So spoke the doting mother. But the doting aunt and friend could hardly disagree; both boys glowed with health and intelligence and good looks and were the joy of their families. And Sally's rounded belly proclaimed the imminent arrival of a new sibling for Jonathan.

Speaking of which—Circe shifted again.

"We should have brought you more cushions," Psyche said, her tone sympathetic. "Is there anything I can get you, Circe? A little lemonade?"

"No, thank you." No one had warned Circe that backaches were so common when one was increasing, though at least she had been spared nausea as severe as Psyche's had been. She was about to speak her thought when she heard male voices approaching.

The three men came up over the hill, all carrying rods and tackle and strings of fat trout from the stream just beyond the meadow. Everyone turned to greet them, and the two small boys barreled toward their fathers.

"Here, mind the trout," Gabriel said. "You'll get all fishy if you don't take care."

Young Alexander paid no attention, wrapping his arms around his father's waist. "Want to fish, too!"

"You did promise," Psyche reminded her husband.

Gabriel grinned. "Just give me a moment to spend with your mother, then I shall take you back to the river and help you hold the rod. But you can't jump into the water, this time. We have no more spare clothes with us." He put his tackle on the grass and sat down beside Psyche.

Sir John and little Jonathan had joined Sally. Circe smiled at her own husband as he dropped down beside her. His cravat was loosened, his hair tousled by the breeze, and his trousers were spattered with mud. How very freeing mutual love and respect could be!

David could no longer be considered a conventional earl, but then, she was hardly the average countess. They seldom went into society, obliging only Psyche or Sally when either held a dinner party or ball and desired their company, though Circe was fond of theater and gallery outings. But Circe's weekly salons were the most popular with artists and writers and statesmen—since David continued to be sought after for help with confidential diplomatic situations—in all of London.

And her paintings were attracting a widening crowd of admirers, despite her exclusion from the Royal Academy because of her sex. But as to that—their loss, as David said. She continued to paint, delighting in it as much as ever, and even Sir Thomas Lawrence himself had commented favorably upon her last work. To think she had once feared her art would be compromised by the demands of marriage. Marriage to David had only enhanced her creativity. Circe grinned at her sister. Psyche had been very wise, after all.

"Do you need anything, love?" David asked, his tone solicitous.

"A back rub?" she suggested hopefully, and smiled up at him.

He shifted so that he could massage her back. His hands were cool from the river water he had just washed them in, but still, the familiar feel of his strong hands sent shivers of pleasure through her. That part of marriage would never change, the delight his touch gave her.

They were creating their life together just as she had predicted, painting it with broad strokes of joy and contentment and mutual consideration, and she had no doubt that it would be a masterpiece.

She relaxed as the too frequent ache eased, and when he sat back beside her, she flicked a bit of mud off his trousers. "Fish put up a fight?" she asked, smiling.

"Of course. A big one, too," he agreed.

"But it got away?" She laughed at his grimace.

"No matter. I have the prize I wanted most," he said, his tone low. He touched her swelling belly and leaned forward for a kiss. And, as in all things, Circe met him halfway.